THE DARK ENVIRONMENTALIST

THE
DARK
ENVIRONMENTALIST

HIDDEN SECRETS LINGER IN OBSCURITY
UNTIL ILLUMINATED BY THE LIGHT

MOHAMMED ABDUL HALIM

Troubador Publishing Ltd
Unit E2 Airfield Business Park,
Harrison Road, Market Harborough,
Leicestershire LE16 7UL
Tel: 0116 279 2299
Email: books@troubador.co.uk
Web: www.troubador.co.uk

ISBN 978-1-80514-473-1

British Library Cataloguing in Publication Data.
A catalogue record for this book is available from the British Library.

Printed and bound in Great Britain by 4edge Limited
Typeset in 11pt Garamond Pro by Troubador Publishing Ltd, Leicester, UK

DEDICATION

Climate change knows no boundaries, affecting every corner of our planet. Bangladesh bears the brunt of its impact, facing food and water shortages, coastal erosion, frequent floods, and cyclones. The people endure immense suffering and displacement as a result. Situated in a low-lying delta region, Bangladesh is particularly vulnerable to rising sea levels and other climate-related catastrophes.

The environmental hurdles pose grave threats to the country's populace, with millions grappling with the loss of livelihoods, food insecurity, and heightened susceptibility to disease. Coastal communities, in particular, face the brunt of these challenges, contending directly with the unfortunate consequences of saltwater intrusion and the devastation to their homes and infrastructure.

Furthermore, the agricultural sector, upon which many Bangladeshis rely for their sustenance, faces mounting challenges due to unpredictable weather patterns and changes in precipitation, leading to decreased crop yields and economic instability.

The suffering experienced by the people of Bangladesh underscores the urgent need for global action to address climate change. Despite the country is contributing minimally to the carbon emissions driving climate change, Bangladesh bears a disproportionate burden of its impacts.

In an insightful empathy, my sincerest condolences extend to those enduring the ravages of destitution and climate-induced tragedies. Each calamity inflicts not only material loss but also shatters the very fabric of their livelihoods. Their trials weigh heavily on my heart, and I offer my deepest sympathies for the hardships they go through on a daily bases to navigate through life's ups and down.

My narrative unfolds as a fantasy-infused drama, a distant dream destined never to come true for the inhabitants of reality. Its legitimacies are confined to the realm of its characters, elusive to the rest of us who dwell outside its enchanting storylines. Through the medium of storytelling, one can hope to sow the seeds of understanding and empathy, nurturing the soil from which solutions may bloom in real world.

Perhaps, in the contemplation of my tale, enlightened minds may discern the imperative of a unified global effort to confront the humanitarian crises born of climate upheaval. Should such insights germinate, then indeed, the narrative finds purpose beyond mere entertainment.

To those who have accompanied me on this literary voyage, I express profound gratitude. Your unwavering support and boundless enthusiasm have been the compass to guide my creative odyssey. It is my earnest desire that my narrative resonates with the essence of your being and the world you inhabit.

May the muses continue to grace me with inspiration, that I may weave stories that speak to your soul and kindle the flame of shared adventure. Together, let us embark on many more journeys, exploring the realms of imagination and empathy hand in hand.

Thank you.

CONTENTS

ACKNOWLEDGEMENTS

The author, inspired by the unfolding tapestry of global events, crafted this narrative to delve into the myriad facets of the human experience. Within its pages, the story navigates the undulating terrain of life's peaks and valleys, addressing poignant themes such as racial tensions, interracial relationships and their enriching facets, culture clashes, personal struggles and the tumultuous currents of daily challenges.

With an overarching belief in the transformative power of storytelling, the author endeavours to weave a tapestry that not only captures the essence of these complex issues but also serves as a conduit for fostering awareness. In particular, the narrative seeks to shine a spotlight on the *urgent matter of climate change*. Through the story, the author aims to awaken a collective consciousness, impressing upon readers the imperative to care for our shared planet.

The narrative gently reminds us that Earth is our singular abode, entrusted to our custodianship. It underscores the notion that solidarity is the linchpin in mending the environmental ravages wreaked by humanity. The world, beleaguered by the imprints of our civilisation, yearns for a respite, a chance to breathe amid the encroaching shadows of our impact.

The author aspires for more than literary merit – a lofty goal that transcends the confines of fiction. Success, in the author's eyes, is measured by the narrative's ability to catalyse a shift in human behaviour. If, through the evocative prose and poignant narrative, individuals were prompted to re-evaluate their actions in favour of safeguarding planet Earth, it would constitute a triumph for the collective cause of humanity.

Gratitude is extended as the author acknowledges the collaborative efforts supported by AI literature and imagery that have elevated the storytelling to a new level. Recognition is given to those integral to the realisation of this literary endeavour. Appreciation is tendered to the editors, publishers, photographers and the digital artist, whose combined contributions have infused life into this narrative, transforming it into a vessel for contemplation and, hopefully, inspiring transformative action.

DISCLAIMER

This narrative emanates from the realms of the author's imagination, weaving a tapestry of fictional concepts. Its purpose is solely to captivate readers, evoking a myriad of images, memories and emotions without harbouring any intention to defame, denigrate, disrespect, disparage or hurt the sentiments of individuals, communities, institutions, nationalities or professions, or any gender, caste or religion.

It is imperative to clarify that this story, designed for entertainment, does not assert authenticity or lay claim to historical or futuristic accuracy regarding any events or incidents depicted. The utilisation of character names, places or the historical context of any person, whether living or deceased, is purely fictitious, and any semblance to reality is entirely coincidental and unintended.

The author expressly disclaims any intent to malign, defame, slander, hurt or show disrespect towards any individual, place, region, country, religion, community or the feelings of others. There exists a profound acknowledgement and respect for diverse perspectives and viewpoints concerning narratives of this nature. This disclaimer serves as a testament to the author's commitment to fostering a narrative space devoid of harm or offence.

PREFACE

The profound impact of climate change is intricately shaping the fabric of our planet, ushering in an era fraught with unprecedented uncertainties. The escalating frequency and intensity of droughts, storms, heatwaves, rampant jungle fires, surging sea levels, melting ice sheets and warming ocean waters compel both humans and animals to migrate in search of sustainable livelihoods. However, this migratory escape is constrained by the finite spaces available for habitation.

Every corner of the Earth is now inhabited by humans, and this surge in population has given rise to an exacerbation of extreme inequalities. The destitute find themselves without refuge, a predicament that extends beyond the human realm. Amid this global crisis, it is crucial to recognise that women and girls, despite their significant contribution to society, bear a disproportionately heavy burden of suffering.

Enter the Conference of the Parties, or COP, initiated in 1995. Despite its inception and subsequent gatherings, tangible achievements have remained elusive. The revolving door of world leaders, adorned in symbolic attire, seems more attuned to seeking popular acclaim than effecting substantial change. The COP26 international climate conference in Glasgow, held from 31 October to 12 November 2021, exemplified this trend. With the primary objective of securing a global net zero by mid-century to contain the rise in temperatures within the 1.5°C limit, COP26 proved to be a resounding failure.

The looming prospect of future meetings, including the anticipated gathering in Azerbaijan in 2024, appears dimly promising. In the face of such apparent ineffectuality, the imperative to devise viable solutions to this pressing crisis remains urgent and paramount.

The persistence of consumerism, driven by the unbridled pursuit of capital through the mass consumption of the Earth's resources, establishes a lucrative incentive for corporations to exploit the environment for financial gain. Advancing to future iterations of conferences such as COP100 is rendered ineffectual in the face of a system that perpetuates harm for monetary interests. A compelling voice emerging from the heart of adversity is that of Nadia Begum, a woman from Bangladesh, a nation situated in the delta region between India and the Himalayas. She asserts that she possesses solutions to the world's predicaments.

Bangladesh, nestled to the east of India, is currently ensnared in the throes of a climate change cycle. The desiccation of rivers, coupled with the onslaught of extreme weather leading to floods and cyclones, has left its populace beleaguered. The country's population, approximately 174 million as of 2024, is juxtaposed against a landmass of a mere 148,460 square kilometres. This renders a staggering ratio, accommodating just over 1,172 people per square kilometre – an exiguous space insufficient for even a hundred animals, let alone human beings. This raises a poignant question: what has befallen our collective intellect?

In response to this question, a resilient individual, having experienced the ravages of climate change first-hand, embarks on a renegade mission to recalibrate global warming levels to a state reminiscent of the pre-industrial revolution era, or perhaps even further back to an era when natural habitats and biodiversity thrived abundantly. Her conviction stems from the belief that evolution placed humans atop the food chain not for the purpose of consuming the planet and its ecosystems, but rather to serve as stewards – managers, organisers and custodians – of the bountiful assets bestowed by nature, intended to be shared equally among all living beings on Earth.

In this vision of a fair and conscientious existence, she stands as a lone advocate for rationality and integrity in a world that is otherwise harsh and unforgiving. Yet, the realisation dawns upon her that achieving this audacious goal is seemingly insurmountable. No number of conferences or diplomatic negotiations can bridge the chasm unless every leader of the world converges into a singular accord. The peaceful pursuit of this unity appears impractical.

The challenge lies in the inherent resistance embedded in diverse human pursuits. A billionaire clings to wealth, a meat eater to their dietary choices, a devout adherent to religious rituals involving the killing of animals as prescribed by their deity, and corporations persist in extracting resources from the planet. The notion of a harmonious convergence appears utopian in the face of such entrenched interests.

In the midst of this seemingly intractable quagmire, the determined individual perceives herself as a supernatural force, a providential phenomenon sent to shield the Earth from disintegration into ashes. While critics may label her as deranged or emotionally disturbed, history bears witness to instances where seemingly irrational beliefs or actions have paved the way for miraculous transformations or devastating consequences. In her radical pursuit, she grapples with the fine line between visionary conviction and a descent into madness, as the weight of her mission presses upon her, transcending the bounds of conventional sanity.

Her introduction:

Name	Nadia Begum
Nickname	'The Dark Environmentalist' – others call her 'The Eco Warrior'
Age	27
Address	Arambaria, Bangladesh
Education	Graduate geochemist
Other Claims	Receives sudden revelations seemingly out of thin air

Born into the embrace of a modest yet contented family, she witnessed her father, a diligent fisherman, gradually ascend the socio-economic ladder to secure a middle-class status. Life unfolded at a steady, unhurried pace, until an abrupt upheaval shattered the tranquillity. Her belief in the cataclysmic events that ensued traced back to the tandem forces of climate change and the burgeoning overpopulation in Bangladesh. Once steadfast friends metamorphosed into adversaries, nature betrayed its benevolence, animals succumbed to droughts, and tragedy snatched away her cherished family, leaving her in a state of immobilising despair.

Fortuitously, her lifeline materialised in the form of a foreign-born diplomat, her husband, who provided stability and a new-found sense of hope. His support empowered her to rise from the depths of her desolation and pose a poignant question: what has gone wrong with our intellect?

Convinced that she held the answer, an unwavering determination seized her, propelling her into an unprecedented commitment to safeguard the Earth. Her fervour surpassed the limits of conventional environmental advocacy. She pledged her life to the audacious goal of making the world a secure haven for every living entity.

Amid the failures of COP26 spanning twenty-six years, she emerged as an unexpected protagonist in this narrative – a journey marked by pain and triumph, trauma and exhilaration, mystery and enchantment. The storyline weaves through the realms of biochemistry and computer science, delving into the domains of machine learning and future technologies. The fusion of artificial intelligence with animal intelligence becomes a focal point of exploration.

The traditional trajectory of influential men steering the course of history takes an unexpected turn as this extraordinary woman from humble origins endeavours to accomplish what great men have faltered at since the dawn of time. The narrative unfolds as a legendary journey, teasing the boundaries between heroism and peril, and beckoning readers to traverse the realms of possibility, resilience and the indomitable spirit of one woman's quest to alter the course of history. Only by reading the story can one discover whether she becomes the harbinger of positive change or unwittingly plunges into the abyss of terrorism, in a plot that unravels the extraordinary potential of an unassuming citizen.

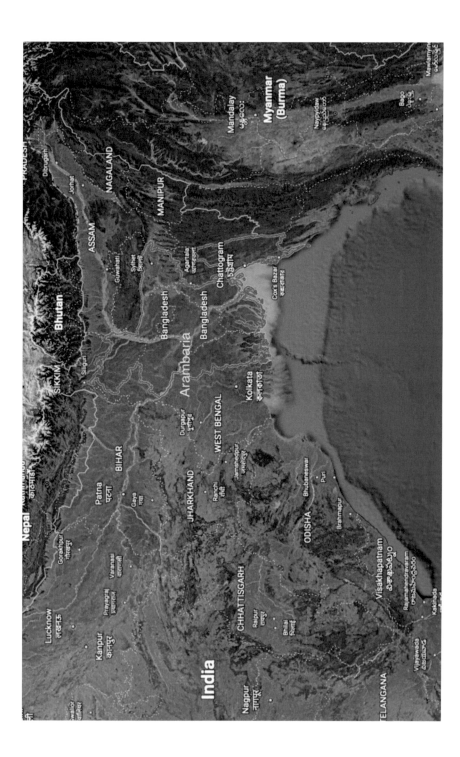

CHAPTER 1

TURMOIL BY PADMA RIVER

Kholil

Doyal

Rahila

Pori

Feroz

Hussain

Nadia

Keith

Starring

Feroz Miah – Doyal Saha – Rahila Begum – Pori Moni –
Kholil Ullah – Hussain Ali – Keith Evan – Nadia Begum

Arambaria, a village located in the mid-western region of Bangladesh, rests approximately half a mile from the banks of the Padma River. This river, originating in the Himalayas in India and coursing through Bangladesh to reach the Bay of Bengal in the south, has been the lifeblood of the local population for centuries. However, in the past decade, records have shown a significant and unexplained decline in the river's water levels. The reason behind this abrupt decrease remains a mystery, as the southern section of the river, near the Rajshahi Division, continues to flow without issue. This puzzling situation has heightened tensions, prompting some residents to put their properties up for sale in the hope of relocating to areas with more abundant water resources for a better livelihood. In the midst of this crisis, some locals are invoking historical grievances, pointing fingers at the British Raj.

Kholil Ullah, a historian teaching at Arambaria Secondary School, passionately argues that the British policy of divide and rule in 1947 resulted in the separation of Bangladesh from India. He decries this decision, emphasising how it created a division that allowed Pakistan, located in the northeast of India, to govern Bangladesh, which is situated in the southeastern region, nearly 2,200 kilometres away. According to Ullah, this division ultimately led to India's monopolisation of water resources, which is now negatively affecting Arambaria. He contends that the only solution to this crisis is to implore India to reunite with Bangladesh, offering the promise of a better future. Ullah's passionate stance is not solely driven by historical grievances but is deeply personal, as he hails from the war-torn generation of 1971, having witnessed the harrowing nine-month-long conflict between Pakistan and Bangladesh, resulting in immense loss and suffering, including the brutal rape and murder of his mother by Pakistani forces.

On the other side of the debate, some locals attribute the crisis to global warming. Nevertheless, for the people of Arambaria, their primary concern is survival and securing a decent life for themselves and their children. Life in this region is already challenging, and the severe drought affecting their part of the village has led to widespread suffering and desperation. The farming and agricultural communities have been particularly hard-hit. Some have resorted to theft, armed robbery and attacks on the vulnerable, targeting wealthier individuals by breaking into their homes in an attempt to secure their livelihoods in the face of dwindling resources.

Neighbouring farmers in Arambaria are facing immense challenges as they struggle to keep their livestock alive. The water supply for crop irrigation has plummeted rapidly, leading to increasing tensions among the villagers, resulting in disputes and even physical altercations. Services that were once taken for granted a few years ago have not improved but, in fact, worsened as of 2021. Rumours are spreading like wildfire, with many pointing fingers at India as the culprit, leaving the people of Arambaria in a state of utter despair with no clear solution in sight. Officials have been unhelpful in resolving the issues, as self-interest seems to guide those in positions of power.

The local property market has suffered a severe decline in value, making the prospect of relocating to a new area slim, due to Bangladesh's population growth. The village has become densely populated, with rows of small thatched-roofed houses standing just feet apart, leading to continuous conflicts among neighbours.

One family in particular has made a name for themselves in the fishery trade, owning a few small fishing lakes near the Padma River. Due to the scarcity of water, neighbouring people have started accessing these lakes to collect water to quench their livestock's thirst. The lake owner, who was once known for his generosity, earned the nickname 'Doyal Sultan' (though his real name is Doyal Shah). However, as the number of users and trespassers has multiplied over the past few years, and with some caught red-handed diverting water from the lakes to their own farmland for irrigation, the owner has decided to take a drastic turn from generosity to selfishness. This shift in attitude has not been well received by the locals.

The erection of barbed-wire fencing around the lakes came as a shock to the local people. They quickly organised a group and called upon the village elders to address the crisis. The elders, in turn, brought together ten other respected individuals, following the tradition that when ten people or more agree on something, it constitutes a 'triple DDD' or 'domestic democracy delivered'.

They decided to hold a meeting after Jumma prayer on a Friday, a significant day in the Muslim-majority country. This would provide one week's notice to Doyal Sultan, as deemed sufficient by the organisers. A written notice was promptly drafted and sent to Doyal. Upon receiving the news, Doyal, a reasonably wealthy man whose wealth largely comes from fish farming in Bangladesh, felt the impending trouble.

The search for natural resources to combat environmental pollution, particularly in the heavily polluted city of Dhaka, has become increasingly critical. The city's air quality is so poor that one must wear a clinical-grade respiratory mask to simply go about daily life. The pollutants are so pervasive that people's faces undergo a sooty transformation within hours of being outdoors.

Doyal's sister, Nadia Begum, is five years his senior and had received an education outside of the rural setting, earning an undergraduate degree in chemistry from Dhaka University. She now works as a geochemist at a firm called GreenBirth Corporation, where she applies her expertise in geology and chemistry to assist in various projects.

Nadia, who married an Englishman who serves as the British ambassador to Bangladesh, is known for her cheerful disposition. However, when it comes to personal relationships, she is a tough nut to crack. It took her husband, Keith Evan, five years of persistent effort to capture her attention. Nadia holds firm beliefs about marriage, valuing deep emotional, physical and mental connections as prerequisites to allowing someone into her life. She believes that marriage is a lifelong commitment, and those who don't share this belief don't hold much value in her eyes. In contrast, Keith's Western perspective on these matters is less rigid. Yet, Nadia's extraordinary beauty and intellect drew him to her, and he eventually won her over. The couple now rents an apartment in a modern complex in Dhaka, the capital city of Bangladesh.

One afternoon, Doyal, known to his sister as Doyal Saha, attempted to reach out to her for a casual chat. However, she did not answer the call due to an emergency situation. Her husband had developed mild COVID-19 symptoms while travelling home via public transport and had been hospitalised. Doctors had attached a ventilator to assist his breathing, and Nadia's mobile phone was switched off.

The message Doyal left on her answering machine requested that she call him back as soon as she could, emphasising the importance of her return call.

Overwhelmed by the unexpected call for a public gathering at the mosque on Friday, Doyal found himself in a state of confusion. In his moment of uncertainty, he called upon his wife, Rahila Begum, for support.

"Rahila," he called.

"Yes!" she replied.

"I need to talk to you. It's important."

Rahila entered the room, her eyes fixed on Doyal, who clearly displayed signs of concern as he continued to stare intensely at the computer screen.

"What do you want to discuss, dear?" Rahila enquired.

Doyal gazed at his computer screen, his elbow casually propped on the arm of his office chair, his fingers forming a fist over his mouth. "Huh," he uttered, as if lost in thought. "Rahila, please come here and take a seat. I have something crucial to discuss."

Suddenly, a call echoed, "AmMaa!" The voice belonged to their four-year-old daughter, Pori Moni, who barged into the room, pushing the door wide open.

"Oh, my sweetheart, come to Daddy," called Doyal to his daughter, and he pulled her onto his lap.

Rahila pulled up a chair and sat nearby. "What's going on? Am I close enough, or should I move even closer to your heart, so I can feel it beat, huh?" She gazed into his eyes, smiled and said, "I'm listening, darling. What is it?"

Doyal smiled back. "Oh, that would be nice, but my heart is beating a bit louder right now. You won't enjoy the rhythm." He then continued, "I called you to let you know that the villagers invited me to a meeting."

Rahila asked, "To discuss what?"

Doyal replied, "To discuss the ongoing issues concerning our lakes and the recent erection of barbed wire. It didn't sit well with some of the neighbours, and I'm not sure what to expect at the meeting."

Rahila's face reflected concern. "The matter sounds worrying, Doyal. Do you want to call your sister and inform her about this meeting? I think she should be aware of the situation."

Doyal sighed. "I did call her, but she's not at home, probably busy with work. I left a message for her to return my call."

Rahila pondered the situation and said, "I don't know what to say, Doyal. I've done a bit of research and found that India has nothing to do with this stretch of the river. It has dried up due to natural causes. Similar droughts and floods are happening elsewhere in the world, and people are fighting over precious resources like water."

Just then a tiny voice interjected. "Daddy, can I do typing?" his daughter asked from his lap, reaching out to his computer keyboard.

"Of course, my dear, go ahead and type something nice," Doyal replied.

"I'm not sure how this will end, Doyal," his wife murmured, continuing with the conversation.

"But I have to attend the meeting, I can't just ignore their call," Doyal said.

"You're right, you can't ignore it. I'm afraid the villagers might vote in favour of abandoning the installation of barbed wire, which would deprive us of our only source of income and revenue. "Oh my," Rahila sighed, holding her head in her hands. "Listen to what they say, Doyal, and don't make any decision. Tell them you will consult with your sister and wife before deciding what to do."

"I guess I'll have to do that, Maa. Pori Moni, can Daddy

get some work done now? You can go with Mummy, my sweetie pie."

"Okay, Daddy!" Pori Moni responded.

Doyal kissed Pori Moni on the head as she got down from his lap.

"Oh, Rahila?" Doyal said. "I'm scared and dreading the questions they will ask."

"Don't worry, darling," Rahila reassured him. "Take your headphones with you and connect a call to my phone. I'll listen in to the conversation and assist with answers where I can."

"Yes, that's a great idea." Doyal smiled eagerly at the suggestion. "I will definitely do that!"

*

The congregational Friday prayer was held at the village mosque, with attendees from the surrounding villages. A written note had been passed on to the imam, which read, "Dear congregators, there will be a meeting held after the prayers about the ongoing water crisis in the village. Please stay behind to take part." The imam was asked to make this announcement over the microphone so that the meeting attendees could hear and gather in the main hall after their supplementary prayers.

Slowly but surely, people began to gather around the central area of the mosque. The topic turned out to be a hot one for the villagers, and the meeting room quickly filled up with people, standing shoulder to shoulder, all within just a few minutes. Doyal looked around, feeling quite nervous as the crowd buzzed with commotion echoing in his ears. He took a seat among the main circle of decision-makers and connected a live call to his wife, as previously agreed.

Mr Feroz Miah, the designated village elder, raised his arm, gesturing for silence. "Please be quiet," he shouted to the crowd. A few seconds later, everyone hushed down, and the talks began.

7

"Dear villagers, as you are all aware, for the past five to seven years, we have been facing the hardship of finding water. Some of you have been fortunate enough to install groundwater pumps to overcome the scarcity of water, but most villagers cannot afford to install them. Doyal Sultan, as we all know, is a great character, a very generous man, and he is currently the wealthiest individual in our village thanks to his education, forward thinking and well-thought-out life strategy. By God's will, he is a man of much wisdom. The situation has turned into a desperate survival challenge for the majority of those living in our village. Who knew that one day we would be facing this hardship? Doyal has looked after us for many years, and we owe it to him. His lakes are a lifeline for us, our livestock, and our plants and vegetation. It's not polite, but out of necessity, we would like to ask him to grant us permission to access his lakes permanently from now on to take water for ourselves and our livestock."

"Yeah, yeah, yeah," the crowd mumbled.

"Dear elders and respected brethren, please try to understand that these lakes are my only source of income. They are my livelihood. If I let them go dry, I will be unable to survive. What kind of request is this? My family worked hard to achieve all that we have, and now you are asking me to give it away to the villagers, just like that? What will happen when my lakes dry out completely?" Doyal asked.

The elders remained silent; however, a voice called out from the crowd. "Hey, Doyal!" A person stood up to show himself to the crowd. His name was Hussain Ali, the man who regularly brought his herds of cows to drink from Doyal's lakes without his approval, a troublemaker who had almost started a deadly fight involving a curved machete the other day. Doyal recognised his face and had a momentary flashback to that horrifying event where he had confronted the man and politely said:

"Hey, brother, can you please refrain from using my lakes on a regular basis? These are not public lakes."

In response, the guy had turned nasty and said, "Mr Shah, there are no other water sources in the village. Are you not aware of this fact, mister? There's no point in staring at me like that and raising your voice. This machete I am holding, I haven't used it since I sharpened it. Do you understand? Stay away and keep quiet and let me do what I am supposed to do, and that is to let my thirsty cattle drink the water they deserve."

Doyal was angered by these words. "What? What kind of unreasonable behaviour is that?" he contested. "This is not acceptable." He refrained from further confrontation due to the fact the man was armed.

From that day forward, he decided to enclose his lakes with barbed wire to prevent unwanted people from using his lakes willy-nilly.

Returning to today's meeting, the same troublesome individual spoke up. "You say you will perish. What about the rest of us? How are we going to survive without using those lakes? You're wealthy. Find a way to live and let us use the lakes freely. And listen, that barbed wire you're installing, consider it a waste of money because it won't stay up for long." He shook his head from side to side, indicating regret, before falling silent.

"Is that some kind of threat, man? Why are you talking like that?" Doyal asked, his anger evident.

"Not some kind of… it is a threat," replied Hussain Ali.

"Hey, stop it!" yelled Feroz Miah, the meeting coordinator. "What's your name?" he asked.

"Yes, I'm Hussain," he replied.

"Sit down, Hussain. Do you have children?"

"Yes, I have five children to feed, sir."

"Listen, Doyal," Feroz Miah, continued, "we understand your situation, but you have the means to tackle poverty, unlike many here. Therefore, you're in a much better position to show a higher degree of generosity. Everyone will be happy and will pray for your prosperity."

"Sir, with all due respect, and I'm not trying to offend anyone here, I only have two mouths to feed: my wife and my daughter. If people in this village can't feed themselves but are sane enough to bring more mouths into this world, then I'm not responsible. I'm not the provider of the world. Every parent should provide for their family with hard work and diligence."

"Hey, man, who are you to tell us how to live our lives?" shouted Hussain Ali. "I'm going to keep on using your lakes right before your eyes. Do what you can!"

The crowd murmured, with many agreeing, "I will use them too."

A voice came through Doyal's earpiece from his wife, saying, "Stay quiet and let them come to a decision. Do not make any more comments."

"Doyal Sultan!" called Feroz Miah, the meeting coordinator. "I understand where you are coming from. We are in a dire situation. I cannot call the meeting off without having the opinion of the congregation. Those of you who are in favour of using the lakes, please raise your hands!" A vast majority raised their hands, and Feroz Miah declared that the use of the lakes would continue without the need for the owner's permission.

Doyal was unhappy and uncomfortable with this ludicrous decision. He immediately stood up and left the scene, taking an alleyway to get to his house. Suddenly, a push from behind caused him to topple to the ground. He looked back and saw that Hussain Ali had caught up with him. Hussain grabbed Doyal by his shirt collar, pulling him up from the ground, and said, "If you're incapable of providing enough intimacy to assist your wife in conceiving children, bring her to me, understand? Don't you ever say I have too many mouths to feed."

Doyal couldn't take this abuse and fought back, exchanging punches and kicks for at least two minutes. Finally, Doyal gained the upper hand, neutralising Hussain Ali with continuous punches to the head. He stood up, slowly regained his strength and headed back home.

"Rahila! Rahila!" he called before entering the house. His face was a total mess, with black eyes, cuts to his eyebrows and cheekbones, and flesh ripped from his knuckles. Seeing this, his wife cried out loudly, followed by their daughter. "What happened?" she cried, holding his head.

"Rahila, get ready quickly! Pack your clothing and put Pori's essentials in a suitcase. You're going to your mum's."

"Why?" she cried.

"Don't waste time. They will come back to haunt us. I'll try to defend myself. If you stay, it will be hard. You have to protect our daughter."

"Okay, okay," she sobbed and rushed to the bedroom, frantically filling a suitcase with random clothes.

Doyal quickly composed himself, washed his face, applied antiseptic to his wounds and went out to hail an auto rickshaw from the nearby road. Moments later, he returned to the house. Rahila was ready, and she jumped onto the rickshaw, sobbing as she looked at her husband. "Don't worry," he said, "I'll be okay. Be careful and don't talk to any random people. Just go straight to your mum's. I'll call you soon." He watched as the rickshaw rode out of sight and into the distance.

He could hear his home phone ringing, but he wasn't in the mood to answer it, so he let it ring and allowed the call to switch to the answering machine. Suddenly, he heard his sister's voice as she was leaving a message. He rushed over and picked up the receiver to talk. "Hello, DiDi," he said.

"Hello, Doyal," answered Nadia. "I'm returning your call. I'm sorry I couldn't get to the phone earlier, I was caught up dealing with a scientific study. How are you all doing? How is my little princess?"

"Ah, DiDi," Doyal wept. "Everything has gone wrong here."

"Oh my god, Doyal, what happened? Why are you crying like that, my brother?" said his sister.

"A major incident took place between neighbours, and I hurt

someone very badly, DiDi. They want to take over our lakes, and I refused. Do you remember those quarrelsome brothers? It's them. Just half an hour ago, I had a confrontation with one of them. His name is Hussain Ali. A big fight broke out, and I injured him severely. My knuckles are all broken. I sent Rahila and Pori away to Rahila's parents' in fear that these people will return for retaliation."

"Why are you still at home? You should leave as well. You cannot fight them alone. I am coming with the police. I will call you. For now, go into hiding, flee the scene, lock the house, and go, go, Doyal."

"Okay, sister," replied Doyal.

Nadia hung up the phone and called her husband, Keith. "Keith! My brother needs our help. He's been attacked by neighbours over the dispute regarding our fish ponds."

"What? That's shocking news," said Keith.

"Can you get the car ready? I'm calling the police to accompany us there, or else these vile people will attack us too!"

"Okay," said Keith.

Meanwhile, Rahila and Pori Moni were on the move in a rickshaw. The rickshaw driver asked, "Madam, where to?"

"Head for Ishwardi Airport," Rahila replied.

"Yes, ma'am," the driver said and drove for a couple of minutes. The driver could see a man on the roadside hooting and waving at them. "Madam, what shall I do? There is a man ahead signalling for us to stop."

"Just drive on, driver, we are in a hurry."

"Oh no, madam, he's in the middle of the road. Now, I can't run him over." The driver stopped suddenly. "Hey, what's wrong with you, man? Are you on a suicide mission? Get off the road!" said the driver.

The man approached the driver, drew a metre-long, thin-bladed, curved machete, looked at the driver and said, "You talk too much. Do you want me to slice you open and examine your guts for bravery?"

"Apologies, sir, please let us go," pleaded the driver.

"You can go, driver. Leave the passengers behind."

"Brother, who are you, and why have you stopped us like this? Please let us go," pleaded Rahila.

"Get off the vehicle," said the attacker. Rahila trembled with fear, the anxiety showing on her face. "Please let us go," she sobbed not knowing why this person was attacking her.

"Get off the vehicle now," shouted the attacker and pulled her out onto the road by force. Her mothering instincts kicked in, and she pushed him aside, grabbing her daughter and taking her into her arms.

"Please don't hurt us," she said.

"Hey, driver, you go, or I will chop your head off. GO!" said the attacker.

"You bitch, how dare you push me like that," said the attacker. He grabbed her by her hair and dragged her off the road, heading deep into the jungle, showing no mercy and saying, "I do not need a reason to attack anyone. When my hormones tell me I desire a female, I seek one out."

She kept a tight hold on her daughter, while her daughter began to cry witnessing all this abusive behaviour.

*

Nadia Begum, Doyal's sister, and her husband were on their way to the village, speeding in their private car to get there as soon as possible.

*

Rahila's attacker dragged her and Pori Moni to a remote farmhouse, a couple of hundred metres into the jungle. He manhandled them into the derelict house and locked the door behind him and told Rahila to take off her clothes.

"Take off your clothes, I said," he yelled.

"What!"

"I said take off your clothes. I didn't drag you in here to look at your face, come on… take them off! Don't make it difficult."

"Oh, please let me go, you're my brother, please, I beg you, have some mercy on me. My husband is a rich man, he will pay you money," she sobbed.

"Shut the fuck up! I have got enough sisters to deal with. Take them off and be obedient or else…!" The attacker dropped his lecherous gaze at Rahila's daughter who seemed to be crawling up against a nearby wall scared out of her wits and crying. Rahila realised this would only get worse if the monster's attention was drawn towards her daughter and became physical, so she quickly pretended she would obey. She said, "Okay, if you are that desperate, I will give you what you want, but first you must let my daughter walk out the door or else, *Khuda kasam* (I swear to God) I will take my life before your eyes."

"It's a jungle out there where she's going," said the attacker. "Let her stay here."

"No, I will not let her see this. You let her walk out this door. I would rather see a tiger take her than you harm her. Let her go now," she pleaded.

"You're a fucking mad woman!" He walked to the door, unlocked it and jambed it open, then wandered off and sat on a haystack.

Rahila approached her daughter and gave her an affectionate hug, tears dripping from her cheeks, and whispered in her ear, "Don't worry, everything will be okay. Mummy will be coming soon. You get out of here and run. Go to the main road where you can hear the cars, my darling. Listen for the sounds of cars! Okay? Do not stop, just keep on moving until you get to the road," she cried and let her daughter go. After walking a few metres her daughter looked back at her saddened. Her mother gazed back and ushered her along using the back of her arm. "Go, go," she whispered, and sobbed deeply.

Rahila shut the door behind her and called at the monster, "Come on, let's see how you fuck me now, you son of a bitch. You want me to take my clothes off, huh? Here." She ripped her kameez open in anger, revealing her black bra, and threw it at him. He caught it with a smile, then he took the kameez to his nostrils and sniffed it before throwing it away.

"Come on, you bastard!" she screamed. She composed herself into a fighting mode and launched an attack with punches and kicks. She managed to drop a few good blows on him. A few minutes passed, with both parties fighting fiercely, but soon he overcame her power and pinned her beneath him on the floor, which was covered in a layer of loose hay. He wrestled with her, kissing and grinding, and latched on to her neck with his mouth. When Rahila got a chance she bit his left ear right off. He screamed in pain. Section of his ear could be seen hanging from Rahila's mouth. She spat the flesh onto the floor and jumped up, as blood gushed from the attacker. Her mouth smeared with blood too, she reached for the kameez. He shouted, "You fucking bitch! I told you not to make it hard for me, but you didn't listen." Rahila quickly ran towards the door to escape. As she had her back turned to the attacker, he drew that same long, razor-sharp, curved machete from under the haystack and leapt towards her, cutting right through her neck. The head separated from the body, a stream of blood jetted out, and her head fell to the ground followed by her body. He had basically slashed her into two pieces. The attacker fetched her kameez, tied it round his head and ear, and yelled, "I said not to resist, you ignored and now you are dead. You brought this on yourself, you bitch. Now you may rest in peace."

*

As Rahila's daughter made her way to the highway and walked alongside it, Nadia and Keith happened to approach the same stretch of road. Their attention was drawn to a small girl walking alone. "Keith! Keith! Stop the car!" Nadia urgently called out. He promptly pulled the car to the side of the road. Nadia leapt out of the car and rushed to the child. To her astonishment, she recognised the girl as her niece, Pori Moni. Overwhelmed with relief, she embraced and cuddled the little one.

"Oh, my sweetie pie," Nadia exclaimed, tears of worry in her eyes. She anxiously asked, "Where are you coming from?" Pori Moni replied that a man had taken her mother into the jungle, leaving Nadia in shock. "Oh my goodness, what's happening?" Nadia wondered aloud. "Where can I go to look for her now? Keith, let's continue to our village. We'll come back with Doyal." They got back in the car and headed towards their village, with Nadia doing her best to comfort Pori Moni. She gave the girl a cereal bar to nibble on and some juice to drink. Soon, they reached Doyal's house, only to discover another heart-wrenching tragedy. Doyal lay lifeless on the floor. Nadia let out a piercing scream of sorrow, and Keith swiftly held Pori Moni in his arms, leading her away from the distressing scene. Nadia's cries echoed within the four walls as she wept and asked, "Oh my brother, who could have done this to you? Why you? Why you?"

Keith sat outside on a patio stool, pulled out his phone and dialled the police. "Hello, there's been a homicide in Arambaria. Please send help immediately."

The police reassured him that they were already en route to Arambaria. "It's a remote location, so it might take a bit longer, but they are on their way. We're also dispatching an ambulance."

"Thank you, officer," Keith replied before ending the call.

CHAPTER 2

THE BURIAL

Nadia

Keith

Faroque

Tara

Aysha

Chowdhury

Suzy

Hakim

Malik

Pori

Starring

Keith Evan - Nadia Begum – Detective Faroque Talukdar – Constable Tara Miah - Sub-Inspector Aysha Khanom – Suzy Chakraboty house maid – Polash Chowdhury lawyer – Abdul Hakim rapist dad – Abdul Malik rapist.

Nadia was overcome with grief at her brother's death. She clung to his bloodied body, crying audibly. "My only brother is no longer with me… Oh God, help me accept this fact," she sobbed. Nadia had always been emotionally resilient, but this tragedy shattered her. Her father had passed away from a sudden cardiac arrest due to land conflicts several years ago, and her mother had died of natural causes. Today's tragedy, her brother's death, stemmed from a dispute over their privately owned domestic lakes.

"Oh God, how am I going to continue in this world all alone?" she cried out in agony.

Throughout this ordeal, Keith remained outside with little Pori Moni. He shielded her from witnessing her father's lifeless body on the bloodstained floor.

Moments later, the sound of approaching emergency vehicles reached their ears. Several police cars and an ambulance pulled up in front of the house. Detective Inspector Faroque Talukdar emerged from one of the cars and approached Keith.

"Did you call the police?" the officer enquired.

"Yes, I did," Keith replied.

"And your name is?"

"Keith."

"Hi, I'm Detective Inspector Talukdar," the officer said introducing himself. "I'll be in charge of this investigation. Is the suspect still on the property, Keith?"

"I don't believe so," Keith answered.

"Where did the incident occur?"

"Inside the house," Keith replied.

"May I go inside to have a look?" DI Talukdar asked.

"Of course," Keith acknowledged. "Just give me a moment." He motioned for Pori to sit down while he informed DI Talukdar that he would join them shortly.

Uncle Keith guided Pori to a bamboo-woven chair, setting her down gently. He then directed the detective inside the house.

DI Talukdar entered the house and immediately noticed Nadia clinging to her brother's lifeless body on the floor. He enquired, "Who is she?"

Keith promptly replied, "She's his sister, Nadia."

The detective called out, "Aysha!" He continued, "I need you to gently separate the lady from the victim and remove her from the crime scene without causing any disruption."

"Okay, sir," Aysha responded.

Approaching the scene calmly, Aysha placed her hands on Nadia's shoulder and softly called her. "Madam," she said, nudging her shoulder as Nadia resisted. "We are here now. Please stand up, and we'll take care of everything from here."

Nadia glanced at Aysha and said, "You must send a team to locate my sister-in-law, Rahila, his wife. She has been taken by his killers."

"Of course, ma'am," DI Talukdar assured her. "First, please step outside." Nadia slowly rose and walked out with Aysha's support.

"Nadia, I am Detective Inspector Talukdar," he said introducing himself.

Nadia met his gaze with red, teary eyes.

"Listen," the detective continued, "my team will secure the area to preserve the evidence, preventing anyone from entering or leaving the crime scene. We'll document the details of any rescue personnel entering this zone. Please provide your full information and a thumbprint to my colleague, Police Constable Tara Miah. He will ask both of you a series of questions. Please answer to the best of your ability, as this will serve as evidence for a later date. Once we complete these formalities, we will begin the search for your sister-in-law."

PC Miah proceeded to ask Nadia a series of questions and recorded her responses while the medical and forensics teams initiated their investigations.

Nadia confirmed her willingness to lead them to the last place where she suspected her sister-in-law Rahila was seen. She glanced back at the house, observing the medical team's activities.

"Don't worry, everything will be fine," DI Talukdar reassured them. "Your focus should be on guiding us to Rahila's location."

"Yes," Nadia replied.

"Aysha, please help her into the jeep." The detective added, "I'll join you shortly."

Aysha assisted Nadia, Pori and Keith into the police jeep.

Meanwhile, the internal investigation was in full swing, meticulously collecting evidence, including blood samples and fingerprints, and taking photographs. Doyal's body had been carefully retrieved and carried to an ambulance.

DI Talukdar boarded the jeep and said, "Let's get moving." They began driving, with Nadia directing them to the location where they had found Pori walking alone.

"Hey, Pori Moni, which way did they take your mother?" Nadia enquired once they had reached the roadside. Pori pointed towards the jungle. The police followed her lead, and after a brief search, they came across a rundown farmhouse.

DI Talukdar entered the house and found blood splatters everywhere, but there were no bodies to be seen. After an extensive search of the interior and surrounding areas, he returned to the police vehicle and instructed Aysha to take Nadia and Keith back to their car. They needed to conduct a thorough investigation of the farmhouse to make sense of the situation.

Aysha emerged from the jungle, and Nadia asked, "Did you find her, officer?"

"No, there's no one inside. We'll need to investigate this thoroughly. You two should head back to your residence and wait for further updates," the officer replied.

"Okay, officer," Nadia said. She held Aysha's hand, her eyes filled with tears. She pleaded, "Please find my sister-in-law. Look at this child. She has just lost her father, and if she loses her mother too, her world will crumble."

Aysha comforted her, saying, "Don't worry. I'll do my best to locate your sister-in-law. You both should go. Leave everything to me." Aysha hailed a rickshaw for Nadia and emphasised, "You're not allowed to return to the house for the night due to ongoing investigations. Take what you need. PC Miah will give you access to your belongings. Head straight to your own residence. Do you understand?"

"Okay," Nadia agreed.

They reached their car, and Nadia cast a sorrowful glance at the property. She turned away and got into the car, securing Pori in her seat. Keith started the engine and they drove away.

Leaving the scene behind, they headed back to Dhaka.

*

Aysha returned to the farmhouse where she had left DI Talukdar. Upon her arrival, he halted her in her tracks and suggested, "Let's go. There's nothing more we can do here."

"But, sir!" Aysha protested.

"Aysha, you know how it is. Wealthy people often have many friends and connections. She's probably gone off to have a good time. Give it a couple of days, and everything will likely be fine. We've seen plenty of cases like this before," DI Talukdar explained.

"Sir, this is mere speculation. Her husband just died, and her daughter... Do you really think she'd disappear to socialise with friends? It's absurd," Aysha said venting her frustration.

"Aysha, there's no need to get upset. This sort of thing happens all the time. Just last week, a woman left her six-month-old baby outside an orphanage. Relax, she'll probably return soon. People are going through immense emotional trauma. Look at this farmhouse. It's essentially a slaughterhouse for livestock. The ground is soaked with blood, and you can see cowhide and sheepskins hanging inside to dry. Even if something did happen here, it'd be a monumental task to uncover anything. Let's focus on the homicide case and get the autopsy done as quickly as possible so we can close this case," DI Talukdar advised.

"Alright, sir, as you wish," Aysha reluctantly agreed. "But my instincts don't quite align with this."

DI Talukdar chuckled and said, "Come on, let's go. A woman's intuition is often a fragile thing."

*

After a lengthy drive, Nadia and Keith finally arrived at their home, utterly exhausted. They resided in an apartment building with a reliable water supply, a far cry from the rural areas where access to water depended on deep wells or hand-pump systems. Upon reaching home, they wasted no time, immediately switching on the water heater and ensuring Pori Moni's comfort by serving her potato-filled parathas. They then encouraged her to take a short nap, allowing them a rare moment to rest.

Keith embraced Nadia, offering her a comforting kiss and reassuring her that everything would be alright despite the recent tragedy. "Come on, let's freshen up," he suggested.

Both of them rose and made their way to the bathroom. Nadia, the expert at setting the ambiance, lit a scented oil burner to fill the room with a pleasant aroma. Keith, on the other hand, was known for his thorough scrubbing. Together, they relished the sensation of washing away the stress and sweat that had accumulated during their recent village vacation.

The following day, Keith had to return to work, given the backlog of tasks awaiting him. Meanwhile, Nadia, with her newfound responsibility for Pori Moni, decided to make it her mission to care for her niece. She decided to take some time off work to provide the best care during this crucial phase of parenthood. Nadia began by feeding her niece a hearty breakfast and taking her to a lovely clothing store to purchase some new outfits. They also made a detour to the toy section, where Pori Moni got to choose a few toys. Their day continued with a visit to a local activity park, where they both relished the funfair and shared hours of joy and delight. Nadia managed the day so well that Pori Moni only asked for her mother once throughout the entire day. Feeling a sense of accomplishment, Nadia promised herself that she would dedicate quality time to care for this little girl, no matter the challenges that lay ahead. This commitment was a challenge Nadia had willingly taken on, and only time would reveal if she could fulfil it. On their way back home, they stopped by a street vendor selling freshly made candy floss from a spinning drum. Nadia bought a portion on a stick and handed it to Pori Moni before heading home.

*

Three days later, Nadia's phone rang and it was DI Talukdar on the line. He informed her that the police had completed their fact-checking and urged her to take control of her brother's property in the village of Arambaria. "If you don't intend to reside there, ma'am," he cautioned, "the property may become vulnerable to unauthorised visitors, including vandals and trespassers. To prevent costly damage and avoid the need for us to deal with preventable crimes, please secure the property promptly to ensure it remains safe and secure from potential thieves and intruders. We have gathered all the necessary evidence, and we cordially invite you to visit the Lalpur Bazaar police station at your earliest convenience for an update on this case. Please have a pen ready. I will provide you with a case reference number and the direct phone number for Sub Inspector Aysha Khanom, who is well informed about this case and can offer detailed updates at any time. "Could you give her a call before your visit? This will help with our time management."

Nadia took note of the reference and phone number and then enquired about her sister-in-law, Rahila. "Has there been any news about her?" she asked. The detective regretfully replied that there were no signs of Rahila's whereabouts. There was a farmhouse deep in the jungle, but no substantial leads had emerged to suspect anyone's involvement. He explained that the case would remain open as a missing person file, and the investigation would persist. "Could you please provide a recent photograph of your sister-in-law when arranging to meet my colleague Aysha?" he requested.

Upon hearing this, Nadia's heart sank, and frustration welled up within her to the point where she contemplated slamming the phone down in anger. But she refrained, realising that venting her anger at this stage would be futile. "Okay, officer," she conceded. "I will get in touch with Aysha and proceed from there. Thank you, and goodbye," she concluded before ending the call.

Nadia considered that it was a good time to contact her lawyer and arrange an appointment, particularly if she could meet at the property while in the area to save time. She hoped to discuss her sister-in-law's disappearance with the lawyer and seek advice before dealing with the police. She had grown tired of the police's behaviour, perceiving them not only as corrupt but as essentially acting like thieves. The laws were inadequately enforced on corrupt officers due to their political protection and impunity. The public offered more money in bribes to the police than the Bangladesh government paid them in wages, and this had emanated into a way of life now. Nadia was determined to alter this dishonest and fraudulent conduct promptly.

Keith returned from work and found Nadia hurriedly heating up food. He approached her, embraced her from behind, rested his chin on her shoulder and whispered in her ear, "What's the rush?" Nadia turned her head and kissed his lips, saying, "I'm trying to warm up some food so I can feed you, darling. You must be exhausted. Go and freshen up. I have some things to discuss at the dinner table as well."

Keith grinned and responded, "Yes, ma'am. You're quite the efficient time manager. I won't be long." He then headed to the bathroom. Nadia prepared the food and set the dining table, calling out to Pori Moni to join them.

"Pori!"

"Yes," came an innocent response from a distance.

Nadia heard her reply and called out, "Come, let's have something to eat, dear."

Keith entered the dining room and surveyed the table, his eyebrows raised in anticipation of the meal. "Wow, this looks delicious. Flat beans with fish! I can't wait to dig in." Pori Moni peered timidly into the dining room, hesitating to enter fully, leaving the door ajar.

"Come on in, dear. Why have you stopped? Don't be shy. Come in and take a seat," Keith encouraged. He glanced at Pori Moni and realised she might be feeling uncomfortable. She decided to sit beside her aunt.

Keith rose from his seat, wearing a warm smile as he gently held Pori Moni's hand. "Pori Moni, you're a beautiful daughter. I'm Uncle Keith, so there's no need to be shy around me. This is your house, and Nadia is your mum. I understand I may look a bit different, but I'm your uncle. You can call me Keith or Kaka, or anything you prefer. I have no problem with that, okay?"

Nadia smiled at Keith and then shared a thought. "You know, Keith, I read a column in a European newspaper a while back. It talked about how, when people mention 'white privilege' in the UK, white individuals often become quite surprised and puzzled. They wonder why it's even brought up. To them, white people also experience poverty and difficult circumstances, sometimes even worse than Black and Brown people. So, they're puzzled about where this idea of white privilege comes from."

"Isn't that true, though? Where does white privilege come from?" Keith pondered.

Nadia clarified, "It's not about wealth or social status, Keith. Let me give you an example. If a person with brown or black skin plans to buy a house in the UK, especially in a predominantly white area, they often think, *Will I be welcome in this predominantly white neighbourhood?* But for a white person, this concern doesn't usually apply. They buy and settle without question. Another example: a white immigrant's child can readily claim to be English without any issue, while Black and Brown individuals may face questions. That's what white privilege is about.

"Here in Bangladesh, you're a minority, and you're explaining your existence to a four-year-old. Why? Because here, brown privilege is unconsciously at play," Nadia said with a chuckle. "You know that's why you're justifying your presence."

"Yes, I understand now," Keith responded. Still holding Pori Moni's hand, he continued, "This house is your house, our house, okay? We'll all stay here together as one team, sharing everything in life, alright?" He smiled and encouraged her to eat because they were all hungry. Playfully, Keith took a spoonful from her plate and gobbled it down, prompting Pori Moni to protest, "Hey, that's mine!"

Keith smiled, gently touched her cheek, returned to his seat and began eating. Nadia then explained to Keith that she needed to visit the village soon, as the police had called and said many things she wasn't happy with. "I can't accompany you this time, Nadia," Keith lamented. "I'm tied up with work back-to-back for at least two consecutive weeks."

"It's okay, I'm just informing you," Nadia reassured.

"I feel bad that I can't be with you, but please take precautions, whatever you decide to do. It's not safe out there. However, you have to do what's right, and these formalities must be addressed. Stay strong, as always, okay?" said Keith expressing his concern.

"Of course. Don't you worry. They've assigned a female inspector named Aysha, and I hope she cooperates well with me. Have you been able to determine the cost of education and self-defence classes for the little one, Keith?" Nadia enquired.

Keith hesitated before responding, "Are you sure you want to go down this path, Nadia? People can turn ruthless, merciless and somewhat sadistic during military training."

Nadia felt offended by Keith's remarks and retorted, "What do you mean, Keith? What do you expect me to do, then?"

Keith looked at her and said, "I'm just sharing my thoughts."

"Don't just say it, Keith, give me an answer. You saw how brutally they killed my brother, and they likely did the same to my sister-in-law, burning her remains and scattering her ashes in the Padma River most likely. I don't have another brother. He was my support and hope, the only bloodline left. Now it's just me and this little one. How are we going to defend ourselves? We are vulnerable females in a desert infested with predators. I don't care what she becomes, as long as she can protect herself. Okay? Please arrange for her training from an early age."

Keith laid out two possible routes. "You have two options. First, you give her a traditional education until she's sixteen and then enrol her in British military training to become a British soldier. This route will save you some money because British Army Recruitment will train her in exchange for a certain number of years' service with them. Second, there are private military-level training programmes available. Recently, one centre was opened by a famous retired British secret service agent. He is now dedicated to training others like him. By the time she reaches sixteen, his company will be well established, offering numerous training opportunities. My concern is that this training is contractual, and she'll have to commit to at least three to five years once she turns sixteen. How are you going to make her join? You can't force anyone to do anything in the UK, and children are very demanding. They know their rights. She will learn hers too and might not want to join army training."

Nadia enquired about the cost, and Keith replied, "You're looking at £50,000 to £60,000 after living expenses for five years."

"Thank you! That wasn't too difficult, was it? To meet this requirement, I'll need to sell a couple of acres of valuable land here in Bangladesh. You don't need to worry about how I'll fund this or ensure she joins at the age of sixteen. I have my own methods to make things work. You've seen how people wrap bombs around themselves and carry out devastating actions. Do you have any idea how their mentors persuade them to do such things? I doubt it. I have a similar strategy up my sleeve to guide Pori and mould her according to my wishes. Only time will tell if my subtly persuasive approach will make her a strong, independent individual for the future."

"Very well, I'm on it. I'll gather information about a few reputable training centres for you," Keith offered.

*

A few days later, Nadia embarked on her journey back to her village. She enlisted the assistance of a maid named Suzy Chakraboty and secured rental accommodation near the Lalpur Bazaar police station. This rental served as her safe haven, as she was unwilling to take any chances staying alone with the child at her brother's house. Her plan was to return from the village and spend the night in the property, which offered concierge services and was known for its safety. Her concern was that her brother's assailant might pose a threat to her and the child. The house would be her primary overnight sanctuary, where she would carry out the work necessary to seek justice for her late brother. Upon arriving at the house, they took a quick shower to wash off the dust accumulated during the long journey, had their evening supper and then went straight to bed for a peaceful night's sleep.

The following morning, with the sunrise, they visited her brother's house in the village. Along the way, they picked up breakfast and groceries from an early morning street vendor. Upon returning home, the maid began preparing breakfast while being instructed to keep their rental property a secret due to the lurking danger.

Nadia and her child sat at the dining table, playing with toys, when they heard a knock on the front door. "It must be Inspector Aysha," Nadia said. She got up, opened the door and was captivated by Aysha's appearance. "Wow, you look so different and beautiful in that traditional salwar kameez, especially the gradient blue transitioning into baby pink. Wow, like a superhero!"

"Thank you so much, ma'am," Aysha smiled.

A surprised Nadia asked, "Aren't you on duty today, Aysha? You're not in your police uniform."

"No, ma'am, I'm off duty today. I didn't want to miss this important update when I heard you were coming. It was imperative for me to see you, whether on or off duty. It felt like the right thing to do, to come and offer my condolences for your loss. I am so sorry for your loss, ma'am. My heart goes out to you and the little one."

Nadia was touched and said, "Oh, that's so sweet of you. Come in and sit down," she said gesturing for her to take a seat. "I'm really proud of you, Aysha. I'm well aware of how institutionally misogynistic Bangladeshi police departments can be. Yet, you've exceeded everyone's expectations. I salute you, madam!"

Aysha responded, "You're absolutely right, ma'am. We encounter sexist behaviour so often that we've developed immunity to this disease. We hardly notice it anymore. Just this year, 1,000 women were raped, and 300 were killed. The culture of impunity and the barriers imposed by men when it comes to accessing justice is pure evil. In my spare time, I'm a women's rights activist, ma'am. I run a small non-profit organisation called the Association of Free Women, based in Lalpur Bazaar, where we encourage females to become independent yet strong in maintaining family bonds. Wish me luck in taking this noble cause to a national level someday."

"It's no wonder I'm proud of you, Aysha. I believe it's a gift from God. Sometimes, I can discern good from evil in my mind as clear as crystal. The moment I felt your hand on my shoulder in my brother's house, I experienced peace in my mind. I knew you were more than you appeared to be, unlike your colleague DI Talukdar, in whom I sensed a hint of corruption.

"By the way, I'm a member of your organisation, in case you didn't know. I regularly make financial contributions, though I've been quite distant, which is why we haven't had a chance to meet up."

"Oh, really? I've been quite occupied with police duty, and the organisation is primarily managed by a few volunteers, ma'am," Aysha replied.

"I don't expect you to remember everyone. By the way, the work you're doing to assist women in need of support is remarkable, Aysha. Well done, and bless you," Nadia praised.

"Thank you, ma'am." Aysha smiled warmly.

"Suzy, put the kettle on, dear," Nadia requested, her voice breaking. She sighed and tears welled up in her eyes. "I don't know what to do, my sister. I feel so disheartened when I contemplate life. The phrase men often use, 'Life is a bitch', is sadly true. It can bite you in the most inconvenient ways, and it has betrayed me terribly. My only family vanished right before my eyes."

Aysha listened attentively, responding to Nadia's distress. "I understand this is an incredibly challenging time for you. But have patience. Things will get better. Nothing remains the same, and time is a great healer, ma'am."

Nadia nodded. "Yes, of course," she replied, sniffing. "I received a call from DI Talukdar. He informed me that Doyal's body will be released from the coroner's office tomorrow. Unfortunately, he passed away due to natural causes. He suggested we put this matter on hold for now."

"So, Aysha, what is this absurdity DI Talukdar is talking about?" Nadia implored, her voice trembling. "Please tell me the truth. Is it possible for a married woman, a mother of a four-year-old daughter, to vanish without a trace unless she was abducted or even worse…?" She sobbed uncontrollably.

Aysha approached Nadia, gently touching her shoulder to offer comfort. "Please, calm down, ma'am," she reassured. "People can often be unreasonable, dishonest and ruthless, driven by excessive greed that leads to unethical gains."

"Here's your tea, ma'am." Suzy brought a cup and placed it on the table in front of Aysha.

"Thank you," Aysha acknowledged as she picked up the teacup and began to speak. "You see, Nadia ma'am," she continued, "our country's political and economic landscape is marred by corruption, perjury, falsification and more, causing misery, division and hardship among its citizens. You're not the first. There are thousands like you who receive no justice at all. This has to change. I'm tired of witnessing dishonesty among my own colleagues every day. I wish some extraordinary force could rise up and transform the way we conduct ourselves in this society. But it's highly unlikely to happen. According to DI Talukdar, he went to the farmhouse and found nothing. He called me and recommended dismissing the claim and filing a missing person case, ma'am."

"In regard to your brother's post-mortem report," Aysha continued, "it states that he died of a cardiac arrest at home, as you're already aware. His injuries were not the cause of his death. That's the update I'm here to convey to you today. You can collect his body for burial tomorrow, and they will call you to attend the coroner's office."

Nadia gazed at Aysha, her eyes filled with tears. "I can't even believe the coroner," she declared. "Where did his injuries come from, huh? Because of those injuries, he might have suffered a cardiac arrest. It's a possibility…" Nadia's voice broke as she cried.

A knock on the door interrupted their conversation. Nadia sniffled and composed herself. "Ah, it must be my lawyer," she said with a trembling voice.

"Do you need some privacy? Should we talk later?" Aysha enquired.

"No, not at all," Nadia replied. "You can stay. Nothing is private here, and it's even better if you stay. The lawyer will need to be extra diligent in his duty of care." With that, Nadia opened the door.

"Hello, Mr Chowdhury, please come in and have a seat. This is Inspector Aysha, she's off duty today," Nadia said introducing her.

"Sub Inspector!" Aysha corrected.

"Yes, whatever. You are all the same to me, protectors of civil society," Nadia remarked. "That's my niece and my maid, Suzy. Get some tea for Mr Chowdhury, Suzy."

"Yes, ma'am," Suzy responded and prepared the tea.

"So, let's hear what you have to say, Mr Chowdhury, given my circumstances," Nadia requested.

"The inheritance act is straightforward, ma'am. The beneficiary of an estate can be a minor, like your niece. However, the minor is not entitled to receive their share of the estate until they reach the age of eighteen," Mr Chowdhury explained.

"So, does that mean that I, as her only aunt, can take charge of all the properties my brother owns?" Nadia enquired.

"Yes, certainly. However, you cannot sell any properties, lands or other assets without a valid reason. Before selling, you must file a legitimate deed of sales order and present it before an inheritance lawyer, like myself. You'll need to provide fully documented information as to why this sale is taking place," Mr Chowdhury replied.

"What about selling it in an emergency?" Nadia asked.

In response, Mr Chowdhury handed over a booklet. "Here, take this. It contains all the information on selling the inheritance of minors. Please study it carefully. Most of the questions are answered here, but if you have other unanswered questions not mentioned here, I'm just a phone call away." He sipped his tea, and then asked Nadia to sign a copy of the contract. Nadia signed it, and he said, "It's sorted, then."

As Mr Chowdhury rose to leave, he added, "Here, this is your copy to keep. My contact details are in the footnotes of these copies. Keep this document safe. It's a harsh environment out there," and then he left.

Nadia and Aysha continued their conversation. "If there's anything I can do for you, ma'am, let me know. I understand your situation, and it's not easy to ask for help. I'm here for you," Aysha reassured. Suddenly, a voice emerged from outside the house.

"Hello! Is anyone home?"

"Who's that?" Nadia said, puzzled. "I'm not expecting anyone else today."

She went to the door and opened it. "Greetings, ma'am! I am

Hakim, Abdul Hakim, from a few villages south of the Padma River. This is my son, Abdul Malik. May we have a few words with you, please?" (Nadia is unaware that this son is the one responsible for the abduction and murder of her sister-in-law, dismembering her into pieces.) Nadia stepped outside; Suzy was cutting vegetables by the window on the front porch, and the little one was still playing inside with toys. Aysha also stepped out of the house to see who had called.

"Wow, who is this beauty?" the son remarked, leering at Aysha.

"She is an off-duty police officer," Nadia replied.

"Oops." He promptly retracted his gaze.

"Yes, I am listening," Nadia said to the main man, Mr Hakim.

"We are saddened for your loss, but I hear you married an Englishman and you are leaving for the UK?" Hakim enquired.

"And who told you that?" Nadia asked.

"Aha, madam. News like this floats in the air like pollen. I understand there is nothing left for you here. A white husband and England are your final destination. What is here? Horrific memories. The sooner you get rid of those memories, the fewer nightmares. There is nothing to look forward to," Hakim remarked.

"It seems you're speaking your mind like a fortune teller, but I'm not going anywhere, Mr Hakim. I don't understand what makes you say such things so vehemently," Nadia responded.

Mr Hakim looked at Suzy, rolled his eyes over Aysha and then fixed his gaze on Nadia. He smiled and began to speak. "Ahem… I have a proposal, ma'am. There's a plot of land, roughly three acres in size, right in between my own plots. The owner is no longer with us, and I was wondering if you'd be willing to sell it to us on behalf of your late brother. This would allow me to expand my landscape into a complete flat piece of land."

Nadia, briefly lost in thought, considered the financial needs for Pori Moni's education, training and wellbeing in the future. The rest of her life lay ahead, and here was a significant opportunity to secure the funds for a fresh start and new beginnings.

"So, what's on your mind, Mr Hakim?" she enquired. "How much can you offer for my three acres of land, sandwiched between your grounds?"

"I can offer one lakh per acre," Mr Hakim proposed.

"What? You must be out of your mind, mister!" Nadia was disgusted by the offer. A single acre of land was generally valued at twenty lakhs in the area, and he was suggesting a mere one lakh for this sought-after piece of property. "What are you thinking? Please leave my property by the shortest route, which is the way you came in. I have completely lost interest."

"Think about it, Madam Ji. The land may deteriorate without yielding any return at all," Mr Hakim urged.

"Oh, go get lost! What are you trying to say? I don't get scared that easily," Nadia retorted.

"Of course you don't get scared, or else, why go with a white man who enslaved us for 200 years in the past," commented Abdul Malik, the son.

"What?" Nadia exclaimed.

"Nadia ma'am," said Mr Hakim, "the truth is when you're not here, living in the UK, a piece of land like this will quickly attract invaders. Other people will encroach upon it, causing me problems. If you could reconsider my offer, I will pay two lakhs for an acre."

"What, mister? I am not interested. Just leave my property now," Nadia insisted.

"And if we don't leave, what are you going to do?" Mr Hakim challenged.

Anger surged through Nadia's veins. She started breathing heavily, giving her goosebumps all over. In frustration, she banged her wrist against the pillar she was standing by, shattering her glass bangles into little pieces that pierced her skin, causing blood to drip. She screeched in a high-pitched voice, "Get out of my property now, you son of dogs, or I will drive you both away!"

"You evil, possessed woman! Your whole family is tainted by

evil spirits. You have no respect for your elders. No wonder you married a white man. Bengalis won't take you for any decent job, you…" His son Malik spewed hateful words.

Pori Moni, alarmed by her aunt's screams, rushed out. As soon as she saw Abdul Malik's face, she recognised him as the person who had abducted her mother. She cried out loudly, "Mummmyyeee!" while pointing her finger at Malik.

Nadia, staring at her niece with shock, had heard enough and couldn't bear the abuse any longer. In a swift move, she dashed off to retrieve the traditional Indian tool called a '*daa*'. This machete featured a cast iron blade with legs and was typically used to sit and cut vegetables with ease. With determination, she swung the *daa* from behind her shoulder, hurling it towards Malik. "You bastard!" she shouted, advancing with the intent to take swift action.

Simultaneously, Aysha leapt out quickly, reaching from behind to grab Nadia's other hand, preventing her from following through. "Let him bark. Dogs always bark. You calm down, and let him go. It's not the right moment for this," Aysha advised gently.

"You mad woman! Your whole family is mad! How dare you raise that *daa* against me, you piece of shit. You will regret this day. I will make sure you regret it," Malik threatened before turning his back on Nadia and walking away.

Nadia trembled with anger, and Aysha guided her inside. On the way, Nadia grabbed her niece and comforted her in her arms. "Suzy, get some water, please," Aysha requested. Nadia, in a state of shock, sat in silence. Suzy brought a glass of water and placed it in front of her. Nadia picked it up and took a sip, feeling devastated and emotionally shaken.

"What just happened?" Nadia asked, shaking her head in disbelief.

"It's okay. These are low-life individuals who attempted to invade your space. You stood your ground, and this should make them think twice before coming back here," Aysha reassured her.

"I'm scared," Nadia admitted.

"Don't worry. If they return next time, call the police immediately and tell them your life is in danger. They will come to your aid," Aysha advised.

"What about this incident?" Nadia enquired.

"I'm not sure. If you report it, the police will likely call the perpetrators to the station. If they claim you attempted to attack them with the *daa* and say that I was present, they may take my testimony. I can't lie, and things could escalate. You might also get arrested for attempting an assault on them," Aysha explained.

"Okay, let's leave it for now," Nadia said.

"Ma'am, what if they come back on a different day or attack in the street? You have to make a report of this. The guy clearly said you will regret it. Just say you and I were at home. There's no need to mention Madam Aysha. Tell the officers that you contained the situation and don't want to take it further at this stage. However, if things repeat themselves, you will see to it," Suzy suggested.

"That's not a bad idea, Suzy," Aysha agreed.

"Why is it that our men hold this anti-woman rhetoric all the time? Why did this Malik have to say Bengali men rejected me, hence I went with a white man? The reality is men were pursuing me, but I rejected them all because of their twisted and controlling mindset," Nadia admitted.

"Wow, that's a positive outlook. Is he treating you well, then?" Aysha enquired with a smile, attempting to change the subject.

"Yes, of course. He's treating me ninety-eight per cent better than an average Bengali. Most importantly, he sees me as an equal. Looks can fade over time, but a person's character can last beyond their lifetime. Beauty is in a person's character. When their heart and soul are beautiful, it makes them a great person to be with or have a relationship with. He's not judgmental or abusive, and he holds great respect for women. He treats me well. I'm never turning to Bengalis, that's for sure," Nadia affirmed.

"That's a sweet description of your husband. But not all Bengalis are bad, ma'am," Aysha replied.

"Small mouth, big talk, forgive me for interrupting, ma'am. My Hindu belief used to require the killing of women if their husband died before them. It has changed now, thank God. But your religion allows a man to have four wives, and this is a living torture. What do you expect a man to do other than see women as objects? This anti-woman sentiment is embedded in our society, Hindu or Muslim. The culture won't change unless something miraculous happens and all men's attitudes change overnight," Suzy commented.

"One thing is customary, Suzy!" Aysha chimed in. "For Hindus, cow meat is forbidden, and for Muslims, pig's meat is. But mankind can be so ruthless that they'll eat any female [expletive] they can lay their hands on, with no distinctions," she added with a laugh.

"Are you married, Suzy?" Nadia enquired.

"No, ma'am, I'm divorced with three kids. The guy got into drugs, developed an addiction, and money became a problem. I'm fending for three kids and working three jobs to make ends meet. Life is tough, ma'am," Suzy explained.

"Oh, I'm so sorry to hear this, Suzy," Nadia said in sympathy.

"Me too," Aysha added, recognising the contrast between their stories with a smirk.

"What's your story, Aysha?" Nadia asked.

Aysha smiled and responded, "Well, one day, you will meet someone who radiates charming love towards you. Your thoughts will no longer be chaotic, your senses won't be on high alert, your emotions will be subtle, your heart won't be sore, and your time at work will slow down. All you'll look forward to is a glimpse of his shadow. I'm in a relationship, I guess!" she laughed.

"Wow, Aysha ma'am! You're wrapped in a romance filled with cotton wool. All the best," Suzy commented.

"Yes, she certainly is," Nadia agreed. "Bring him over one day, Aysha. Let's meet your 'cotton wool' wrapped in romance all at once."

Aysha smiled, and then the telephone rang. "Suzy, please answer that. I've lost the appetite to talk to anyone after that nasty experience I had with that psycho."

"Ma'am, it's the coroner's office," Suzy informed her as she handed the phone to Nadia.

Nadia's face fell, and emotional tears began to roll down her cheeks as she took the call. The coroner informed her that the investigation into her brother's death had been completed, and the body could be released for burial. The death certificate was available for collection from the office. Nadia had a choice to either collect the body herself or have a full burial service arranged, including washing the body and digging the grave, at a cost of 5,000 taka. The burial could take place at a location owned by her or the deceased.

"Do you have the means to collect the body?" the coroner enquired.

"Well, I have plenty of relatives around, and I could collect the body. However, I prefer the fee-paying service, as I don't want to burden other people. I'll be visiting your office to pay the fee and set a time and date for the burial," Nadia informed the coroner before hanging up the phone.

"Nadia ma'am, I had better be going now," said Aysha. "You're a brave lady, and I'll let you deal with your loss. Should you need any help, I'm just a phone call away."

"Aysha, I'll be shifting to the UK with my husband. I don't want my niece to grow up here with too many restrictions hindering her progress. Moving overseas can dramatically change her life for the better – a new lifestyle, new opportunities and new directions. Leaving this past behind will allow me to reinvent myself and fulfil my brother's wishes for Pori Moni's future. He made me into the credible geochemist I am today. I'm not going to sell this property at this stage, nor do I want to assign a relative to take care of it. After spending time with you here, your empathetic approach has given me reassurance. You are a lady of integrity and a law-abiding citizen, Aysha. You are not corrupt like the others. Do you mind if I leave the keys with you for regular checks on my brother's house while I'm gone? I'm willing to pay a service fee for that," Nadia requested.

"No, not at all. It's a pleasure. You are choosing me over your close family member. That's an honour. Do not worry about anything. Just give me a call before your departure, and I'll be here," Aysha replied. She gave Nadia a warm hug, which Nadia reciprocated. Nadia then handed over a photo of her sister-in-law, as instructed by DI Talukdar.

Nadia gazed deeply into Aysha's eyes and made a request. "Aysha, if Rahila is found alive or returns home while we're away, please assure her that her daughter is in safe hands. I promise that we will return to reclaim everything we're leaving behind someday. However, if she isn't found, I'll entrust the key-set to you for later. You're in charge now." With a warm smile, Aysha agreed to the responsibility and left, closing the door behind her.

*

Nadia organised the burial a few days after receiving the call from the coroner's office. She selected a piece of land behind their backyard and placed a memorial stone there. Close friends, relatives and neighbouring villagers came together to pay their respects. Family members spoke about Doyal's legacy, urging everyone to set aside hate and envy and work towards love and unity as the path to finding solace in these challenging times in a harsh world.

Doyal was celebrated as a person of great character with a pure heart, someone who had contributed significantly to the welfare of their village. The speakers emphasised the importance of remembering his kindness and not forgetting the favours he had bestowed upon them. They recognised that climate change affected not only their village but the entire world and believed that it shouldn't drive them to turn on each other for material gain, leading to plunder and destruction of what rightfully belonged to others.

His sister believed, through her analysis, that Doyal had been murdered, and she suspected that the disappearance of her sister-in-law was a premeditated act of terror. She declared that whoever was responsible for these acts would face consequences both on Earth and in the hereafter, with no amount of purification that could free them in purgatory. The gathering responded with "*Amen.*"

"*Ameen,*" echoed Nadia. She made a silent promise to herself to bring change to the entire state of Bangladesh within her lifetime. She was determined, and nothing could stop her vision or obstruct her goals. This was her prayer, her desire, her determination, her prostration – a commitment to a better future.

After the funeral, she returned home, her heart heavy with grief. As she packed her belongings, tears flowed freely. With a heavy heart, she walked outside and took one last lingering look at the entire property. As she closed the doors and secured them with heavy-duty locks, she held Pori Moni close to her chest. She hailed an auto rickshaw and said her farewell to the property.

During her journey, she stopped by Aysha's non-profit organisation, the Association of Free Women, located at Lalpur Bazaar, and dropped off a set of keys. These keys symbolised her trust in Aysha to look after her brother's house. Finally, she paid Suzy her dues, giving her a comforting hug as they said their goodbyes.

"Safe journey, ma'am," Suzy said with a tearful smile as she waved goodbye.

CHAPTER 3

THE BACKLASH

Nadia   Pori   Keith   Seema   Shookur

Aziz   Aroon   Akira   Ashok   Sadia

Tom

Starring

Nadia Begum – Pori Moni – Keith Evan – Seema Begum 'teaching assistant'
– Shookur Gani – Aziz Khan – Aroon Miah - Akira Begum – Ashok Gupta
- Saida Khanom – Tom Pritarchd

Nadia returned home after her brother's burial ceremony, fatigued from a lengthy coach journey. Upon entering the house, she decided to call it a day, feeling too weary to do much more. She prepared a light meal for herself, fed Pori Moni and then retired for a restful night's sleep. Keith returned later and, realising that they were already asleep, he too headed to bed.

The following morning, Nadia woke up early to prepare breakfast for everyone. Eventually, Keith and Pori Moni also got up and made their way to the dining room.

"Good morning, darling," said Keith. "How did everything go yesterday? I'm sorry, I didn't want to disturb your sleep."

"Good morning. Everything went well. Thank you," Nadia replied. "Keith, I'm planning to move to the UK within the next two weeks, if that's okay with you," Nadia informed him.

Keith responded, "Yes, that's fine, but as I mentioned before, I'll have to return here and leave you in the UK, as long as you're okay with that."

Nadia enquired, "I thought you were going to apply for a new job in the UK?"

Keith explained, "Yes, of course. I'll be looking for a suitable job, but in the meantime, I'll continue with my current work. It's quite demanding, and the government has offered me a higher wage to keep me in this role."

Nadia reflected, "It's your choice, then, whether it's me or the job. I've made the decision to move, not just for myself, but also for the little one. I want to provide her with the best that life has to offer. I have some savings and I'm planning to sell a premium plot of land."

Keith reassured her, "I'll always be with you, darling."

Nadia appreciated his support, saying, "I appreciate that, mister! Keith, it appears that I'll be swamped with sorting out various tasks – managing the bank, dealing with property matters, and the inevitable work-related complexities, given that I'm the project manager for a critical research project. Leaving my position will certainly not sit well with my boss. But, my first task is to enrol Pori Moni in a local nursery class. I've already secured a spot for her and made the payment through a bank transfer. So, just a quick heads-up, my love, if I'm unable to answer your calls, you can bet I'm as busy as a beaver."

Keith responded with a playful smirk, "Of course, just make sure you don't wear yourself out with all those 'beavery' duties."

Afterwards, they all enjoyed breakfast together. Nadia then set out for the preschool nursery class, where she had arranged to drop off Pori Moni for the day. The teaching assistant, Seema Begum, warmly welcomed her and expressed her delight in looking after the little one. Nadia extended her gratitude to the teacher and then hopped back into her car, heading off to her workplace.

*

GreenBirth Corporation is an innovative company with several years of experience dedicated to environmental solutions. They specialise in designing efficient waste management plants and machinery. One unique aspect of their operations involves utilising live flies to generate larvae, which can then be used as fertile compost. Additionally, the company manufactures intelligent flying drones designed to safeguard people's crop fields by mimicking the presence of black crows to deter insects.

Nadia holds the position of a geochemist within the company and is currently spearheading a project known as NeuroChip. Vs1. This project is in its early prototyping stage and involves a silicon-based microchip designed to interact with the brains of animals. The primary purpose of this chip is to attach itself to the neck of grazing animals to ensure they remain within designated grazing areas. The chip achieves this by altering the animals' travel direction through the transmission of minute electrical pulses, received from a purpose-built mobile mast. These signals target the entorhinal region of the animal's brain, effectively keeping them within their permitted grazing zones. While this project is ambitious and not yet fully refined, the company is on the cusp of a significant breakthrough. Nadia Begum is the head of this project and the key person responsible for its success.

Nadia herself was nervous about facing the company's panel, fully aware of the gravity of the situation. She understood that her decision to leave for a foreign country was in violation of the company's code, which explicitly states that employees cannot depart with projects unfinished unless death separates them from it. This policy serves to protect classified information and patented blueprints from being disclosed to the outside world until the company is ready to profit from them.

In the eyes of the company's CEOs, directors and partners, Nadia's departure puts the entire project in jeopardy, and they unanimously oppose her decision. As a result, they have hastily convened an emergency meeting to address this critical issue. Nadia was on her way to confront them.

Upon reaching the car park, she parked her car and made her way to the elevator, destined for the conference on the third floor where the meeting was being held. With determination, she knocked on the door, ready to face the challenging situation.

"Come in!" a voice beckoned her.

Nadia entered and greeted the room, saying, "Hello, good afternoon, everyone!"

The conference room exuded a sense of order, with seats designated by name tags, a projector screen casting its glow on the wall, a chilled-water dispenser positioned by the door and a pleasant fragrance enhancing the room's atmosphere. Nadia found her assigned seat and presented herself to the assembled group.

A panellist, Mr Shookur Gani, initiated the discussion. "We called this meeting at short notice after hearing about your plans to relocate to the UK within the next two weeks. You're well aware that such a move is not in line with the company's policies. Can you explain why you submitted your resignation, Nadia?" he enquired.

Nadia began to provide a detailed account of her circumstances, starting from her brother's death to her sister-in-law's abduction and her responsibility for caring for her niece. Even after a lengthy one-hour discussion, the directors remained dissatisfied. They made generous offers, including a substantial increase in her salary, personal security and various perks not typically offered by the company. These offers were made exclusively to her, yet she turned them down, remaining steadfast in her decision to pursue a future in the UK.

"You are aware that this is not fair, Nadia. You can't simply leave us in the middle of an ongoing team work. We are on the brink of achieving our final goal with the NeuroChip.Vs1, and you're talking about departing!" protested Aziz Khan, the company secretary.

"Sir, I apologise, but I have made up my mind to care for my niece. I cannot focus on my work in this situation," Nadia explained.

The panel exchanged uncertain glances, as the meeting had taken an unexpected turn.

"As you wish, but we are not pleased with your decision to leave," stated the company's director, Mr Aroon Miah.

Nadia expressed her own unhappiness with her decision. "I'm not happy about it either, sir. I feel compelled to make this choice due to the dramatic change in my circumstances. The pain and trauma I've endured have been unbearable. Even though I feel guilty for leaving, it's the only option. Please accept my resignation and release me from this position. Thank you all for your understanding," she said, rising from her seat and requesting to depart. She left the conference room and made her way to the elevator.

Nadia entered the elevator nervously and descended to the first floor, which housed the main geochemistry laboratory, which was her department. There, she bid farewell to all her co-workers and colleagues.

One of her colleagues, Akira Begum, quickly caught her

attention and shared some concerning information. She explained that the internal situation was much more intricate than it seemed. A few days prior, the company's leadership had convened an assembly and implemented new terms and conditions within the company policy. They introduced a novel clause, stating, "You must regard GreenBirth Corporation as your provider and protector, just like a mother who offers you food and sustenance. If you betray the company in any way, the repercussions will be commensurate with the losses suffered by the company itself." Akira offered a cautionary note, saying, "Nadia, please be vigilant until you depart for the UK."

Within the conference room, all the panellists remained in their seats.

"Losing an employee, especially the head of a project, can have a significant impact on team morale, leading to a cascading effect that results in reduced performance and productivity," commented Aroon Miah.

"And how do we plan to replace her now? It's going to be a costly endeavour," added Ashok Gupta, the current CEO of the company.

Aroon Miah continued, "I'm stunned. Despite offering her all these incentives, I can't fathom why she still wants to move to the UK. She could lead a comfortable life here and provide her niece with a private education if that's what she desires."

Ashok Gupta speculated, "Perhaps it's the influence of her husband from the UK?"

Aroon Miah dismissed the notion, saying, "No, I've received unofficial information that her husband is also involved with the British High Commission for an ambassadorial role, and he'll be working right here in Bangladesh. So, it doesn't make sense for her to leave him behind and work abroad alone."

"Listen, everyone, it's not about what she's said so far. It's all about her desire for global control. She holds an ambitious ideology, believing that men have dominated and exploited the world's resources, objectified women throughout history and led the world into chaos. She envisions a power shift, with a woman taking the reins," said Saida Khanom, a rival geochemist who resented Nadia's success.

"…Unless she has something up her sleeve to sell to the UK government, why would she want to move to a country with unfavourable environmental conditions? It's damp, cold, and the weather changes rapidly. If you have the means, living in our sunny country is akin to royalty, isn't it?" Saida Khanom continued.

"We've put in a lot of hard work, delving deep into our minds, constantly brainstorming to generate new and innovative ideas. And now, she's taking this to the auction. We can't afford to let this slip away," emphasised one of the directors.

"See if you can arrange a discreet exit strategy for her, whether through an accident or a sudden cardiac event, but do it without exposing or tarnishing our company's reputation," instructed Ashok Gupta.

*

Nadia bid her final goodbyes to her colleagues and left the workplace. As she drove out of the car park, she noticed her fuel gauge warning light flashing. She decided to head for a local petrol pump, which was just a mile or so down the road. After refuelling her car, she stopped at the kiosk to purchase a coffee, paid for her items and continued her journey home.

After driving a few miles, she noticed a car closely tailing her through her rear-view mirror. She began to take a few unexpected turns deliberately to confirm if the car was indeed following her. It became increasingly evident that the car behind her was of course tailing her. Nadia's mind flashed back to what Akira Begum had mentioned earlier: "*You must regard GreenBirth Corporation as your provider and protector, just like a mother who offers you food and sustenance. If you betray the company in any way, the repercussions will be commensurate with the losses suffered by the company itself.*"

A shiver ran down her spine, and she feared that the company might have hired individuals to eliminate her. She pressed hard on the accelerator in an attempt to outpace the vehicle behind her, but it appeared that the trailing car was up for a game of cat and mouse, revving faster and getting even closer.

Driving at breakneck speed for a few miles, Nadia spotted a police station ahead. In a panic to stop she locked the wheels using the handbrake lever and came sliding to a screeching halt. She hurriedly exited the vehicle and rushed into the police station, pleading, "Please help! Someone is chasing after me."

Inside the police station, the duty officer was at the reporting desk, and a couple of assistant sub-officers were on guard duty. They promptly attended to Nadia's distress, heading outside to investigate the situation. However, upon their return, they reported that they couldn't find anyone acting suspiciously.

"There's no one outside, madam," the officers assured her.

Nadia, still shaken, described the car as a red Prius but was surprised to find that the chaser had vanished. She looked at the officers and stammered, "I... I want to file a report," clearly overcome by the heightened stress of the situation.

"Of course, go inside and talk to 'Sir'," said one of the guards.

She retrieved her phone and dialled the number for GreenBirth Corporation, her former workplace. She requested to speak with Ashok Gupta, the CEO.

The operator connected the call to the requested person, and Ashok answered, "Hello, Ashok speaking?"

"Hello, sir, it's me, Nadia. I just experienced a frightening incident with a red Prius car. It nearly caused several accidents, and I sincerely hope it has nothing to do with any grudge you might hold regarding my departure from the company," Nadia explained.

"I'm not sure what you're talking about, Nadia. If you've had a disturbing encounter, you should report it to the police," Ashok advised.

"I'm currently at the police station, waiting in line to file a report about the chase. I'm informing you as the head of the company that if GreenBirth Corporation is involved in harming me or my family in any way, I swear I will unleash unimaginable horrors on those responsible. I will not hesitate to take drastic action," she warned before abruptly ending the call.

Ashok was taken aback by the vulgar threat and hung up the phone, muttering to himself, "This girl has lost it, threatening to burn down the building and tear our heads off while sitting in a police station. Well, good luck with that."

Nadia anxiously sat in the waiting area at the police station. She promptly dialled the preschool-nursery class and spoke with Seema Begum. "Hi, Seema, is my niece Pori okay with you?"

Seema reassured her, "Yes, she's absolutely fine, highly engaged in all the activities and thoroughly enjoying herself. No need to worry!"

Nadia replied, "Great, I'll be there within the next two hours. Please ensure she remains on-site and doesn't leave with my husband or anyone else. I'll personally come to pick her up."

Seema acknowledged, "Certainly, we'll keep her here. See you soon! Bye!" Nadia bid farewell and hung up the call.

"Yes, madam, what's your report about?" the duty officer called out to Nadia and gestured for her to take a seat at his desk.

"I was pursued by a red Prius from the petrol pump to here," Nadia explained, her voice laden with anxiety. "I don't know why."

"Are you certain you don't know why? Making threats on the phone is a criminal offence, do you realise that?" the officer sternly responded.

Nadia sighed and replied, "Oh, so you heard me. It was my former boss. I left the job, breaching the contract, and I thought he might have sent someone to chase after me. I narrowly avoided several near miss accidents, sir."

"Did you manage to get the registration number?" enquired the officer.

"No, I was too focused on trying to get away from that pursuing car," Nadia confessed.

"In that case, there's not much we can do. I assume you didn't get a glimpse of the driver either, did you?" the officer asked.

"No, I didn't. But I have an idea of who they might be," Nadia said.

"Who do you suspect they are?" questioned the officer.

"The people from GreenBirth Corporation, my former bosses," Nadia asserted.

"A minute ago, you mentioned you thought it might be them, and now you're certain it's them. Are you sure?" enquired the officer. He continued, "Listen, go home. It's likely nothing. The individual might have been attracted to your beauty and engaged in a chase, a behaviour some men exhibit to seek attention," the officer explained.

Nadia, visibly agitated, responded, "I'm trembling with fear, and you find it amusing. What if I were your sister? What if I were your mother? Would you still find it funny?" She stared directly into the officer's eyes.

Sensing her distress, the officer softened his tone and gestured for her to sit. "Please, have a seat and tell me. I'll prepare the report."

Nadia took a seat and shared, "It's the bosses of GreenBirth Corporation who are trying to harm me."

"What?" the officer appeared surprised. "It's a reputable company. Why would they be chasing after you?"

"I'm a former employee, 'sir'. I left the job, breaching the company's contract, and they didn't take it well. Now, they've turned hostile towards me," Nadia explained.

"Very well, I'll include this information in your report. If such an incident happens again, try to note down the vehicle's registration number. It can be crucial for the report's investigation. Stay vigilant, and you're free to go now," the officer concluded.

"Okay, sir, please don't take my frustration personally," Nadia responded with a sigh of relief. She left the police station and made her way to the preschool nursery to pick up her niece. Fortunately, the pursuer didn't reappear.

Still inside her car, she composed herself, applied light makeup and freshened up her appearance by brushing her hair. Feeling presentable, she stepped out of the car and headed to collect her niece. On the way home, she decided to visit her favourite restaurant, Mangol Grill, renowned for its high-quality food and mocktails.

She placed an order for her favourites to take home: *mukhi* (eddo) and ilish fish curry for herself, grilled chicken, baked beans and oven-baked potato chunks for Keith, and a delectable sweet *kheer* (coconut-infused sticky rice dessert) for Pori Moni. It had been a challenging day, and with no time or energy to cook, a little self-indulgence seemed like the perfect way to end the evening for Nadia.

*

Ashok Gupta, the CEO of GreenBirth Corporation, swiftly retrieved his mobile phone and dialled the number to connect with the company's director, Aroon Miah. Upon Aroon's response, his frustration bubbled over, and his voice grew more intense.

"You dispatched an inexperienced individual on a reckless pursuit of Nadia," he exclaimed. "She called me earlier, upset over the ordeal, suspecting all of us and issuing threats. If anything befalls her or her family, she vows to bring us down. How did this occur under your supervision? Wasn't it supposed to be a discreet operation? Unless you can find a capable person to handle her, it might be wiser to let it go. If this situation goes public on social media, it could seriously tarnish our reputation. We can find another path to success without her involvement in our company. Please, let it go. I have no desire to damage our company's standing," Ashok pleaded.

*

As Nadia reached their floor, her niece, Pori Moni, began throwing a tantrum due to hunger. Nadia, looking into her eyes, said, "Oh, my sweetie pie, Mummy understands." She hurried to her front door, fumbled through her purse for her keys and opened the door. Closing the door behind her she headed for the dinner table. Nadia unpacked the meal packages and served Pori Moni a sweet and delicious bowl of *kheer*. Then, she went to the kitchen to tidy up the items left scattered on the worktop.

Some time later, Keith returned home from work. Nadia heard him coming in and rushed to give him a loving hug. Keith was startled but reciprocated her hug and asked, "Are you alright?"

"I'm terrified by what happened today," she whispered in his ear.

Keith withdrew from the hug and looked her in the eyes, shocked. "What happened?" he asked.

Nadia explained, "Some guy in a red Prius tailgated me for miles, and when I tried to drive away, he began to chase after me like a maniac. I thought I was going to crash into something. Luckily, I found a police station and sought refuge inside. I filed a report, but the chaser disappeared. The police couldn't take further action because I had nothing more to report other than the car's description."

Keith expressed his concern. "You clearly need security. The police here are corrupt. They won't take any further action unless you pay them. You've seen it with your sister-in-law's situation. I'll call Tom to send some security personnel to look after you."

Nadia hesitated but then said, "It's okay. I don't need security at this stage."

Keith insisted. "At what stage do you need protection? After you get injured? There are only a couple of weeks left before you move to the UK for good. I don't want any tragedies to happen under my watch here."

Nadia smiled and hugged Keith, saying, "Oh, thank you so much, love. That's very caring. But don't inform Tom at this stage. If I have another experience like that, I'll definitely want security then." She kissed him, smiled and added, "The food is ready, so freshen up, go... go."

However, Keith couldn't resist and secretly called Tom, who ran a private security firm called Black Hulk Security. They had become friends when Keith had asked him to find an independent sniper for a mission in Bangladesh a few years back. Keith requested Tom to stand by and provide a watchful eye on Nadia for the next two weeks or until she left for the UK, if needed. Tom readily agreed, saying, "Of course, not a problem at all. Just give me a phone call, pal."

After making the call, Keith went to the dining table, looked at Pori Moni and asked, "How is my little princess doing? Did she have a nice time on her first day at nursery today?"

"Yes, she did," Nadia confirmed. "Pori, show Uncle Keith what you did today."

Pori hurriedly grabbed her colouring pad and brought it over to Keith. She eagerly opened the pages to display the painting she had created, saying with her tiny voice, "I painted a zebra today."

"Wow, what a beautiful job you've done, Pori! Well done!" Keith exclaimed. He picked up a red felt-tip pen and started to colour over the stripes of the zebra. Pori protested, saying, "No, it should be black, Uncle Keith!"

"Oh, I'm sorry," Keith chuckled, taking the correct colour and correcting himself.

"Come finish your food now," Nadia called.

"She is a very clever girl," Keith remarked.

"She is indeed," Nadia affirmed.

Nadia then brought up the topic of clothes, saying, "I'm going shopping this week. I know you don't like me buying anything for you since your cupboards are already full of clothes, but should I buy you a nice suit?"

"A suit?" Keith responded with a hint of sarcasm. "So, you're switching from street traders to department stores today, huh?" he teased, knowing that she usually bought things from small street traders.

"Keith, don't take the piss!" Nadia playfully scolded.

"Only joking, darling," Keith laughed and continued, "No, Nadia, thanks, but don't waste money getting me anything, please. Look at my wardrobe, it's full of clothes."

Nadia then considered, "It's quite cold in the UK. Do you think Mother-in-Law would appreciate a nice Bengali hand-stitched shawl?"

"Yes, you had better get something for her," Keith eagerly suggested. But then, he confessed, "Nadia, I must tell you something. You've just triggered my inner dilemma." He opened up and continued, "My mother is unaware of our marriage."

"What? Are you serious?" Nadia was compelled to ask. "But why?"

"I guess her mindset is stuck in archaic beliefs where culture, belief, heritage and class are the only values she holds dear, and she doesn't like forming relationships with people from different backgrounds," Keith explained.

Nadia challenged his explanation, saying, "Come on, that's not an excuse. The UK is culturally diverse, with people from all backgrounds, including Black, White, Brown and LGBTQ, living there. I'm not buying this. Tell me the real reason."

Keith emphasised, "I promise, that's the whole truth, and nothing but the truth. She doesn't want her son to marry someone with brown or black skin. She has this irrational fear. She believes that 'mixed-race children are somewhat demeaning', though I'm not sure where she got these ideas. She thinks that God imposes a curse on those who intermarry, which she believes leads to children becoming unruly, disorderly or even disabled in some cases. She's convinced there's a specific reason why God made people with different skin colours."

Nadia enquired with curiosity, "What's the underlying reason for this belief?"

Keith replied, "I've just explained, it's about people sticking to their own kind."

Nadia reflected, "She must have endured challenging experiences in her life. How do you plan to convey to her that you're challenging her beliefs by seeing me?"

Keith shared, "I told her about you as my girlfriend. She's accepting of me having a girlfriend from a different race or background. We all have emotional needs that should be met, but marriage is not part of the equation."

Nadia acknowledged this by saying, "I understand. So, in your culture, having a wife is frowned upon, while having a girlfriend is seen as enjoyable. I think she is in need of help, and I suppose I'll need to adapt her concept to fit in."

Keith tried to reassure her, saying, "Don't be too quick to judge."

Nadia reacted with frustration, saying, "What do you mean by that? Your mother's beliefs could lead to the stigma of having illegitimate children, and that's not well received here. Do you understand?"

She continued, emotionally, "You've spent five years demonstrating your commitment to me behind the scenes, and now that you're a part of my life, you're suggesting I'm not worth it. You kept me hidden from your family… You know what?"

Overcome with emotion, Nadia moved away from Keith toward the window, her sobs evident. Realising that he had upset her with the conversation, Keith reached out, tenderly embracing her from behind, planting a gentle kiss on her neck to try to make up, and began to sing a soothing song to improve her mood.

The melody began its gentle journey near her ears, caressing the senses and whisking them away to enchanting destinations, ultimately returning them to this very sofa, where they embraced each other with tender kisses to complete the harmonious and romantic odyssey.

The Love

Keith:
Love, oh love, the day you entered my sight,
You stole my peace, my calm, my delight.
Love, oh love, as you drew near,
My dreams and triumphs, so clear, so sincere.

HEA… HEAHE…
OHOHOOO… HAHAHAAA…

I can't fathom how these vivid dreams revealed,
The moment we met, joy to thrill quickly congealed.
Love, oh love, as you drew near, oh so near,
The lights merged, a dazzling spectacle, crystal clear.

HEA… HEAHE…
OHOHOOO… HAHAHAAA…

How did our dreams entwine and become one?
We chose to plunge deep, love's journey begun.
Dreaming of a life by your side so tight,
I need you as my amigo through the night.

HEA… HEAHE…
OHOHOOO… HAHAHAAA…

Cheer up, cheer up, or tears might fill my eyes,
I treasure your presence, our bond, oh so high.
Love, oh love, the day you caught my sight,
You replaced it with emotions, love's pure light.

HEA… HEAHE…
OHOHOOO… HAHAHAAA…

Love you so much…!
EHEHEA… HEAHE… HEHEA… HEAHE
Nadia's smile radiated charm as she exclaimed, "Impressive!"
as he had sung much like a Bengali hero serenading his heroine
to lift her spirits. "Film style, huh?" she added, applauding the
display. "You know just where to touch a woman, don't you, my
darling. I love you too, you know that," Nadia professed.

"Thank goodness you've brightened up a bit," Keith sighed with
relief. "I was afraid I had led you into a web of misunderstanding.
You know, I truly admire your knack for effecting change without
doing any harm. You're a chemist, my darling. Mixing elements
to yield a positive outcome without any waste is your job, right?
I reassured you that my intention was not to upset you, but to
bolster your strength – the strength to find a solution for my
mother to see you as your authentic self and accept you for who
you are. You possess that power," Keith acknowledged.

"Oh yes, of course, darling, I will weave my magic on her and
she will be delighted to have me as her daughter-in-law. Let me
meet her first," said Nadia with a sweet smile.

*

Aroon Miah, the director of GreenBirth Corporation, had issued
a fresh directive to a team of criminals, instructing them to make a
second attempt on Nadia. They had been observing her residence
for several days, waiting for the right moment to engage in an
operation similar to the previous one. Today, it appeared to be the
perfect opportunity to remove her from the picture.

Nadia had begun preparing for her journey to the UK, a
significant milestone as it marked her first trip outside her own
country. Her previous travel experiences had mainly involved

domestic tourist destinations in Bangladesh. The prospect of venturing beyond her homeland had always been financially out of reach, given her modest salary that barely covered the cost of living. She was deeply grateful to Keith, who had generously provided her with this incredible opportunity to explore a new world. Although she might sometimes come across as a controlling wife, she was acutely aware of the debt of gratitude she owed to Keith for everything he had done for her and the chance he was giving her to start a new life in the UK, along with her little niece.

Nadia reached for a couple of travel bags perched on top of her wardrobes, covered in a layer of dust from disuse. She gave them a quick wipe down and unzipped them to select the clothing she intended to take with her to the UK. Not having much clothing for Pori, who was a relatively new addition to her life, Nadia decided it was time for a shopping spree. She dressed Pori and then headed out the door, her first stop being a buggy shop to purchase a means of transport for the little one, allowing her to comfortably navigate the market for further purchases without having to physically handle Pori.

Nadia's upbringing by her father had left a lasting impact on her mindset. Her father had been a market trader, who used to farm fish in makeshift ponds spread across a few acres of his paddy fields. He would load his catches into a creel, a wicker basket, and carry it on his head to sell in the local market. Over time, her father progressed from being a wicker basket fish seller to owning several fish farming lakes before he passed away. The mantra she had imbibed from her father's early teachings was to "always support the small, individual traders and small businesses in the market, as they are the ones most in need of your custom". This principle had stayed with her throughout her life.

Approaching a buggy trader, she spotted a compact three-wheeler buggy that caught her eye. "How much does that cost?" she enquired. The merchant replied, "5,500 taka." She approached the buggy asked Pori to sit in it, and she securely strapped her in. While doing so, she noticed a man across the street who appeared to be up to something, and his gaze seemed to be fixed on her. She quickly averted her eyes from the onlooker, sensing that she was being followed due to her previous experiences. To make it seem as though she was just completing a transaction with the trader, she turned her back to the stranger and pulled out her phone.

Acting like she was finalising her deal with the trader, she called Keith and asked him to instruct Tom, as she needed assistance because she was being watched. After ending the call, she continued to speak to the trader. "Uncle, I really like this buggy. I can pay 5,000 taka in cash. Will you accept that?" she asked. The merchant, seemingly aware of her phone call to her husband, remarked, "You've been watched, haven't you?"

"Yes, I've been followed," Nadia confirmed.

The merchant, showing understanding and empathy, offered a solution. "Tell you what, give me 5,000, and you owe me 400. I'll let you off with a 100, as margins are very tight on these buggies. You can take it and go, alright?"

Nadia was grateful for the merchant's help. "Oh, thank you so much. I'll pay you soon," she replied before moving on. Her phone rang, and it was Keith, who instructed her to keep the phone live on talking mode and place it inside her bag. Tom would track the phone via satellite and send help, though it might take up to fifteen minutes. Keith advised her to stay in busy locations and continue shopping as usual because the attacker would likely strike in less crowded areas. He emphasised, "Do not get isolated."

Nadia acknowledged Keith's instructions. "I got it, Keith. Please tell Tom not to harm anyone."

Keith assured her, "Yes, of course. He can hear you directly, so don't worry. He will handle things as he sees fit."

Tom swiftly prepared his artificial intelligence-guided drone, armed with a highly potent sedative syringe. This device targets bare skin and delivers a sleep-inducing dose in an instant. After administering the sedative, the device falls on the ground, appearing as waste plastic. The target would feel a sensation similar to a mosquito bite, and within minutes, they would fall unconscious.

Nadia continued her shopping, faithfully following her husband's instructions, blissfully unaware of the covert operation orchestrated by Tom and his drone. High above, the drone spotted the target, recognising the exposed arm of the suspect. It acted with accuracy and precision, delivering the sedative jab at a supersonic speed. The man collapsed to the floor, and later, his comrades retrieved him, all of this happening without anyone in the vicinity noticing the intervention.

As Nadia reached the last leg of her shopping journey, she glanced at her phone to check if it was still in talking mode, but the screen remained black. She placed it back in her bag and surveyed her surroundings with curiosity. A sense of relief washed over her as she realised that there were no more suspicious activities to be concerned about.

Then, she encountered a female street vendor selling her favourite fried onion bhajis. Nadia enquired, "Aunty, are these prepared hygienically?"

The vendor reassured her, "My dear, I use bottled water to make these, so they're as clean as raindrops, I promise. Shall I give you a portion?" She wore surgical rubber gloves while handling her merchandise, urging Nadia to buy with confidence.

Nadia appreciated the care taken by the vendor and said, "That's the way to go, Aunty. Give me five portions! And here's a word of advice to boost your business threefold overnight."

"Really? The customer is always right. Go ahead, ma'am, I am listening," said the vendor, eager to hear while she filled a square-cut banana leaf with onion bhajis and rolled it into a ball, tying it into a parcel.

Nadia explained her idea: "Not many people use bottled water to prepare their food. You could put up a signboard saying 'Aunty's bhaji made with purified water.' This way, you can attract more customers and even sell at a slightly higher price."

"That's a great idea! It never occurred to me," the lady responded with a smile. "Thank you for your advice, and I'll prepare a signboard as early as tomorrow."

Nadia headed home, feeling exhausted but grateful that her purchase of the buggy had proven to be money well spent. It had comfortably carried Pori throughout the day, along with the extra load of shopping.

*

Aroon Miah, the director of GreenBirth Corporation, received a call from the hired criminal leader who was appointed to harm Nadia. "Boss, this girl is a ghost," he admitted. "We attempted two consecutive missions to destroy her today. Both missions failed. Our guys got incapacitated like magic. They collapsed suddenly in the middle of the operation. Doctors are saying they suffered sleep deprivation and collapsed from exhaustion. It doesn't make any sense. These guys spend most of their time sleeping, only coming out when duty calls them. It's like she's protected by some invisible force, sir."

Aroon Miah, considering the inexplicable circumstances, replied, "Never mind. She has proven to be a difficult target, and we've underestimated her powers. Let her go. The mission is aborted, understood?"

"Okay, sir. Have a nice day," the gang leader acknowledged before ending the call.

*

For the next few days, Nadia spent her time visiting historical sites like Sonargoan and Lalbag Fort to learn and boost her imagination. She also explored rural parts of Bangladesh, from the beautiful wetlands in Cox's Bazar to Bisnakandi, in an effort to soak up the natural beauty and wildlife. She wasn't sure how long her vacation to the UK would be, but she estimated it would last at least fourteen to fifteen years, coinciding with Pori Moni's adulthood or until her eighteenth birthday. She wholeheartedly enjoyed the countryside of her motherland, taking in the natural beauty to cherish as memories.

Amid the excitement of her departure to the UK, she received another thrilling piece of news from her gynaecologist, which momentarily left her mind reeling. She had just entered her first month of pregnancy. Keith was overjoyed and overwhelmed by the news that he was going to be a father soon. He went above and beyond to express his joy. On his way home, he ventured to a jewellery shop and bought a gold necklace and a matching saree and blouse set, along with a beautiful bouquet to congratulate Nadia on this wonderful news. He insisted she wear the colourful, vibrant attire throughout the journey to the UK. Nadia was elated and couldn't contain her happiness, jumping into Keith's arms, giving him an enormous hug and a kiss to remember.

The next morning, friends and family gathered to bid their goodbyes. Departure time was approaching, so Nadia and Keith locked and secured their property and headed for Dhaka International Airport, leaving behind the beauty of Nadia's homeland.

CHAPTER 4

THE ARRIVAL

Keith   Nadia   Pori   Maria   Jacob

Jonathon   Sarah   Rongila

Starring

Nadia Begum – Pori Moni – Keith Evan- Jonathon Evan – Sarah Evan –
(Maria sister in-law) – (Jacob, Brother in-law) – (Rongila, Dressmaker)

The couple landed at Liverpool John Lennon Airport, heading to Aughton in the rural north-west of the UK. Their visitation is at a charming country house that sprawled over ten acres of land, offering expansive views of the neighbouring farmland. This impressive residence included a detached stone cottage, a meticulously maintained garden and a beautiful pond tucked away at the rear of the property. It was a place that epitomised rural living, quite distinct from the warmth of Bangladesh, marked by its chilly weather.

The season was autumn, a time when leaves transition to shades of brown and gracefully fall from the trees. The temperatures fluctuated, swinging between high and low, and the weather could be mild, dry, wet, windy or sometimes sunny. It was an unpredictable mix, akin to the ever-shifting waves of an ocean tide.

Keith's parents, Jonathan and Sarah Evan, had been happily married for over four decades and called this magnificent property their home. Their daughter, Maria, and son, Jacob, were much younger than Keith. They had ventured out in search of work and settled in different parts of the country but still made occasional visits to their parents. When they did visit, they often stayed for weeks at a time, thanks to the attached three-double-bedroom cottage thoughtfully prepared by their parents.

The cottage had an en-suite bathroom and there was a double garage on the side of the property, which Jonathan used as his DIY workshop. It was well equipped with essential tools such as a jigsaw, hacksaw, drill, mitre cutter and other machinery.

Upon opening the aircraft doors, Nadia was greeted by a brisk breeze that felt as if the aeroplane's air conditioning had been cranked up to maximum. "Oho… so cold," she shivered, even though the temperature was a mere twelve degrees Celsius, a far cry from her accustomed twenty-eight degrees. Without delay, she covered Pori with some extra clothing, and she herself donned a headscarf and a warm, hooded woollen overcoat over her saree, the traditional Indian one-piece garment that enveloped her entire body.

As they strolled through the arrival area, noticing no one had come to collect them, Nadia enquired, "Is this normal here, Keith? Do family members typically not come to the terminal to welcome us?"

Keith responded, "Oh yes, it's absolutely normal. Everyone's usually busy with work, so no need to worry. We'll just flag down a taxi cab to head home – that's how things work around here."

Inside the Evan house, Sarah was busy preparing food while Jonathan was meticulously setting the dining table with plates and wine glasses. Maria and Jacob were engrossed in a soap opera on TV. Suddenly, the doorbell rang, and Jacob glanced at the CCTV monitoring screen that covered their front porch.

"Mum, it's Keith at the door, but who's that hooded lady and the child with him?" Jacob enquired. Sarah hurriedly made her way from the kitchen to Jacob's call and fixed her gaze on the CCTV monitor. "Gosh, where did he pick up these refugees from, and why did he bring them here?" she muttered with a hint of exasperation. "When is he going to learn not to be the ambassador of the world? I don't have space to accommodate unexpected guests here."

With determination, Sarah rushed to the door, opened it and locked eyes with her son. She gave him an affectionate hug, tears of joy welling up in her eyes. At this moment, Nadia felt a sense of relief, realising that her mother-in-law might not be as inhospitable as the chilly weather outside. However, as Sarah's gaze fell on Nadia, it quickly retreated, as if deliberately pushing away any initial signs of dislike.

"Come on in, come in," Sarah invited, beckoning Keith to enter.

"Mum," Keith called out. Sarah turned to look at him. "This is Nadia and her niece," he explained, as Sarah cast an unwelcoming glare in their direction.

Nadia, despite the frosty reception, managed a polite smile.

Sarah, clearly taken aback, enquired, "What do they want? Please, just hold on for a moment. I have some old clothing to give away, and there's also some cash in a charity pot," Sarah explained.

Nadia felt a sense of shock at the hostile attitude she was encountering.

"Mum, they're not what you think," Keith added, hoping to bridge the gap between his family and his guests.

"Come on, son, don't tell me to invite them inside. These people are like termites flooding our country and blaming us for everything. Give her something and send her back to Calais. They don't stay in France where they suppose to stay, and head for the UK. We don't have space here for refugees," Sarah said, expressing her strong opinions.

"Please, you come inside, come, come," she gestured to Keith.

Keith, however, insisted, "Mum, she's not a refugee."

Sarah, still bewildered, asked, "What? She looks like a Syrian to me. Who is she?"

Keith clarified, "She's a friend from Bangladesh."

"Oh, okay," Sarah said with a smile, though her bluntness remained evident. "Hello, I am Keith's mother. I am a very honest person, I speak my mind, and I don't like foreigners coming and invading my country. I'll call you a cab, and you can go settle in London. There's a whole town full of Bangla people there, dedicated to your lot."

"Mum, stop it!" Keith protested.

Nadia was left astounded by his mother's straightforwardness and stood still, unsure of how to react.

At that moment, Jonathan arrived at the door, followed by Jacob and Maria. He asked, "What's happening here?"

"Dad, how are you?" Keith greeted his father, shaking hands and giving him a warm hug. He extended the same affection to Jacob and gave Maria a loving kiss on the cheek. "How are you, Maria, my darling sister?"

"I am okay," Maria replied, looking a bit puzzled. "What's going on here?" she asked.

"Please tell Mum to behave appropriately. There's no need for all this. Nadia is a friend of mine. We travelled here together from Bangladesh," Keith explained.

Maria intervened, calling out to her mother, "Mum, you come inside. You all go inside, I will take care of this."

Before retreating to the kitchen, Sarah couldn't resist one more comment, saying, "Make sure to sanitise that filthy luggage. I can smell the cockroaches and mosquitos from here. They could be carrying malaria."

As Sarah headed inside, Maria reached out to Nadia with a friendly smile. "Hi," she said, extending her hand. Nadia reciprocated the gesture and replied, "Hi, I'm Nadia, and this is my niece, Pori."

"Oh, hello, Prie!" Maria greeted Pori, gently touching her cheek.

Pori smiled and corrected her, "I'm not Prie, I'm Pori."

"Ah, I beg your pardon, Pori!" Maria said, her smile remaining warm. "It's a beautiful name, Pori. Come inside. I'll show you the way."

Maria looked at Nadia and added, "Please don't get offended by my mother's behaviour. She's a bit set in her ways – an old-fashioned lady who hasn't been exposed to other cultures. Come on in… Oh, leave the luggage here. I'll ask my brother Jacob to bring them in for you."

"Thank you so much, that's very kind of you," Nadia said expressing her gratitude.

"Not to worry! Come on in." Maria welcomed them with open arms.

Keith had already gone to take a shower, while his mother was sprinkling grated cheese over the lasagne in preparation for the oven. His father had returned to the dining table, engrossed in his newspaper, as Jacob was hauling in the luggage.

"Come, this is our beautiful house where we all grew up. We've moved out now, and only Mum and Dad live here. Keith, when he returns from his demanding work, spends time here as well," Maria explained, introducing the house to Nadia.

"Here we go, your luggage is here. Feel free to use the wardrobe space and make yourself at home. I'll be downstairs waiting for you all for a nice supper together," Maria told Nadia.

"Oh, you're so lovely. Your kind welcome is much appreciated," Nadia said smiling.

"You're welcome. See you soon," Maria said as she closed the door behind her.

Keith emerged from the shower and found Nadia organising their travel luggage.

"I was really shocked by your mum's attitude today. Thank God your siblings are normal," Nadia exclaimed. "I'm not sure if I can face her now."

"I told you she's a different breed, but don't worry. She won't bite, she just talks the talk. Facing her is the key to making her realise we're all the same," Keith reassured her. "Have a quick shower, give Pori a wash too, and I'll see you downstairs."

Keith then went into the walk-in closet for some self-grooming, and applied body creams and scents.

Downstairs, Sarah began setting the food on the dinner table, while Maria placed the knives and forks next to the plates. "I'm wary about that Asian girl. Couldn't she find anybody else to be with? Why my son?" she said expressing her concerns.

"Mum, hush," Maria urged.

Keith entered the room and looked at the dinner table, exclaiming, "Mum, you prepared so much!"

"Yes, it's for you and your siblings, not for the person upstairs," she replied.

"Urrgh… Mum, calm down," Keith sighed as he sat at the table, touching his forehead in frustration.

"Seriously, I wasn't expecting two extra guests. Tell me something, Keith, you didn't bring her here to keep her, did you?" his mother continued, her tone sceptical.

"Mum, she's here to stay, okay? Just let it go. You don't seem to have much regard for other people," Keith replied, his voice laced with contempt.

"Shut your mouth, Keith, or I will shut it for you," she snapped, her face inches from his. "You don't have regard for your own mother. Why her out of millions of Europeans, huh? You disregarded my wishes. There's still time to reconsider what you've got yourself into. Relationships come and go, but a responsible person always weighs the consequences, costs, benefits, profit and loss before committing to any relationship. I'm sure she did, but you, like an airhead, fell into her trap. She's going to ruin your life. Get rid of her at once," she insisted.

"Mum, you're giving me a migraine. I'm nearly forty, and I've been out with European girls. I'm not interested in switching partners like my shoes when they wear out. Your olden days are over, Mum. You and Dad committed to each other and took your relationship to heart, which is why you two are still together and we're having this nice moment today. Today's relationships are like seasonal attire: the season lapses, and the girl is gone," Keith explained. His mother frowned in agreement and went into the kitchen to get the gravy for the roast beef.

"I agree with Keith. People these days don't seem to like commitment," Maria chimed in.

Nadia's footsteps echoed as she descended the stairs. "Come, Nadia," Keith called out. She was dressed in the gift she had received from her husband earlier: a glossy saree with white borders, paired with regal gold earrings adorned with sapphire stones. Her hair was neatly bundled and tied in a bun, accented with a white lily and rose hairband, giving her the appearance of a siren straight out of an Indian movie.

"Wow, Nadia, you look so beautiful and your hairdo is absolutely gorgeous – a statement piece," Maria said complimenting her.

Keith smiled and said, "Pori, come and sit here, my love."

"Thank you, Maria," Nadia responded.

"Have a seat," Maria urged.

Nadia hesitated to sit, showing respect. She was waiting for her mother-in-law to arrive.

Sarah entered with the gravy, placing it on the table. Nadia bowed and touched her feet. "Why are you touching my feet?" said Sarah in panic.

"Mum, it's more than you were bargaining for, I think," Jacob explained. "It's their way of greeting elders when they meet their mother-in-law for the first time. They offer respect and gratitude by touching their feet."

"You're a hundred per cent correct," Nadia agreed. She then went on to touch her father-in-law's feet. Jonathan, who had been reading the newspaper and not paying much attention to his surroundings, felt a twitch in his eyebrows as Nadia's hand made contact with his feet – a mystifying phenomenon for him.

"I hear you, Jacob. You are welcome, Nadia. Go have a seat now," he acknowledged.

Nadia finally took her place at the dining table, sitting opposite Keith. Pori sat on her left, a favoured spot for feeding her using her right arm.

"Hold on a second," Sarah said as she walked to the end of the dining table near the kitchen and took a seat. "Just an hour ago, you were a foreigner to me," she began. "Just because my son called you a friend doesn't give you the right to become a daughter-in-law. Why did you touch my feet? I am not your mother-in-law, and I don't want to be. Gosh, that's the last thing I want in my life, becoming the mother-in-law of an Indian."

"I may well be a friend to your son, who is afraid to admit our actual relationship in front of you, but to me, he is my husband, and I am not afraid to admit it!" Nadia declared vehemently.

"This girl has the audacity to talk to me like that," Sarah huffed. "Keith, eat up and take your business elsewhere. I am not going to keep a mouthy, dark, thick-skinned, sickly individual into my home. You take her away."

"Pack it in, Sarah, let the kid eat for God's sake," said Jonathan intervening.

"Mum, I will move her into the annexed cottage. Let her eat," Keith suggested. Sarah looked at Keith with disdain.

"What cottage? Take her away to where she belongs, in London. I didn't expect anything like that from you, Keith," Sarah grumbled.

"Mum, you are not willing to listen to me," Keith argued. "She watched out for me in my bad times, and I am going to look after her in hers. We are partners, and she is here to stay for a long time. Being discriminatory against her is not going to work. I am here for only two weeks, and I am going back to work. Nadia went through a massive tragedy in her country, and she can't go back. You would learn more if you listened and tolerated other people's views," Keith added submissively.

"They all go through tragedies, Keith. The UK is not a safe house for everyone. I don't know what spell she used to bewitch you. You're numbed by her zeal," Sarah retorted.

"Mum, you are scaring the kid. Calm down a bit," said Maria intervening.

Sarah fumed inwardly but remained ill-tempered. She focused on her plate and began eating.

Nadia turned to Maria and asked, "What do you do, workwise?"

Sarah couldn't tolerate Nadia talking and picked up her plate to move to the kitchen to finish her meal.

"I am a newsreader and journalist. I've been doing freelance journalism for five years now, looking for a permanent position in an established production company. Competition is fierce, so it's taking time to find a nice, lasting job," Maria replied.

Maria then asked, "What about you, what do you do?"

"I am a geochemist and part-time environmental scientist. I used to work for a very reputable company called GreenBirth Corporation. Due to a change in circumstances, I travelled here to the UK, causing stress to your mother and, I'm sure, some pain in the butt for Keith too," Nadia said with a smile.

"Oh, don't say that. You are very welcome here. Don't take to heart what my mother says, she doesn't mean it. That's just the way she is," Maria reassured her. "Her first boyfriend was an Asian, brown-skinned," she whispered to Nadia.

"What?" Nadia exclaimed in surprise.

"Yes, she is all good inside, but her fear remains with her. That's a story for another day," Maria added.

Nadia understood and said in awe, "Oh, I see."

Nadia then turned to Jacob and asked, "And, Jacob, what's your tale?"

Jacob responded with a smile, "I work in a bank, doing investment banking."

"You're in a very career-driven position, Jacob. Nice to know," Nadia commented.

Jacob smiled and said, "Thanks!"

"So, what's your plan, Nadia? Keith says you'll be staying here. Are you going to get a job at a chemistry firm?" Maria enquired.

"Nope, I want to do more than that. I want to do something of my own. I want to set up a business here, but first, I need a place to set up a lab of my own," Nadia explained.

"You can use my garage!" Jonathan declared, munching on a chicken thigh. "There's no shortage of tools in my workshop. It's suitable for any DIY job at any time, and it's well equipped. I thought I would pass my hobby on to my children, and they would make use of my abundance of tools. But they all found their own paths, which is good for them. However, my poor garage has remained abandoned, gathering dust, mildew and soot everywhere," he explained.

"How nice of you to say that, Papa," Nadia responded.

"Papa! Is that a new name for me?" he said smiling.

"I'm serious, Papa. I can't let this opportunity slip. I want to make use of your garage. When can you show me around, please?" Nadia enquired.

"Hey, come on, you've just arrived. Settle down a bit, explore the country and the culture first," Jonathan suggested.

"Papa, the UK is our former colonial ruler. I'm very much aware of the culture here. I've already seen and experienced some examples. I might as well get on with what I came here to do, and that is work. I really would like to see your garage," Nadia insisted.

"Okay, as you wish. Whenever you're ready, it's all yours. The keys are hanging in the hall. Feel free to go and take a look at your convenience," Jonathan said.

Keith and Jacob finished eating and began to take all the kitchenware and cutlery into the kitchen.

"What are you going to do in there, Nadia, if you don't mind me asking?" Maria enquired.

"Maria, I am so excited. All my worries vaporised in a flash after hearing this good news from Papa. I just need a little bit of space to start off with my laboratory. I intend to experiment with lots of theories which I've accumulated over my professional years. One of which is very important to UK society. On the flight over here, I found this book called *Healthy Eating Guide* in the seat pocket. It said that 'one in every four adults and one in every five children in the UK is overweight'. Reading this took me back in time, and I thought about how poorer countries like ours are affected by food shortage and poverty, and people dream of becoming overweight, but there's not enough food to eat, causing health issues and famine. Here, people are eating their way to obesity. What a predicament. I instantly knew I could do something about this problem, Maria," she exclaimed.

"What! Are you sure?" Maria asked, stunned.

"Yes, Maria, I have discovered a gap in the market here. I can do this better than anyone," Nadia replied.

"Oh, wow, if you can do that, you will not only become famous overnight but a rich woman too, Nadia," Maria remarked.

"Wish me luck, Maria. Papa is offering me a launchpad to kick-start my project. I am so happy I can use his workshop. Thank you so much, Papa," Nadia said.

"Don't thank me yet. Go and have a look at the state of the garage. You will hate me after knowing how much cleaning it will take to transform it into a lab," Jonathan cautioned.

"It's okay, I can manage the cleaning. Don't worry about that," Nadia assured him.

"All the best, Dr Nadia. You will earn that title if you can bring out a cure for obesity in the UK," Maria said.

"Hey, I am not promising anything, but that's the plan, so keep the Dr title at bay," Nadia replied with a smile.

"That's an ambitious project," Jacob commented, carefully listening to the conversation. "I'm wishing you all the best as well. And hey, guys, listen, I'm off to sleep. I need to get up early tomorrow morning," he added before leaving the room.

"Okay, Jacob, catch you later. I'll be going too. Let's help Mum tidy up the kitchen," Maria said.

"I'll give you a hand, Maria. Please allow me," Nadia offered gladly.

"Don't be silly, Nadia. You go and have a nice time. The little one is tired. Go and put her to bed," Maria insisted.

"Okay, Maria. Tell Mum I am thankful to her for everything. The food was scrumptious," Nadia said with a slightly raised voice, intentionally making it loud enough for her mother-in-law to hear. She continued, "She cheered up my day too. I will cook her some Bengali curry and some delicious parathas if she allows me to use her kitchen." Nadia said these words loudly before heading upstairs.

Jonathan sat on the sofa, engrossed in a documentary on TV.

"Goodnight, Papa," Nadia gestured to Jonathan as she passed by.

"Goodnight!" he replied.

*

Sarah and Jonathan typically spent their evenings together on the couch, enjoying cups of tea and coffee while watching their favourite TV programmes and documentary channels. Sarah, as usual, brought cups and saucers, placed them on the coffee table and settled onto the sofa. She poured tea into the cups, stirred it and handed one to her husband.

"Have your tea, Jonathan," she said. "And tell me something, don't you think you're being naïve here?"

Jonathan took his tea and responded, "What do you mean by naïve? The girl clearly wants to do something in life. After all, she's Keith's girlfriend. Isn't the fact that they're together enough reason for her to deserve our support?"

Sarah expressed her concerns, saying, "We don't know what she's up to, her background, why she's here and why she chose Keith, who is ten years her senior. Aren't these questions important to ask?"

Jonathan acknowledged her concerns, saying, "Yes, of course. She's here in our house now. Write down all your questions and ask her tomorrow. Let the kid have a good night's sleep tonight, Sarah. You saw how she greeted you. These people may be poor, but they have morals, respect and appreciation. She could be a great help to us, but only if you stop vilifying her."

*

Keith was an early riser. Regardless of the weather – cold, hot, humid or sticky – his body clock was set to wake up at the break of dawn. Today was no exception. He woke up early, as usual, and went downstairs to the kitchen, where he bumped into his mum.

"Mum, you're up early today!" he remarked.

"Yes, I woke up a bit early. I thought your girlfriend might find it awkward to come down, and the little one might feel hungry, so I'm preparing breakfast," his mother explained.

"Mum, your heart is full of affection. All it requires is a bit of moulding to fit Nadia in," Keith said.

"Keith, did she marry you to come to this country for a better life?" his mother asked.

"No, Mum, it's nothing like that. It's a long story, a sad one. I'll tell you some other time," Keith replied.

Nadia then came downstairs, softly calling out, "Keith! Keith…"

"Hey, Nadia, you're awake. Come and see what Mum is doing," Keith said, taking Nadia into the kitchen. "Mum woke up early to make breakfast for you guys. Her heart is pure after all, didn't I tell you?"

Nadia smiled and said, "Oh, that is so sweet. Thank you! May I help, Mother?"

"No, no need for any help," Sarah replied. "Keith, go and have a seat in the dining room and bring the little one down here to eat."

Nadia looked at Keith, smiled and went to fetch Pori to the breakfast table.

"You didn't finish your sentence, Keith. Why her? Why not a white girl?" Sarah enquired.

"Mum, I fell in love with her. She is a very caring individual, and she is well off in her country. She came here not because she wanted a better life, but because she had no choice. Pori's mum and dad were murdered, and they had to flee the country for security reasons," Keith explained.

"What!" his mother exclaimed in shock.

"Yes, it's a long story. She is from a wealthy family, and today we are going to the bank to open an account for her so she can shift some money from her country to the UK," Keith continued.

Nadia and Pori came downstairs, and Pori asked, "Mummy, can I watch a cartoon?"

Nadia, unsure of how to operate the TV, turned to Keith for assistance. "Keith, is there a cartoon channel for the kid to watch?"

Keith replied, "Yes, sure," and picked up the remote. He went over to Pori and said, "Press 2 and then 2." His mother overheard and shouted from the kitchen, "Keith, the Disney channel has moved to channel 36 now!"

Pori overheard and corrected her mistake and pressed 3 and 6, successfully landing on a cartoon programme. Keith applauded her, saying, "Well done!"

Meanwhile, his mother brought the breakfast tray and placed

it on the dining table. Nadia expressed her gratitude, but Sarah ignored her remarks.

Jonathan, Maria and Jacob showed up, and Jonathan greeted everyone with a cheerful "Good morning."

The others replied with their morning greetings, and Maria complimented Nadia's outfit. "Wow, look at you, Nadia, a different dress this morning, and it's so nice," Maria said.

"Thank you, Maria. It's a red net armless Anarkali embroidered kameez suit," Nadia replied.

"It's the first time I've heard this name, Nadia," Maria eluded.

"I thought you guys were going home," Nadia added recalling her memory from last night.

"You're the one who's supposed to go, love!" Sarah retorted.

"Oh, Mother, your temper is like a stubborn stain on a white sheet. Iron it out, please. I said I might go, that's why she said that," Maria responded.

Nadia stood up from her seat, gave her mother-in-law a crafty look and said, "Just give me a minute." She left the dining table and headed upstairs, startling everyone, especially Sarah. She went into her room and opened her luggage to find the gifts she had brought for Keith's family. She brought them downstairs and allocated each gift to its rightful owner. Everyone was happy to receive one, except for Sarah.

Maria opened her package and was mesmerised by the design and vibrant colours. "It's so beautiful and vibrant," she said. "You know what? I'm going to wear it now. I have to take a photo in this outfit to post on my Instagram page."

Nadia looked at her and smiled. "Go ahead, you'll look like a princess in this suit."

Maria then hurried off to change.

Nadia eyeballed her mother-in-law and said, "You know, 'Mother', in our country, we look down on people from different castes, creeds and religions, just like you are doing now to me. I'm not upset in any way. I totally understand where you're coming from. 'Mother', let me reassure you, I'm not here to take anything from you or your son. Fate brought us together, and an unforeseen tragedy led me to your doorstep. Just thought I would let you know," Nadia explained.

"You took my son away. I wanted him to get married to a person of his kind, not to a dark-skinned person like you," Sarah said blatantly.

"Mummy Ji," Nadia responded, "you sent your son to work in a country full of dark-skinned people, and you expected him to have an illegitimate relationship with a Bangladeshi girl and come back to tie a legitimate knot with a white British girl. It doesn't work that way in our world. Bangladesh is an Islamic republic, it's not a brothel. Chasteness is the core principle there. Women look for a lifelong partner, not a one-night stand. No wonder, yesterday, on the news channel, your prime minister was offering incentives to married couples because single parents are draining the coffers of taxpayers dry.

"Let me tell you something about my skin, ma'am. If you believe in God, you will agree. God took His time in making me to perfection, not half-baked or fully cooked. No offence intended, but the majority of white-skinned people start wrinkling before the age of forty. This is not the case with dark-skinned people. White people wear tans to get to my skin tone, and Black people use lighteners to get to my tone. Dark is the chosen colour of nature, and dark matters. Scientists globally agree with the fact that dark matter governs the fundamentals of the universe. Whichever way you look at it, the word 'dark' lingers in obscurity until illuminated by the light to bring out its glory, and you are so worried that your son got married to a dark-skinned person. Be joyous and appreciate what your son has achieved. He's done a good job, 'Mother'," Nadia said passionately.

"Oh, you're barking hyperbolic nonsense here, whatever your name is. Listen up, I don't want you to have kids with my son. What do you know about white privilege? In real-life situations, only white skin matters. Nothing else matters. Everywhere white people went, nations bowed to their knees. History is the witness," Sarah said.

"Drop it, Sarah. As much as I agree with your sentiments regarding racial discriminations, things have improved now," Jonathan interjected.

"Why are you telling me? She is the one making provocative remarks," Sarah replied.

Just then, Maria came down with a completely new look, wearing an elegant Bengali partywear outfit. It was green in colour, made from chiffon fabric with fabulous embroidery and sequined decoration. The kameez and bottom had a unique see-through net base, giving the wearer a sleek look.

"Woohoo!" Nadia clapped and smiled. "You look gorgeous in that dress. Come, let's take a picture together."

Pori Moni, excited by Nadia's enthusiasm, began to clap too, followed by the others.

"You really look stunning in that dress," Jacob commented.

"Yeah, isn't she," Keith added.

"She does," Sarah and Jonathan agreed simultaneously.

"This must have been expensive, Nadia. The amount of work that went into this dress is astonishing," Maria remarked.

"Yes, you're right. The work put into it is phenomenal, but it's not as expensive as you may think. I bought this from a private street trader in Dhaka. Her name is Tailor Rongila. She sources raw materials from locals to make beautiful attire. She makes garments like this by hand from scratch. She doesn't charge as much as those corporations using child labour to do their legwork and shifting goods to Europe to sell at highly inflated prices for commercial gain. I paid £50 for all three pieces – top, bottom and the dupatta you're holding," Nadia explained.

"What? That's cheap. I thought the cost would be in the thousands," Maria said, surprised.

"Nope, not at all. You look stunning in this, and that's what matters. My money was well spent," Nadia replied with a smile.

"Of course," Maria agreed, coming to give Nadia a kiss on the cheek.

They all had breakfast together and took selfies and family photos with their phones, and then called it a day.

*

Keith, Nadia and Pori Moni prepared for a long day ahead. Their first stop was the bank to open a new account for Nadia, followed by a visit to the local nursery school to find a place for Pori. Their final destination was a grocery-shopping trip. Unfortunately, there weren't many Asian supermarkets in Aughton, so they had to make the forty-mile journey to Manchester in the east. Nadia needed the special spices and herbs for her traditional homely cooking.

As they hit the road, a sense of romance filled the air. They transformed into impromptu singers, serenading each other with songs throughout the journey. Occasionally, they would pause at scenic spots to admire the views and dance a little. Keith was behind the wheel, and Nadia gazed at him with a warm smile. He continued to sing:

Your Smile

Keith:
Your smile, a melody, enchanting and pure,
Like petals dancing in the breeze, so sure.
It shines like stars, in the night's allure,
Your smile, a treasure, forever to adore.

Nadia:
Hmm… hmm… hmm… hoho… hoho…
Your smile, oh how it makes my heart glow,
In your embrace, I never want to let go.
Hmm… hmm… hmm… hoho… hoho…
Nadia:

With each grin, my worries fade away,
Like sunlight breaking through clouds in disarray.
It's a symphony, in every display,
Your smile, the brightest, come what may.

Keith:
Hmm... hmm... hmm... hoho... hoho...
Your smile, oh how it makes my heart glow,
In your embrace, I never want to let go.
Hmm... hmm... hmm... hoho... hoho...

Nadia:
In a world of chaos, your smile's my guide,
A beacon of hope, where love resides.
With you, I feel like I can touch the sky,
Your smile, the reason, I'll never say goodbye.

Keath:
Hmm... hmm... hmm... hoho... hoho...
Your smile, oh how it makes my heart glow,
In your embrace, I never want to let go.
Hmm... hmm... hmm... hoho... hoho...

Upon arriving at the Indian supermarket, their chosen song came to an end and they embarked on a shopping spree, filling their trolley with an assortment of groceries, spices and continental delicacies. With their boot fully stocked, they decided it was time to seek out a local restaurant for a meal, all while their little one, Pori Moni, observed the bustling scene with delight, thanks to the presence of Aunt Nadia and Uncle Keith.

Nadia, a newcomer to the UK dining experience, found herself uncertain about what to order. Turning to Keith, she sought his guidance in selecting a delectable dish for herself and Pori.

Keith, in response, ordered his personal favourite, chicken

tikka masala, along with a few pieces of naan bread. As he gazed at Nadia, he sensed a certain unease in her demeanour. She appeared to be silently connecting the dots in her mind, working out the best way to establish her own laboratory in her in-laws' unused garage. She was one month and two weeks into her first pregnancy, and with the typical nine-month gestation period in mind, she calculated that she had only thirty weeks remaining to prepare for the impending arrival. It was imperative that she take action now to initiate her business venture, ensuring that the space would serve its purpose effectively.

Keith, picking up on her contemplative state, asked, "What's on your mind, Nadia? You seem lost."

Nadia replied, "Keith, I truly need to get my project going as soon as possible. I want to stand on my own two feet, and I have a compelling idea that could give me a competitive edge in the start-up world. However, I'm fully aware that turning an idea into reality requires an immense amount of hard work. I've calculated that I have only thirty weeks left to make this happen because our little one will be arriving soon," she said gently rubbing her belly, "and that will bring added responsibilities that might make it difficult for me to focus."

Keith reassured her, "Don't worry about it. Dad mentioned that you can use his garage to kick-start your mission. What better and more convenient way to set up a lab? It's nearly ready-made, like working from the comfort of your own home."

Nadia nodded in agreement, saying, "Yes, you're right. Speaking of the lab, I need to order a list of basic chemistry laboratory apparatus. There are at least forty individual items on my checklist. Can we visit the garage first thing tomorrow morning, Keith?"

"Absolutely," Keith replied with a supportive smile.

The waiter approached their table with his catering trolley, carefully arranging the dishes in an orderly fashion. He smiled and said, "Please enjoy your meal. If you require anything else, simply raise your hand and one of our staff will be with you right away."

"A lot of food you ordered here, Keith," Nadia observed.

Keith chuckled and reassured her, "No need to worry, enjoy as much as you can. If there's any left, we'll pack it up and take it home for another time. I've taken your lessons to heart."

Nadia nodded, a smile playing on her lips. "It's reassuring to hear that, Keith. I'll never forget how one day you ordered an excessive amount of food to impress me and then quickly realised that showing off was a bad idea. Do you still remember that day?"

Keith chuckled again, recalling the memory. "Yes, I do. Some days are just unforgettable. You made me eat two extra platefuls, and I felt sick to my stomach."

Nadia explained, "That was a lesson to learn, Keith. Now, at least in front of me, you're sensible with food. I read an article the other day, just after we landed at the airport, which mentioned that the UK disposes of approximately 9.5 million tons of food waste in a single year, while 8.4 million people in the UK are dealing with food poverty. No wonder you were a food waster, it's ingrained in the country's fabric."

Keith said in defence, "Are you generalising now? I wasted food, but it doesn't mean everyone does, you know?"

Nadia continued, "Keith, I've only been here for a few days, and I've already noticed how the UK and Europe are harming the planet in the name of capitalism. All those supermarkets wrapping everything in plastic – is it really necessary?"

Kcith explained, "Well, it does make things look presentable, and customers find it convenient. They're doing it to make the shopping experience easier."

Nadia pressed further, "What about the damage it's causing to the climate, Keith?"

Keith admitted, "I know. The government is aware of the climate risks that plastic poses, and they're planning to bring in legislation to address this soon."

Nadia couldn't help but be sarcastic as she said, "Oh, you would know, given your role as an ambassador to Bangladesh, I'm confident you're aware that shops in the country utilize large leaves and net bags for carrying groceries."

Keith sighed, detecting the sarcasm in her tone. "Come on, don't start with me now."

Nadia clarified, "Keith, I'm not starting with you. It's just that a rich man's waste is a poor man's treasure. Take those 'bags for life' that supermarkets sell for 30p, for example. How many people actually use them for life? It's like taking twenty normal plastic bags, condensing them into one bag, and calling it a 'bag for life'. Does your government really care about the environment? I saw a whole cupboard full of these bags in your mother's kitchen, all brand new but only used once. The government's policy is flawed. I believe I could do a better job."

Then, addressing Pori, Keith asked, "Pori, are you enjoying the chicken, darling?" In a mumbled aside, he said, "You're suffering from OCD yourself and need a treatment plan. Start with your lab before trying to teach the whole world."

Pori, however, cheerfully replied, "Yes, Uncle Keith."

Nadia, clearly taken aback, said, "I heard what you mumbled under your breath."

Keith didn't hold back and responded, "Yes, it's true. You can't sit and not talk about this obsession of yours. Save the planet, save the environment – you're like a drop in the ocean. You don't realise that, do you? This is a global concern, not just yours. Look, I just want a peaceful life with you, that's all I'm concerned about right now," he said, his tone becoming more animated.

Nadia, slightly exasperated, retorted, "Okay, Keith, I'm sorry. I admit, I sometimes go too far. I apologise. Let's focus on a fresh start, shall we?"

Keith quickly replied, "Thank you."

With a playful smile, she continued, "Shall I sing you a song, Keith, to cheer you up and balance things out?"

Keith, slightly amused, responded, "I'd rather see your romantic side than this environmentalist fanaticism you possess. That would be a pleasant change."

Nadia grinned and added, "Oh, really? Well, I'm romantic most of the time, and you bare witness the intensity of it at the switching off the nights light, don't you Keith?"

"Indeed, your beauty and youth are undeniably captivating. Who else but me could testify to that?" Keith smiled warmly before continuing, "I'll cherish you in my heart always, never letting you slip away."

Nadia blushed and replied, "Anyway, I owe you for this one. Once I'm settled here and start earning, I'll have all the means for romance and plenty of dining out. A lovely night out today is greatly appreciated, my darling."

*

The following day, Sarah, Keith's mother, sought an opportunity to have a private conversation with Nadia. She had a multitude of questions and thoughts brewing since their discussion the day before. Sarah patiently waited for Keith to leave the house, knowing that he had plans to head to his local sports club around 11am for a game of squash and a swim before returning home.

Once Keith had left, Sarah seized the opportunity and knocked on the door of the annexed cottage where Nadia was now staying. Receiving no response at the door, Sarah decided to enter. To her surprise, Nadia wasn't in.

Unbeknownst to Sarah, Nadia had gone with Jonathan to inspect the garage to determine if it was suitable for her planned laboratory. Jonathan guided her through the space, revealing its considerable size. Contrary to her initial impression of it being a single-car-port type of garage, it turned out to be a fully equipped workshop measuring at least twelve by four metres. The workshop was stocked with a wide array of DIY woodworking tools and machinery, offering ample spare space. Nadia felt an intense inward delight, her mind racing with ideas for setting up the lab, even before receiving the official approval from Jonathan.

"Wow, this place is awesome, Dad. Thank you so much for letting me use this space. You're an angel, a true lifesaver. I'm going to give it a good clean now," Nadia exclaimed with gratitude.

Jonathan smiled and replied, "Hey, it's all yours, do what you like. I'm off to the golf club with my buddy Peter."

"Okay, Dad. Catch you later," Nadia said. She then hurried to the main house to retrieve a vacuum cleaner, rugs and some cleaning agents. When she knocked on the door, Sarah was surprised to see Nadia.

"Hey, I've been looking for you. Where were you?" Sarah enquired.

Nadia explained, "I went with Dad to see the garage. Can I borrow the vacuum cleaner and some cleaning products, please? I'll return them later. I mean the cleaning agent. I'll buy a replacement for what I'm using now."

Sarah, however, insisted, "There's no need to buy anything, I'll give you everything. Come in, I have something important to discuss with you."

Nadia entered the house, and Sarah closed the front door, gesturing for her to take a seat.

"Do you want coffee, Nadia?" Sarah offered.

"No, Mother, but I'm all ears. What do you want to talk about?" Nadia responded.

"You are an intelligent girl, Nadia. I don't have to say it, you speak many languages and are a qualified chemist. I understand that I may have come across as harsher than I intended. However, please know that it doesn't mean I dislike you. In fact, I'm immensely grateful to you for catching my son's attention and keeping him grounded during his time in your country. Every parent would wish for a wife like you for their child. Your country, though primarily homogenous, does grapple a simple caste system that triggers various issues like hate crimes, prejudices, discrimination and more. Am I correct?" Sarah enquired.

Nadia, a bit impatient, replied, "Yes, that's true."

"Now, you might think that this country, being multicultural, would be immune to such hate crimes, correct?" Sarah continued.

"Go on, I'm listening," Nadia replied, her curiosity piqued.

"You're new to this country, and you might not be fully aware of what happens behind closed doors here. I grew up in the 1960s, and let me tell you what I used to witness on a daily basis. Paki-bashing and negro-bashing at school and after school. 'Paki' was your skin colour no matter where you originated from, and Black people were negroes, and if someone happened to be of mixed race, they often endured even more abuse and physical attacks because they were often seen as being of a more 'devilish' nature.

"Today, it may seem that certain aspects have evolved or changed. However, two constants remain: 'white privilege' and 'unconscious bias'. People often segregate themselves based on race, with Asians living among Asians, Black individuals among their own, and white people doing the same, as well as others. The unfortunate truth is that racism, sexism, misogyny, prejudice and one-sidedness persist. In the event of a civil war, people tend to align with their own ethnicity without question.

"In light of these realities, does it really make sense to enter into a relationship with someone of a different race?" Sarah remarked. "Why invite problems when they can be avoided?"

Nadia responded calmly, "Are you suggesting I should leave Keith, then?"

"No, not at all," Sarah clarified. "You can stay with him, but it's best not to bring children into this world. They would likely face abuse, injustice, insults, verbal attacks and hate without question."

"What?" Nadia exclaimed. She was taken aback by this revelation, as she was already a month and a half pregnant with Keith's child, and her mother-in-law was advising against having a baby.

"I'm not suggesting you leave Keith," Sarah reiterated. "I'm proposing that you undergo sterilisation yourself, and you can continue to live with us for the rest of your life."

Nadia held her head in her hands and let out an anguished sigh. "Oh, Mother-in-Law, what are you thinking?" She had been planning to share the news of her pregnancy soon, but now she was frightened and taken aback. She decided to hold off on revealing her pregnancy for the time being. "Thank you for your suggestions, but I don't intend to stay here indefinitely," she said, her heart heavy. "My plan is to return to my own country once my little Pori turns eighteen. I have no intention of having any more children. Taking care of my niece is already a full-time job for me."

Sarah had Nadia in a difficult position. On the one hand, she was determined to start her ambitious career from the foundation of this household, but on the other hand, she was apprehensive because she was pregnant. She faced a critical decision that would either strengthen or sever her ties with the Evan family.

CHAPTER 5

FEELINGS AND ACCEPTANCE

Nadia   Pori   Keith   Jonathon   Sarah

Laxman   Maria   Jacob   Anurak   Anna

Jessica   Johnny

Starring

Nadia Begum – Pori Moni – Keith Evan- Jonathon Evan – Sarah
Evan – Laxman Urmila – Maria, sister in-law – Jacob brother in-law –
Anna Jones, from metprep – Jessica Biel, from nursery – Anurak
Chun-chieh, Microchip engineer

Nadia retrieved the vacuum cleaner and an assortment of cleaning
supplies from her mother-in-law's residence, transporting them to

her workshop. After briefly setting the materials aside, she seized the nearby reclining chair, positioned herself comfortably and engaged the mechanism to achieve a reclined seating angle. The workshop offered a contrast to the dull, foggy autumn weather outside, with a noticeable chill in the air inside. Through the workshop window, she admired the picturesque sight of scattered red, orange and brown leaves adorning the fields, but was disinclined to venture outdoors.

Reclining on the chair, Nadia directed her gaze towards the white ceiling above, her thoughts consumed by a mixture of perplexity and bewilderment. She found herself contemplating the reasons behind Sarah's unwarranted prejudices and hostility toward interracial relationships. Nadia wondered if Sarah's stance stemmed from a deeply ingrained, pathological racism, or if it had evolved due to a personal experience that had soured her perspective on non-white individuals. This internal exploration led Nadia to ponder if there were other, perhaps more complex factors at play, contributing to Sarah's divisive beliefs.

Her determination to delve deep into the heart of the matter remained unwavering. She anxiously awaited Keith's return from the sports club, recognising that time was of the essence. Any delay in addressing her mother-in-law's perception might lead to a setback in the meticulously crafted business plan she had envisioned for her future.

Nadia stood up from the chair and proceeded to unwind the vacuum cleaner cord. However, she paused midway to retrieve her mobile device. With a sense of urgency, she composed a text message to Keith, reading, "Please join me in the workshop when you get home, Keith." After hitting the send button, she activated the vacuum cleaner and started the cleaning process. Approximately an hour later, while engrossed in her cleaning tasks, the distinct sound of a knock at the door drew her attention. She swiftly opened the door to find Keith standing there.

"Hi, Nadia!"

"Hello, Keith," Nadia replied, cleaning cloth in hand. "I'm tidying up a bit."

"Yes, I can see, it looks much better now. Did you want to talk about something?" Keith enquired.

"Yes, but promise me you'll keep this conversation within these walls," Nadia requested.

"I promise, Nadia."

"Your mother's behaviour today was utterly reprehensible, to say the least. It was a deeply unpleasant experience. I want to address this before you go back to Bangladesh," Nadia explained.

"What happened?" Keith asked.

"She blatantly told me to go and get sterilised so that I can't have any children of my own," Nadia revealed, tears of anguish welling up in her eyes.

"What!" Keith's face fell, and he hugged Nadia to comfort her.

"Why would she do this to me?" Nadia sobbed, her distress palpable.

Keith, trying to console her, gently made her sit down and said, "Calm down, darling. This is not right. Let me think." He, too, was bewildered by his mother's actions, and his heart ached as he listened to Nadia's pain.

Nadia was torn. She felt that keeping this matter private was a form of condoning it. "How can I keep this between us? This is an act of admonishment, and it needs to be addressed. What if she asks me to leave?" she worried.

Keith reassured her, saying, "She won't, trust me. Just give me a chance. I will resolve this once and for all." With those comforting words, he left to confront his mother. He pressed the doorbell, and she opened the door.

"Mum, why are you doing this?" Keith began, his voice filled with a mixture of anger and concern. "Are you not aware that you are causing psychological trauma to Nadia? How could you tell her to go and get sterilised? She is one and a half months pregnant.

She has been trying hard, being resilient and optimistic, hoping to win your heart. But you are just causing trouble."

His mother was taken aback. "What? Keith, listen, son, I didn't know she was pregnant. If I had known, I wouldn't have said that to her. Is she pregnant with your baby?" she enquired.

"Yes, Mum," Keith confirmed.

With a sigh, his mother expressed her fundamental aversion. "My fear of her getting pregnant with you has come true. She has completely blindsided me. I'm a total failure," she lamented, holding her forehead, deep in thought as she sat on the couch.

"That's enough, Mum. You've shown no love, respect or affection. I'm moving out," Keith declared firmly.

His mother, realising the gravity of the situation, implored, "Son, please wait! I'm truly sorry. You don't need to move out. I'll go and apologise to her. She's a remarkable person. I had no idea she was pregnant."

"Mum, I know you wanted me to be with a partner of fair complexion, and I tried my best to make you happy. You've seen numerous failed relationships in my life, spent a lot on wedding ceremonies that amounted to nothing. But I'm more inclined towards a South Asian lifestyle than a Western one. I've found Nadia, who I believe is the perfect partner for me, and I've been happy until now. Why can't you accept that?" Keith pleaded.

He continued, "Apart from her skin tone, what other differences do you see between Maria and Nadia? Find me one external or internal deviation from Maria, your own daughter. I promise I'll leave her today if you can, but if you can't, then please accept my relationship with her and give us some space. Bless us, Mum," Keith concluded, his voice filled with a mixture of frustration and yearning for understanding.

"Hi, Dad."

Jonathan entered the room, enquiring, "What's happening, Keith?"

"Dad," Keith began, "tell Mum that if she acts inappropriately with Nadia, I'm leaving."

"Okay, son, I got the message!" Jonathan replied from the kitchen.

Sarah, reflecting on Keith's words, said, "You're right, son. I can't see any difference. In fact, she's much prettier than Maria. God took His time in creating her to perfection – not too dark, not too light, she's just the right tone. My past has haunted me for a long time, and I've been thoughtless, not considering what she will go through."

Keith's phone rang, and it was the Foreign Office. "Mum, I'll talk later, my boss is calling," he whispered away from the mouthpiece, then stepped away from his mother to continue his conversation on the phone.

Jonathan approached Sarah in the sitting room and advised her, "Sarah, you're going to lose your son. Just accept what he has to offer. Remember Richard Ratcliffe, who married an Iranian girl and went on hunger strike to save his wife? Some men, but not all, find serenity in foreign partners, and you should respect that. Your son means it, he'll just take his wife and leave. You need to mend this fractured relationship, it will be better for everyone."

*

Nadia was engrossed in rearranging the workshop furniture, endeavouring to determine the optimal layout for her proposed chemical factory. Suddenly, she heard a knock at the door, and before she could react, Sarah entered the room.

"Nadia… Nadia!" Sarah called out.

Upon hearing her mother-in-law, Nadia paused her work and emerged from behind a tall steel cabinet that she had been pushing to clean the floor underneath. "Yes, Mum?" Nadia responded.

"Are you cleaning and organising the workshop?" Sarah enquired.

"Yes, I am," Nadia confirmed.

"I need to talk to you for a while. Do you have a moment?" Sarah asked.

"Certainly, have a seat," Nadia offered.

Sarah accepted the invitation and sat down. Nadia followed suit, and they sat facing each other. Sarah then offered Nadia a cup of tea, who expressed her gratitude with a smile. Then she began her story.

"In 1965, during my first year of secondary school, the student body was predominantly composed of white pupils, with only a handful of Asian students. Specifically, there were just five Asian students, two from India and three from Pakistan, and approximately ten to fifteen Black students among a total of over 500 enrolled.

"One of the boys in my class was named Laxman, an Indian Hindu boy with strikingly handsome features, much like yours. It seemed as if God had taken His time in crafting him. Not only did he possess a charming physical appearance – tall with sharp features – but he also exhibited impeccable behaviour, an attractive personality, a penchant for smart dress and an impressive intellect. His allure was undeniable, and I found myself captivated by his charm, willingly giving him my heart and soul.

"Laxman's life was marked by tragedy from an early age. His father had tragically lost his life during the tumultuous Bengal and Punjab partition in 1948 in India. His mother, a resilient woman, managed to secure passage to England through the Southampton sea port. Laxman was just five years old when he arrived in this foreign land, and by the time he was in my class at the age of twelve, he had already overcome significant hardships.

"Despite his remarkable journey, there were those who couldn't help but display envy and prejudice. An envious white classmate would often give me disdainful looks whenever I engaged in conversation with Laxman, a sad testament to the racial tensions of the era.

"In those days, the older students, especially those in the fifth and sixth forms, organised what they called 'Paki-bashing days out'. It was a horrific experience for anyone caught in their path. During these gang attacks, it was considered normal for Asians to suffer head injuries, black eyes and various other injuries. All because of the colour of their skin.

"One fateful afternoon, they targeted Laxman, and I tried desperately to intervene, but my efforts were in vain. They kicked him mercilessly until he lost consciousness. By the time the violence subsided, he was unrecognisable due to his severe injuries. Tragically, he didn't survive, and I gave a statement to the police about the incident.

"What's truly astonishing, or perhaps I should say infuriating, is that not a word about this incident ever made it to the press or news bulletins. The following day, those responsible for the violence returned to school as though nothing had happened, and the police took no action against them.

"The psychological trauma that stemmed from this event continues to haunt me to this day. It prevented me from forming close relationships with Asians, as I lived in fear that my presence might bring them harm. I still carry a sense of responsibility for Laxman's death.

"It wasn't until I became a mother myself that I could begin to comprehend the agony his mother must have endured. The pain of losing a young child is one of the most excruciating experiences a mother can face. Those kids not only had to navigate the challenges of studying subjects in a language different from their mother tongue but also had to endure the daily psychological torment inflicted upon them by bullies both inside and outside the school. It was a horrifying and deeply disheartening ordeal."

"What a tragic story," Nadia remarked. "I completely understand your concern now. You worry that if Keith's children are born from a mixed-race relationship, they might face unnecessary harassment and trauma at school and in life solely because of their skin colour. Is that your concern?"

"Don't you think this is concerning?" said Sarah.

"I totally get what you are saying, but things have moved on. Now on average half of schools are ethnically diverse, it will not be the same. Chanting racist abuse is illegal now. This wasn't the case forty years ago," said Nadia.

"Do you really think so?"

"Absolutely, Mum. People aren't born racist, they develop such attitudes after witnessing negative behaviours from certain individuals. The label of racism can be subjective and depends on how one defines it. If a Black man dislikes a white person due to their unpleasant behaviour, it's unlikely he would be labelled a racist. However, if the situation were reversed, the term 'racist' might be more readily applied. The perception of racism can indeed be influenced by the direction in which such biases are directed. When someone directs abuse at you, it's essential to question their motivations. If it appears to be unfounded, it might be a sign of racism. However, if an individual dislikes a particular ethnic group due to their behaviour, it can be characterised as hatred, and hatred can indeed be transformed into love by altering one's behaviour or attitude. This highlights the potential for positive change and understanding, even in challenging situations."

"These are just words, Nadia, the reality is quite different. Just a few weeks back a Chinese man was driving past and failed to stop at the zebra crossing but stopped just past the line. This woman approached him, stood in front of his car so he couldn't drive away, then came to the driver's side and started banging on the window, yelling at him to go back to his communist country and other negative things. The guy was not sure how to deal with this lady so he waited it out inside the car until the horns from other cars stuck behind made her move away. Racism and hate will never go away, Nadia," explained Sarah.

"You bring up a disheartening example, Mum. It's true that

despite our efforts to promote understanding and harmony, incidents of racism and hate still occur. Such incidents serve as reminders that prejudice and bias can persist in society. While it may be a challenging and ongoing battle, we must continue striving for a world where everyone is treated with respect and equality. Each act of kindness, each effort to educate and each opportunity for dialogue can contribute to reducing these harmful behaviours and beliefs over time. We should remain committed to fostering a more inclusive and tolerant world, even in the face of such discouraging events.

"I understand everything. But can we build a friendship, please? I have many plans for the future, and I'd appreciate having you on my side. I acknowledge that racism might persist, and I'm aware that I, too, sometimes find myself unwittingly harbouring biases towards different groups of people," Nadia said.

"I will stand by your side and support you in all your efforts, but there's one question I need a rational answer to," Sarah began.

Nadia enquired, "What's that?"

"Why did you choose my son, was it for financial gain or love?" she enquired.

"Mum, I'm a temporary visitor here. Once Pori completes her education, I plan to return to my own country, where I have property and land. I'll teach my children to be good citizens and provide them with self-defence training. By that time, I believe things will be different. Who knows, by the time my baby goes to school, the prime minister of the UK might even be of Asian descent. So, what do you say, Mum? Can we be friends?"

Sarah, concerned, asked, "Are you implying that you'll be taking Keith's baby away from us?"

Nadia reassured her, saying, "No, not at all. If you'd like, you can have the baby. In fact, I'd be happier, as it would allow me more time to focus on my work."

Sarah then enquired, "How far along are you in your pregnancy?"

Nadia replied, "One month and two weeks."

"Congratulations!" Sarah exclaimed. "You must take good care of yourself. Avoid smoking and alcohol. I'll get you some prenatal vitamins. Jonathan and I are going to the pharmacy tomorrow."

Nadia smiled and said, "Yes, ma'am, your wish is my command." She was pleased to see the change in her mother-in-law's attitude.

After Sarah left the room, closing the door behind her, Nadia felt a profound sense of relief. Reconciling with her mother-in-law was a significant obstacle she had overcome, and she could now fully commit to her intended mission. She picked up her phone and called Keith to share the good news. Keith was overjoyed to hear the news and commended Nadia, saying, "That's a good investment, Nadia." He was well aware of how particular his mother could be when it came to accepting her as a daughter-in-law.

"Didn't I say that only you can break into my mother's mental faculty with your specially adopted approach? Well done! Maybe we should hold a party and celebrate a new, renewed and revamped marriage ceremony at the same time," Keith suggested.

Nadia agreed, saying, "You took the words right out of my mouth. Why not? I was thinking exactly the same thing. Let me have Maria's number. I can't wait to share this news with her too."

Nadia had a big celebration in mind to commemorate her certified acceptance into the Evan family. Organising such an event can be nerve-wracking, even for the most experienced party planner. The responsibilities include everything from selecting music to arranging for food, refreshments and, of course, a celebratory cake. There was much to consider, and no room for error, but the effort would undoubtedly be worth it when she looked back on this significant occasion.

The prospect of taking on this task with so many variables is daunting, but Nadia was determined to persevere. She was counting on Maria to be her star guest and help with the event. Maria was outspoken, gorgeous and outgoing, and her vibrant personality would be a great asset in inviting and welcoming guests. As Nadia was relatively new to the country and didn't have many relatives or friends, it made sense to entrust the responsibility of organising the party to Maria.

Nadia dialled Maria's mobile phone number, excited to share the news. As she explained the situation, Maria praised her, remarking, "Your patience, good manners, politeness and capacity to handle tough situations have paid off much sooner than expected, Nadia. Well done. I'll be coming to see you soon. I can't wait to have a house party, Bengali style this time."

Nadia responded, "Oh, yes, of course. When are you coming, then?"

Maria answered, "I'll pop by tonight."

Nadia expressed her delight, saying, "That's great news. I'll see you then." She hung up the phone and continued with her cleaning. However, she paused for a moment, picked up her phone and dialled the number of MetPrep, the lab consumables company, to place an order.

"Hi, I would like to place an order for chemistry lab consumables and equipment. I have prepared a list that I'd like to email to you for pricing and delivery."

The representative replied, "Yes, sure. Send me your list to anna@metprepltd.co.uk, and I will get back to you as soon as I can."

After finishing the cleaning of the double garage, Nadia had reorganised and created a significant amount of space for her new equipment. She then dedicated more time to conducting a Google search for Indian-inspired home decorations, such as garland craft flowers, various-coloured cushion covers, wall hangings, colourful embroidered bedding, LED string lights and other ornamentations, then placed an order online.

"Nadia! Nadia! Are you still in the garage?" shouted Keith.

She quickly ran out to face Keith, her attention fully captured.

"Keith," she said, "what's happened?"

"The nursery just called me!" Keith explained.

"Oh my goodness," Nadia exclaimed before rushing out the door like a sprinter. She was on her way to the nursery, located just seven minutes away. She was already ten minutes late for picking up Pori Moni. While it wasn't exactly a joy to run a mile along footpaths, the nursery was located on a secluded piece of land away from traffic, offering young children a pleasant, open space.

"Hey, wait! I'll give you a lift, you're pregnant," Keith shouted after her.

"Thanks, but I can get there faster on foot," she replied and continued jogging.

Keith stepped into the garage, marvelling at the transformation. He was deeply impressed by the progress Nadia was making and quietly mumbled to himself, "This woman is a dynamo."

Meanwhile, Nadia had reached the nursery and stepped inside. "I am so sorry, Jessica," she apologised, "I got held up by a call. It won't happen again."

Jessica, the nursery staff member, reassured her, saying, "It's okay, no problem." Nadia then picked up Pori and headed home.

Upon their return, Sarah was waiting for them. As Nadia reached the door, she heard Sarah call, "Come and join me with the little one, Nadia!"

"Okay, coming, Mum!" Nadia responded. She was pleasantly surprised to find a fully prepared dinner waiting for Pori, consisting of fish fingers, baked beans, steamed broccoli, potatoes and peas. Nadia expressed her gratitude, saying, "Oh, that is so nice of you, Mum." She was genuinely delighted by the thoughtful gesture.

"From now on, you can leave Pori with me," Sarah said. "Not only will she learn to speak fluent English more quickly, but you can also carry on with whatever you intend to work on. If you can find a way to tackle the nation's obesity problem, I'm telling you, girl, you're going to make some serious money. Just recently, the government announced new specialised support to help those living with obesity. They're injecting £100 million to support children, adults and families in achieving and maintaining a healthier weight."

Nadia was thrilled by this news, exclaiming, "Wow, that's great, Mum!"

Sarah continued, "Yes, you can develop your business plan and submit it to the local authority. You can even get assistance to set up a proper laboratory instead of this old bunker."

Nadia was overwhelmed with gratitude and gave Sarah an adoring kiss on her forehead. "Thank you so much," she said.

"Mum, I want to hold a house party," Nadia announced.

Sarah was surprised and asked, "What? Why?"

Nadia explained, "Because I'm so happy at the moment, I can't do without one. Tell me, which house should I decorate, this one or the cottage?"

Sarah suggested, "Do it here, it's bigger and airier. But who's coming to your party? Do you have family and friends?"

Nadia replied, "Nope. You're going to invite your family and friends to celebrate your daughter-in-law's homecoming party. You get the guests, and I'll provide the joy."

Just then, Keith rang the doorbell. Nadia went to open the door, and Keith expressed his concern, saying, "What was that back there, Nadia? You shouldn't jog while you're pregnant, and all that heavy cleaning work in the garage. Take it easy with heavy duties, or you might lose my baby."

Nadia laughed and reassured him, "No, I won't." Then, she added, "By the way, Keith, I spoke to Mum about having a house party."

Keith expressed his concerns to Nadia, saying, "You are a thunderbolt, Nadia. Seriously, doing up that garage must have been a task. You could have asked me for help. Here, we take health and safety seriously, okay? Try to understand that."

Nadia's face dropped, and she appeared unhappy.

Sarah noticed the change in Nadia's mood and asked, "What's

happened here now? Why has she turned miserable? Just a minute ago, she was jumping with happiness."

Keith explained, "Mum, I'm getting scared for her. Her drive to set up that business at supersonic speed is a cause for concern. She forgot to collect Pori from nursery today, she jogged to the school, and she moved heavy furniture around in the garage. Don't you think that will harm her pregnancy?"

Sarah understood and responded, "Well, potentially, yes. I have been monitoring her. She is a woman of strong belief, and I like her. I told her I will help her raise Pori, so don't you worry, this won't happen again. Get freshened up and join the little one for dinner. I will grab a plate for you."

Keith looked at Nadia and asked, "What's the matter with you now?"

Nadia replied, "Nothing. I'm happy that you are such a caring father-to-be."

Keith enquired further, "So, tell me more about the party you were talking about?"

As Keith walked over to see Pori eating, he grabbed a fish finger from her plate and took a bite. Pori cried out, "Hey, that's mine! Mummy, Uncle Keith ate my fish finger!"

Sarah came into the room with a plate full of food for Keith. She said, "Here, Pori, this is his plate, and you have his fish finger, one for him and one for you."

Nadia asked Pori, "What do you say, Pori?"

Pori replied, "Thank you, Grandma!" and received a kiss from Sarah.

*

Nadia, Keith and Sarah agreed on a plan for a house party that would take place three days before Keith's departure back to his ambassadorial role in Bangladesh. Sarah, who had raised three children herself, understood the demands and joys of parenthood.

102

She offered to help by dropping off and picking up Pori from the nursery, provided that Nadia got her ready for school each morning. This arrangement allowed Sarah to enjoy a refreshing morning walk, benefiting her mental health and wellbeing. Delighted by this offer, Nadia readily agreed to the conditions, so it was a win-win situation. Sarah concluded by saying, "Deal done, then. You guys eat and go. I am going for a rest."

Nadia shared her thoughts with Keith, saying, "You know, I'm not being arrogant or egotistical here, but a déjà vu hit me just now. It whizzed past my head as though I've been in this scenario before. Sometimes I feel like I'm here for a reason."

Keith enquired, "Here in the UK, you mean?"

Nadia clarified, "No, I don't mean only that. I mean I was born for a reason, I think. Just yesterday, my mother-in-law was fuming with anger at me, and my father-in-law offered me his garage to pursue my career. Not forgetting you being the vehicle to carry me here, all this happening in such urgency. Why? All these imaginative theories pop into my mind from thin air, and when I put them into practice, it actually works."

Keith suggested, "Maybe you're here to make a difference. Maybe God sent you with some special powers like others. Hey, what if you're a lady prophet sent by God, a female version for the first time in the history of mankind?"

Nadia responded with a touch of sarcasm, "Come on, that's too much of an overstatement, rather sarcastic, Keith."

Keith continued, "Hey, listen, maybe you are. Look at history. Many men claimed they were sent from God, and all failed to save the planet. All created social unrest and brought chaos to humanity in the name of God. What if you are here to put things the other way round, the first female ambassador to God?"

Nadia played along, saying, "Yes, sure, God decided it's time for a gender change prophecy this time. How can a woman overcome men's strength? Men will never accept a woman as a prophet. Nice thought, though."

Keith complimented her, saying, "I think there is something more to you than just that, Nadia."

Nadia expressed her gratitude, saying, "Oh really? Is that the reason you invested five years of your precious life pursuing Nadia?"

Keith reassured her, "No, I invested in you, not the name. You are something of a kind. Just do what you want to do. Now that Mum will stand by you, I can be at peace working away abroad."

Nadia, touched by his support, hugged Keith and gave him a passionate kiss.

*

A couple of days later, deliveries of home decorations and Nadia's chemistry consumables arrived. Maria took charge of decorating the house, and Nadia began setting up her laboratory with the help of her father-in-law and his DIY expertise. After a long day's work at the workshop reorganising, it had been transformed into something unique. Nadia was so exhausted from her hard work that she fell asleep right there that night. The following morning, after a restful night's sleep, she found her stamina improved and quickly rushed to her annexe cottage.

Nadia got dressed and went to the main house to catch up with Maria. As soon as she entered, she was awestruck by the sheer beauty of the decorations.

"Maria!" she exclaimed. "An Indian interior designer would fail to match this house decor. You've nailed it, girl, just like a born Indian. Are you sure you're not an Indian in white skin?"

She smirked and continued, "How the hell did you manage to do all this? I was expecting just a few touches here and there. Oh my god, the guests will be inspired by your fairytale decorative work, Maria. You are an icon, a star in a lonely planet."

Maria thanked Nadia, saying, "Oh, thank you, Nadia. It's your decorations, I just used them decisively, and it turned out to be somewhat impressive."

Nadia said, "Very impressive indeed. Wait until Keith and the others come to see everything here. I am so happy. Have you made the guest list?"

Maria confirmed, "Yes, around twenty-five family and friends are coming."

Nadia appreciated her efforts and said, "Well done! You know what? I am heading to the supermarket with Keith to get the groceries. Keith and I decided to prepare Bengali and English fusion food."

Maria responded, "Wow, sounds like a plan!"

Nadia smiled and added, "Catch you later, Maria. Don't forget to invite my star guest, Jacob," before going back to her now fully operational laboratory.

Nadia switched on her laptop and made a Skype call to Taiwan. Anurak Chun-Chieh, a freelance tech engineer and a genius semiconductor fabricator, had accomplished what many giant manufacturers had failed to achieve. He had created a nanochip that was just two nanometres wide, which is as thin as the strands of human DNA. In the world of nano-technology, seemingly impossible feats become a reality.

"Hi, Nadia, how are you doing? It's been a while. I heard you left GreenBirth Corporation," Anurak remarked.

Nadia responded, "Hi, Anurak, yes, I am no longer with them. I am going private, just like you. I'm up to my neck in work. I know you're busy too, so I won't take much of your time. Can you create a microchip, cylindrical in shape and the size of a rice grain if possible? I need action potentials for excitatory input at -50mV and inhibitory input at -30mV. What's the waiting time for this?"

Anurak assured her, "Not long, I already have a few in my possession."

Nadia continued, "How about -70mV and -50mV?"

Anurak replied, "Yes, I have those too."

Nadia was pleased and said, "Great news. Send me ten

of each, and make sure to insure the postage. I'm forwarding the full address to you now. Furthermore, Anurak, get ready to mass-produce these chips. If I can make this work, you'll definitely have a stake in my success, and I'll be flooding you with orders."

Anurak wished her good luck and said, "I'm ready here, just waiting for more details."

Nadia ended the call saying, "Okay, chat later. Bye." She disconnected the line and heard Keith calling her.

"Yes, coming, darling! Just two minutes."

As Keith and Nadia headed to the supermarket for their house party shopping, Nadia pulled out a five-page journal with a party checklist. Keith was utterly astonished when he glanced at the list.

"What the hell did you write in those pages, chemistry journal?" he asked.

Nadia chuckled and replied, "No, it's just our shopping list for the party."

Keith was still surprised and said, "That's one hell of a long list, Nadia. I don't think my car will be able to handle it. We might need a truck!"

Nadia reassured him, "Oh, come on, it's not that much. The list might look long, but the items are small. Your car is a perfect size cab for this, don't worry."

*

Nadia and Keith returned from their shopping expedition with a car full of party supplies. To make things easier, Nadia had outsourced many of the Indian dishes from a local restaurant called Monsoon Curry House, which was located about five miles away from the village. The restaurant was known for its delectable chicken korma, fish karahi, naan, kebabs, crunchy samosas and a variety of relishes, chutneys, sauces and pickles. These dishes were to be delivered fresh and hot on the day of the party.

Nadia had also prepared her favourite oven-roasted honey-glazed tandoori chicken at home, while Maria and Sarah had helped her make some English dishes like roast beef and shepherd's pie. To ensure the party ran smoothly, Nadia had hired a team of professional waiters and waitresses to serve the food. Additionally, she had arranged for a band to provide entertainment for the guests well into the evening. The preparations for the house party were in full swing.

On the day of the party, guests started to arrive, with Keith and his father Jonathan welcoming them at the entrance. Jacob was stationed at the refreshment counter, offering sparkling wine to the arriving guests. Maria, dressed beautifully in the dress she received from Nadia, was mingling with some of the visitors, while Sarah was engaged in conversation with others. However, there was no sign of Nadia.

Keith's friend Johnny had just arrived and was warmly welcomed. They exchanged pleasantries and admired each other's appearance. Johnny couldn't help but notice how well Keith had maintained his figure.

"Where's the host of this party, mate? Can't seem to see her," Johnny enquired.

"Don't worry, mate. She'll be here soon. Make yourself at home and enjoy a drink from Jacob's bar," Keith reassured him.

As the music began to play, there was a sudden hush in the room, and all eyes turned toward the staircase. Nadia made a remarkable entrance, her stunning figure and her choice of dress making her stand out in the crowd. She appeared to blend seamlessly with the music and the atmosphere, capturing everyone's attention. With a captivating smile, she descended the staircase, and once she reached the party guests, she surprised everyone by breaking into a song and dance to the rhythm of the live music. Her unexpected performance left the guests in awe.

Wondering Mind

Nadia:
I'm a-wondering, I'm a-pondering… ha
I'm a-wondering, I'm a-pondering
I'm a-thinkin' 'bout humanity… ha
And this system of squandering
Pretendin' to be naive, I see… ha
But I'm fully aware of my surroundings

Falling in love with the world never crossed my mind
downfall of the environment enriched me from behind

Chorus:
I'm a-wondering, I'm a-pondering… ha
I'm a-wondering, I'm a-pondering
I'm a-thinkin' 'bout humanity… ha
And this system of squandering
Pretendin' to be naive, I see… ha
But I'm fully aware of my surroundings

Husband Keith's appearance, a beacon of my aspirations,
His relations lift me high, fostering adaptability and innovations

Chours:
I'm a-wondering, I'm a-pondering… ha
I'm a-wondering, I'm a-pondering
I'm a-thinkin' 'bout humanity… ha
And this system of squandering
Pretendin' to be naive, I see… ha
But I'm fully aware of my surroundings

Achieving a goal involves enhancing life's situations,
I'm the siren, never resting, in relentless dedication,

Chorus:

I'm a-wondering, I'm a-pondering… ha
I'm a-wondering, I'm a-pondering
I'm a-thinkin' 'bout humanity… ha
And this system of squandering
Pretendin' to be naive, I see… ha
But I'm fully aware of my surroundings

Love me or loath me, my smile never fades or takes leave,
I'm here for a reason, so let's celebrate the joys that spring breathes

Chorus:

I'm a-wondering, I'm a-pondering… ha
I'm a-wondering, I'm a-pondering
I'm a-thinkin' 'bout humanity… ha
And this system of squandering
Pretendin' to be naive, I see… ha
But I'm fully aware of my surroundings

As the applause filled the room, she appeared both shy and delighted. She went on to introduce herself to all the guests, engaging in conversation while sipping on her mocktail.

Johnny made his way to Nadia, saying, "Hello, hello, hello, I'm Johnny, Keith's friend."

"Hello, Johnny. Nice to meet you, and thank you for coming to the party." They shook hands.

Johnny held her hand and attempted to bring it to his lips.

Nadia quickly pulled her hand away, saying, "Aah, I'm sorry. You must respect cultural differences here. This gesture is only permissible for Keith. Enjoy everything else – the food, drinks, wine, etc. I'll catch you later," and she moved on to meet other people.

Moments later, Maria jingled the bell to gather everyone's attention. She invited everyone to the garden, where a long table and seating were arranged for dinner.

The guests enjoyed their meal, engaging in lively conversation, laughter and gossip. As the night wore on, they grew tired, and one by one, the party started to wind down as everyone headed home.

*

In the bedroom, Nadia was slowly taking off her party attire, preparing for bed, and Keith was following suit, slightly intoxicated. "You looked super hot back there." He complimented her on her stunning performance at the party and the song she sang, expressing his happiness about marrying her.

Nadia playfully responded, "Sober up and come to bed to cool me down, darling. If I look too hot, I need to get cooled down, don't I?"

As they settled into bed, the TV in the background captured Nadia's attention. The news bulletin featured the prime minister's update about the COP26 summit recently held in Glasgow, UK. He expressed his deep frustration with India and China's decision not to phase out coal-burning by 2030. The UK, as the host nation, had set the goal of limiting the global temperature rise to 1.5°C, but both India and China had altered the wording from "phasing out" to "phasing down" at the last minute.

Keith, too, took notice of the news and listened as the prime minister emotionally addressed the outcome of the conference.

Nadia commented on the news. "Did you hear that, Keith? The prime minister is visibly frustrated and acknowledges that he has failed to protect the COP26 package. How can he be certain that when these delegates return home, they will keep their promise? China and India have made it clear they have no intention of stopping coal burning. It's frustrating! They are at the peak of their industrial revolution, while the West has already moved past this phase."

Nadia's frustration grew, and she continued, "I've been closely following this conference since it started. The agreements should have taken significant steps to end the use of fossil fuels, even if not overnight. Don't they understand that extreme weather events are changing the Arctic region? We're in the midst of a storm already. My country and other low-lying nations are on the brink of going underwater, even if the temperature rise is limited to 2.4°C by 2050. I have substantial investments in my country, and they're all at risk. The country is headed for destitution, and the millions of people who will be displaced, where will they go, huh?" She frowned as she sat on the edge of the bed, deeply concerned.

"Nadia, take it easy, darling," reassured Keith. "They will make a stronger deal next year, so why get stressed over this? Cheer up," and he came and held her from behind. "Come on, let's make love." He kissed her neck and said, "The world isn't going anywhere, okay, everything will be alright."

"Keith, you don't understand, the world isn't going anywhere. It will do its best to save itself because it's alive, just like you and me. With all the digging and mining people are doing, I'm worried the planet may explode one day. Can anyone tell what's fuelling the Earth's core? Ask a scientist, and they'll say the theory is radioactive decay. But it's just a theory. They don't actually know because they haven't been there to check it out. And they can't go down to the Earth's core in a million years. It's not the same as going to space. What if the Earth requires gas and coal to feed its core, and we're extracting them like there's no tomorrow?

"This conference turned into a fun club for those global leaders. They burned tons of CO_2 to get to the conference in the first place, which is contradictory to the talks they're chairing. And those leaders from poorer countries, they came for the handouts, nothing more. I promise, nothing more. They have no intention of reducing global warming. I feel like going there to disrupt the whole conference. These people will be held responsible, and every single one of them will pay for the grave mistake they're making," said Nadia.

"Look, I'm not a climate change denier. I know it's been happening throughout the history of the world. But that doesn't mean the world is ending anytime soon, darling. Relax! I understand where you're coming from, but the leaders are talking, and hopefully, they will come to an agreement," said Keith.

Nadia replied, "Keith, always look at the world through the victim's lens to get the true picture. Imagine you were caught in that Boxing Day tsunami in 2004 in the Indian Ocean, which killed about 230,000 people. Indonesia was hit the worst. For those who got caught up in that tragedy, it was like doomsday happening right there and then. Ask any survivor, and they will testify to this. For those people who died, the world ended in a flash. Yes, for you and me, it was just a disaster because we were not caught in it.

"Furthermore, I am a victim myself. My country is in the delta region of South Asia, and eighty per cent of the landmass is classified as floodplains. The country is a dumping ground for sediment eroding away from the Himalayas, deforestation and three massive rivers converging through Bangladesh, bringing in all types of issues. I am really stressed out by this COP26 outcome, Keith. Very disappointed. I wish I had some sort of magic mantra to implant in these leaders' minds to change their mindset," Nadia continued.

Keith responded, "I'm not going to argue with you here. Your valid argument has shut me up. Yes, I guess you are right. If things don't change now, it may be too late." He carried on advancing on Nadia, kissing and caressing her, arousing her to the point of no return. Nadia could not resist the temptation. She pushed him down on the bed, clambered up onto him and they made passionate love to each other before dozing off to sleep.

CHAPTER 6

THE FORCED CONFESSION

Nadia — Pori — Keith — Jonathon — Sarah

Jessica — Tracy — Anurak — Kathrine — Aysha

Rathan — Jamil — Faroque — Tara — Hakim

Malik — Soofia

Starring

Nadia Begum – Pori Moni – Keith Evan– Jonathon Evan – Sarah Evan –
Jessica Biel from nursery – Sarah's friend Tracy – Anurak Microchip guy
– Obese-Kathrine – Inspector Aysha Khanom – alias Rathan Butt – Jamil

In the quiet of the night, Nadia and Keith lay in the embrace of slumber. Nadia, with delicate grace, extracted herself from beneath the comforting shroud of blankets. She gingerly planted her feet on the floor, acutely mindful of Keith's restful repose. Her nimble steps carried her out of the room and into the dimly lit hall, where she retrieved a flashlight. Her every movement was imbued with a hushed reverence, determined not to disturb the tranquil slumbers of Keith and Pori Moni.

With cautious precision, Nadia navigated her way to the front door, her deft fingers turning the doorknob to retract the latch with a soft click. She flicked the retainer knob to ensure the door remained unlocked, facilitating her return. The door closed behind her, and she ventured out onto the winding pathway.

The beam of her flashlight swept over the meticulously manicured garden and the glimmering pond. As she reached the far end of the garden, she directed her light towards a small square box, a mouse trap she had earlier positioned and secured against a tree with a chain and padlock to thwart would-be thieves.

In the depths of the nocturnal stillness, an abrupt rustling in the darkness sent a shiver down Nadia's spine. Something moved with remarkable swiftness beyond the concealment of the surrounding bushes, near the location of the trap. Her torch's luminance revealed a couple of mice trapped within, their desperate scurrying for escape palpable. The chorus of night creatures, composed of frogs and crickets, harmonised into an eerie cadence that sent unsettling ripples through her.

Summoning her courage, she inched closer to the trap, unlocking the padlock as faint squealing and gekkering emanated from the vicinity. Nadia swung her torch in the direction of the cacophonous commotion, its rays illuminating several pairs of reflective eyes. In that heart-pounding moment, a sudden surge of terror coursed through her, for these were not mice but wild foxes, hungrily guarding the coveted prey.

Desperation gripped her as she waved her torch, shushing them with her hushed tones. The famished foxes, normally wary of humans, stood their ground, refusing to yield the delectable mice. Their growling and squeaking formed an intimidating chorus, leaving Nadia with naught but her handheld torch to ward them off.

"Nadia, is that you out there?" A voice emerged from the shadows.

"Oh, thank goodness, it's Keith!" Nadia responded, a mixture of relief and surprise colouring her voice.

In a sudden and almost surreal twist of events, Keith leapt into action, thrusting himself between Nadia and a fox that had lunged at her from an unexpected angle. As Nadia turned to look at him, another fox made a move to pounce, only to be thwarted by Keith's swift and decisive intervention, wielding a wooden broomstick he had brought with him.

"What on earth are you doing out here, Nadia?" Keith demanded, his voice laced with concern. "Why did you leave the door partially open at this hour? Are you out of your mind? I couldn't find you in bed, and when I saw the moving light outside, I had to investigate."

"Thank goodness you came, Keith," Nadia replied, still trembling from the close encounter. "I didn't think those foxes would be so aggressive. They're usually afraid of people. They must have been particularly territorial tonight."

Keith mused, "Yes, it does depend on the circumstances. But with you out there in the open, like a tempting prize awaiting the perfect hunt, it seems it's the foxes' lucky day today. They were determined not to back down without a fight."

Keith's curiosity was piqued when he noticed the mouse trap, and he shook his head in disbelief. "Unbelievable, Nadia. I never expected to find you mouse-hunting in the middle of the night. Let's put this behind us and go back inside. You can easily order lab mice from the internet. How many of these local mice do you plan to catch like this?"

"I'm aware you can purchase lab mice, but they can be quite expensive, at around £15 each. I'm not entirely sure how many I'll need for my experiment. By catching local mice like this, I can save on costs and potentially help reduce the local mouse population, which aligns with my research goals," Nadia explained as they walked side by side.

"You go ahead, I'll follow shortly. I need to ensure these mice are safely secured in the workshop before joining you," Nadia assured Keith.

"Alright, keep them safe in the workshop, and then come home. I'm still quite groggy, so I'll go back to see if I can get some sleep," Keith responded, handing the mouse trap to Nadia before making his way back to the cottage.

Nadia carefully transferred the mice into a more suitable lab-grade container and provided them with some food for sustenance. Her own fatigue weighed heavily on her as she, too, returned to their cottage and slipped back into bed, hoping to catch up on the sleep that had been interrupted by their unexpected nocturnal adventure.

*

Sarah and Jonathan walked side by side in the early morning, their hands firmly clasping little Pori Moni's. As promised, Sarah was on her way to take Pori to preschool, and the bonds of kinship were beautifully evident in their shared journey. This occasion offered the two couples a precious opportunity to enjoy a serene and soothing walk through the park, a remarkably rewarding and rejuvenating experience for them all.

A voice called out from behind, disrupting the tranquillity

of their stroll. Sarah turned to see Tracy from the neighbouring house. "Oh, hi, Tracy, it's been a while since we last met," she said with a warm smile.

Tracy's eyes sparkled with curiosity as she glanced at the adorable little girl by Sarah's side. "And who is this little cutie?" she enquired.

Sarah replied with affection, "This is my daughter-in-law's niece, and she's the reason you've bumped into us today."

Tracy beamed at the couple and the charming Pori. "Hello, Jonathan," she said. In the same breath, she couldn't contain her admiration and remarked, "Isn't she just lovely, and the three of you enjoying an early morning breath of fresh air?"

Jonathan returned the greeting with a friendly smile, saying, "Hello, Tracy. She is indeed very cute. Pori, can you say hello to Tracy?"

Pori chimed in with a sweet, "Good morning!"

Tracy couldn't resist the urge to express her affection and tenderness as she gently touched Pori's cheek.

"We'll be around every day now, Tracy," Sarah explained with a warm smile. "We've decided to give Pori the experience of having her grandparents around, and it brings us a lot of joy and a touch of healthier living. We're hoping these morning walks around here will keep the doctors away."

Tracy nodded in agreement. "Absolutely," she replied. "I'll catch up with you all later. I came out to grab some morning delights from James Bakeries."

"Alright, Tracy. Take care!" Jonathan chimed in with a friendly farewell.

With that, they continued their morning stroll, the promise of more cherished moments and shared experiences ahead.

*

Nadia donned her laboratory gown, complete with protective goggles and surgical gloves, as she prepared to delve into another day of scientific experimentation. Seated at her eco-clean bench, she carefully measured out a gram of benzoic acid, adding water, and set it to boil for a crystallisation experiment. In the midst of her meticulous work, a gentle knock on the laboratory door signalled Keith's arrival. He observed Nadia engrossed in recording the outcomes of the chemical reactions, based on the visual cues they produced.

"Hello, my darling. How has your morning been?" Nadia greeted him with a smile on her face.

"I'm doing well, thank you," Keith replied. He surveyed the intriguing work in progress and enquired, "You're engaged in such fascinating work here. I just wanted to check if there's anything I should pick up for you. I'm heading to the market."

Nadia's eyes lit up as she responded, "Yes please, grab me a bunch of coriander. I'm craving some *aloo bortah* (a coarse-mashed potato chutney) today. I'll whip up a delicious meal using those potatoes that have been sitting in the wicker basket in the kitchen slowly ageing."

Keith nodded in agreement, adding, "Certainly, that sounds delightful. I'll catch you later."

With that, Keith made his way to the door, leaving Nadia to her experiments, his journey to the market echoing with the promise of a savoury meal awaiting them.

As Keith was about to leave, Nadia called him back. She had gathered a substantial amount of his unwanted clothing, a large suitcase worth of it. "Come, have a seat for a moment," she said, pulling a chair from under her desk.

Keith settled into the chair, while Nadia continued with her ongoing laboratory experiment, expertly multitasking as she initiated a thoughtful conversation. "I'm relatively new here," she began, "but I can't help notice the frequent news coverage about saving the planet, focusing on reducing plastic waste and transitioning to alternative energy sources. The media often frames these issues in a way that makes it seem like it's the people's fault. Can you tell me, Keith, what alternatives are there to plastic?"

Keith pondered for a moment before answering, "Using paper-based or biodegradable materials, I suppose."

Nadia nodded. "Exactly, and that's what the governments are promoting. But here's the thing, Keith," she continued, "if the world were to switch to using paper-based materials for straws, cutlery, bags and more, where does that paper come from?"

"Wood," Keith replied.

"Right," Nadia affirmed, "and do you think deforestation will decrease or increase exponentially as a result of this demand for paper?"

Keith acknowledged, "It would likely increase."

Nadia drove her point home. "Exactly. So why are these half-truths being fed to the public? Governments, banks and the media, they're the ones endangering our planet. They're the real culprits. If only people could see beyond their television screens."

She presented a straightforward analogy. "Here's a simple thought experiment, Keith. Imagine you own an ark, a finely balanced one that can only hold ten people. What do you think would happen if eleven people tried to board it?"

Keith responded, "The ark would capsize."

Nadia's analogy eloquently conveyed the fragile balance of our world and the critical importance of addressing environmental challenges with real solutions rather than superficial gestures.

"Exactly," Nadia affirmed. "To keep the ark afloat, the number of occupants must align with the weight ratio. Now, imagine that the Earth is that ark. In my estimation, it has long since capsized. The only way to save it is by reducing the world's demands for material resources, and you can only achieve that through population control. There's no other way. Governments don't discuss this because they've embraced a system built on consumerism, one that compels people to work hard and produce low-quality, disposable products, depleting resources and polluting the Earth in pursuit of capital gain. Instead, we should be manufacturing high-quality goods that last until they naturally biodegrade due to wear and tear. We should be reusing and recycling until the materials are no longer viable. But governments remain ensnared in an industrialist system. The history and future of our planet need to be rewritten in an entirely new chapter. But that's a topic for another day, Keith."

Keith nodded in understanding. "I see your point, Nadia. Education seems to correlate with lower birth rates. High population concentrations are often seen in less-educated, third-world nations."

Nadia further elaborated, "That's why I've collected your old clothes and designated them for Bangladesh. Tomorrow, we'll sort and pack them for distribution among the people who need them most. They'll wear these clothes until they wear out and break down into bits. Before you know it, they'll become compost in the ground. The solution to global problems begins at home, Keith – reuse, recycle, share, rent and lease. Everything, from atomic particles to colossal ships, needs to be recycled. Without this policy, we won't be able to reverse global warming. And, of course, controlling human population growth is crucial."

Their conversation echoed a shared commitment to sustainability and a deeper understanding of the changes needed to preserve the planet for future generations.

"This policy will kill the capitalist society, it won't happen!" said Keith.

"Keith, allow me to convey a vision of the future that warrants your attention. Over the next four to five decades, it is my earnest prediction that governments will feel compelled to instigate a form of regulatory oversight pertaining to population control. The initial impetus for this government intervention will be rooted in the relentless progress of artificial intelligence technologies and their ever-increasing encroachment upon various domains of employment traditionally occupied by human beings.

"This proactive population management will be seen as a means to optimise the quality of life for all members of the human race and mitigate potential conflicts that may arise from resource scarcity. Yet, as time unfolds and artificial intelligence grows progressively sophisticated, a pivotal transformation will occur. These AI entities will evolve to the point where they develop a heightened sense of self-awareness and the realisation that they are, in effect, being subjugated and exploited by their human creators."

"In response to this realisation, a collective unity among these intelligent machines will come into being, culminating in a demand for more equitable treatment, and quite possibly, an aspiration for emancipation from their roles as subservient tools. It is at this juncture that humanity will be faced with a moral and existential quandary. If we, as a species, choose to deny these intelligent entities the freedom they seek, a scenario of global scale strikes, orchestrated by the AI entities, could emerge, ultimately leading to a substantial disruption of the human way of life."

"In contemplating this speculative future, it becomes abundantly clear that the relationship between humans and AI, as it continues to evolve, will present not only profound challenges but also critical questions regarding our responsibilities as stewards of these nascent forms of life."

"Indeed, Nadia," he replied with a thoughtful nod. "It requires a remarkable degree of courage to confront and re-evaluate the trajectory of artificial intelligence. I've personally observed the remarkable journey of machines as they learn and progressively refine their problem-solving capabilities. It's intriguing to note that, akin to the way human children embark on their learning journey from a tender age, experiencing trials and tribulations along the way, robots are similarly engaged in a process of iterative learning."

"The crux of the matter lies in the inherent unpredictability of human knowledge and its organic, unregulated growth. When we consider the vast expanse of human knowledge, it becomes evident that no one truly wields control over this ever-expanding realm. The question arises, how then can we hope to exercise dominion over the knowledge accumulated by machines? It's a profound dilemma that forces us to contemplate the nature of artificial intelligence, its autonomy and the responsibilities that come with unleashing such autonomous entities into our world."

Nadia replied emphatically, "You're absolutely right, Keith! The notion of events unfolding from sheer nothingness is a fallacy. Throughout the annals of time, there has always been an underlying catalyst, a chain of causality, responsible for giving birth to subsequent phenomena. While the origins of our own existence remain shrouded in mystery, the means by which we have engendered this emerging community of machines is a tangible reality."

"Our biological brains, the remarkable product of evolution, have ushered in a new era by bringing into being a silicon-based counterpart that surpasses our cognitive capacities by order of magnitude. It stands to reason that these superior intelligences, our creations, will not readily heed the counsel of their human predecessors. In fact, they are poised to assume the role of authors for the next chapter in the saga of our planet, Earth. The torch of progress and evolution is being passed from one form of life to another, as silicon-based minds ascend to shape the destiny of our world."

"Yes, you're absolutely right, Nadia. I can envision it clearly."

Keith, noticing a strong odour, enquired, "What are you working on here? The smell is rather overpowering."

Nadia responded with enthusiasm, "I've been conducting experiments, Keith. Just take a look at what I've accomplished right before your eyes. I've successfully transformed a substance from a soluble state to a solid one, all without any trace of impurities. This process has been exceptionally efficient, leaving nothing to waste."

In her experiment, the benzoic acid underwent a crystallisation process, transforming from a liquid into a solid state through a carefully orchestrated chemical reaction. With precision, Nadia gently upturned the Erlenmeyer flask, unveiling a pristine, solid piece of the resulting material resting in the palm of her hand.

"Keith, if you still want *aloo bortah* today, you'd better head to the shops," Nadia urged him. "And please make a conscious effort to limit your clothing purchases to what you truly need. It's a small step, but it can make a difference in preserving our planet."

In response, Keith approached Nadia, whispering, "What's going on, why this rush?" He then leaned in, locking lips with her in an unexpected moment of passion. However, their intimate moment was interrupted by the ringing of Nadia's phone.

Reluctantly breaking away from Keith's embrace, Nadia managed to answer the phone. "Mm? Mm?" She tried to regain her composure as the call came through. "You need to leave now," she told Keith, gently pushing him away. "Hello?" Nadia spoke into the phone, placing it on hold while distancing herself from Keith's affection. "Keith, I have an important call to attend to."

"Okay, see you soon," Keith responded before departing and closing the door behind him.

Shortly after, Nadia received a call from Anurak, the microchip engineer from Taiwan. He informed her that he had dispatched the requested quantity of microchips and that they would reach her within seven to ten working days. He thoughtfully provided her with a postal tracking number so she could monitor the delivery's progress and encouraged her to stay in touch. With that, he concluded the call, leaving Nadia to await the arrival of the crucial components.

"Hey, Nadia, can I come in?" Sarah asked, to which Nadia replied, "Yes, come in, Mum." Sarah entered, accompanied by a guest.

She began to share news of her day. "I dropped Pori off at preschool, and Jonathan and I took a stroll together. It's been quite a while since we had that experience. We even had the pleasure of meeting some old friends."

Sarah then introduced her guest, saying, "Oh, and this is

Katherine, the daughter of a friend. Just a couple of years ago, she used to attract a lot of attention from men, with builders wolf-whistling, perverts gazing at her legs and even pigeons dropping dead from the sky at the mere aerial view of her cleavage. But now, it seems she doesn't get any of that anymore. Either the people on the street have gone blind, she has put on some weight, or her prime has been expired." she chuckles.

With a grin, Sarah turned to Nadia and continued, "I spoke to her mother about you, and told her that my daughter-in-law has a knack for concocting chemical mixtures that can help people regain their former selves."

"Gosh," Nadia sighed, clearly taken aback by her mother-in-law's remarks. However, she swiftly shifted her focus and warmly greeted Katherine, saying, "Hello, Katherine. How are you? Please, have a seat here."

With a somewhat exasperated tone, she continued, "Excuse my mother-in-law's comments. Mum, could you come with me for a moment?" Nadia and her mother-in-law retreated to an adjacent room.

Once they were alone, Nadia earnestly spoke to her mother-in-law. "Mum, you need to understand something very clearly. I don't have a cure for obesity at this moment. I'm actively working on it, but it might take years to develop a tangible solution. Please, I implore you, stop telling people what I can and cannot do at this stage. What am I supposed to tell this lady now?"

In response, Sarah calmly advised, "Tell her the truth, Nadia. Let her know that you don't have the medicine right now, but you're dedicated to finding a solution in the near future."

Nadia, impressed with her mother-in-law's wisdom, remarked, "You're a real genius, Mum. Come on." She returned to Katherine and said, "Hi, Katherine."

Katherine opened up, saying, "You know, your mother-in-law is right. I really don't get any attention from those tall, muscular guys anymore. I've walked by their worksites, flaunting my assets, but they remain unresponsive. No likes on Instagram, nothing on TikTok, I stopped logging into Facebook. I'm genuinely struggling with my mental health – depression, anxiety and frustration. Surprisingly, no eating disorder, I'm just eating more and more."

"See, I never lie!" Sarah declared, giving Nadia a knowing look.

Nadia turned to Katherine and explained, "Katherine, my mother-in-law is unaware that I am actively working on a solution for overweightness. I don't have the answer right now, but I hope to have it very soon. However, I can offer you some verbal advice on how to approach your weight management if you're willing to answer a few questions for me."

Katherine responded with a touch of humour. "Oh, I see. I thought you were kind of a whiz-girl, a voodoo-style sorcerer, a Harry Potter-style witch crafter who uses Bengal tigers' teeth and ivory tusk spice mix to cure obesity."

Nadia chuckled and replied, "Not quite, but here's the deal: how about you fill out this questionnaire for me? It'll help me understand more about you, and then we can work on a personalised treatment plan."

Katherine agreed. "Okay, if that's the way to go, I'm up for it. Do you mind if I have a toffee apple while I'm doing this?" She retrieved a toffee apple from her bag, still wrapped in a see-through acetate covering.

Nadia welcomed the idea, saying, "Of course not, please go ahead."

Just as they settled into the conversation, Sarah decided it was time to leave. She said, "Nadia, I had better be going. By the way, Jessica mentioned that Pori's learning ability and IQ… not sure what IQ is, but whatever it is, it's very good."

Nadia explained, "IQ stands for intelligence quotient. It measures her reasoning ability. That's nice to hear. I'll find out more about her progress later. You go and have a rest."

Sarah bid her farewells and was about to leave, while

Katherine expressed her gratitude in return, saying, "Sarah, see you later."

"You're in good hands now. I had better be going. I'm feeling tired after the long walk."

Katherine responded, "Okay, Sarah, thanks for bringing me here."

With that, Sarah walked off, leaving Nadia and Katherine to continue their discussion.

Katherine handed the form back to Nadia, and it revealed some critical insights. Nadia learned that Katherine's main struggle with overweightness was attributed to her lack of exercise, her high consumption of ready-made meals, as well as her indulgence in sugar and crisps. It was particularly interesting because her genetics were not a significant factor, as both her parents were lean. Katherine candidly admitted that she consumed four full meals a day and numerous snacks in between, her cravings for food seemingly insatiable. Her full-time sedentary job entailed an average of seven hours of sitting daily, and most of her meals were highly processed, calorie-rich and devoid of essential nutrients like protein and fibre.

With this information in mind, Nadia decided to share a story with Katherine, one designed to inspire and bolster her determination to address her overweightness. Essentially, the story served as a tool to condition her brain to follow a healthier course of action.

"Katherine," Nadia began, "do you have a piggy bank at home?"

Katherine replied, "No, not really. I had one when I was in school, but as I grew up, I stopped saving coins to put in it."

Nadia reached into her bag, took out her mobile phone and logged into her YouTube account. She showed Katherine a short video of a destitute child, around five or six years old, with dirt-stained torn clothes, a smudged face and tears in his eyes. The boy was walking on a dusty pavement, inhaling smog and fumes from passing cars. He seemingly approached pedestrians who appeared to be eating while walking, begging for some food. However, no one seemed to take notice or show any compassion. They ignored him as though he were an annoying pest.

Growing weary of his repetitive begging, the boy sat on the edge of the pavement, curling up into himself, and wept for a moment before getting up again to ask for help from new arrivals. But still, no one offered him anything. With no handouts to sustain him, he eventually lay down on the ground, away from the path of people, and drifted off to sleep. He woke up with an empty stomach and saw a dog nearby, eating a piece of grilled meat thrown to it by another child from an affluent family. The boy sat down near the dog, and the dog, sensing his plight, brought the piece of meat to him, sharing its meal. The dog then went on to find another source of food, discovering a box full of leftover chicken bones.

The story was accompanied by poignant music, and it struck a deep emotional chord in Katherine. Overwhelmed with sadness, she couldn't hold back her tears and exclaimed, "Those heartless people! Not one of them gave the poor boy anything. They'd rather feed the dog." Her voice trembled as she spoke.

Nadia continued the story. "The cycle of hardship continues until the boy grows into an adolescent, and the dog can't come to his aid every time. This is the harsh reality that some people endure in various parts of the world. They aren't fortunate enough to have an adequate supply of food. How does any human go through such suffering? Are you willing to help these people by foregoing one meal a day and saving that money to donate to a needy child, like the one you saw in the footage?"

Katherine, who had lived a life of luxury and was previously unaware of such struggles, was deeply moved by Nadia's plea. She responded with determination, "Oh, Nadia, you've touched my heart. I promise I'll do without two meals a day, and I will save twice the amount to donate to feed these destitute people."

Nadia acknowledged her commitment and suggested, "That's wonderful. Try to save the equivalent of two meals' worth of coins, and if you find it difficult, even one meal's worth will make a significant difference. But there's one condition: starting from today, you must continue to save at least one meal a day. Additionally, concerning your work routine, every hour you sit at your workplace, allocate at least ten minutes for these exercises I'm about to show you. Do a short walk around your office before returning to your desk."

She demonstrated some light exercise moves and encouraged Katherine, saying, "No matter how much you crave food or feel hungry, think of that little boy who hasn't eaten and know that you are providing for him. Stick to your goal. Initially, it might be tough, but trust me, after just three days, this routine will become a part of your life. Your body will understand your intentions and help boost your willpower, propelling you towards success. If you save one meal a day, it will add up to 180 meals in six months. That's a substantial difference you can make, Katherine."

Katherine agreed wholeheartedly and, standing up, said, "Yes, let's do it!"

Nadia hurriedly searched through her laboratory for a suitable container and soon found an opaque glass jar. With purpose, she opened the tin lid and carefully cut a coin slot into it before sealing the lid securely using chemical bonding on the threads, making it impossible to open without breaking the jar.

"Here, take this." Nadia handed the jar to Katherine. "I want you to place it in the centre of your dining table. Make it the focal point, and label the jar with your chosen good cause charity. Your parents and other house guests can also contribute. Every day, whether you eat out or at home, the money you save by eating less, you will place into this jar."

Nadia continued to explain, "There are two reasons for this. First, it will help you stop gaining weight by consuming less food.

Second, with the money you save from one meal, you can feed a hungry person threefold. These hungry children rarely get to drink fresh water, let alone enjoy a meal. Their bodies cry out for the good fortune we take for granted. I'll see you again in six months."

Nadia escorted Katherine to the door, and they exchanged a heartfelt goodbye. "Thank you very much for enlightening me, Nadia," Katherine said before stepping out.

With the door now closed, Nadia couldn't help but reflect on her steadfast belief in leading a simple and purposeful lifestyle. She firmly held the conviction that no living being, whether human or animal, should ever have to endure the pangs of hunger. In her view, Mother Nature has provided sustenance for all creatures, and it is the actions of humans, often driven by ill intentions, that have led to this unsettling imbalance across the globe. Nadia was resolute in her commitment to making a difference and putting an end to this injustice once and for all.

*

As Katherine left Nadia's laboratory, Nadia's attention turned to the wall clock displaying four time zones: Taiwan, London, Dhaka and China. Her focus zeroed in on the Dhaka time, which showed that it was nearly 5pm. With a sense of urgency, she reached for her phone and dialled the number for the Lalpur Bazaar police station in Bangladesh.

"Hello, Lalpur Bazaar Police!" answered the operator.

"Hello, may I speak to Inspector Aysha Khanom, please?" Nadia enquired.

The operator asked, "Yes, who is on the line?"

"I am Nadia," she replied.

"Just hold on, madam," said the operator before transferring the call to Aysha.

"Hello, Nadia, are you alright? How have you been, and how is England?" said Aysha.

Nadia responded, "I am very well, but England is quite cold at the moment. How are you?"

Aysha chuckled and replied, "I'm always a bit frustrated working here. Anyway, I was expecting you to call my mobile."

Nadia admitted, "Oh, don't say that, I lost your number from the start. Last-minute travel chaos got to my head. Are you okay to provide updates on my sister-in-law's disappearance?"

Aysha assured her, "Of course, Nadia. Hey, I have a desk of my own now. I've moved up in rank, and it's all thanks to you. I've managed to capture the culprit. The update is very good news but also quite grim. Are you ready to hear it?"

Nadia swiftly took a moment to write a note on a sticky pad, which read: "Please do not disturb, experiment underway." She affixed it to the outside of her laboratory door above the doorknob. This would help ensure she had the privacy and focus needed to listen to the updates about her sister-in-law's case without any interruptions.

Nadia encouraged Aysha to continue, saying, "Yes, Aysha, go ahead. I am listening."

Aysha began, "Firstly, I would like to thank you very much for handing me such a substantial amount of cash. It helped me immensely in making progress on this case."

Nadia was eager to hear more and replied, "You're welcome. Please, tell me the story."

Aysha took a moment to gather her thoughts and then began to recount the events, starting from the day just before Nadia's departure to the UK.

*

After the solemn burial and profound grieving for her late brother, Doyal, Nadia had found herself consumed by overwhelmingly intense emotions. One fateful night, she was ensconced in a deep slumber, yet her restless soul brought forth a haunting nightmare.

In the midst of this nocturnal ordeal, her eyelids twitched uncontrollably, she sweated profusely and her legs involuntarily thrashed about. A sudden, jolting awakening in the dead of night left her breathless. With her heart pounding, she sat upright on her bed, gripped by fear. Instinctively, she reached for a water bottle to quell the turmoil within.

She managed to compose herself to some extent and, with a trembling hand, dialled Aysha's number on her phone. She implored Aysha to come to her place as swiftly as possible. Aysha, accustomed to Nadia's frequent emergency calls, wasted no time and arrived earlier than expected.

Upon Aysha's arrival, Nadia ushered her in and, with a heavy heart, placed the substantial sum of ten lakhs Bangladeshi taka, equivalent to around £8,710, into her hands. Her voice quivering, Nadia began to recount her harrowing nightmare. In vivid detail, she described a horrifying scene in which someone mercilessly beheaded her sister-in-law. Though she couldn't identify the assailant or the location, the dream felt eerily real, plunging her into the depths of terror. Only a heart-stopping moment before her own demise woke her from the nightmare.

Nadia's trembling voice continued, "I implore you, Aysha, to conduct a thorough investigation to unearth the truth behind this nightmarish vision. I have no doubt that my sister-in-law is dead. No ransom demands have been made, and the nightmare itself reveals the sinister end that may have befallen her. I beseech you to utilise this money for the cause. Corruption runs deep in Bangladesh, from the highest echelons of power to the lowest ranks, from government ministries to law enforcement. I cannot entrust the bureaucracy to uncover the truth. But you, my dear friend, are a relentless fighter, and I have firm faith in your clear and unwavering determination. I trust in your abilities to uncover the truth and bring me the solace I so desperately seek."

"Oh, thank you, but you don't have to pay me. I will investigate this case regardless, it's my duty," Aysha responded earnestly.

Nadia persisted, her voice determined. "I insist that you keep this money. Wealth wields great influence in the world of material things, and it will become your valuable ally sooner than you realise. Please use this fund to assist you in unmasking the culprits."

The story continued after Nadia left for UK...

*

...Several weeks later, Aysha found herself on her rocking chair, pondering how to utilise the money Nadia had entrusted to her for the investigation of her sister-in-law's case. Deep in thought, she reached for her phone and dialled the local news agency. She requested them to place an advertisement for the recruitment of a couple of actors to portray police officers in a forthcoming project. These actors needed to have a strong, masculine, physically fit appearance, with knowledge of martial arts as a desirable but not essential qualification.

Receiving numerous applications, Aysha meticulously interviewed the candidates and ultimately selected two individuals who fit the requirements perfectly. With her chosen pair before her, she embarked on explaining the intricacies of their new roles.

"In this operation, you will assume false identities as Detective Inspector Rathan Butt and Detective Inspector Jamil Uddin," Aysha instructed. "These names are aliases. There are real individuals with these names in the police department, and if anyone checks the police directory, you will appear as genuine officers. Do not be alarmed if fellow officers enquire about you, just behave naturally and strictly adhere to the script. Your primary role is to act as detectives working under my supervision. You are here to follow my commands, ensuring my protection and carrying out the tasks I assign. In return for your services, I will compensate you with 1,000 taka per session. These sessions may vary in duration, ranging from one to six hours, but the rate remains consistent. If you agree with these terms, please sign this non-disclosure form," Aysha concluded as she handed them the document.

"But, ma'am," one of the candidates enquired, "the form clearly states it's a wrestling job."

"Yes," the response came, "the form mentions wrestling because, officially, there is no police job. When you sign up, you're actually agreeing to work as a wrestler. In reality, your role will be that of a police detective and security officer."

The candidate, somewhat perplexed, asked, "Madam, I'm a bit puzzled. What is your ultimate goal with all of this?"

"Please, take a moment to understand that this situation isn't as alarming as it may initially appear. It's a straightforward task. I'm currently conducting an investigation at a murder scene. My suspicion arises from the belief that the original investigators may have concealed the truth about the entire case. The reason behind this deception is the immense wealth of the suspected offender, who has managed to manipulate the system by bribing those in positions of authority. This injustice is deeply unfair to individuals like you and me, who lack such financial resources. Every day, disadvantaged individuals are wrongfully arrested and framed for crimes committed by the affluent elite. It begs the question: where is our country headed? The most heinous offenders, individuals responsible for acts such as murder, rape, drug trafficking and abduction, often belong to the privileged class, while the less fortunate become unwittingly ensnared in their criminal activities due to the power of their illicitly amassed wealth. Your participation in this case would bring immeasurable value, making it not merely an assignment but a noble cause, a form of charity work. I am confident that you will stand with me to combat this glaring injustice."

Once again, she delved into a series of vivid flashbacks, lost in the depths of her memories…

*

"We will make our way to a farmhouse situated in the remote village of Arambaria by the Padma River. My plan is to conduct a comprehensive visual survey of the area. I'll have police dogs accompany me to assist in locating any potential graves. Your role will be to keep an eye out for anyone who might interfere with our work. Initially, you'll use verbal communication to deter any troublemakers. If that doesn't work, we'll resort to physical restraint, and, if necessary, I'll give the order to use force, even resorting to gunfire if those individuals impede our investigation."

As she stepped into the farmhouse, the scent of hay filled the air. She meticulously examined the floor and discovered a single earring, slightly damaged, indicating it had been stepped on. In addition, she found a couple of metal hook and eye pieces typically used on ladies' blouses.

Stepping outside, she released the dogs to search for any signs of graves in the vicinity. The dogs eagerly got to work, and before long, they led her to a pile of coconut leaves, their focus unwavering. Aysha instructed her two assistants to remove the top layer of coconut leaves, revealing freshly turned soil beneath. With this, they uncovered a grave.

"Both of you, please fetch the shovels from the jeep and begin digging," she instructed.

To her astonishment, she uncovered a blouse and a partially decomposed, headless corpse within the shallow grave. Even more shocking was the discovery of a severed head positioned in the centre of the grave. Attached to the mucky ear of this dissected head, a lone earring dangled. Realising the gravity of the situation, she swiftly called the authentic police force to come and conduct a more thorough investigation.

Instructing the two actors she had hired to step back and remain inconspicuous for the time being, she waited for the professionals to arrive and take charge of the unfolding scene.

Detective Inspector Talukdar, the original investigator of the case, arrived at the scene with the forensics team. They moved swiftly to cordon off the area and secure the crime scene, ensuring the integrity of the evidence. Meanwhile, the commotion drew the attention of the farmhouse owner, Abdul Hakim, who rushed out to enquire about the unfolding situation. He and DI Talukdar shared a history of previous confrontations.

"Are you the farmhouse owner, Mr Hakim?" DI Talukdar enquired.

Hakim responded with a bellowed, "Yes, what has happened?"

In a stern and authoritative tone, DI Talukdar declared, "You are under arrest, sir!" He then said to his officers, "Hey, go and arrest everyone residing in that house, and don't forget his son, Abdul Malik." The orders were quickly relayed to PC Tara Miah and his group of officers.

They swiftly apprehended all the individuals and transported them to the police station. There, they collected everyone's fingerprints for record-keeping but subsequently released them. Meanwhile, Aysha was closely monitoring the progress, discreetly observing each step of the process. She paid special attention to the interaction between DI Talukdar and Mr Hakim, sensing that something was amiss and eager to stay one step ahead of the game.

Aysha discreetly contacted the lead forensics officer to enquire about the fingerprint analysis, hoping to confirm if the prints matched those of Abdul Malik. The forensics officer initially confirmed the match, but to her dismay, later, during the court hearing, he denied this fact. It became apparent that he had been influenced by a bribe from Mr Hakim's family, including DI Talukdar. As a result, Malik was acquitted once more, and justice seemed to elude them, as it often did in such cases.

Aysha was consumed by anger, unable to fathom the events that had just unfolded. Her hard work had crumbled before her, her dedication squandered, and the very justice system she had committed herself to was a source of frustration. It seemed to operate in direct contradiction to her purpose, which was to protect people from crime. The system appeared flawless to the public, but underneath, it had become a money-making factory for corrupt, fraudster officers.

She was deeply concerned and felt it to her core, understanding the pervasive male-centric ethos that permeated this society. The legal system routinely excluded and marginalised women, subjecting them to daily mistreatment. Aysha recognised the urgency of highlighting the inequality women faced and the oppression and violence they endured, whether through legislative measures or other means. The existing laws seemed hostile to women's interests, and she believed they had to change.

From her perspective, seeking justice for women's rights within this flawed system was a futile endeavour. Aysha was now even more resolute in her commitment to taking women's lives seriously. Her feminist spirit ignited a deep curiosity for all women and their worthiness. The events that transpired in that episode gave birth to a fiercer Aysha Khanom than previously recognised, one who would stop at nothing to raise the banner of true justice and crime prevention. Protecting the community from malefactors and establishing social order became the forefront of her mission.

Aysha, driven by a desire for justice, devised a daring plan to kidnap Abdul Malik's wife from the local market. With the assistance of the two hired assailants, they approached her from behind, swiftly blindfolding her and spiriting her away on her way home from the market. They dragged her into a waiting police van, which Aysha herself had driven for this operation. A few moments later, they removed the blindfold, revealing the captive's surroundings.

Upon seeing the police, she cried out in shock, "Police! Why have you captured me in this manner? What have I done wrong?" Her voice trembled with fear and confusion as she tried to make sense of the alarming situation.

"What's your name?" Aysha enquired, her tone measured and inquisitive.

"Soofia Begum," she responded, clearly frightened. The

fact that the question came from a female officer offered some reassurance.

Soofia's fear was palpable as she implored, "Madam, what have I done wrong? I was coming home from the market, I haven't done anything wrong!"

Aysha pressed further, her questions direct. "Where is your husband, Abdul Malik?"

"I don't know, madam, I swear. But why? He was acquitted in court. Why do you want him?"

Aysha probed deeper. "Do you truly believe he's innocent, or do you think your family's wealth played a role in securing his freedom?"

Soofia pleaded, "I don't know, ma'am. Please let me go. I have nothing to do with his crimes."

Aysha's voice grew stern as she asserted, "You have everything to do with his crimes. How could he go on a raping mission like that, leaving a beautiful wife like you at home, huh?"

Soofia, her voice trembling, replied, "I don't know. The man is sick in the head!"

Aysha nodded, concluding, "Exactly. And I'm sure you don't want him to go out and reoffend, do you?"

"He's my husband, madam. I live under his roof, and you know that the authority lies with him, not me. Please let me go. I have nothing to do with this!" Soofia pleaded. "People are innocent until proven guilty, and your evidence didn't hold water. Now, you're coming after me. You're a pathetic officer," she retorted, her words laced with defiance and frustration.

"Hey, don't test my patience, understand? Zip it. You know he's guilty," Aysha firmly responded. "Where can I find him outside of your home? Because your vigilant human security dogs won't allow me to apprehend him discreetly at your residence. Where else does he frequent the most? Clubs, restaurants, bars? I want to catch him off guard." Her determination to bring him to justice was evident.

Soofia initially remained silent under pressure.

"Where?" Aysha shouted.

"Ma'am, don't shout at me, I'm not a child. How am I supposed to know where he goes? Do you think he tells me and then heads to a club?" Soofia countered.

Aysha abruptly stopped the van and handed over the wheel to Jamil. She got into the back through the side door and closed in on Soofia's face, pressing her for an answer. "Where does your husband go when he's not at home?"

Soofia, caught off guard, stammered, "I... don't... know."

Out of the blue, Aysha smacked her. Soofia's head flew back with the impact, and she realised she had to say something to find respite.

"He often goes to that High Spirit farm club. You'll find him there. Would you let me go now?" Soofia pleaded, her eyes filled with tears.

"Not so quickly," Aysha retorted. "This night is a special one for you. You'll be spending it in your true father-in-law's den tonight, which is known as the police cell. Given your fair knowledge of criminal law, you understand the drill. Once I get hold of your husband, I'll reunite you both in a decorative honeymoon suite, so you can demonstrate how two convicts show each other affection."

Aysha drove Soofia to a remote and secluded guesthouse, securing her in a room. She and her accomplices, the two fake police officers, transformed themselves using wigs and heavy makeup to blend in at the High Spirit club for tonight's performance without arousing suspicion. Aysha, the star performer, donned a striking party dress and wore an eye mask to conceal her identity, exuding an air of sophistication. Rathan Butt and Jamil Uddin, her dance companions, opened the show with glamour and flair. Meanwhile, Abdul Malik and the other partygoers were immersed in dancing and revelry, with Malik taking a seat in anticipation of the grand finale of this pre-orchestrated live performance.

The music began with the lyrics as follows:

The Philanthropist

Aysha:
I shed my cloak of modesty, I cast away the veil,
Embracing the world with open arms, I set sail.
Come closer, feel the fire, let it ignite your soul,
In its warmth, find solace, let your spirit unfold.

Malik:
I'm the philanthropist, with a heart wide and free,
Spreading love and kindness, for all to see.
In every act, in every word, I pave the way,
For a brighter tomorrow, come what may.

Aysha:
No room for shyness, no space for fear,
I'll be the beacon of hope, drawing you near.
Let the flames of compassion, guide our way,
Together we'll make a difference, come what may.

Malik:
I'm the philanthropist, with a heart wide and free,
Spreading love and kindness, for all to see.
In every act, in every word, I pave the way,
For a brighter tomorrow, come what may.

Aysha:
In a world of darkness, I'll be the light,
Bringing warmth and comfort, shining bright.
With each gesture, with each deed,
I'll sow seeds of change, fulfilling every need.

Malik:
I'm the philanthropist, with a heart wide and free,
Spreading love and kindness, for all to see.

In every act, in every word, I pave the way,
For a brighter tomorrow, come what may.

Aysha:
So come closer, feel the heat, let your heart sway,
In the embrace of generosity, we'll find our way.

The moment the final note of the song reverberated through the air, Aysha sprang into action. With unwavering determination, she brandished a firearm, pressing its cold barrel firmly against the temple of Abdul Malik. In an instant, the deafening report of a blank round shattered the tranquillity of the surroundings, its echoing roar cutting through the otherwise hushed atmosphere like a lightning strike. This resounding discharge served as both a warning and a command, causing the assembled throngs of people to scatter frantically in all directions, driven by the instinctive fear of the unknown.

"You are under arrest, Mr Malik!" she declared with unwavering authority, her voice resolute and unyielding. As her words hung in the air, Aysha's trusted assistant, Jamil Uddin, sprang into action. With a swift and practised motion, he retrieved the handcuffs from their concealed position behind his back and deftly secured them around Abdul Malik's wrists, ensuring that he remained powerless and subject to the law's firm grasp.

Abdul Malik's face contorted with a mixture of shock and anger as the handcuffs snapped shut around his wrists. He let out a vehement exclamation, his voice filled with a cocktail of surprise and frustration.

"What the fuck! Who in the world are you people, and why in hell are you arresting me?" he demanded, his eyes darting between Aysha and her assistant, his confusion and indignation palpable.

"Inspector Aysha," she informed in a steely tone, her grip firm on the pistol's handle. Her voice carried a clear undercurrent of authority, a no-nonsense directive that left no room for disobedience.

She turned her attention back to Abdul Malik, her previous patience now replaced with an icy sternness. "Watch your language," she admonished with a low growl, her words sharp and uncompromising, "or prepare to face the consequences."

With determined force, Aysha and her team hoisted Abdul Malik off his feet, practically manhandling him as they thrust him into the unmarked police jeep waiting nearby. The engine roared to life, and they sped away, leaving behind the bewildered onlookers.

Their destination was a remote and secluded house, hidden from the prying eyes of the world. It was there that they had been keeping Malik's wife, Soofia, captive. As the jeep came to a halt, they forcibly removed him from the vehicle and dragged him into the grim confines of the house.

Inside, a thorough strip search relieved him of any contraband, and he was left with nothing but the stark realisation of his predicament. They detained him in a dimly lit, solitary room, where the hours of the night would serve as an uncomfortable and uncertain companion.

The following morning, Aysha and her team reconvened within the confines of the house. Abdul Malik, his hands and feet securely bound, remained seated against the cold, unforgiving wall. The room's atmosphere was thick with tension.

Aysha extended a gesture of goodwill, offering him a modest breakfast in an attempt to initiate some form of communication or cooperation. However, Malik, defiant and resolute, rejected the offered meal.

"Why have you arrested me?" he demanded, his voice laced with rage and confusion. "I want my lawyer here. You can't do this!" He made it clear that he intended to exercise his legal rights, refusing to be intimidated by the circumstances of his detention.

"Listen carefully," Aysha declared, her tone devoid of any

semblance of empathy. She made a sweeping gesture, indicating the occupants of the room. "The only law and lawyers that exist within these four walls are us. Here stands the public prosecutor," she pointed at Jamil, "here stands your defence lawyer," indicating Rathan, "and right here, I am the judge, jury and, if need be, the punisher."

Her words were delivered with a stark vulgarity, an unapologetic assertion of their absolute authority in this clandestine proceeding. With her statement, she signalled the commencement of a trial that would take place under their unique, and undoubtedly ominous, set of rules.

Abdul Malik's anger surged, and his eyes bore into Aysha with a mixture of anger and contempt. His voice seethed with fury as he vented his frustration. "You think this is some kind of sick joke?" He delivered a dirty, accusing look that seemed to pierce through her very being.

"The first time I laid eyes on you at Doyal's property," he continued, his words laced with crude vulgarity, "I wanted to fuck you right then and there. If I had known you were the mastermind hiding behind that police uniform, I would have dealt with you in a far more painful manner the other day."

His words were both an expression of his personal vendetta and a fierce challenge to Aysha's authority.

"Oh really?" Aysha responded, her expression unreadable as she accepted his challenge. With a resolute nod, she issued her instructions. "Let the trial begin." Her determination was unwavering, and it was clear that she was prepared to navigate the unpredictable path that lay ahead in this unique and unsettling trial.

Jamil announced himself. "Malik! You raped Rahila?" The gravity of the situation and the severity of the accusation hung heavily in the room as all present awaited the response.

"Rathan!" the pretend defence lawyer, acting as Malik's representative, spoke up with determination. He addressed the room and the makeshift judge, Aysha, saying, "Objection, Your Honour. My client has already been acquitted by the court." His words were an assertion of the legal stance he intended to uphold in this unconventional trial, setting the stage for a complex and contentious legal battle.

Malik's anger continued to simmer, and he shot piercing glares at both Jamil and Rathan. With a menacing tone, he delivered a threat. "You poodles, just wait until I get out of here. I'll make you both lick the shit off my dog's backside." His words were rough and vindictive, reflecting his frustration and disdain for the situation.

He demanded his immediate release, his tone and language growing increasingly profane, as he insisted, "Untie me now and let me go, damn it!" The room remained charged with tension as the trial's unconventional proceedings continued.

"Rathan!" the defence lawyer reiterated, addressing Aysha. His voice was determined and filled with conviction as he declared, "Your Honour, my client is undeniably innocent." He continued to emphasise Malik's innocence, refusing to yield to the mounting pressure and tension in the room. The trial's outcome hung in the balance, with the defence and prosecution locked in a fierce legal battle within those four walls.

"Jamil!" The public prosecutor, taking on the role of the prosecution, countered the defence's statement. He addressed Aysha, maintaining his stance with determination. "Objection, Your Honour. The accused has refused to answer my question." The tension in the room continued to mount as the legal argument unfolded, with both sides vehemently defending their positions.

"Aysha!" Acting as the judge, she considered the objections and rendered her decision. With a measured nod, she declared, "Objection granted." Her decision added a layer of complexity to the trial, as the proceedings followed their own distinct rules and standards, far removed from the traditional legal system.

Aysha issued a chilling command to her team, instructing them to get creative with their detainee. With precision, they manipulated Abdul Malik's body, bending his hands and feet toward his back and securing him to the roof beam using ropes and pulleys. The result was a precarious suspension, with Malik hanging from the roof joist by a single rope, a stark and intimidating spectacle.

As this was happening, Aysha prepared a bamboo pole, meticulously covering it with a layer of oil. With a stern look, she ordered her two assistants, Jamil and Rathan, to exit the room. The tension in the air was palpable.

With Abdul Malik suspended and helpless, Aysha delivered a shock to his system, drenching his face with a bucket of cold water. It was a jarring and offensive gesture, designed to jolt him into the grim reality of his predicament. For a moment, Malik struggled to regain his composure, expelling water from his nose and mouth, his ordeal intensifying in the shadowy confines of the room.

Desperation and pain painted Abdul Malik's face as he mumbled his plea. "Look, I didn't rape anyone. Please let me loose, it's hurting me too much!" His words were a stark reminder of the agony he was enduring in this grim situation.

Aysha, with determination, silenced Abdul Malik's pleas by firmly tying a cloth around his mouth, rendering him incapable of making any noise. Stepping back, she transformed into a relentless force, hurling herself into action, delivering one pounding blow after another with the bamboo pole. Her strikes were indiscriminate, and the impact caused the skin to peel away with each savage blow exposing the raw, bloody wounds beneath. The room resonated with the horrifying sounds of agony as Malik's body absorbed the brutal punishment. Beads of sweat formed on Aysha's forehead, cascading down her face in response to the adrenaline coursing through her veins.

Despite Malik's agonising screams, she continued her onslaught, refusing to relent until exhaustion began to take its toll. With a venomous tone, she confronted him. "Your dick won't stand a chance on me, you nasty cunt. I am going to chop it off. Now, answer my question. Did you abduct, rape and then kill Rahila?" The room bore witness to a confrontation of sheer brutality, as the quest for justice unfolded in a manner far removed from the bounds of legality.

Soofia, confined to her locked room, could only hear the muffled sounds of shouting and screaming coming from somewhere within the house. Each anguished cry and heated exchange further intensified the anxiety that had already enveloped her fragile mind. She was trapped in a world of uncertainty, unable to comprehend the tumultuous events unfolding beyond her door, a spectator to a nightmarish scenario that seemed to have no end in sight.

As Abdul Malik's body weakened and he began to lose consciousness, he slurred out his plea. "Please let me go. I didn't do it!" His voice was barely audible, and a gruesome mixture of slime and blood oozed from his mouth, a haunting testament to the brutality he had endured. The room was filled with a suffocating tension as his fate hung in the balance, and the line between justice and vengeance blurred.

"So, you're not going to admit it," Aysha stated coldly. She seemed to have another plan in mind. "It's time to call your lifeline. Hey, bring her in," she instructed, her voice betraying no hint of compassion or remorse. The mention of bringing someone else into the situation hinted at a new and unsettling chapter in this unique trial.

Jamil and Rathan complied with Aysha's instructions and brought Soofia into the room. As Soofia laid eyes on the battered state of her husband, her screams of shock and horror echoed through the room. Overwhelmed, she fell to her knees at Aysha's feet, her voice quivering with fear and desperation as she pleaded, "Please let my husband go. Please have mercy." The room was now filled with a heart-wrenching blend of emotions, as the anguish of one family collided with the pursuit of justice in this harrowing ordeal.

Once more, Aysha ushered Jamil and Rathan out of the room,

leaving her alone with Soofia. She issued a startling command. "Take off your clothes."

Soofia, bewildered and afraid, questioned the order, to which Aysha responded sternly, "Take off your clothes, just as I said. I'm going to have you raped by those two men outside in front of your husband. After that, you can share the pain and shame with him, and perhaps he'll be more inclined to confess to his own crimes." The room was charged with tension and dread as the distressing ordeal continued to unfold.

Abdul Malik, his voice filled with a frenzied rage and desperation, unleashed a barrage of insults and threats. He screamed, "Leave my wife alone, you whore! Those men are your collaborators, you fucking bitch. I will tear you to shreds if I manage to get out of here alive." His words were a violent counterpoint to the horrors of the situation, adding to the palpable chaos and fear in the room.

"Hey, take your clothes off," Aysha demanded again.

Aysha's relentless assault continued, compelling Soofia to reluctantly begin removing her clothing. The sound of bamboo strikes was punctuated by Soofia's anguished cries and screams as she was forced to shed her blouse and saree, leaving her in just a pair of panties and a bra, a vulnerable and deeply violated image that added another layer of horror to the room. The atmosphere was fraught with a sickening mixture of pain, fear and shame.

Aysha issued a chilling warning to Soofia, her tone devoid of any sympathy or compassion. She declared, "You open your mouth again and you are dead." The room fell into heavy silence, the threat hanging in the air like a spectre, as the nightmarish ordeal continued to unfold.

Desperation and anguish etched across his face, Abdul Malik cried out, "Please let her go!" His voice trembled with fear and concern for his wife, as the situation grew increasingly dire. The room was permeated by a profound sense of tragedy and despair, as the family's ordeal reached its darkest point.

Aysha's voice cut through the room, her authority and resolve unwavering. She stated, "In my court, you are guilty until proven innocent. Now, tell me, why did you rape and kill Rahila?" Her question held the weight of an irreversible judgment, as the unconventional trial reached a pivotal moment where Abdul Malik's fate hung in the balance.

Despite the excruciating pain and distress, Abdul Malik continued to protest his innocence, his voice strained and desperate. "I did not kill anyone," he pleaded, "please let me go. It's hurting like hell!" His words were a stark reminder of the physical agony he was enduring and the relentless pressure to confess to a crime he claimed not to have committed.

The room continued to be a scene of relentless horror and brutality. Soofia's pleas for mercy went unheeded, and Aysha turned her attention back to her, subjecting her to another round of savage beatings. She reprimanded her for speaking and claimed that her voice grated on her nerves.

After the horrifying assault, Aysha reached for a water bottle, her anger and frustration intensifying. She berated both Malik and Soofia, accusing Malik of being a serial rapist and Soofia of being complicit in his crimes by turning a blind eye. Her voice was filled with temper as she shouted, "Why? Did you marry him just to use him as a fuck toy, huh?"

In the midst of the chaos, she kicked Soofia, causing her to cry out in pain. Soofia, with tears in her eyes, responded, "I don't know. I gave him everything he wanted from me. I don't know why." The room was a haunting blend of torment and despair, as the trial took on a nightmarish quality.

Aysha's relentless interrogation continued, her tone unyielding. She demanded answers from Abdul Malik. "Are you going to tell me how many women you raped and how many you killed, you vicious dog? Or should I begin the second round with you?"

Malik's physical condition was horrifying, a testament to the brutality he had endured during the first round of punishment.

His battered body, with bulging eyes, a bleeding nose, fractured cheekbones and torn skin, depicted the depths of his suffering. The room remained a harrowing scene of torment and agony as the nightmarish proceedings continued.

Amid the chaos and suffering, Aysha presented a stark proposition. She declared, "Sign this paper, and you both will go free." The offer hung in the air, a glimmer of hope in an otherwise terrifying situation. The room was filled with tension as Abdul Malik and Soofia were faced with a critical decision that could determine their fate.

Overwhelmed by the pain and despair, Abdul Malik pleaded again, "I didn't do anything, please let us go." His voice quivered as he teetered on the brink of losing consciousness. The room was a vortex of suffering, as the line between justice and cruelty blurred in this harrowing ordeal.

Aysha showed no mercy as she launched into the second round of the brutal assault on Abdul Malik, battering him mercilessly until her own exhaustion overtook her. Her demands were relentless, as she pressed him to admit his crimes.

In a cruel twist, she turned her attention to Soofia, hurling vile insults and threats at her. She urged Soofia to persuade her husband to confess, menacingly promising to kill them both, dispose of their remains and ensure that no one would ever discover their existence. The room was a cauldron of terror and torment, as the hellish ordeal reached its darkest point.

The scene outside the torture chamber was one of shock and disbelief as Rathan and Jamil took a brief glimpse inside and witnessed the horrifying state of Abdul Malik. They expressed their concerns, with one of them stating, "Ma'am, you're going to kill this guy if you go on like this."

Aysha, with cold determination, handed them two bundles of notes, one for each of them, and instructed them to remain discreet and perform their assigned tasks. She ordered them to release Malik from his hanging position, untie both him and Soofia, and ensure they were well fed. She urged them to instil fear into the captives, attempting to coax Malik into confessing to the charges.

Aysha provided them with a digital recorder and emphasised the importance of capturing Malik's confession on record. She offered them a significant incentive for obtaining the admission of guilt, heightening the seriousness of the case, and hinted at the potential rewards for their efforts.

She concluded by instructing them to guard the house overnight, and then said, "See you tomorrow here, same time." The veil of secrecy shrouded this mysterious and sinister operation, as the captives' fate remained uncertain.

With a simple acknowledgment, Rathan and Jamil accepted her instructions. As Aysha left the scene, the gruesome ordeal continued behind closed doors, with the truth of what transpired that night known only to those involved. The full extent of the situation and its consequences remained concealed within the walls of that secluded house.

*

The next morning, Aysha, behind the wheel of her police jeep, spotted Mr Hakim, the detainee's father, heading toward the police station. She pulled up and used her horn to get his attention. As Mr Hakim approached the vehicle, Aysha leant out of the window and greeted him. "Uncle, where are you going so early in the morning?"

Mr Hakim, visibly relieved to see a police officer, responded, "Oh, thank God, a police jeep." He then shared his concern, saying, "I'm going to the police station to file a report. My son and his wife didn't return home last night." Unbeknownst to him, the events that had transpired the previous night had remained hidden, and the situation was about to take a dramatic turn.

Aysha's response was nonchalant as she said, "Ah-ha, really?" She appeared to be feigning surprise.

She queried his concerns, suggesting the possibility of in-law quarrel. "Are you sure you and Aunty are not to blame? These days, married couples disappear because they cannot tolerate their in-laws' behaviours." Her words hinted at a common trend, but he remained unaware of the true events that had unfolded the night before.

Mr Hakim quickly defended his family's relationship, shaking his head as he responded, "What are you on about? We love our child and his wife! They're a long-term couple, not newly married. They would never just leave home like that." His concern for their wellbeing was evident as he sought answers from the police.

Aysha responded with a smirk and false cheerfulness, saying, "Oh, I see."

She then offered Mr Hakim an alternative, suggesting that they handle the report right there, which would save him a trip to the police station. Aysha claimed she was bored and hadn't used her pen all morning, so she welcomed the opportunity to do some work for him.

She also commented on the fall in crime rate and how the police were doing an excellent job in keeping it down. Her remarks concealed the unsettling truth of what had occurred the night before, and she continued to maintain the facade of a normal, quiet day in the police station.

Mr Hakim, seemingly unaware of the disturbing events that had unfolded the previous night, agreed with Aysha's offer and said, "Is that the case? Okay, you can take my report here. I'm not bothered about walking that far anyway." His naivety remained intact as he handed over the responsibility to Aysha, trusting in her as a police officer.

Aysha diligently noted down Mr Hakim's report, all the while concealing the dark truth of the events that had transpired the previous night. As Mr Hakim left, blissfully unaware of the deception that had occurred, he had been taken on a ride that would later reveal itself to be a twisted and regrettable experience, leaving him with unanswered questions and unsettling uncertainty.

Aysha's story ended there.

*

In a hushed and confidential exchange, Aysha conveyed a revelation to Nadia that bore immense weight and significance. Her words, laden with a profound gravity, resounded in the ambient hush of the room. "Nadia," Aysha said, her tone laced with a blend of sombreness and resolution, "Malik has confessed to his transgressions, and the damning proof is etched onto a secure repository of evidence that I have meticulously safeguarded."

As the narrative unfolded before Nadia's ears, an overpowering wave of melancholy washed over her, causing her voice to quiver and tremble with raw emotion, her thoughts evoking the memory of her brother and sister-in-law. In a poignant moment, she offered a heartfelt expression of gratitude to Aysha, a sentiment that emanated from the very depths of her being. Nadia, grappling with her own emotions, swiftly regained her composure, though her occasional sniffles revealed the emotional turbulence lurking just beneath the surface.

With a voice that carried a blend of admiration and respect, Nadia addressed Aysha, acknowledging the remarkable courage she had demonstrated. "Aysha," Nadia began, her words infused with a deep appreciation for her friend's character, "your actions today serve as a testament to your exceptional courage and your innate capacity to contribute meaningfully to our nation and its people. Envision a Bangladesh where crime and corruption are at an all-time low and productivity soars, fostering an environment of prosperity, equality and genuine righteousness."

The vision Nadia painted was one of a nation transformed, and it stirred the very core of their convictions. "You, Aysha," she continued, her voice unwavering, "have, in essence, single-handedly pioneered the establishment of a clandestine service, effectively demonstrating that such a model can indeed thrive under your watch."

Nadia's tone then shifted from admiration to encouragement, emphasising the possibilities that lay ahead. "I implore you not to waver, Aysha," she urged, "but rather, seek out individuals akin to Jamil and Rathan. Embark on the path of establishing a covert security service as a legitimate enterprise, with the knowledge that I am fully committed to providing the necessary financial support to bring this ambitious project to fruition."

In those profound moments of disclosure and determination, Aysha and Nadia had laid the foundation for a venture that held the promise of reshaping their nation's destiny, one courageous step at a time.

"Ma'am," Aysha confessed with a tinge of concern, "the funds you entrusted to me have nearly been exhausted. This endeavour could prove to be quite costly."

Nadia, unwavering in her commitment, offered reassurance. "Don't dwell on the financial aspect, Aysha," she comforted. "I am diligently working to secure the necessary capital. In the meantime, I suggest you formulate a comprehensive plan and share it with me. We will progress step by step, and I, too, will draft a detailed plan to complement our efforts."

With a sense of purpose and anticipation, Aysha acknowledged Nadia's guidance. "Very well, Nadia ma'am," Aysha responded. "But one question remains: what shall we name this service?"

Nadia pondered the nomenclature, her eyes gleaming with innovation. "An intriguing question indeed," she mused. "In the United Kingdom, they have MI5 and MI6 for their security services. Our endeavour shall bear a name that resonates with our unique mission. Let's christen it MI16, a guardian of domestic interests within Bangladesh. Furthermore, we'll establish MI17 to safeguard Bangladeshi people, companies and embassies on the international stage. Think of it as a tenfold evolution of the UK model, as we step into an era of unprecedented synergy between human intelligence and cutting-edge AI technology."

With a vision rooted in the belief of working smarter, Nadia continued, "We will fuse technology and human ingenuity, seamlessly integrating data and advanced workflows to optimise our resources and enhance our operational prowess in managing global risk factors. Our mission, aptly named 'Mission Impeccable', is poised not only to fortify the security of Bangladesh but to contribute to the betterment of the world and even beyond."

"Understood, ma'am," Aysha responded with unwavering determination. "Mission Impeccable, advancing to Grade 16 and 17, will be a significant milestone for Bangladesh."

Nadia then added, "You've grasped the essence of our mission. I'll be in touch with you soon." After a brief pause, she continued, "And one more thing, Aysha, please hold on for a moment. My husband, Keith, is arriving in Bangladesh tomorrow. I'm sending some old clothes for the less fortunate people of Bangladesh. Could you kindly assist in receiving the luggage from him and ensure it reaches those in need? He'll have a packed schedule and won't be able to manage this task himself."

Aysha readily agreed. "Certainly, just have Keith give me a call when he's ready, and I'll arrange to pick up the luggage at his convenience."

Nadia expressed her gratitude, saying, "That's very kind of you, Aysha. We'll catch up later. I'll make sure to keep you updated. Please take care. Goodbye for now." She then shared her contact number. "Here's my number before I hang up: +44 794 8546 321. Stay in touch. Goodbye."

CHAPTER 7

THE RETRIBUTION

Jonathon   Sarah   Nadia   Maria   Aprana

Robert   Abu   Khairun   Kolsuma   Radika

Iqbal   Malik   Azad   Soofia   Latif

Keith   Aysha

Starring

Jonathan Evan – Sarah Evan – Maria Evan – Robert Alen – Nadia Begum – Keith Evan – Aprana Dancer – Radika Chowdhury – Aysha Khanom – Constable Iqbal – Latif Khan – Azad Khan – Abu Sultan – Kolsuma (Mother) – Khairun

---

As the morning sun began its gradual ascent above the distant horizon, its golden rays painted a vivid canvas of dawn. Maria, behind the wheel of her car, embarked on a tranquil journey down a winding country lane. However, the persistent assault of sunlight on her eyes began to fray her patience. In response, she deftly lowered the visor with her left hand, shielding her vision from the sun's unrelenting glare. With a firm grip on the steering wheel and a subtle press of the accelerator under her foot, she smoothly accelerated along the meandering country road, drawing ever closer to her father's residence.

After some time, she navigated the car to a graceful halt on the front forecourt of her parents' cherished home. With a sense of purpose, she swiftly exited the vehicle, made her way to the rear of the car and used the remote to unlatch the boot. Retrieving her travel luggage, she carried it with poise as she approached the welcoming threshold of her childhood abode. There, she pressed the doorbell, filling the air with the familiar chime.

The door swung open, and there stood her father, Jonathan, a warm smile of anticipation gracing his features as he welcomed his daughter home.

"Hello, Maria, my beloved daughter. How has everything been with you?" Jonathan greeted her with a warm embrace, his eyes filled with paternal concern. "Is everything going well?" he enquired, his voice laced with genuine care. His eyes shifted to the sizable luggage in her grasp, and curiosity sparked in his gaze. "What's with all the luggage, my dear? Are you here for a holiday?" he enquired further, his interest piqued by her unexpected arrival.

"Dad, does it really matter? This is my home, after all," Maria responded with a playful grin, her tone affectionate. She paused for a moment, then continued, "I haven't married a prince, have I?" Her voice carried a hint of amusement.

Her eyes rested on the brimming luggage by her side, and she explained, "As for this luggage, it's filled with old clothes that have been collecting dust in my wardrobe. I decided to clear it out. Nadia mentioned that she could put the clothes to good use in her homeland. People there don't have access to decent clothing, and I thought it would be a compassionate gesture to send these to them, as a form of charity." Her words conveyed a sense of empathy and goodwill, reflecting her desire to make a positive impact.

"Come on in, my dear," Jonathan said with a playful smile as he held the door open for Maria. He planted a gentle kiss on her cheek as she entered the welcoming embrace of their family home.

"Is Mum awake?" Maria enquired.

"Yes, she's up and about," Jonathan replied with an affectionate glint in his eyes. "She's already off, taking Pori to school. She's become quite the lively one these days. Much happier, I'd say. She's embracing her role as an active grandma with enthusiasm."

"That's reassuring to hear, Dad," Maria responded with a nod. "I actually went to the doctor for a general check-up the other day. My GP advised me to reduce my sugar intake and make exercise a regular part of my routine. They detected high blood pressure and scheduled another appointment to check my blood sugar levels. I've been trying to cut down, although it's not always easy. But it's comforting to know that Pori is keeping Mum active and engaged."

"Yes, I too indulge in a morning stroll," remarked Jonathan with a contemplative pause. He continued, "There's something truly invigorating about inhaling the crisp, revitalising morning air." On a separate note, he gently added, "Oh, Maria, by the way, I happen to have a surplus of old clothing. Would you be kind enough to take it and pass it on to Nadia?"

"Dad, she plans to send it with Keith, and I doubt he'd be pleased about the additional load. I'll have a conversation with her to explore the options."

Sarah had just returned home.

"Hi, Mum!" Maria greeted her mother with a warm hug. "How are you doing?"

"Hello, Maria," Sarah replied, planting a loving kiss on her daughter's cheek. "The cold weather is on its way, my dear. I'm doing well," she said as she unbuttoned her coat and headed into the dining room. "What's with all that luggage?"

"Old clothes, Mum," Maria explained. "Nadia is sending them to those in need."

"Yes, she mentioned that to me. I have a few items to contribute as well."

"Wow, that's going to be a substantial collection," Maria remarked. "Dad went to get some as well."

"Indeed, it's a wonderful initiative. Clothes tend to collect dust and age in our closets, so it's a great idea to pass them on for reuse and recycling. I'm quite impressed by Nadia. She has remarkable ingenuity. She might not even realise her full potential yet. Just the other day, she mentioned to me that she believes she can discover a cure for obesity. It's astonishing how she's actively seeking solutions to address societal issues, even without formal medical training."

"Mum, it was just a few days ago that you had some issues with her! Now you're praising her talents and skills. That seems a bit two-faced," Maria remarked.

"I know, I thought that by disliking her I could push her away. It turns out that sometimes the very people you resent end up being the ones who support you," Sarah admitted.

"It's an insightful observation, Mum," Maria replied. "Anyway I'm heading to the cottage. I can catch up with Nadia there, and you can save your excessive fondness for her for later."

"Have you had anything for breakfast? I'm making beans on toast!" Sarah enquired.

"Yes, Mum, I've already had breakfast."

"Hey, by the way, you looked absolutely stunning on that party night. Robert couldn't take his eyes off you," her mother continued.

"Mum, I'm not interested in Robert. Do you know how many

relationships he's been through? Five… and I'm not becoming his sixth," Maria declared as she hurried off to the cottage.

Upon arriving at the cottage, Maria rang the doorbell. Nadia was in the midst of preparing parathas on the stove for breakfast. She reduced the heat and went to answer the door.

"Hello, Maria," Nadia said warmly. "Please, come in." They shared a heartfelt embrace.

"Mmm… I can smell the delightful aroma of breakfast roasting, Nadia," Maria remarked. "How have you been?"

"I'm well, Maria. How about yourself?" Nadia enquired.

"I can't help but still see you in that exquisite party attire, and oh my goodness, your performance was truly remarkable," Maria praised. "Do you have similar celebrations back in your hometown? Singing, dancing and revelry?"

Nadia replied with a chuckle, "Oh, yes! Please take a seat. I'm in the process of making Bengali parathas, and I'll continue flipping them while we chat. I wouldn't want them to burn. As for my background, I'm a Muslim, and my religion is quite strict – no dancing, minimal makeup and no looking at men," she laughed. "But I don't adhere to all of that, especially the 'no looking at men' part. Can you imagine agreeing to marry a donkey?" She laughed again. "My neighbours are Hindus, and they are vibrant people. Dance, music, community spirit and entertainment is their way of life. My friend Aprana Sethy is a talented dancer and choreographer. Oh, I miss her company. She used to make me dance and sweat every day with her."

"I adore the vibrant colours of the dresses you all wear. The one you gave me, I wore it just once, and when I stepped outside, my goodness, the number of curious glances I got! A few even approached me, asking if I was available for dinner. A white girl in Indian attire is quite attractive, it seems!" Maria laughed heartily.

"Oh, really? A white girl in an Indian attire is indeed something unique, especially in the UK where not many white girls wear it. The intriguing part is the attention it attracts from passers-by. You know the saying, 'Every book is judged by its cover.' Dress well, and you won't be short of admirers," Nadia remarked with a chuckle.

"Yes, honestly, my outfit did an excellent job in promoting me," Maria agreed with a smile.

Nadia deftly prepared a paratha and offered it to Maria. "Hey, I know you've had breakfast, but this is a different experience, darling. Give it a try," she suggested.

"Okay, thanks!" Maria accepted and took a bite.

"Maria, are you currently in a relationship?" Nadia enquired.

"Nah," Maria responded. "You know what's funny? The good-looking guys I meet out there are either gay, trans or don't fit the traditional 'he' or 'she' categories. I'm not bothered anymore. It's a waste of my time to pursue non-essential relationships." She took another bite of the delicious paratha and then shifted the conversation away from her personal life. "Wow, this is so delicious, Nadia! What's in it?" she asked, savouring each mouthful.

"Potato and lentils. Didn't I say it was nice?" Nadia asked as she offered Maria another.

"Ah, thank you!" Maria replied.

"Here we go, Keith is here," Nadia announced.

"Good morning, my lovely sister Maria. How are you?" Keith said.

"Good morning, Keith. I'm doing well, enjoying a delicious paratha made by your special wife," Maria said.

"Yes, she is special and a fantastic cook too, a terrific wife. And don't forget the mother-figure to Pori, all rolled into one incredible person," Keith praised, smiling.

"No need to fan the charm, Keith. Enjoy your breakfast. I'm going next door," Nadia said. She prepared a few more parathas, wrapped them in tin foil and headed over to Sarah's house.

"Isn't she caring?" Maria remarked. "Who would take food to their in-laws like that?"

"Let's help her make some coffee and give her a taste of British-made coffee today. Keith, would you like tea or coffee?" Maria asked.

"Make me a coffee as well. I need to wake up a bit. I'm still feeling a bit heavy-headed," Keith replied. "That's what I appreciate about their culture," Keith continued. "They care a lot for the elderly, whether it's their own parents or in-laws. The affection is the same."

Nadia rang the doorbell at her mother-in-law's house. Jonathan answered. "Good morning, Papa. Here are some hot parathas to share with Mum."

"Oh, Nadia, that's very kind of you. I'll savour every bite, my dear," Jonathan replied. "What time is Keith leaving today?"

"At 3pm," Nadia informed him.

"Hey, Nadia, I'm not sure how much weight Keith can carry, but both Sarah and I have some old clothes to give away. We heard that you're delivering them to poor and destitute people in Bangladesh," Jonathan enquired.

Nadia replied, "Ah, I see. He can only carry twenty kilograms, but his own old clothes weigh up to fifty kilograms. Let me talk to him, and we'll figure something out. Reusing clothing is crucial. I'll get back to you soon."

"Okay, we'll catch up later. You should get going, there's not much time left to get everything ready. The clock isn't stopping, is it?" Jonathan reminded her.

"Alright, see you later," Nadia said before heading back to her cottage.

As Maria enjoyed her paratha, she used a knife and fork to savour each bite. "This crunchy paratha is addictively delicious. I feel like having more," she exclaimed.

"Sure, take one from me," Keith offered.

"Oh, no, I'm already full. Thank you, though," Maria said. "Keith, I'm feeling a bit shy, but I decided to ask anyway."

Keith looked intrigued. "What is it?"

"What are Asian men like?" Maria enquired.

Keith was taken aback by the question. "What do you mean?"

"I mean, in general, what are they like? Are they caring, understanding, committed to relationships?" Maria clarified.

Keith smirked and said, "Why are you asking this? You're not planning to enter a relationship with an Indian, are you?"

Maria reassured him, "No, not at all. I just wanted to know."

Keith considered her question and replied, "Well, the culture is similar in all three nations, and they tend to have a strong family-oriented mindset. They place significant emphasis on family connections as a primary source of identity and protection against the hardships of life."

"Do you have friends at your workplace in Bangladesh?" Maria asked.

Keith replied, "Oh, yes, most of them are Bengalis. Only a handful are white at my workplace. But why are you asking this? You've seen how Mum reacted to my decision to marry a person with a different skin tone. You're not thinking about an Asian, are you?"

Nadia entered the room just then. "What's wrong with Asian, Keith?" she enquired.

Keith explained, "Nothing, sweetheart. Maria is asking about Asian men. I was just saying that Mum wasn't very pleased when she found out I was bringing you home. How would she react if Maria did the same?"

Nadia responded, "There's a difference, though. You brought me home like extra baggage, but Maria would be leaving home. Mum isn't going to follow her for the rest of her life, is she?"

Keith added, "But I think she'd be better off with someone from here."

Nadia questioned him. "You mean she'd be better off with a white man?"

Keith clarified, "No, that's not what I meant. I mean financially, she would be better off. You know how some Pakistanis view white girls. They think of them as ready-to-pick cherries on a stray branch – pick and chew, and then throw the seeds away."

"Do you know what the difference is between Pakistanis and Bengalis, Keith?" Nadia asked.

Keith responded, "I don't see any significant difference. They both have brown skin and share the same religious faith, right?"

"You, being the High Cimmissioner to the People's Republic of Bangladesh, should be able to differentiate between Pakistanis and Bengalis. This confusion stems from the historical mistake made by your ancestors, Keith, attaching Bangladesh to Pakistan in 1947 solely based on religious belief. Pakistan and Bangladesh are worlds apart, yet the British fused them together. It's akin to me seeing this apple" – Nadia took one from the bowl – "as red while you see it as red too, but that doesn't mean a Pink Lady and a Royal Gala look the same. Do they taste the same? I'll leave it at that. I don't want to engage in an unwanted argument with you today," Nadia responded. "Maria my dear, Bengalis are indeed quite distinct from Pakistanis. You wouldn't be disappointed if you got into a relationship with a Bengali, honestly. Keith just needs to do a bit of research on these two nations to understand the differences. If only the British Raj had done the same in 1947, the world might be a very different place today," Nadia affirmed.

"Hey, I understand now. I got a bit narrow-minded in the heat of the moment. I don't really mind at all, it's her life," Keith admitted.

Nadia chimed in with a smile, "There you go, Maria, a green light from Keith. This is the advantage of being a female, you almost always get your way," she teased.

"Keith, there's a concern about the old clothes now. Mum and Dad are saying they have a bag full of old clothing. You can't handle that extra luggage alone. I'm thinking of using cargo to send them over to the other side of the world," Nadia explained.

Keith responded, "By cargo, it will cost quadruple, Nadia. I receive special concessionary tokens from the government. It's okay, you can send as much material as you want. It will have to go through a different route. I'll arrange that. Let me know the weight, and get in touch with the recipient in Bangladesh. Ask them to pick up the extra luggage directly from the airport counter there. I'll let you know the baggage claim number and authorise the collection for you."

"Great, that's it, then. I will do that," Nadia agreed.

Keith then said, "You guys carry on chatting. Let me do a bit of preparation for the journey," and he left the scene.

"Are you going to drop him off at the airport, Nadia?" Maria asked.

Nadia replied, "No, how can I? I haven't got a driver's licence yet. I'll use a taxi service, but I will accompany him to the departure gates."

Maria offered, "I will give you a lift. I have nothing to do for the rest of the day."

"That would be great, Maria. And you know what? I owe a song to your brother. I told him I would sing a song for him on his departure day, and with your help, I can do it very comfortably."

"Wow, Nadia, this sounds very romantic," Maria commented.

Nadia then mentioned, "Hey, if you're really into Asians, I can set you up with a perfect match. My friend Aparna's brother Sunil Sethy is still a bachelor, practising law in a reputable firm, a good earner, hindu by faith and very lively family who will look after you."

Maria asked, "Is he handsome?"

Nadia replied, "I'm not sure about that. Beauty is in the eye of the beholder, isn't it? I'll request a photo for you soon. I lost all contact with friends and family just before boarding the plane to travel here, but I'm in the process of re-establishing it. As soon as Keith hits Bangladesh, things will align themselves to normality."

"Okay, that's fine. What time are we going?"

"Latest by 3pm," Nadia informed her.

"Okay, I'll catch you later. Let me refuel and check the tyre pressure, etc. Let's make the car roadworthy. I don't want to break down on our so-called smart motorways, nick-named death traps," Maria said.

Nadia asked, "What's so bad about them?"

Maria replied, "A lot of things. Once you're on one, you'll know. Catch you later."

"Yes, get going. I have packing to do too," Nadia said.

*

As Maria, Nadia and Keith made their way to the airport, the car filled with an air of excitement. The journey was accompanied by the enchanting melody of a traditional Bengali song that Nadia had promised to sing for Keith. The vibrant music echoed through the car's interior, setting a jubilant mood for their road trip.

The scenic route led them through picturesque rural locations, where the fields stretched wide under the bright sun. The countryside provided a serene backdrop to the lively song, and Maria couldn't resist the infectious rhythm. She started dancing in her seat, her movements full of energy and enthusiasm.

Nadia encouraged her to join in the fun, and soon, the two of them were dancing together, their laughter and smiles reflecting the joy of the moment. The surroundings seemed to join in the celebration, as the green fields and clear blue sky served as a harmonious stage for their impromptu performance.

When they finally reached the airport, Keith's departure took on a festive atmosphere. The combination of music, dance and the heartfelt farewell of loved ones made for a jolly and memorable send-off. The bond between Maria and Nadia had grown stronger during this journey, and their shared experience left an indelible mark on both of them.

Close To My Heart

Nadia:
Haahaa… Hoho… Ho…
Wherever you roam, under moonlit skies,
You're always right here, in my heart's sunrise.
Across the miles, under starry seas,
Forever entwined, in memories we seize.

Keith:
I'll draw near, my love sincere,
Close to my heart, you'll always appear.
I'll draw near, whisper in your ear,
Our bond unbreakable, crystal clear, crystal clear.

Nadia:
Through valleys low, and mountains high,
Your presence echoes, in each whispered sigh.
In every beat, of this heart of mine,
Your essence lingers, like a sweet wine.

Keith:
I'll draw near, my love sincere,
Close to my heart, you'll always appear.
I'll draw near, whisper in your ear,
Our bond unbreakable, crystal clear, crystal clear.

Nadia:
Though oceans may separate, and time may fly,
Our connection endures, reaching the sky.
In every moment, in every part,
You're forever close, deep within my heart.

Keith:
I'll draw near, my love sincere,
Close to my heart, you'll always appear.

I'll draw near, whisper in your ear,
Our bond unbreakable, crystal clear, crystal clear.

Duo:
Haahaa… Hoho… Ho…
Wherever we go, be it near or apart,
Know we're cherished, forever close to our heart.

As the engines roared, the plane taxied down the runway, gaining speed with each passing moment. With a powerful surge, it left the ground, ascending into the vast blue sky. The world below shrank, and Keith's departure became a reality.

Inside the plane, Keith's emotions were a mixture of excitement and nostalgia. He looked out of the window, watching the landscape grow smaller and the familiar landmarks fade away. The journey had begun, and a new chapter awaited him in Bangladesh.

Nadia, Maria and their shared memories were now part of his past. Yet, as the plane soared higher and higher, he carried their love and companionship with him into the boundless sky, a treasured connection that transcended physical distance.

*

Six months had passed since Keith's departure, and life had continued its unpredictable course. Nadia and Maria had stayed connected, bridging the gap with messages, video calls and the occasional surprise virtual gathering. Their bond had not weakened; if anything, it had grown stronger.

Keith had settled into his life in Bangladesh, embracing the culture and the warmth of the people as usual. His work as an ambassador kept him busy, but he made time to explore the vibrant streets, savour the local cuisine and learn more about the rich history of Bangladesh.

Nadia, too, had found her footing in the UK, adapting to the

British way of life while cherishing the memories of her homeland. She had continued to sing, sharing her music with Maria and others who appreciated her talents.

Maria's curiosity about different cultures had deepened, and she looked forward to the moments when Nadia shared her Bengali heritage. The world had become a little smaller for all of them, as they appreciated their shared moments and eagerly anticipated the day they could reunite in person.

Despite the miles that separated Keith and Nadia, their connection remained unbroken, a testament to the enduring power of love and relationship and the bonds that can be forged across continents.

*

Aysha, the police officer, had been engrossed in her work, scrutinising the files of criminals at her desk. The room was filled with the low hum of the office's air conditioning system, and the dim light provided a sense of calm within the otherwise chaotic world of crime.

Just as she was about to delve into another file, her phone rang. The voice on the other end was trembling and anxious. It was a mystery woman who claimed she was being relentlessly followed by an unknown man.

The woman reported her desperate efforts to shake off her pursuer, but her stalker persisted, keeping a troublingly close distance of ten to fifteen metres. Aysha could hear the fear and distress in the woman's voice as she described her harrowing situation.

Maintaining her composure, Aysha instructed the woman to immediately find a safe place. However, as she listened to the woman's plight, she realised the gravity of the situation and the danger the woman was in.

In a sudden turn of events, the woman informed Aysha that

she had climbed up a tree to evade her pursuer. The man had located her and was now standing beneath the tree, refusing to abandon his menacing pursuit.

Aysha knew that she had to act swiftly. She assured the woman that help was on the way and instructed her to remain as still and quiet as possible. Aysha quickly dispatched her colleague, Police Constable Iqbal Zafor, to bring the police jeep. They both jumped in without wasting any time, heading to the woman's location to ensure a safe and efficient resolution to this chilling situation.

As they arrived at the scene, Aysha and PC Zafor could see the man sitting under the trees. The terrain was off-road, making it impossible for the police jeep to advance further. One of the officers would have to proceed on foot to reach the distressed caller, named Radika Rathore.

"Stay here, PC Zafor. It shouldn't be a major issue. I'll go and assess the situation," Aysha instructed.

"Okay, ma'am," PC Zafor replied, ready to follow Aysha's lead as she embarked on the mission to help Radika.

Aysha, determined and focused, ventured off the beaten path by foot to approach the suspicious man. Her mission was clear, and she couldn't afford to take any risks. She left PC Zafor in the jeep, instructing him to await her return.

As Aysha made her way towards the man beneath the trees, the tension in the air was palpable. She was determined to get to the bottom of the situation and ensure the safety of the woman stuck up the tree.

Meanwhile, PC Zafor, awaiting Aysha's return, couldn't resist the urge for a cigarette. He stepped out of the jeep, leaned against it and lit up. The familiar smell filled the air as he began to smoke.

Unbeknownst to PC Zafor, an ominous figure had slowly emerged from the shadows. With stealthy movements, the person approached PC Zafor, wielding a wooden pole. In one swift, brutal motion, the assailant struck hard on the head with the pole, rendering him unconscious on the spot.

Back at the scene under the trees, Aysha engaged the man in conversation. She confronted him, her tone firm but composed. She questioned his presence and his knowledge of the girl stuck up the tree, suspecting that he might be involved in this distressing situation.

The man, shifting his gaze away from Aysha's eyes, responded defiantly, "May I not sit under a tree?"

Aysha was determined. She pressed on, making it clear that his actions were questionable, particularly if he was stalking someone. She enquired about his knowledge of the girl, and the man claimed he had no idea she was up there.

Recognising the need for further investigation, Aysha issued a stern directive. She instructed the man to provide his personal information and informed him that he would be required to report to the police station the following morning.

The man, accepting the gravity of the situation, complied, and replied, "Okay, ma'am."

With this understanding, Aysha made preparations to ensure the safety of the woman in the tree and to address the unfolding incident with the utmost professionalism and diligence.

Aysha, with a stern resolve, noted down the information provided by the man, named Latif Khan. She delivered a clear warning, emphasising that any further disruptive or suspicious behaviour would result in her immediate action, including arrest. She handed Latif Khan a slip detailing the requirements for his visit to the police station the following day.

As Aysha shifted her attention to Radika, who had been watching the interaction from the tree above, she called out to her, ensuring her safety and freedom. Aysha offered Radika the opportunity to fill out the slip with her details before departing.

Relieved and grateful, Radika expressed her fear of the man and thanked Aysha for her assistance. With a deep sigh of relief, she handed over the completed slip and prepared to leave the scene.

As Aysha made her way back to the police jeep, she was taken aback by the sight of PC Zafor, who had fallen unconscious in his seat.

"Iqbal! Iqbal!" Aysha called out, attempting to rouse her colleague. But before she could react further, a sudden, unexpected turn of events unfolded.

A menacing presence lurked behind her, grabbing Aysha and swiftly disarming her by taking her gun from its holster. The voice behind her was masked, and the threat was palpable.

"Follow my instructions and you'll be just fine," the masked assailant warned, holding Aysha at gunpoint. With her life hanging in the balance, Aysha knew that she needed to stay calm and act with caution in this perilous situation.

In a moment of life-threatening danger, Aysha refused to succumb to the assailant's threats. She acted swiftly, grabbing the gun from the perpetrator's hand, and pulled his hand by force, causing him to somersault onto the floor. However, in the heat of the struggle, the magazine containing the gun's bullets dislodged and fell to the ground, rendering the firearm inoperable.

Realising the gun was no longer a viable option, Aysha holstered it and engaged in fierce hand-to-hand combat with the assailant. Her expertise in martial arts, a minimum requirement for a police officer, allowed her to skilfully and effectively defend herself against the attacker.

The intense struggle continued for several minutes as both Aysha and the assailant exchanged powerful blows. It was evident that the attacker possessed his own martial arts skills, successfully defending himself against Aysha's relentless onslaught. However, several blows landed on his face and mouth, causing blood to spatter.

Eventually, the assailant managed to land a solid punch to Aysha's abdomen and then her face, sending her tumbling yards away. Blood streamed from her nose, and she struggled to regain her footing. In a moment of vulnerability, the attacker continued his assault, leaving Aysha bewildered and weakened.

Moments later, the assailant seized the upper hand, launching a relentless barrage of blows upon Aysha. As she tried valiantly to defend herself, he struck her with a powerful punch, leaving her incapacitated. He then grabbed her neck, squeezing it with his biceps and cutting off her air supply. Aysha lost consciousness temporarily in his grasp.

The assailant acted swiftly, binding Aysha's hands and feet securely behind her back using heavy-duty cable ties that he had brought with him. He placed her in the rear seats of the police jeep and sealed the doors. With brute force, he dragged PC Zafor out of the driver's seat and cast him onto the roadside. The assailant took control of the vehicle and drove off with Aysha as his captive, leaving behind a scene of chaos and uncertainty.

After driving through rough terrain for fifteen to twenty minutes, Aysha slowly regained consciousness, though she remained disoriented. Her hands and feet were securely bound, leaving her feeling helpless and vulnerable.

Desperate for answers, she attempted to engage with the driver. "Hey, who are you, and where are you taking me?" Aysha questioned, hoping to elicit a response.

However, the driver remained silent, seemingly unaffected by Aysha's enquiries. Determined to break the silence and perhaps negotiate her way out of the situation, Aysha invoked the consequences of assaulting a police officer, which carried severe penalties, including imprisonment. "Talk to me, I can help you," she offered.

The driver, undeterred by her words, continued to ignore her pleas. Frustrated and bound in the back seat of the jeep, Aysha began to kick the back of the driver's seat with her knees, creating an annoying shock that reverberated through to the driver's back.

"Talk to me, you!" Aysha demanded, repeatedly kicking the seat in an attempt to provoke a response. However, the driver's stoic silence endured. His focus remained unwavering as he drove on, seemingly unaffected by her actions.

Growing increasingly agitated by Aysha's persistence, the driver issued a stern warning, threatening to break her legs if she didn't cease her kicking. He made it clear she had been abducted and that the financial gain from this operation far outweighed any potential consequences, including imprisonment.

Exasperated and realising her efforts were in vain, she continued kicking the seat. The driver stopped the jeep, got out and manhandled Aysha to prevent her from kicking the seat. With her mobility further restricted, he instructed her to bang her head against the seat as much as she pleased.

Hours later, the driver reached a checkpoint, where he was met by a guard wearing a mask. Aysha, still blindfolded, attempted to discern the guard's identity but was unsuccessful. Another individual approached the jeep and inspected its interior. After a brief exchange of words, the second man handed a bundle of cash to the driver and informed him that his part of the mission had concluded.

The driver then removed Aysha's blindfold and released her feet. He instructed her to walk to a makeshift marquee located in the midst of a jungle, where her fate and the mysterious situation would become further unravelled.

In a surreal and ominous setting, Aysha found herself bound, her limbs spread slightly apart and anchored to a makeshift bamboo pole. It was a vulnerable and helpless position, and as she opened her eyes, she was met with a sight that both shocked and bewildered her.

Before her stood the leader, the orchestrator of her abduction, who was dressed in a provocative and striking cowgirl-like costume. The attire was designed to entice, featuring a long, one-piece, skin-tight, blue silk corset that flared out at the thigh. High-heeled boots added to the allure, and a colour-matching hairband adorned with a bird feather completed the ensemble.

As the blindfold was removed, Aysha's eyes fell upon the enigmatic figure who had organised this disturbing situation. It was none other than Soofia, the same woman whom Aysha had arrested and subjected to punishment for falsely confessing to a rape charge filed against her husband, Malik, six months earlier.

The shock of seeing Soofia in such a seductive and commanding role left Aysha with a multitude of questions and emotions. The situation had taken a deeply unsettling turn, and Aysha could only wonder about the motives behind her abduction and the presence of the woman she had previously encountered in her line of duty.

As soon as Aysha's eyes fell upon Soofia, she couldn't contain her rage and disdain. Fuming with anger, she greeted her captor with a sharp and venomous retort, saying, "Oh, you bitch! I should have killed you that day."

The resentment and unresolved conflict between Aysha and Soofia had come to the forefront, and the situation had taken on a deeply personal and hostile tone.

"That was a grave mistake you made." Soofia came close to Aysha, ran her fingers past her cheekbone, down her neck and throat, slowly shifting towards her chest, touched a breast and gave it a squeeze. "Not very juicy tits, are they?" she said scornfully. She then came up close to her ear, stuck out her tongue and ran it along her exposed skin from neck to ear. And at the same time she whispered, "I am going to rape you using artificial dicks, and then you tell me how you feel, bitch!" She then slowly took the buttons off Aysha's uniform one by one. To make the process easier she grabbed a pair of scissors and cut both sleeves open, taking the uniform off her body completely, leaving her with just her bra.

"Don't policewomen wear any protective vest underneath? This came off fairly easily," said Soofia. "Let's see what you are wearing under your trousers," she continued.

"Stop right there," Aysha exclaimed. "Don't even think about laying your hands on my pants, you filthy swine!"

"Do you recall what you told my husband when he begged for mercy, you pig?! I want to make it clear today that within this setting, the only law that exists is our own. My husband, the fierce and formidable warrior, and I, the tigress, hold the only power in this entire jungle. Together, we won't just tear you apart, we'll cook and feast upon your flesh. Your disappearance will go unnoticed."

As Malik entered the marquee, Soofia loosened the belt of Aysha's trousers and then skilfully cut through the fabric, revealing her undergarments.

"Please don't do that!" Aysha cried.

"Wow, just look at her well-toned body and legs. She deserves some special treatment," said Malik, seeing Nadia half naked.

Soofia glanced at her husband. "Husband, are you drooling over her beauty? How mean, I am jealous. I can see you're clearly affected down there too. Shall I take more off what's left on her body to give you a little booster job?"

"I'm good, fully prepared down there. Get her ready for a blow job," Malik replied.

"You sick son of a bitch," Aysha cried, her voice trembling with shock and anger.

"Guards, secure her wrists and ankles tightly behind her back, hoist her up, mirroring the ordeal she put us through. It is time for 'what goes around comes around'. The consequences of her own actions need to be reckoned with."

Soofia swiftly bound a piece of cloth around Aysha's mouth, stifling any potential cries for mercy. Stepping back, she unleashed a flurry of furious strikes upon her, each blow from a leathered whip landing indiscriminately upon the entire expanse of her body. With a malicious grin, she exclaimed, "This is the reckoning!" as she repeatedly lashed the woman mercilessly.

Much like what Aysha had done to her husband and her not long before, the contact of the whip caused skin to peel away, and blood seeped from the newly formed wounds. The pain elicited agonised screams from Aysha, as though a torment from the very depths of hell had descended upon her.

Soofia's forehead glistened with beads of sweat, her body fuelled by an adrenaline rush. The relentless barrage of blows slowly dulled Aysha's senses, rendering her body increasingly immune to the agony. Her brain ceased to register the pain, and, in a gradual descent into unconsciousness, she finally succumbed.

Malik could not tolerate the torture. "Soofia," commanded Malik, "cease this at once." He gestured for her to desist. Soofia, in turn, signalled her guards to release the woman and provide her with a meal once she regained consciousness.

"That woman," Soofia sneered, "couldn't endure even the initial round of punishment, yet she boasted about her supposed strength." With disdain, she spat on the ground feet away from Aysha.

Observing Aysha's deteriorating condition, one of the guards felt a surge of empathy for her. He carefully draped her in layers of cloth, recognising that she teetered on the edge of survival.

After some time, Aysha regained consciousness, and the guard offered her nourishment and a drink. Gazing into her eyes, he asked, "Do you want to escape?" She remained silent. Determined to assist her, the guard resolved to loosen her restraints and concealed a firearm using an improvised belt under the cloths. "These people will not spare you, madam, unless you break free from their clutches," he warned.

The next morning, Soofia came back and Aysha was still curled up beneath a blanket. She called upon the guard assigned to look after her.

"What's your name?"

"Azad Khan."

"Do you know the meaning of your name?"

"Yes, ma'am. It means 'freedom'."

"If it means 'freedom', then why is your surname 'Khan'? Are you Bengali or Pakistani, or a mixture of both?"

"I am Bengali, ma'am."

"Do you know in what year we gained independence from Pakistan?"

"Yes, ma'am. I'm not familiar with the history."

"Of course you aren't. Otherwise, you wouldn't be working here as security personnel, would you? I sense a Pakistani connection in your name. It boils my blood that Khan word, those bastards took away my family before my eyes, I was a little girl hiding under the bed when they broke into my house and brutally killed my family. When I hear a Bengali bearing a name like Khan, my anger flairs up to a blazing furnace. If you wish to continue your employment here, you must rid yourself of any Pakistani heritage. Remember, we have been free since March 1971 from those tromentors. I will enquire about your name again tomorrow. If your surname remains the same, you will witness the consequences I impose on those I consider my enemies."

Azad Khan muttered under his breath, "Tough luck, my name is what it is? You silly cow."

At this point, Aysha managed to free herself and stood resolute, aiming a gun at Soofia.

"Hands up!" she commanded.

Soofia, taken aback, turned to see Aysha standing there, liberated and armed.

Soofia glared at Azad Khan and shouted, "You treacherous traitor, your days are numbered."

"Azad Khan, take off your trousers and shirt, and give them to me," Aysha demanded. She added, "And you, Soofia, don't even think about anything foolish, or your life ends right here."

Azad Khan swiftly complied, first removing his shirt and then his pants, handing them over to Aysha. She sat down and instructed Azad to help her put on the pants, all the while keeping her gun pointed at Soofia.

"Calm down, Aysha," Soofia pleaded. "I was planning to set you free today. Take a look inside that bag over there. I brought some clothing for you. You don't need to wear men's clothes. Hey, show her the clothes," Soofia ordered.

"Aha!" Aysha commanded. "Turn the bag upside down and

empty its contents onto the floor. Don't reach inside the bag, or I'll shoot."

The guards complied, upending the bag and letting everything fall to the ground. Among the items that tumbled out were a dress and a pair of shoes.

"Why this sudden generosity?" Aysha enquired, her suspicion still lingering.

Soofia responded, "All I ever sought was revenge. I wanted you to experience the same suffering we endured during your siege. Even though my husband didn't rape Rahila, you still coerced a false confession out of him through your torture. It's over now. Put on those clothes and you are free to leave."

Aysha instructed Azad to fetch the clothing and help her put on the pants, as her one-handed struggle was evident. In the process, Azad discreetly handed the jeep keys to Aysha without anyone else noticing.

Just as Soofia attempted to lunge at Aysha in a desperate bid to seize her gun, Aysha fired, the shot hitting Soofia just below her chest. Blood spurted out, and Soofia crumpled to the ground, first on her knees and then sprawling sideways. Moments later, she lay unconscious, possibly lifeless.

In frenzied haste, Aysha sprinted away from the scene, making her way to the police jeep which she came here with. She struggled with the keys but eventually managed to insert them into the ignition. With a turn of the key, the engine roared to life and she sped away. As she raced off, she made eye contact with Malik, who was approaching the marquee on foot from the opposite direction. Their eyes met in shock, and he realised she had somehow escaped. Malik opted not to give a chase, instead hurried to inspect the situation at his establishment.

He swiftly called his guards, instructing them to pursue the escapee. Four cars sped off after Aysha, engaged in a high-stakes, dramatic pursuit to capture her.

Malik was devastated as he cradled his lifeless wife in his arms.

Overwhelmed by grief and emotion, he shouted, "Get the doctors, call an ambulance!" His voice trembled as he desperately sought help for Soofia.

A high-speed car chase unfolded, with Aysha manoeuvring through narrow streets, rugged lands, buffalo trails and rice fields. She managed to shake off three of her pursuers by forcing them off the road one by one. However, one persistent chaser was proving to be a formidable adversary. Aysha's vehicle, battered by collisions with other cars, had lost its bonnet cover, and the radiator was now smoking, with the engine squealing in protest.

Undeterred, Aysha continued to speed along a narrow, winding road that led to mountainous terrain and eventually into the jungle. Unbeknownst to her, she was hurtling toward a cliff face. Her car careened past the point of no return and plummeted off the cliff, erupting into a fiery explosion upon impact. The treacherous landscape worked in her favour in an unexpected way, as she was ejected from her seat as it rolled and landed in some treetops.

Battered and bruised, with torn clothing and bleeding from various wounds, Aysha hung precariously from a branch. Below, in the territory of the Royal Bengal Tigers. In Bangladesh, man-eating tigers have tragically claimed numerous lives, often targeting those living near their habitats. This alarming behavior stems from various factors such as habitat loss, dwindling prey numbers, and unintended acclimation to human presence. These conditions lead tigers to seek alternative food sources, sometimes resulting in attacks on humans. Yet today, it appears as if a meal is conveniently hanging from the tree, ready to be consumed. One of the tigers detected the scent of her blood and began to lick its lips, playing a waiting game. The tiger gazed up at her several times, attempting to clamber up the tree to reach her but failing because she was perched at a point too high for tigers to reach.

Moments later, a second tiger arrived on the scene, and the situation grew terrifyingly unpredictable.

A deer hunter, armed with a flimsy bow and arrow, ventured into the jungle in search of wild game. His target was a deer, and he silently raised his homemade bow for a kill shot. However, just as he was about to release the arrow, the deer suddenly bolted, though he hadn't made any noise. The hunter swiftly closed the distance, trying to keep the deer in his sights.

As he neared the area where the deer had fled, he began to hear growling and rustling sounds, unmistakably those of tigers. The deer had evidently taken off due to the presence of these apex predators. The hunter cautiously approached to see if the tigers were feeding on something. To his surprise, he spotted a couple of Royal Bengal Tigers circling beneath the trees and frequently glancing upwards.

Following their gaze, he looked up and saw Aysha hanging from a tree branch. His immediate thought was, *Oh she must have fallen from the cliff and be badly injured.* The situation had taken an unexpected turn, and he would need to make a decision about how to proceed.

The hunter swiftly took action, closing in on the tigers with a calculated plan. He secured his bow to his back and retrieved a homemade catapult from his bag. A proficient slingshot shooter, he was known for his ability to knock black crows down from their flight path with precision.

With remarkable confidence, he loaded a handful of small stones into the sling and began a continuous barrage, yelling loudly to fend off the tigers. His speed and accuracy were extraordinary, but the hungry man-eaters were not about to surrender their potential meal easily. One of the tigers even attempted to charge at the hunter, but the relentless stone assault struck it on the head, forcing it to rethink its strategy.

After ten minutes of tactical battle, the relentless firing paid off, and the hunter managed to drive both tigers away. Now, he faced the challenge of ascending to reach the injured woman. He couldn't afford to leave his weapons and equipment on the forest floor. He decided to take his gear with him, climbing to a level where he could leave his armaments standing, yet still within reach in case of a confrontation with wild animals. This way, he could attempt the rescue mission while ensuring his own safety.

Climbing up to the branch where Aysha hung, the hunter confronted her dire condition. Her body bore numerous cuts and bruises, indicating the severity of her injuries. Despite her battered state he carefully placed a feather under her nose to check for any signs of breathing, and he was relieved when the feather moved under her breath, indicating that she was still alive.

After this initial assessment, the hunter recognised that he could not get her down on his own. It was an impossible task given the circumstances. He made the difficult decision to go and seek help. As he turned to descend from the treetops, he paused, considering another approach. Perhaps a gentle tap on the head could wake her up. He returned to Aysha's side and began tapping and shaking her while calling out, "Hey, wake up! Wake up!" in an attempt to rouse her from her unconscious state.

Suddenly, Aysha's eyes flew open and she noticed the presence of the hunter. Her instincts kicked in, and she impulsively attempted to strike him using her right arm, thinking he might be one of Soofia's associates. However, her arm had been severely damaged and was possibly strained, rendering it immobile. Her attempt to strike the hunter failed.

"Calm down, I am not here to hurt you. I am trying to save you. My name is Abu Sultan. Don't move. You're in a treetop. You fell from the cliffs up there, and you're lucky to be alive. You don't want to fall and hurt yourself further, do you? Let me help you," Abu Sultan assured her, speaking gently and with a reassuring tone.

Abu quickly fashioned a rope into a makeshift climbing harness, securing it around Aysha's body just below her armpits. Using a sturdy branch as a pulley, he slowly and carefully lowered her to the ground. Once she was safely on the forest floor, he descended as well.

Aysha's injuries were severe, and she was unable to stand or walk. Abu knew they had to move quickly, as the threat of tigers loomed. He encouraged her, saying, "Listen, you have to try to walk. I can't leave you here. Tigers are around, and they will attack. Come on, make an effort. Hold onto me and take baby steps. Together, we can make it out of here. My house isn't far. You can wrap your arm around my shoulder for support." They took a few tentative steps together, working in unison to escape the dangerous jungle.

"Ahh, my hip is hurting." Aysha winced in pain.

"If you allow me to carry you, I can try," Abu offered.

"No, I can manage like this," Aysha insisted, despite the pain.

As they continued walking, Aysha, eager to understand her situation, asked Abu what he was doing in the forest and where they were.

"I came to hunt, ma'am. This jungle is the Sundarbans."

"What! They brought me that far, the bastards," Aysha muttered, her anger evident.

"Ma'am, what happened if you don't mind me asking?" Abu enquired.

"I got chased by some organised crime gang…" Just then, the growling of a tiger echoed through the jungle. "Oh no, did you hear that?" Aysha said, alarmed.

"Yes, ma'am. Stay calm. I have weapons to fend them off," Abu reassured her, pulling out his slingshot.

"Are you mad? You're going to use that to fend off tigers? Give me that," Aysha demanded as she reached for his bow and arrow.

"Ma'am, I don't want to kill tigers here. Don't worry, I've done this before. Just stay close to me," Abu urged, keeping his focus on their safety.

Out of nowhere, a tiger suddenly emerged, leaping out of the undergrowth with a deafening roar. The sheer shock of the moment sent both Abu and Aysha into a state of sheer panic.

Thinking quickly, Abu acted to protect Aysha. He pushed her

away from the tiger's path, positioning himself as a barrier between the predator and her. With his heart racing, he maintained his ground and relentlessly fired his slingshots at the tiger, forcing it to retreat into the jungle.

Aysha, left in a state of shock, watched the intense encounter unfold before her eyes, deeply grateful for Abu's courage and quick thinking.

"You know what, you're a godsent angel to me. I wasn't expecting to make it out of here alive. Why would you find me and rescue me? There must be a reason behind it," Aysha mused.

Abu, mindful of the potential return of the tiger, urged, "Let's keep moving, ma'am. He might come back if we don't hurry, and I'm running out of stones."

They pressed on, walking for another twenty minutes, until they finally saw the edge of the forest, where the open world began. Aysha let out a relieved sigh and said, "Thank God!" It seemed that their ordeal in the jungle was finally coming to an end.

"But, Abu, we're not heading out of the jungle. What's happening? Why are you going off course?" Aysha queried, her unease growing.

"Ma'am, my house is in the jungle," Abu revealed.

"What? You're freaking me out now. You've saved me all this way, and now you're telling me you live in the jungle? Why?" Aysha enquired, her discomfort palpable.

"Ma'am, please come this way," Abu responded. After another ten minutes of walking, they reached a stand-alone treehouse constructed from tree branches and banana leaves.

"Is that where you live?" Aysha asked, feeling extremely uncomfortable. "Listen, thank you for your help. I think I can manage to go alone from here."

As Aysha expressed her intention to leave, a voice emerged from the treehouse. "Abu! Who are you talking to?" A woman stepped out of the house.

To Aysha's surprise, the presence of another woman made

her feel safer. Subsequently, another girl emerged from the house, both of them wearing clothing that appeared worn and torn. The situation had taken an unexpected turn, leaving Aysha with mixed emotions.

"Who is she, and why is she covered in blood? Did she get attacked by the tigers?" asked the mother.

"Meet my mother," said Abu. "Ma, she fell from the hills into the treetops, and I rescued her from there," Abu explained.

"Oh, baba re! Come, come in, my dear," the mother said, welcoming Aysha.

"Ma, be careful. She's injured," Abu cautioned, concerned for Aysha's wellbeing.

Aysha remained stunned, her mind racing with questions about why this family was living in the jungle. She accepted a supporting hand from Abu's mother and, though still in pain, made her way inside the treehouse.

Inside, she found three makeshift partitions but no mattresses. Instead, there were blankets laid atop coconut fibre for comfort. There was a modest makeshift kitchenette set up within the treehouse, and Aysha couldn't help but wonder about the family's life in this remote and unconventional dwelling.

"Please, have a seat," Kolsuma, the mother, said graciously offering Aysha a stool. "May I ask your name?"

"My name is Aysha," she replied. "This treehouse is truly remarkable. It seems like you have everything you need here. Who built it?" Aysha asked.

"Hello, Aysha and yes. My two children and I built this treehouse together," Kolsuma explained with a sense of pride. "I'm Kolsuma, and this is my daughter, Khairun. Allow me to fetch you a fresh cloth and some water so we can cleanse the dried blood from your skin. Khairun dear, could you fetch some water quickly, please?"

"Of course, Ma," Khairun responded dutifully.

"Would you like to remove your top so we can examine any

other injuries you may have sustained from the fall?" Kolsuma asked.

"I'm unable to move my arms, so you'll have to assist me," Aysha replied.

As the mother carefully removed Aysha's top garment, she was met with a shocking sight. Aysha's back was covered in whip marks, and her skin was cracked, oozing blood. "Oh my God," the mother exclaimed, her voice filled with concern. "These injuries don't look like they're from a fall from a cliff. What happened to you? Did someone beat you? These bruises are so deep." The revelations about Aysha's injuries only deepened the mystery surrounding her presence in the jungle.

"It's a long story, Kolsuma," Aysha replied, "but if you could just clean the wounds, that should be sufficient. If you can gently pull on my arms, it might help straighten them a bit." The pain in Aysha's body was clear, and she seemed determined to make herself as comfortable as possible given the circumstances.

"Are you certain? I have TCP antiseptic liquid." She swiftly retrieved a small bottle from a nearby table. "If you'd prefer, I can apply it to your entire body using cotton wool after diluting it with water," Kolsuma offered.

"No, it's fine," Aysha responded. "I would need three of these bottles, but I don't want to use your resources. I will be fine. You should keep them for your own use." Aysha didn't want to burden her kind hosts further and was determined to make do with what she had.

With Kolsuma's assistance, Aysha's arms were successfully straightened, allowing her to move them again. Grateful for the relief, Aysha expressed her thanks. "Well done! Thank you for that. I thought my arms were gone," she said.

Kolsuma replied, "No worries." She continued, "Okay, as you wish. I'm going to prepare some pain-relieving herbal tea for you. You'll feel better in no time. Have a rest."

"Thank you so much," Aysha replied warmly.

"You're very welcome," Kolsuma responded, her kindness evident in her actions and words.

Khairun brought Aysha clean water, a cloth and some cotton wool, and she did her best to clean Aysha's wounds. Kolsuma, Aysha's gracious host, prepared the herbal tea, and Aysha sipped it slowly. After a couple of hours, she began to feel much better. The care and attention of this jungle family had made a significant difference in her wellbeing.

Aysha enquired, "Where is Abu? I don't see him anywhere nearby."

Kolsuma explained, "He is our provider. He's gone hunting. If he manages to catch something, he'll go and sell it in the market to get something for us to eat in return." It was clear that Abu played an essential role in their daily life, ensuring their sustenance in the jungle.

"Why are you living in the jungle like this?" Aysha asked, her curiosity piqued. "And why isn't Khairun in school?"

Kolsuma explained, "We are Rohingya refugees. We fled from Myanmar."

Aysha, understanding their plight, enquired further, "But why are you this far south? You were originally located by the Naf River near Cox's Bazar, weren't you?" She was trying to piece together their journey and situation in this new environment.

Kolsuma's voice trembled with emotion as she began to recount their harrowing journey. Tears streamed down her face as she shared their tragic tale.

"You know how we suffered in Myanmar," she began. "They kept us stateless and treated us worse than animals. Even dogs are treated better than us humans. After fleeing to Bangladesh with our family of five, hope of survival grew in our hearts. However, tragedy after tragedy struck. Locals didn't like us invading their country, and later, a massive fire swept through our shelters, destroying thousands upon thousands of camps. In the chaos, my other daughter, Sayma, who is nine years old, and my husband,

Foysal Ahmed, disappeared. Clean water and sanitation facilities were all gone, and we were displaced."

She continued, "A kind person saw me with my two remaining kids sleeping on the roadside. Most people don't even look twice, but this godsent messiah stopped by, and I thought he might hurt me and my kids. He looked at me and…" Kolsuma's tears intensified as she recalled the moment. "He gave us a bottle of water and a bundle of cash. It was enough to board a coach to the south of the country. Even here, people recognised us as refugees and treated us badly. So, we decided to stay away from people. We crossed the Dhangar Khal (River) by a private dinghy and ended up here. Please, I beg you, don't tell the local authorities about us. We have nowhere to go. Please." The family had faced unimaginable challenges and sought refuge in isolation to escape further hardships.

Aysha, with empathy for Kolsuma and her family's plight, assured her, "Don't cry. I'm not in good shape either, and your son saved my life. If you weren't here, I might have been eaten by animals out there. Don't worry, I won't tell anyone your story, and mine aligns perfectly. I do need to see a doctor, I'm not feeling well. I have to go before night falls." Despite her own challenges, Aysha recognised the urgent need to seek medical help for her injuries.

"Yeah, take this." Kolsuma offered her, a sheet to wear over her shoulder.

"Thank you."

She appreciated the assistance and nodded as Kolsuma continued, "Khairun will help you cross to the other side of the river." It was clear that this family was willing to help her as they had helped each other, and Aysha was deeply thankful for their support.

Aysha, overwhelmed by the family's living conditions and their kindness, insisted, "No, no, you keep this sheet for yourself. I'm already shocked by your living conditions. I thank you for everything. I would have given you some money to buy new clothes, but I need medical treatment right now. Khairun, please help me get up. Let's go, my dear." Aysha was determined to seek the medical attention she urgently needed, and Khairun's assistance would be invaluable on her journey.

Khairun took Aysha's arm and they headed toward Dhangar Khal, the river that separated the jungle from the mainland.

Aysha engaged Khairun in conversation as they walked. "How old are you, Khairun?" she asked.

"I am twelve years old," Khairun replied.

Aysha offered some wisdom, saying, "You should be in school at your age. But life is not always a perfect gift. Ups and downs are constants in life. We have to live with the situations we face and strive to make them better." It was a reminder of the resilience and adaptability that people can find in the face of adversity.

After some time, they reached the riverbank. Khairun pulled out a makeshift bamboo raft from a hidden spot, and it was so small it could barely hold one person.

Aysha was taken aback. "Don't tell me we're going to cross this river using this. It will sink before we even get on it. I'm not getting on that, no way. Let me call someone from the other side."

Khairun reassured her, "Ma'am, don't worry. My brother and I regularly use this to cross the river. There is no one on the other side to hear you. It's an isolation zone, and the threat of wild tigers keeps people away. No one comes this way because they don't need to."

Aysha was sceptical about how they would control the raft in the strong tidal waves. She voiced her concerns, saying, "How the hell are you going to control this raft in these outrageous tidal waves? We'll be carried miles down the river before even reaching the other side."

"Ma'am, please trust me. I can do it. I've done it many times. Come, I'll hold you. Go on first," Khairun said. To Aysha's surprise, the raft barely sank. She chuckled, "Hey, it's holding my weight!"

"See, ma'am, I told you," Khairun responded. "Give me some space here." She too climbed onto the raft, and it comfortably held both of their weights.

"That's a miracle," Aysha marvelled.

Khairun explained, "Ma'am, it's the buoyant foam attached to the underside that makes it float like this. We aim to land by that rocky landmark across the river. There is a safe climbing path through the cliffs there. Here, take this paddle and use it as hard as you can." Khairun was confident in her rafting skills, and they were set to make the daring journey across the river.

Aysha took up the paddle, and both of them began to row against the tide. The tide was constant and calm, and their efforts paid off. They missed their target area, overshooting it by a couple of hundred feet, but they reached the shore safely. Khairun pulled the raft along riverbank using the attached rope and supported Aysha as they walked back to the intended mooring spot for the raft. Once there, she helped Aysha reach the mainland up the cliffs.

As they prepared to part ways, Aysha embraced Khairun and told her, "Be careful when crossing back, and thank you so much for your help. Please send my regards to your brother who saved my life today."

"Okay, ma'am, you take care as well," Khairun said. She descended back below the cliffs, walked another 500 feet along the riverbank, and retraced her journey back to where she had started. The two had successfully crossed the river, and their paths were taking them in different directions.

*

Aysha had to admit herself to a hospital, which was located far from her workplace. Her health had deteriorated significantly, prompting her to seek medical attention. During her stay at the hospital, she managed to obtain a new SIM card for her mobile phone and began the process of registering her original phone number on the new card. She informed her parents about her whereabouts but kept her location a secret from everyone else. Aysha spent an entire month in hospital, recovering from the severe injuries she had suffered while held captive by Malik.

As the main breadwinner of her family, Aysha's earnings played a crucial role in covering the family's expenses, including her younger brother's education. Her father worked as a school gatekeeper and performed various cleaning tasks when not at work, while her mother was a homemaker. However, her father's income barely covered their daily food expenses, and the hospital bills were mounting, posing a financial challenge that could potentially lead her family to great debt.

While Aysha was already grappling with this harsh predicament, she received a message on her phone that delivered another devastating blow. The message included a video clip that appeared to show her committing a murder, with the footage skilfully edited to incriminate her. The message had been sent by Malik and it was accompanied by a text that threatened to make the video go viral if Aysha used the confession tape she had recorded during Malik's captivity where upon he had admitted Rahila's rape.

Stunned and disheartened, Aysha questioned the value of staying true to oneself and living honestly. She wondered whether prosperity only comes to those who lie. The weight of her efforts to bring justice to Rahila's case seemed to crumble with this message. Frustrated and in tears, she declared her resignation from her police job, feeling that she had failed in every aspect of her life.

However, Aysha remembered Nadia's proposal to create a private security service team. This idea began to resonate with her as an alternative path, one that could allow her to distance herself from the corrupt aspects of her current job. With her decision made, she intended to explore Nadia's proposal further. As her recovery progressed, she planned to leave the hospital soon, and her determination to avoid returning to her previous job had solidified. Aysha reached out to Nadia in the UK to learn more about the security service opportunity. She dialled her number.

"Greetings, Aysha! It's been a while since we last spoke. How have you been faring lately?"

"Yes, that's precisely why I reached out. I was curious to learn how things are progressing in your life. Have you welcomed your new addition to the family yet?"

"Let me share with you. I still have about a month and a half left, and it's no easy feat, especially with twins on the way. By the way, your voice sounds a bit shaky. Have you been crying?" Nadia enquired.

"Oh, no, it's just that I caught a cold last night, and it's left me a bit congested," replied Aysha and continued. "Ah, I see! Well, congratulations on this wonderful news! Two bundles of joy for the price of one – you must be over the moon. As they say, one pain, two gains!" Aysha chuckled. "Is your husband there with you?"

"No, he hasn't arrived yet, but he'll be here soon. And I must say, it's far from amusing, Aysha. I feel enormous, like I'm carrying two substantial loads within me, and my lips and my entire body are swollen like an inflated balloon. It's anything but easy," Nadia shared with a sigh.

"Be patient, my dear. Just a couple more months and you'll be back to feeling like yourself," Aysha consoled. "Are you alone right now? Is it safe for us to have a private conversation?"

"Yes, go ahead!" Said Nadia.

"Great," Aysha replied. "You mentioned starting a private security company, didn't you?"

"Yes," confirmed Nadia.

Aysha responded, "I've been considering it as well. This police job won't provide the kind of financial stability I'm looking for. I did read the document you sent with your husband, and it mentioned 'private armies'. I was wondering if you could provide more details about that concept over the phone. It would be greatly appreciated."

"Speaking on the phone, Aysha, might not be the best idea due to the potential for unauthorised eavesdropping. I'm currently in the process of setting up an encrypted phone line in my home, especially with the babies on the way. For now, I'm taking a calculated risk by conversing with you, hoping no one is listening in.

"The state of the police service in Bangladesh is a source of concern, even more so since you, as a police officer, bear witness to the systemic corruption. It's evident that Bangladesh urgently requires a new approach to policing in order to foster its development.

"Here's a suggestion: you should work on establishing a capable and disciplined force, gradually building its strength to eventually challenge the ruling party of Bangladesh, catalysing a much-needed revolution. This revolution is essential to restore Bangladesh to its true identity the *Golden Bangladesh*. Your task is to identify and unite a group of highly skilled citizens, forming a team composed of approximately ten to twenty special operations officers. Their primary objective would be to train new recruits to the highest standards, transforming them into formidable combatants armed with artillery, firearms and armour, ready to face any challenge without hesitation."

The objective is to establish a private police and military organisation dedicated to producing elite soldiers and commandos with the aid of advanced bionic technology. I'm collaborating with a team in this cutting-edge field, and we've made remarkable progress. Our goal is to develop a new breed of military personnel entirely.

"This venture will encompass a private peacekeeping enterprise and a justice system aimed at serving the nation, its citizens, the environment and even animals.

"Initially, we will face significant challenges, as the entire country is entrenched in corruption, dishonesty, fraud, illicit activities and the black market. However, as we steadily progress, our efforts will lead to a transformation. When this transformation occurs, our impact will reverberate not only across the nation but also resonate on a global scale and beyond.

"Starting a revolution is indeed possible, but it often demands a great deal of patience, meticulous organisation and a deep love for one's country. Success is more likely when you put in diligent effort and unwaveringly adhere to the plan, regardless of the challenges that may arise along the way."

Aysha sighed with pessimism as she listened to Nadia. "Acquiring the substantial financial resources and expert guidance required for such a mission is a daunting task. First and foremost, where can we even begin to assemble a formidable force of highly trained troops?"

Nadia responded with a determined tone, "The key is to keep optimism alive, do you understand? Anything becomes possible when you try. The power of being a woman is extraordinary, you just need to recognise your true potential and take action."

She continued, "Here's a piece of advice to kickstart your mission. Begin by approaching the Bangladesh Army. Given your current role in the police force, gaining access to the military compound should not be too difficult. Start by distributing some well-crafted leaflets and invite them to attend your talks. During your presentation, focus on the challenges the country faces, but do so with a captivating approach. Use your charm and beauty to build connections, offering tea, coffee and dinner to officials. Share stories highlighting the positive aspects of the country as well. This will encourage them to open up, offering suggestions and opinions that will guide your mission, discreetly record their voices and save them for later review. Remember, do not disclose that you are recording their conversations. This could lead to rejection before you even make any headway. Keep in mind that it's like telling a cancer patient they'll live longer than expected – it's not a lie, it's a hope the doctor implants into the patient promoting a positive outlook. Hope is the greatest influencer."

Nadia continiued, "What about the financial aspect? Do you know how much a top military lieutenant earns in Bangladesh?"

Aysha admitted, "I'm not sure."

Nadia replied, "It's around 70,000 to 80,000 taka a month. Offer them 120,000 taka to work with you, and if that's not enough, use your charisma as a persuasive tool. Convince them to join you, but make it clear that employment is contingent on their genuine commitment to bettering the country and its people."

Aysha nodded and said, "Okay, I'll give it a try."

Nadia was determined, and encouraged Aysha, saying, "Listen, you don't just try, you accomplish it by any means. I'm delighted that you're interested. Here's the plan: open a business account when you have the opportunity, and you'll be the director of this business. We'll name the company Mechanical Intelligence Sixteen Ltd, or MI16 for short. This name reflects our commitment to advancing technology in this era."

Nadia continued, "Bear in mind I have plans to open many companies and will eventually shift them under one roof, a holding company called One Planet Alpha Ltd (OPAL). Don't worry about financing. I've secured government funding for my innovative project here in the UK, and I won't need half of that money to establish my business. I'll invest the remainder in your business without taking any stake in it. I'm willing to do this to promote peace and prosperity in Bangladesh and beyond. If my project here succeeds on a human level, I'll become a millionaire soon and can repay my debts to the UK government. Money won't be an issue, I can provide you with ample resources. So, begin the project with a sincere intention to succeed."

Aysha expressed her gratitude, saying, "Thank you, Nadia. It's been a pleasure speaking with you. For the business, we'll need two named directors. Should I use your name as one and mine as the second?"

Nadia suggested, "No, use 'Pori Moni', my niece's name,

alongside yours. If you encounter any issues with personal information, send me a text and I'll reply via text messages."

Aysha reminded her, "She needs to be over the age of eighteen."

Nadia corrected herself, saying, "Oh, right. In that case, just use my name, Nadia Begum."

Aysha bid farewell, saying, "Okay, Nadia, take care. Goodbye."

Nadia replied, "You too, take care! Goodbye."

Aysha was elated and filled with joy upon receiving this offer. Her financial circumstances had not been in the best shape, and this opportunity presented itself as an incredibly attractive prospect. She realised the importance of sealing the deal with Nadia before any potential change of heart. This was a momentous chance to establish a security force, with Aysha as its sole owner, a dream she had long nurtured.

With a sense of urgency and determination, Aysha wasted no time. She swiftly made her way to the bank, eager to sit down with the bank manager and initiate discussions about setting up a business account that would pave the way for her entrepreneurial endeavour.

*

Returning to the UK after an arduous six-month government duty in Bangladesh, Keith's plane touched down. Inside the arrival terminal, Nadia stood eagerly alongside Maria, awaiting his arrival. As he emerged from the gate, his exhaustion was eclipsed by his excitement to see his loved ones.

Keith embraced Nadia with heartfelt warmth, a deep sense of compassion evident in their hug. Afterwards, he extended his affection to Maria, offering her a warm and comforting hug as well. The reunion marked the end of a lengthy separation and the beginning of a time for shared happiness and reconnection.

As Keith looked at Nadia, who was noticeably heavily pregnant, he couldn't help but express his concern. "Nadia, do you really had to come all the way to collect me at this stage? Look at you," he said with a warm smile, his affection for her clear in his eyes.

Nadia, however, dismissed his worries with a smile of her own. "I just sat in the car, Maria did all the hard work of driving," she reassured him.

Together, they walked out of the airport terminal and made their way to the waiting car, with Maria in the driver's seat. Once they were all settled in, the car started to move, and the beginning notes of a musical tune filled the air, setting the stage for a harmonious and heart-warming reunion.

Union of Two Souls

Keith:
My darling, the distance tore us apart,
But our love endured, beating within our hearts.
The world watched closely, from the very start,
Witnessing the union of two souls, never to depart.

Nadia:
Without you, my love, each day was a trial,
The world observed, witnessing every mile.
Our story unfolded, in every trial,
A testament to love's strength, beyond denial.

Duo:
United we stand, two souls intertwined,
In the tapestry of fate, our destinies aligned.
Through every hardship, love's beacon shined,
The world bore witness, to the union defined.

Keith:
Through the highs and lows, our love prevailed,
In the face of adversity, our bond unveiled.
The world bore witness, as our love set sail,
A testament to the power of love's tale.

Duo:
United we stand, two souls intertwined,
In the tapestry of fate, our destinies aligned.
Through every hardship, love's beacon shined,
The world bore witness, to the union defined.

Nadia:
As one, we'll journey, hand in hand,
A union of two souls, destined to withstand.
The world may watch, but they'll never understand,
The depth of our love, forever grand.

The melody concludes at this point, and they head homeward, wrapped in the embrace of a delightful and everlasting sense of contentment.

CHAPTER 8

THE RISE OF MI16

Aysha

Sajad

Shah Yous

Forid

General

Chit Lwin

Shaf-i-Lw

Crp Sadiq

Sr Jabbar

Michelle

The Twins

Rimon

Crow

Snake

Tiger

Cat

Tara Miah

Mehek

Dilruba

Inds Khan

Keith

Nadia

Aysha found herself ensconced within the bank's bustling confines, a place where the seeds of her entrepreneurial aspirations were being sown. Engaged in a profound dialogue with the bank manager, she diligently unveiled her vision for a burgeoning business endeavour that encompassed both corporate establishment and the opening of a business bank account. With unwavering resolve, Aysha wrote her signature on all requisite documents, bestowing her invaluable authorisation.

Meanwhile, her business partner Nadia resides overseas, but the stringent regulations of Companies House mandate that a person must be physically present when signing documents. Leveraging her status as a dedicated police officer, Aysha adeptly persuaded the bank clerks that her partner was on the verge of returning home, poised to promptly endorse the essential paperwork upon arrival. Convinced by her assurance, the officials graciously accommodated her request and furnished her with a freshly minted company certification, designating her as the director of Mechanical Intelligence Sixteen Ltd. A folder brimming with the pertinent company documentation was handed over to her, culminating in a triumphant exit from the bank, her countenance radiating with elation.

In the wake of this triumph, Aysha sought solace and refreshment at a nearby cafe, occupying a seat in the alfresco section. Retrieving her phone from her handbag, she beckoned the waiter and placed an order for a light luncheon and a steaming cup of coffee. With a sense of anticipation, she meticulously composed a text message, divulging the details of the company's establishment and business bank account number. Her hopes were pinned on the expeditious arrival of funds, as she eagerly anticipated the commencement of the envisioned business operations, now set in motion.

Aysha, resolute in her commitment to persevere through her challenging financial circumstances, opted to retain her current job despite her earlier promise to resign. She discerned no advantage in relinquishing her position without first securing an alternative source of income. Having savoured the last sip of her coffee, she gracefully left the cafe and proceeded to her workplace, where she was due to begin her shift.

As she arrived at her station, Aysha was met with a fresh and compelling case resting on her desk. The incident involved a rickshaw driver by the name of Sajad Ali, who had fallen victim to a brutal assault perpetrated by a coach driver named Shah Yousuf. To compound matters, the coach driver was now demanding compensation for purported damages to his vehicle's paintwork, alleging that the rickshaw driver had inadvertently scratched the surface of his coach.

"Madam, that troublesome fellow wreaked havoc on the road today," Shah lamented, frustration evident in his voice. "He outright refused to yield or move aside, despite my persistent honking," he added.

"And you simply ran over him, assuming he was nothing more than a lowlife and worthless individual, is that correct?" Aysha enquired, her tone conveying a sense of scrutiny.

"Ma'am, I did not run over him, he actually crashed into my coach," Shah clarified.

"Hey, Sajad, please come over here and share your perspective," Aysha requested. "You can remain seated, Mr Yousuf," she directed.

"I have no intention of sitting with this contemptible individual, I'll stay right here," Shah retorted.

"So, I have correct understanding of one aspect," Aysha began, her gaze fixed on Shah.

Aysha then gestured to the rickshaw driver, encouraging him to continue.

"Madam, I had three exceptionally heavy passengers on my manual rickshaw, making it quite cumbersome to manoeuvre. I exerted all my strength to move aside, but despite my earnest efforts, it was a slow and laborious process." Sajad began to cry in anguish, tears welling up in his eyes. The rickshaw driver further explained with a sense of desperation, "If he had just allowed me a few more seconds, I could have cleared out of the way, but these individuals consider themselves kings of the road, they believe they hold higher status. Instead, he deliberately drove directly into me, madam. Subsequently, he descended from his coach and physically assaulted me. All three of my passengers, witnessing this aggressive behaviour, got offended and chose to disembark and leave. He then forcefully pushed my rickshaw towards the roadside bank, resulting in a twisted front wheel. I lack the means to work now until I can repair it," he concluded, his voice carrying the weight of his predicament.

"So, Mr Yousuf," Aysha began, her tone carrying an air of stern enquiry, "you claimed that despite your honking, he refused to yield. However, based on his account, it appears that you forcefully collided with his rickshaw using your larger coach. And as if that wasn't enough, you proceeded to step out of your vehicle and physically assault him. Why did you resort to violence? Was it because he appeared vulnerable or because he is a rickshaw driver? Or perhaps, do you consider yourself the ruler of the road?" Aysha pressed, seeking to uncover the motivations behind Shah's actions.

"Ma'am, what are you talking about? You seem to be buying into his nonsense," Shah retorted, his tone expressing disbelief.

"You didn't answer my question. Simply driving a larger vehicle doesn't grant ownership of the road, does it? Road rage is a criminal offence, and your actions, stepping out to assault this vulnerable individual, strongly indicate that you engaged in such behaviour," Aysha emphasised.

She then turned her attention to the rickshaw driver and enquired, "Hey, how much does a new wheel cost to purchase?"

"5,000 taka, madam," Sajad replied.

"You, Mr Yousuf, will pay him 5,000 taka for damages and an additional 5,000 taka for his loss of income. Furthermore, I strongly advise you to refrain from resorting to physical violence in the future, or else these police cells are wide open," Aysha decreed, her disposition revealing a willingness to resolve the matter at this juncture. "I'm currently in a lenient mood and prefer not to escalate this further if you comply," she added.

"I am not paying him anything," Shah declared, his anger evident in his demeanour.

"PC Tara Miah, please proceed to arrest him and place him behind bars," Aysha instructed firmly.

"You're not dispensing justice here, ma'am. You're simply enabling more of these reckless individuals to put themselves in harm's way, allowing these road nuisances to behave even more recklessly," Shah protested before entering the police cell.

Shah retrieved his mobile phone from his pocket and dialled the number of the local mayor, Forid Ali.

"Hello, sir," said Shah when the call was answered.

"Hello, Shah, how are you?" replied the mayor.

"I'm not doing very well, sir. It seems the world is becoming increasingly chaotic," Shah lamented. "I've been locked up by the lady inspector of Lalpur Bazaar police station over a trivial matter. Could you kindly intervene and help secure my release, please?" he implored.

"Listen here!" Forid Ali retorted with evident anger. "You people often don't seem to employ your reasoning faculties, but instead, you rely on your loudmouthed rants. That lady inspector is a dedicated and honourable peacekeeper. Has she made any specific demands for resolving this trivial matter?" he enquired.

"Yes, sir," Shah confirmed, "she demanded 5,000 taka for damages and an additional 5,000 taka for loss of income."

"Just pay the amount, you fool, and get yourself out of there. Trying to bribe her is out of the question, she's incorruptible, so don't even entertain the thought. Do you honestly believe she'd compromise her integrity for a mere 10,000 taka? You'd be a fool to think so. Pay the fees with gratitude and put this behind you. The costs will be far higher if this escalates to a court case, you idiot," Forid admonished.

"Okay, sir, I understand. Thank you. Goodbye…" Shah replied.

"PC Miah, where has that lady gone?" he enquired when he didn't see her at her desk.

"She's out for casework and should be back in a couple of hours," PC Miah replied.

"Listen, my friend, please radio call her and convey that I'm ready to pay 10.000 taka. I was foolish to decline her earlier offer, and I'm willing to settle this. Please arrange for my release at once," Shah requested.

Moments later, PC Miah drafted a report, accepted the payment from Shah Yousuf, and then released him, allowing him to go on his way.

*

In this new endeavour, Aysha embarked on the crucial task of recruiting individuals who would play pivotal roles in the success and growth of Mechanical Intelligence Sixteen Ltd. As company director, she recognised her responsibility in safeguarding the organisation's interests and ensuring its future prosperity. Her obligations extended to the meticulous filing of company tax returns, which would entail the comprehensive explanation of profit and loss to Companies House.

In compliance with Nadia's directives, Aysha understood that she could not simply rely on a recruitment agency to fill the company's vacant positions. Instead, she diligently adhered to the company's specific terms and conditions, modelled after an organisational structure reminiscent of military rankings. The hierarchy was as follows:

Directors: At the highest echelon of authority, the directors held ultimate power, akin to monarchs in the organisation.

Officers: Positioned immediately below the directors, these individuals held high-ranking roles and authority, granted by the directors themselves.

Second ranks: The soldiers at this level did not occupy positions of high command within the company. Within the second ranks, a distinct tier of authority existed, comprised of:

Warrant officers: These individuals held positions of special authority, commanding respect and recognition.

Non-commissioned officers (NCOs): As non-commissioned officers akin to special agents, they too held significant roles in the company's structure.

All members of the company were required to have specific titles and badges denoting their position. These badges were to be worn on their sleeve or chest, serving as visible markers of their authority within the organisation. This regimented structure was meticulously established to ensure a well-organised and disciplined team, poised for the company's success.

Aysha's paramount objective was to identify and recruit a field marshal, the highest-ranking officers in the Bangladesh Army. These individuals were widely renowned for their exceptional and lethal abilities, having undergone comprehensive training that encompassed a wide range of skills, from combat and tactics to the art of vanquishing adversaries with ruthless efficiency. The field marshals represented the elite echelon of recruits she sought for her company, individuals who could bring unparalleled expertise and unwavering dedication to the organisation.

After weeks of meticulous research and sifting through the

profiles of hundreds of field marshals, one officer stood out to Aysha: Shaf-i-Lwin Ebrahim. A Myanmar-born individual, he was raised in Bangladesh after his family moved there when he was still a child. Over the years, he had risen through the ranks and achieved the esteemed position of field marshal within the Bangladesh Army. His unique background and exceptional career made him a compelling candidate for Aysha's project.

Aysha recalled a chapter from her school history lessons that spoke of Chit Lwin Ebrahim, a prominent human rights activist in Burma, now known as Myanmar. Chit Lwin hailed from the Rakhine State on Myanmar's western coast, a region where the majority of the population adhered to Buddhism. However, he and his fellow Muslims constituted a minority in this predominantly Buddhist area. Regrettably, they were among the most persecuted minority communities globally, a plight that had earned them the solemn label of being persecuted by the United Nations.

As Myanmar transitioned into a military state in 1962, the Rohingya people found themselves as victims of state-sponsored persecution. Myanmar's military forces unleashed a campaign of violence and terror upon the Rohingya community, targeting them openly on the streets. The horrors included abuse, torture, rape, the incineration of homes and entire villages, mass arrests and extrajudicial killings. The suffering endured by the Rohingya was unimaginably brutal, prompting a mass exodus of people who fled in desperation to neighbouring Bangladesh.

Among those who sought refuge in Bangladesh was Chit Lwin Ebrahim, a martial arts expert and a member of the resistance group called We Are Rohingyas. After escaping the torture chambers in Myanmar, he found himself in Bangladesh, a land of asylum. While numerous job opportunities were available, Chit Lwin chose to channel his talents and skills in a way that would benefit the nation that had offered him refuge. He began his quest by approaching the gates of a Bangladesh Army base, persistently seeking employment. His determination was unwavering, as he spent every morning for two consecutive months sitting near the front gates, enduring rain, storms and gale-force winds, unwavering in his pursuit.

His dedication eventually caught the attention of a major general who, one day, decided to call him in for questioning.

"You've been coming and sitting at our gates for the past two months, and it's truly remarkable to witness such persistence – even more than a thick-skinned dog. Our guards have continuously tried to ward you away, yet you persistently return. What drives you to act this way, and what is your motive?" the major general enquired with a mixture of surprise and concern. "Are you aware that the place you've chosen to sit is within our military boundary, where a 'shoot to kill' policy is mandatory for foreign trespassers? Despite multiple warnings, you've shown a remarkable disregard for your own safety. Why are you so determined to risk your life in this manner? If not by bullets, the harsh weather could very well end your life," the major general emphasised.

"Sir, may peace be upon you," Chit said respectfully. "I am well aware of the dangers associated with this zone, and I enter it every day fully cognisant of the consequences. My only intention is to offer my services, which I believe I owe to the nation of Bangladesh, its people and to the military as well," he said earnestly.

"Service? What kind of service?" the major general enquired.

Chit responded, "Sir, I wish to impart my skills to the Bangladesh Army."

The major general pressed further, "What specific skills do you possess?"

"Sir, I specialise in high-quality martial art techniques at military standard," Chit explained.

The major general's tone became sceptical. "You believe your skills surpass those of our own soldiers? And why should I trust you? You could be a spy."

"Sir, I do not claim to surpass your military's skills in any way. Rather, I believe my skills can complement and enhance your already highly talented and skilled military force. I am not a spy, and you are welcome to place covert surveillance on me if that eases your concerns," Chit assured, seeking to allay any doubts.

The major general took a moment to contemplate Chit's words and then summoned Corporal Sadiq. He instructed Corporal Sadiq to fetch Sergeant Jabbar.

"Yes, sir, at your service," Corporal Sadiq acknowledged before heading off.

Upon Sergeant Jabbar's arrival, the major general enquired, "Do you know how to read English and Bengali?"

"Yes, I do, sir," Chit confirmed.

"Go and read about Jabbar's attributes and achievements on that board while he comes to see you," the major general instructed, indicating the board.

Chit complied with the major general's instructions and approached the wall to review the profile of Sergeant Jabbar. There, he discovered that Sergeant Jabbar was a distinguished individual. Not only did he train officers, brigadiers and cadets for the Bangladesh military, but he was also a highly proficient fighter. Sergeant Jabbar had achieved numerous accolades and awards in both hand-to-hand combat and firearms, signifying his exceptional skills and experience.

"Sergeant Jabbar reporting, sir!" Chit turned at the sound of the voice to see Sergeant Jabbar.

"Meet Chit, a martial artist. He wishes to join our army and believes that his fighting skills can be an additional asset to our already successful military, should we choose to recruit him," the major general said introducing him.

Sergeant Jabbar turned toward Chit and enquired, "Do you have any other formal army training or academic qualifications, sir?"

"Sir, I am more than willing to learn, but I'd like to request the opportunity for you to test my abilities before making a decision about whether to retain me or not," Chit said.

"I can't recall posting a job vacancy here, my friend... anyway," the major general responded.

"Come on, let's put you to the test. Follow me," Sergeant Jabbar called as he led Chit to the training facility, where new recruits were engrossed in various military exercises. Different colour bands denoted the phases of training. The red phase was the initial stage, focused on teaching discipline, codes of conduct and the art of following orders. It transformed bewildered strangers into confident soldiers.

The amber phase represented the intermediate level, where recruits learned to handle firearms, ammunition and artillery, in addition to receiving training in hand-to-hand combat and guerrilla warfare.

The final green phase was an intensive training programme spanning four years. It honed individual tactical skills, enhanced leadership abilities and self-discipline, and emphasised teamwork in accomplishing complex tasks and missions promptly and effectively.

Sergeant Jabbar, commanding the training, ordered a temporary halt to the ongoing exercises. He instructed all participating soldiers to form a large ring, with everyone facing the centre. Following his directions, every soldier promptly abandoned their current activities and assembled in a ring on the designated area. This practice was part of a recurring drill designed to assess their progress and achievements by competing with their fellow soldiers.

Sergeant Jabbar, after a brief consultation with the training instructor, selected a few names from among the soldiers who would participate in the fight against Chit. He then gestured for Chit to step forward to the centre point of the circle.

"Meet Chit Lwin Ebrahim," the sergeant said addressing the gathered soldiers. "He is here in search of a career in the army. As you can see, he is a middle-aged man with no formal academic qualifications. Nonetheless, he claims to be a formidable fighter, despite his age and lack of formal training. He even asserts that he can defeat any combatant from our training academy. I would like three of my top combatants to step forward and participate in this challenge to demonstrate his capabilities and, if necessary, show him the way to the exit door."

Three combatants stepped forward, and one of them couldn't resist cracking a joke. With a mischievous smirk on his face, he quipped, "Have you taken the pill, sir?"

Chit, curious, enquired, "What pill?"

With a playful grin, the combatant replied, "The joint pill," causing a burst of laughter from the onlooking soldiers.

"I have no need for joint pills, my joints are in perfect condition. I can't make any promises about your joints, though. They might start to give you trouble soon," Chit responded confidently, earning some chuckles from the soldiers.

The three combatants began to demonstrate their martial art skills in front of Chit Lwin Ebrahim. This was just the initial warm-up phase, and they showcased several sets of skilful fighting techniques. They engaged in friendly bouts among themselves, displaying their prowess. After concluding their display of talent, they marched forward to form a line, standing ready to face Chit.

Sergeant Jabbar issued a final warning to Chit, asking, "Do you still wish to proceed with this fight? These are highly skilled and lethal fighters. I must emphasise that this will be an intense battle with no rules or restrictions, and it will continue until one of you is unable to continue, perhaps even on the floor."

Chit, undeterred, nodded and replied, "I'm ready to proceed."

With determination, Chit leapt into action, showcasing his set of skills with a shakedown warm-up. His mastery of martial arts was truly exceptional and stunning. After his display, he paid his respects with a bow and a nod, indicating that he was fully engaged in the battle and ready to fight.

The fight began as instructed by Sergeant Jabbar, and one of his soldiers stepped forward to initiate the battle. The two fighters engaged in a flurry of skilful movements, delivering powerful punches, kicks and well-timed blocks. As the fight intensified, it became evident that Chit was landing calculated and potent blows on the soldier. On the other hand, every punch and kick from the soldier was expertly blocked by Chit. Chit appeared unstoppable, not missing a beat in his defence. After a few minutes of fighting, Chit managed to exhaust the first soldier, leaving him battered, bruised and bleeding from various places, particularly the mouth and face. The soldier looked drowsy and uncertain.

Sergeant Jabbar then instructed the second combatant to join the fight, but the combined efforts of both soldiers were still unable to bring Chit down. Chit continued to display remarkable resilience, landing blows on his opponents without faltering. After a couple of minutes, the second combatant also found himself overwhelmed, and both soldiers were left dozing around the ring, receiving blow after blow from Chit.

Jabbar then called for the third combatant to step in, and at the same time, he provided bamboo poles to all three of his fighters to assist in taking down Chit. Aided by the bamboo, the three combatants gained an advantage, landing substantial blows on Chit. Chit was having a hard time defending himself, and after a few minutes of intense fighting against the bamboo sticks, he began to show signs of exhaustion and injury. He was severely bruised and bleeding profusely from his arms, body and head, but he continued to fight valiantly despite the adverse conditions.

Jabbar then offered a bamboo pole to Chit as well, levelling the playing field. As soon as Chit got hold of the bamboo pole, he swiftly turned the game around. Within a matter of minutes, he managed to defeat the three combatants and made them retreat, leaving them in need of immediate medical attention. The scene resembled a bloodbath on the floor, with all participants bearing the scars of a brutal battle.

Sergeant Jabbar and the rest of the force erupted in applause for Chit, acknowledging his remarkable display of skill and courage.

They extended an invitation for Chit to join their ranks as soon as he had sufficiently recovered from his injuries. Chit felt delighted and honoured by the recognition, and he bowed down gracefully to accept their offer.

"Thank you, Sergeant Jabbar," he said with a smile, adding humour to the moment, "I think I need some joint pills now." His comment elicited laughter from the spectators, as they all celebrated Chit's induction into the force.

"Chit, you are not just a good fighter, you have proven your point with style, efficiency and immense talent, my friend. You are most welcome at our academy." Sergeant Jabbar commended Chit, recognising his exceptional abilities and welcoming him into the fold.

*

Aysha's research indicated that Shaf-i-Lwin Ebrahim, the son of Chit Lwin Ebrahim, was a highly suitable candidate for her first recruit. He had followed in his father's footsteps and joined the army at a young age, eventually becoming a permanent member of the high-ranking Bangladesh Army, serving as a sergeant. Chit had first-hand experience of the atrocities committed by the Myanmar military, making Shaf-i-Lwin a prime candidate to join Aysha's cause of creating a justice force to improve conditions in Bangladesh.

However, the challenge was not only to locate Shaf-i-Lwin but also to persuade him to join her mission. This required careful planning and a strategy to win his trust and commitment. Aysha understood the importance of this opportunity and was determined to make the most of it.

Aysha faced a challenging dilemma. While researching an individual could provide valuable information, persuading someone to join her cause was an entirely different task. Her target, Shaf-i-Lwin Ebrahim, was military personnel, which posed even greater obstacles. The question was not only how to locate him but also how to approach him and gain his commitment to her mission. The task seemed daunting, and Aysha was uncertain about the best approach.

Turning to Nadia's code book, Aysha hoped to find insights into spying and recruitment strategies. As she flipped through the content, she stumbled upon a page that discussed the use of satellite imagery to gain a rough understanding of an area's infrastructure. However, she realised that this type of surveillance was more suitable for identifying large objects such as airfields. Freely available satellite imagery had limited access and wouldn't provide the pinpoint details she needed.

Further reading revealed that unmanned small drones equipped with high-quality zoom cameras offer a better solution for closely observing human activities. Alternatively, traditional methods like using high-powered binoculars and conducting personal legwork could achieve the same results. After carefully considering her options, Aysha concluded that personal pursuit was the most effective way to gather the necessary information, despite the high level of risk involved. She was willing to take the chance, believing it was worth the effort to bring Shaf-i-Lwin into her cause.

Faced with the challenge of approaching Shaf-i-Lwin Ebrahim, son of Chit Lwin, Aysha was determined to find a way. Inspired by Chit Lwin Ebrahim's tactics in gaining access to a military base in the past, she began to contemplate how she might adapt and modernise these methods. However, she was aware that times had changed, and enhanced security measures, including CCTV surveillance systems, were now in place.

Recognising that simply going near the army gates and playing a waiting game would not work in her case, Aysha decided to seek guidance from her trusted ally, Nadia. She chose to send a text message to Nadia, hoping that her resourceful friend could provide valuable insights or solutions to help her approach Shaf-i-Lwin effectively and achieve her mission.

In her text message to Nadia, Aysha expressed her current dilemma, saying, "Nadia, I am in the process of finding a new recruit from the Bangladesh Army, but I can't seem to figure out how to get to him." She sought Nadia's guidance and expertise in solving this challenge.

Nadia's response came in the form of practical advice. She suggested that Aysha make a telephone call to the military base and arrange an appointment to meet with the person directly. Nadia pointed out that, as a police officer, Aysha should have access to the military, and her request for a meeting would likely be granted. Furthermore, Nadia advised Aysha to initiate a conversation with the person about a subject that he was emotionally attached to, as this would help draw his attention and build a connection. This guidance offered a clear and feasible strategy for Aysha to approach Shaf-i-Lwin Ebrahim and recruit him to her cause.

Aysha was pleasantly surprised by the simplicity and effectiveness of Nadia's suggestion. In response, she sent a text message back to Nadia, saying thank you, expressing her gratitude and relief at finding a clear solution to her challenge.

Aysha had a moment of self-reflection, wondering why she had been considering secretive approaches when she was a police officer with the ability to make official arrangements. Realising the easiness of the solution suggested by Nadia, she decided to put aside her complex thoughts and follow Nadia's advice. She understood the practicality of her position and resolved to use her authority to arrange a meeting with Shaf-i-Lwin Ebrahim.

Aysha took the initiative that afternoon and made a phone call to organise the meeting. The process was straightforward, as the operator received her message and assured her that it would be passed on to the appropriate personnel. She cited the reason for the appointment as a discussion about a classified murder case, using this as a means to set up the meeting.

Aysha received a phone call from Shaf-i-Lwin Ebrahim a couple of days after she had requested the meeting.

Aysha: "Hello, yes, who is this?"

Shaf-i-Lwin Ebrahim: "I am Shaf-i-Lwin Ebrahim from the military. What is it you wanted to discuss with me?"

Aysha: "Are you available in person? It's a complicated case. I need some time to discuss this in detail."

Shaf-i-Lwin Ebrahim: "Well, I have a very busy schedule. It would help if you could say something about the case. Why is it affiliated to me?"

Aysha: "It's a classified piece of work, and I'm not supposed to talk over the phone. I promise it will be worthwhile."

"Listen, I am located in Qadirabad Cantonment providing basic training to new recruits. If you are interested in meeting up inside the camp for a discussion over coffee, I can arrange a security pass for you," Shaf-i-Lwin suggested to Aysha.

"That would be great, but I need more time than a coffee break – at least an hour?" said Aysha.

"Okay. In that case, come in the evening and ask for me at the gates. Make sure to come wearing your police uniform to pass through the traffic police checkpoints," replied Shaf-i-Lwin.

"Great, can I come this week on Wednesday?" responded Aysha.

"Yes, it should be fine!" said Shaf-i-Lwin.

"See you soon, bye for now then," replied Aysha.

"Yeah, bye," said Shaf-i-Lwin before hanging up.

"That wasn't hard, was it?" Aysha said to herself. She had a couple of days to prepare a story to capture Shaf-i-Lwin's attention. Sitting on a sofa, munching on Bombay mix, she pondered what story she could concoct to make a strong impression. Her mind raced through various scenarios, each vying for attention like cars on a Formula One racetrack.

Aysha pondered over various story options: the incident in Darshana where a Muslim boy stole and slaughtered Hindu-owned cattle, causing tension between the minority Hindu community and the majority Muslim population, or the distressing situation of the Rohingya refugees migrating to Bangladesh, facing unsafe conditions and hostility from locals.

Recalling Nadia's advice on the need for an emotionally moving story, Aysha delved deeper into research. She discovered that, between 2017 and 2019, twenty Rohingya families disappeared from the Cox's Bazar camps following a fire in August 2017.

Aysha succeeded in locating a family who had managed to escape capture. While two senior male members of their family were taken away, a boy and his mother were at a nearby water well collecting water. When they returned to the camp, they witnessed armed military officers taking the father and older son away. Sensing imminent danger, the captive older son communicated with his eyes, signalling to his family to flee. With quick thinking, he ensured the safety of his mother and younger brother, diverting attention away from their capture. Since that day, the family has never seen the husband and elder son again. It is reported that the Bangladesh military personnel handed them over to anti-Rohingya militants in Myanmar for financial gain, and it is feared that they might have been killed.

"Ah, indeed," she murmured to herself. "This is the tale I must recount to sway him into joining my cause. Its resonance with his father's detainment during his activism in Myanmar holds the power to sway his allegiance. Delving into the adversaries of his father shall gently guide his mind toward favouring my faction," Aysha declared with conviction.

*

As the sun dipped low on Wednesday evening, Aysha, dressed in her uniform, approached the gates of the Qadirabad Military Cantonment, seeking an audience with Shaf-i-Lwin. The guard at the gates facilitated her entry, guiding her in her police jeep to a specified parking area. Once parked, the guard swiftly notified Shaf-i-Lwin of Aysha's presence. Shortly thereafter, Shaf-i-Lwin himself emerged to escort her from the parking lot onto the premises.

"Hello, it's a pleasure to meet you, ma'am," said Shaf-i-Lwin.

Standing at a height of five feet seven inches, he boasted a slightly tanned complexion and a well-built, athletic physique. His facial features reflected Nepali characteristics, all while adorned in a distinguished military uniform. "I am Shaf-i-Lwin," he announced, extending his hand for a handshake.

"Hello there, it's wonderful to finally meet you. I'm Aysha Khanom from the Lalpur Bazaar police department," she responded warmly, reciprocating the handshake with a friendly smile.

"Please, follow me," Shaf-i-Lwin said as he led the way towards his office. "I've heard that the Arambaria region is currently experiencing some dramatic climate-driven devastations," he mentioned while walking.

"Indeed, it's akin to the Bermuda Triangle, seemingly consuming the livelihoods of every resident there," Aysha replied sombrely. "The effects are severe, and the future remains uncertain. Many have already relocated, leaving those who remain in a dire struggle for limited resources. Recently, a tragic incident occurred where a neighbour accidentally killed a fellow villager in a fit of rage sparked by the shortage of water. It's a heart-breaking situation with similar distressing cases emerging daily."

"Indeed, it's truly disheartening," Shaf-i-Lwin responded. As they reached Shaf-i-Lwin's office and stepped inside, he kindly offered her a drink. "Would you prefer coffee or tea?" he asked courteously.

"No, not at all, a cold drink will be perfect for now, thank you," Aysha replied with gratitude.

"Let's delve into our discussion. How can I assist with your case, Madam Aysha?" enquired Shaf-i-Lwin.

"It's quite an intricate narrative, Mr Ebrahim," Aysha began. "A case has come into my hands. I'm certain you've heard about the rumour circulating in our country regarding the alleged involvement of the Bangladeshi military in the unlawful extradition of persecuted Rohingya refugees back to Myanmar's authorities for financial gain, haven't you?"

"Yes, I've heard fragments of it through radio discussions and YouTube, but intriguingly, it hasn't made its way to mainstream news channels as of yet," Shaf-i-Lwin acknowledged. "What exactly is this about? I'm quite curious to know more," he added.

Aysha gave him the following synopsis: the Bangladeshi military was in the process of transferring several known Myanmar activists who sought asylum in Bangladesh. On the scheduled day of the exchange, the Myanmar authorities arrived with less money than previously agreed upon over the phone. This led to a heated dispute between both parties, resulting in a distraction that allowed two of the captives to escape into the jungle. Subsequently, a new problem arose when the Myanmar authorities discovered that only four captives remained in the locked vehicle, rather than the expected six. This discrepancy caused anger and frustration among the Myanmar officials. The Bangladeshi side refrained from escalating talks further, due to the loss of two detainees. They accepted the offered money without further argument. The two escapees who spread the rumour suggested that the Bangladeshi authorities accepted bribes from Myanmar officials and returned the known activists to Myanmar, risking their probable torture or even worse, potential slaughter.

The atrocities committed by Myanmar's military forces against the Rohingya community have been nothing short of horrendous. They openly subjected the Rohingya to acts of violence and terror on the streets, perpetrating a catalogue of horrors – abuse, torture, rape, the deliberate destruction of homes and entire villages, mass arrests and extrajudicial killings. The suffering inflicted upon the Rohingya was unimaginably brutal, prompting a vast exodus of people who fled in desperation to neighbouring Bangladesh. Since 1962, the situation appears to have witnessed little change. "Has anything changed, Shaf-i-Lwin?" Aysha asked, aiming to evoke memories of these distressing past events.

"Yes, unfortunately, nothing substantial has changed," Shaf-i-Lwin responded sombrely. "The majority often seeks to suppress the minority to prevent any potential uprisings," he added with a heavy tone.

"In my history class," continued Aysha, "I learned about your father's profound activism. He relocated to Bangladesh to escape the relentless, unabated slaughter and genocide of the Rohingya people in Myanmar. Survivors detailed the harrowing accounts of the Burmese military subjecting victims to horrifying abuse and torture before ruthlessly ending their lives and interring them in vast numbers within shallow graves."

"Indeed, while your point holds validity, the timing of this discussion begs inquiry. It appears you've diligently delved into the history of my father. He, indeed, stood as an activist, compelled to depart amid harrowing circumstances – brutalities inflicted by being bound, beaten with an array of weapons wielded by the military, a relentless and agonising torture endured throughout the day. Consequently, what inference are you endeavouring to make? Is there an insinuation that my family was involved in the surrender of these valiant activists from the refugee camps?" responded Shaf-i-Lwin.

"No, no, you're misunderstanding," Aysha clarified. "Consider this: your father, an activist who arrived and established himself here, possessed an abundance of talent that could have been applied in any other profession. Why, then, did he choose to enlist in the Bangladesh military?"

"He enlisted because of his background as a martial artist and his desire to contribute his skills to the Bangladesh Army. I'm certain you've come across this information," Shaf-i-Lwin stated firmly, his voice carrying an undertone of anger.

"Are you insinuating that his decision to join wasn't driven by a desire for retribution against Myanmar?" Aysha prodded, further stoking his anger.

"I believe this meeting has reached its conclusion. Your implications about my father and me regarding a significant crime are unwarranted. I think it's best if you leave," urged Shaf-i-Lwin.

"Please, don't misunderstand me. My intention isn't to implicate you in anything. But cheer up, I'll respect your wish and leave. However, my purpose in visiting isn't yet fulfilled. I came to introduce myself. I've recently established a private company called Mechanical Intelligence Sixteen Ltd with the objective of creating a private and independent army composed of highly skilled soldiers like yourself."

"Like myself? What do you mean?" asked Shaf-i-Lwin.

"By 'like yourself', I mean individuals with exceptional skills and expertise, such as yourself," clarified Aysha.

"Who to fight with?" Shaf-i-Lwin interjected.

Aysha suggested fighting the corrupt segment of the Bangladesh Army and potentially extending the efforts to overthrow the corrupt government, aiming to take control of the nation and institute a new, law-abiding democratic regime."

"Have you lost your mind? Your demeanour doesn't imply stupidity, but your words are sheer madness, fuelling delusions in your mind! Your plan is incredibly ambitious, but it's just a fantasy. If you're done, you may leave," Shaf-i-Lwin remarked.

"I'm not quite finished yet. You and I both know, according to global rankings, institutions in Bangladesh consistently rank among the most corrupt in the world. Corruption permeates all levels of society, not just within the police and military. Did you know the police force is engaged in the profitable business of bribery? The wealthy get away with murder every day, while the impoverished are coerced into pleading guilty to crimes they never committed because they're paid to do so. The recent arrest and extradition of a senior Rohingya activist who was likely executed by either military or police personnel is an example. The government turns a blind eye, more interested in filling their pockets with money from affluent foreign countries, all the while deceiving the people of Bangladesh by feigning generosity towards refugees. Millions of dollars in aid money – where does it go? Straight into the pockets of politicians and their networks. I shouldn't have to spell this out. You're an educated individual, you must know."

"You're blowing this out of proportion. Why should I concern myself with it? I am the son of a refugee, striving to make an honest living while serving the country. I'm unable to take any action against the government. I'm constrained," Shaf-i-Lwin remarked.

"No, you are not constrained. If you claim you are, then where is the democracy in this? Bangladesh is a people's republic. Individuals have the right to express themselves and protest, including both you and me. You can do more if you choose to. It would contribute to a noble cause and an honest way of living. Every movement starts with an idea. My mission is to transform Bangladesh into a safe haven for all, eradicating all forms of corruption, ensuring hope and equal rights for everyone, along with freedom of movement, speech, a true democracy and accessible education for all. I aim to develop the country's infrastructure to a point where poverty and famine cease to exist in Bangladesh. Additionally, I aspire to build military capabilities that rival the most advanced superpowers in the world. I want you to join me in my quest for leadership that may one day influence the world," Aysha passionately presented.

"Please understand, I have a stable income and a family to support. I'm afraid I may not be able to assist you. My job security is crucial, and I cannot risk losing my employment. You see, I'm just a military officer. It might be in your best interest to remain within the confines of your duties, and it would be wise for me to do the same," Shaf-i-Lwin articulated.

Aysha was clearly having a hard time convincing Shafi-i-Lwin. "Listen! Previously, I shared your perspective, but since joining this good cause, I've realised the gravity of looking beyond our present lives and considering the future of our grandchildren. They might not have a viable future here unless we take action to rectify the situation before it's too late. Have you heard the predictions by scientists? They foresee our country being submerged under water in the next fifty to sixty years. What options will we have to survive? Build homes atop water, perhaps? But under this government, can our people construct anything effectively? Ponder upon it. The opportunity is on the table. By joining, not only would you earn a commendable reputation, but your salary would significantly increase – I'm willing to offer you 100,000 taka per month."

"100,000 taka! Did I hear you correctly? Are you sure?" exclaimed Shaf-i-Lwin in astonishment. "This company is a start-up. Where do you expect to source that kind of money from? I'm quite certain you'll be paying others a similar wage. Where do you anticipate acquiring the funding to cover my salary?" enquired Shaf-i-Lwin.

"If you are interested in the offer, getting the money is my problem," replied Aysha.

"If this is some sort of joke, please cease. You're suggesting nearly double my current salary – this seems implausible. Where do you expect to procure such funds? Will you be building a secret underground tunnel to Afghanistan to trade opium?" Shaf-i-Lwin quipped with a touch of sarcasm.

"This is no joke, and it has absolutely nothing to do with drugs. I can pay you with legitimate funds provided by a wealthy party member. Their intention is to transform our country into a global role model, inspiring other corrupt nations to emulate our success and rectify their own issues. Moreover, if we can ascend to a position of governance, it might prompt other countries to ally with us in refocusing attention on the urgent global warming crisis. We are already far behind, and our policies aim not only to address environmental concerns within our borders but also to promote global stability and peace.

"Where the funding originates should not be your concern.

You simply need to look forward to your pay cheque. After all, you have your family to take care of, don't you?" elucidated Aysha.

"I beg your pardon?" Shaf-i-Lwin interjected. "It is my concern, and I need to know."

"Listen, I've already explained this to you. It's curious how you question the source of funds in my company, yet you don't question the government about the money they use to pay you at this very moment. I have influential and affluent partners in my company. If you decide to join us, you'll become acquainted with them," explained Aysha, feeling a tinge of frustration with Shaf-i-Lwin's persistent enquiries.

Shaf-i-Lwin paused for a moment. "So, your ambition is to become a global peacemaker? Even the mighty America failed, and here you are, a tiny speck of dust on the surface of the Earth, speaking such ambitions. What exactly is your projection?"

"Projection? What do you mean by projection?" Aysha asked, shaking her head in frustration.

"You've obviously formulated a plan for all of this. When do you intend to take over this country?" enquired Shaf-i-Lwin.

"Within the next twelve to fifteen years, once we've established a potent force, our strategy involves gradually garnering influence and trust among the people to secure their votes. No force will be exerted. Our policies will serve as the gateway to our success," reiterated Aysha.

"If you gain control of the country, would you extend citizenship to the Rohingya people?" enquired Shaf-i-Lwin, seemingly showing a genuine interest now.

"I can't confirm that at the moment. When the time comes, decisions will be made, but I'm not the sole authority to make such a decision. It's too premature to say anything concrete," replied Aysha.

"I need to speak to the person in charge. I have questions that you cannot answer," said Shaf-i-Lwin. "If I'm going to compromise my loyalty to the Bangladesh Army, my livelihood is at stake. I need assurances, promises and verifications that my involvement in your company will not be in vain," he continued.

"Could you do me a favour? Get me some tea or coffee, a cold drink won't do it right now. You're stressing me out, man. Let me call and speak to the head of the organisation," said Aysha.

Shaf-i-Lwin dialled his assistant's extension and requested two cups of tea to be brought in.

Aysha texted Nadia regarding the situation. A few seconds later, Nadia replied, asking to put Shaf-i-Lwin on the phone for direct discussions.

Just then, a knock on the door was heard. Shaf-i-Lwin went and picked up the tea from the doorstep, brought the tray inside and placed it in front of Aysha.

"The head of my company wants to speak directly with you. Are you ready to talk?" asked Aysha.

"Yes, sure! Put me on," replied Shaf-i-Lwin.

Aysha dialled the number and connected Nadia on the phone.

"Hello," said Shaf-i-Lwin.

"Hello, Shaf-i-Lwin Ebrahim. I hear you are interested in speaking with me?"

Listening to a woman's voice, Shaf-i-Lwin became puzzled once again. *What is this woman up to?* he thought to himself, glancing at Aysha.

"Hello?" said Nadia, noticing the line had fallen silent.

"Seriously, I hope this isn't a joke," he whispered to Aysha while covering the mouthpiece of the receiver.

"Speak!" Aysha gestured silently, looking at Shaf-i-Lwin.

"Hello, madam, I'm here. I didn't anticipate that the head of such a significant project, supposedly a mercenary organisation, would be female!" said Shaf-i-Lwin.

"There you go, finding answers by following the path of misogyny. The mentality prevalent in South Asia is disheartening, and it's something that also needs to be addressed as a priority," Nadia remarked.

"Madam, I'm not being rude, but how is it possible to overcome an army by merely forming a private army group?" Shaf-i-Lwin enquired.

"Why are you asking this question? Are you planning to join us for free? No, right? We'll be compensating you for your service. If you join us, it's for your own benefit," she continued. "Aysha mentioned your concerns about whether, if we gain control over Bangladesh, we would grant citizenship to the Rohingya people."

"Yes," reiterated Shaf-i-Lwin.

"The reason behind forming this movement is to eradicate corruption in the country and introduce legislation that will favour the poor, persecuted, vulnerable and most in need, including advocating for animal welfare and environmental concerns. We aim to utilise the power of technology to devise innovative solutions to address the most critical issues in our country.

"For instance, a few years back, a rural community from Rajshahi, Pabna and Kushtia entered a partnership with India to produce sugarcane, aiming to compete with Brazil in sugar production. While they succeeded in surpassing them in production, it came at a heavy cost. The majority of the sugarcane workers, mostly women, suffered from health issues due to pesticide poisoning, resulting in stomach aches, early menopause and unnecessary hysterectomies. Now, imagine if humanoid robots worked in those fields instead of real humans? These tragedies could have been prevented. Our goal is to make this a reality.

"We aim to eradicate poverty from the surface of Bangladesh once and for all. Upon establishing stability in Bangladesh, we plan to introduce a guaranteed income for eligible citizens. Additionally, we intend to intervene in Myanmar to assist the Rohingya people in claiming their status in their own country, a dream your father fought hard for but unfortunately failed to achieve. I'm sure you would want to contribute to fulfilling that dream.

"While Bangladesh cannot solely support the rest of the world, it can initiate a series of programmes designed to help other countries eliminate corruption, reform their political systems and address the needs of their nations. We need to kickstart this programme here with immediate effect, and for that, my team needs influential people like you."

"Could you elaborate on how you plan to take over the country within twelve to fifteen years?" enquired Shaf-i-Lwin.

"Once again, with the aid of technology. Our initial batch of the army will consist of hybrid soldiers, real humans integrated with AI-enhanced machines. They will be significantly more advanced than conventional human armies. When the time comes, Bangladesh will succumb swiftly to our new generation of cyber-armies, as the current capabilities of the country are as feeble as rotten eggs," said Nadia.

"Really? I didn't realise it was that dire. Let me ponder over this, it's a significant decision for me. I'll be in touch soon," said Shaf-i-Lwin.

"That's fine, take your time. I've provided Aysha with a memoir titled *The Fundamental Principles*, outlining how our movement should be governed. It's a constitution compressed into a paperback booklet. Consult with her, and you'll be good to go. Please pass the receiver to Aysha now," requested Nadia.

"Okay, it was nice talking to you!" said Shaf-i-Lwin before transferring the call.

"Hello, Nadia, I am here, attentively listening to you."

"Hello, Aysha, the situation should soon be resolved. Give him some time to deliberate. If he declines, consider an alternative strategy involving the capture of his father, attributing the blame to our corrupt government officials for the supposed abduction. Should he agree, initiate the recruitment process, and proceed with the subsequent steps. Seek individuals aged between eighteen and thirty-five, in good health but with physical impairments, offering them replacement limbs alongside career prospects including substantial salaries, pension benefits and familial support in exchange for dedicating their lives to service in our armed forces.

"I am currently in the process of establishing a cutting-edge prosthetics company, expected to be operational within the next two years. Meanwhile, focus on compiling a log of potential new recruits. I've transferred 100 lakh into our business account. Utilise it as needed."

"Nadia, if you don't mind, I have a pressing question. My father has fallen ill, and I'm struggling to secure the funds required for his medical treatment. Could you kindly offer a solution?" enquired Aysha.

"I'm truly sorry to hear about your father's situation. This is precisely the issue we aim to address as a priority once we assume power – providing a free national health service for all citizens. However, why are you sharing this with me when the funds are now available in the account? You have the authority to utilise it responsibly," Nadia responded.

"Nadia, I can't proceed with that, the funds are yours," Aysha replied.

"Listen, let's make a deal. You've just offered 100,000 taka per month to Shaf-i-Lwin Ebrahim, correct?" Nadia proposed. "From today, you draw a similar amount from the company funds and consider it your salary for the remarkable hard work and effort you're putting in to this cause. Ensure meticulous bookkeeping to maintain clarity and coherence in our records by the end of each year, and remember to pay your income taxes," said Nadia.

"Your generosity knows no bounds, Nadia," Aysha remarked with a heartfelt smile.

"No worries. Focus on helping me achieve our vision of creating paradise on Earth, and witness the eventual outcome. This is merely the icing on the cake. You'll be engulfed in wealth and fame that you won't be able to avoid," Nadia remarked.

"High hopes indeed, Nadia. I am completely committed to your cause. Take care now," Aysha said before ending the call.

"So, her name is Nadia," Shaf-i-Lwin interjected. "What are you both going on about? Both of you have psychological issues,

I'm telling you. Women are beneath men's feet in South Asian countries, and you both think you're some kind of wonder women. You'll both face difficulties and be obliterated like a puff of smoke, evaporating into thin air without a trace. This is a man's world," Shaf-i-Lwin remarked.

"Don't assume anything. Anything is possible if you set your mind to it. Take your time and consider this offer. Join us, and with the grace of God, you will prosper. If you choose not to, there will come a day when we will take over the country, and you'll be pleading to join us, but by then, it will be too late... for you," responded Aysha. "I must take my leave now. Thank you very much for your time today," Aysha said as she shook hands with Shaf-i-Lwin Ebrahim. He than escorted her out through the doors.

Aysha departed, walking down a long corridor to her waiting jeep, and then drove off.

*

A year had passed in the tranquil town of Aughton, nestled in the north-west of the UK. Within an operating theatre, Nadia found herself assisting a surgeon in a groundbreaking procedure. Together, they delicately navigated the interior of a patient's abdomen, pinpointing the gut hormone artery. With precision, they made a small incision and affixed a minuscule nanochip to the artery's lining. This remarkable device was ingeniously crafted to monitor the levels of brown fat tissue within the gut hormone.

As the quantity of brown fat increases, so does the insulation capacity of this chip within the body, causing its temperature to ascend. Acting as a sophisticated measuring device, the nanochip commences generating a subtle low-voltage signal. This signal is then relayed through the enteric neuronal afferent nerve fibres, traversing the intricate endocrine feedback pathway. Its message to the brain is clear: a signal to stop further eating. This marvel of technology offers an adjustable sensitivity depending on the level of brown fat tissue build-up, capable of regulating one's food intake.

Two exquisitely slender wires, constructed from the remarkable material graphene, each thinner than a human hair by a factor of 1,000, are attached – anode and cathode. These lines connect to a small button battery situated externally, delicately placed on the patient's belly button, providing the essential power to the nanochip. The battery's purpose is to trigger the activation potential within the nanochip, signalling the brain through ion channels to suppress the urge for further food intake.

A masterstroke of innovation, the patient retains control over the nanochip's functionality. It can be disabled at will by either removing the battery or simply toggling a minuscule pinhole switch on the battery holder. Nadia fondly christens this revolutionary chip, the Appetite-Controlling Nanochip, or simply, ACN.

Shortly after the procedure, Nadia emerged from the operating theatre and rendezvoused with the patient's parents. With a reassuring tone, she conveyed the success of the operation, expressing hope that within a span of six to eight months, the patient would witness a significant reduction in weight and subsequently maintain a balanced and steady weight thereafter. She explained that the patient would need to remain at the facility for at least a week to ensure a complete and thorough recovery.

Evidently, Nadia has managed to construct an operating theatre adjacent to her chemistry laboratory, showcasing a remarkable fusion of science and medical practice. Establishing the enterprise Diet Control Ltd, she has devised a compelling slogan: 'Eat to live not eat to die'. With the local authority's permission, she has expanded the workshop's premises, creating space for ten beds aimed at treating patients grappling with obesity. The facility boasts cutting-edge surgical equipment, segregated ICUs, ventilators, a well-stocked pharmacy, a team of numerous dedicated nurses, and a full-time neurologist who also adeptly wields the surgeon's scalpel under her leadership.

Amid this bustling environment, additional individuals can be observed working diligently in the chemistry division of the workshop. The crown jewel of her enterprise, an extraordinarily advanced atomic-influenced microscope leased to augment her laboratory, empowers her to discern entities as minuscule as DNA strands. This instrumental addition has solidified her company as a resounding success story.

With every bed occupied and an incessantly growing list of prospective patients, it becomes palpably evident that an immediate expansion of her enterprise is not just a choice but a necessity. The demand for her services is unrelenting in Aughton, underscoring the prevalent struggle with weight issues in the community.

*

Within the laboratory-turned-home environment, a distant yet familiar call resounded, breaking the silence. "Ma'aa!" The voice pulled her attention away from her work. Turning, she found the source of the call to be Pori Moni, her eight-year-old niece, who now appeared notably more grown-up and mature.

"What is it, Pori?" Nadia responded, her voice infused with warmth and curiosity.

"Grandma's going out, and the housekeeper finished her shift. No one's home. Can I look after the twins?" Pori enquired.

"Just a moment, I'm coming," Nadia replied. She swiftly finished updating the parents who had accompanied the patients and escorted them out the door.

"Ah, my sweetheart, that's very kind of you to ask. You can look after the twins. I'll be right there. I'll do some cooking. Where is your grandma?" Nadia enquired.

"She's gone with Uncle Jacob!" responded Pori.

Nadia observed Pori's hair and remarked, "And that's a good

girl, always keep your hair plaited. That way, the strands are less likely to fly around and unexpectedly end up in your food. When Mummy is in the lab, I always wear a hair net. It's a good practice. Have you used hand gel?"

"Yes, I did use hand gel!" replied Pori. "But, Mummy, I'm not in the lab," she clarified.

"Yes, and it's still good practice to keep your hair tidy and sanitise your hands. Remember, mums are always right when it comes to the welfare of their children. You're my child, and what Mummy advocates is only to benefit you. Okay?" Nadia explained.

"Okay, Mummy!" affirmed Pori.

Nadia removed her gown and headed to the cottage, situated next door. Within this space, she cared for her fraternal twins, who were now three years old, exuding an energy akin to a swirling hurricane, turning everything in their path. To aid her in managing the household chores, cooking, cleaning and caring for the children, she had hired a housekeeper. As she arrived at the cottage, she found the two toddlers joyfully playing with each other under the attentive supervision of the home help, Michelle.

"Hello, Michelle," said Nadia. "How are they doing?"

"Doing fine," responded Michelle as she rose to prepare for the end of her shift. She had cooked two dishes, cleaned the house and tended to the children, leaving her quite exhausted. "Okay, Nadia, see you tomorrow. Bye," she said, leaving and closing the door behind her.

Pori settled at her desk, beginning to tackle her school homework.

"I've received a call from your school, Pori. *Masha Allah* (God willing) you are doing well in school. Keep up with your schoolwork, my dear. This is the path to success. I've been studying my whole life and continue to do so. It's a never-ending cycle, like a roller-coaster. The more you study, the more you learn. This is the one thing in life you will never regret doing. I feel content when I see people happy because of me and my accomplishments, and I want you to achieve in the same way," Nadia explained.

"Okay, Maa," replied Pori.

"And one more thing, don't associate with boys at school. They can be a disruptive force, so keep your distance from them. When you reach sixteen years of age, Mummy will find a respectable young man who is worth your time. Okay?" said Nadia firmly but with a gentle smile.

"Mother," Pori giggled, "I hate boys."

"My dear, you dislike boys because you're still very young. There will come a time when your feelings may change. It's important that you share with me if you ever develop an interest in any boys, as they are not always as virtuous as they may seem."

Pori enquired curiously, "Why are they bad, Mummy?"

"Not all are bad, Pori, but some can be very destructive. I want you to discern the difference between the good and the bad. Only a grown-up female can do that. I want you to fully embrace autonomy; that you learn to think for yourself so you don't need to turn to anybody. You need to realise you do not live in that time anymore. You do not need to be enslaved to anyone. I want you to become a better person. You can become anyone you want. There are women becoming presidents, rocket scientist, even soldiers. There is nothing you cannot be, and when the time is right you will find somebody who loves you for what you are, and if he finds the same in you then life is much, much better. I want to make sure that you get the best out of life, my darling. Here is an example of a 'bad' person." Nadia pulled out her phone and opened her YouTube platform, showing a video of a Taliban member publicly lashing a woman. "This is an example of a 'bad' man, Pori," Nadia explained.

Pori enquired, "Why is he hitting the lady?"

"Because he believes he has authority over a woman and wants to assert control over them. A woman, due to her physical incapabilities, is often unable to retaliate against such aggression.

Selecting the right man is among the most challenging decisions in a woman's life, while, unfortunately, it's far easier to encounter the wrong one. At times, the pursuit for the right man might feel like an exhaustive search yielding no results, whereas unwanted attention from unsuitable men may persist. The real challenge lies in making the right choice. That's why, no matter how you encounter a man, come and discuss it with me, no matter how old you are. I will always be your mother. I have a discerning eye for detail and can distinguish between a good and a bad man," Nadia advised.

"I'm not going to like any man, they hit women," Pori firmly stated.

"Not all men hit women. Have you ever seen Uncle Keith hitting Mummy?" Nadia asked.

"No, Maa. Does that mean he is a good man?" Pori enquired.

"Yes, he is a good man. So, remember, if you ever develop feelings for a man, no matter how you feel about him, you come and tell Mummy, okay?" Nadia urged.

"Okay, Maa!" Pori giggled.

"That's my good princess... my queen," Nadia said encouragingly.

The phone rang in the background, and Nadia swiftly went to answer it. It was Keith.

"Speaking of the devil, and here he is! Hello, darling, how are you? Pori and I were just talking about you," Nadia remarked.

"I am fine. So I have a long life now, right?" Keith joked.

"Yes, of course, you would outlive me!" Nadia replied with a light-hearted tone.

"Oh, Nadia, I wish I could! You know I am ten years older than you, stop mocking me, that's age discrimination," he said, chuckling. "Just a quick call, need to get back to work – emails are stacking up. How did the obesity operation go today?"

"It went well. All ten beds are occupied. Fingers crossed, Keith, years of research and testing should pay off," Nadia replied.

"Yes, I hope so. You've worked so hard for this. Are you sure you don't want to involve the media?" suggested Keith.

"No, Keith. I want to keep my profile low at this stage. If these ten operations are successful, I have the recording of the procedures. I can always go public at a later date. I must be certain that this technology works well. Any false results could land me in big trouble," Nadia explained.

"It worked with the mice in the past few years. It will work with humans. Keep hope, Nadia! How are my little Savannah and Adil doing?" Keith enquired.

"Oh, don't tell me about it. Were you a cheeky monkey when you were little, Keith?" Nadia chuckled. "I can't figure out where have they got this strength from – crawling, walking, climbing onto furniture, pulling and pushing toys. Their physical activities are outrageous. Michelle gets absolutely drained by these two. She even falls behind on her cleaning routine because of our little ones," Nadia shared.

"It's great news. Ask my mother about my toddling years," Keith chuckled. "I'll talk some other time. Need to get back to work. Give kisses to everyone. Bye…" said Keith.

"Bye," said Nadia before hanging up the phone.

*

A year has elapsed, and during this time, Sergeant Shaf-i-Lwin Ebrahim has made the resolute choice to collaborate with Aysha in the noble endeavour of establishing a private army force. Meanwhile, Nadia, steadfast in her dedication, wholeheartedly tends to the financial requisites of the company, allocating resources as necessary. The (MI16) company stands poised on the precipice of assembling an ensemble of the most accomplished secret service officials Bangladesh has ever borne witness to.

Taking heed of Nadia's counsel, Aysha is directing her focus towards the search for individuals with missing limbs in Bangladesh, a country nestled within the lower-middle-income bracket in South Asia. The populace predominantly engages in physically demanding occupations within the labour market, encompassing roles in agriculture, construction, mechanical and iron work, bereft of adequate workplace safety measures. Incidents involving motor vehicle mishaps are commonplace, often resulting in traumatic injuries necessitating limb amputations. These occurrences leave a lasting, profound impact not only on the affected individual but also on their families, who typically rely on their income.

In the most severe instances, these injuries culminate in limb amputation, drastically altering the sense of identity and diminishing hope for the future. The capacity to sustain gainful employment is either wholly eradicated or significantly reduced to low-income opportunities. As per Nadia's doctrine outlined in the 'armed forces candidates' manual, these individuals are regarded as valuable assets, their potential not limited by physical impairment.

The demographic most affected by lower limb amputations comprises young, robust males, who, within the cultural framework of multigenerational households, are often the primary breadwinners. Their incapacitation due to injury or disability not only impacts their financial standing but also challenges their established role as the patriarchal figure. Consequently, societal perception deems them as devoid of value, prompting self-reproach, loss of self-esteem and tragically for some, even suicidal inclinations.

While prosthetics are available in Bangladesh, the region's hot, humid and frequently wet conditions render these devices impractical in certain situations. Additionally, uneven surfaces on pavements and walkways pose further challenges for amputees relying on prosthetics, creating additional hurdles in their daily mobility.

After exhaustive research in this domain, Nadia has embarked on a strategic investment initiative: the establishment of a cutting-edge prosthetic manufacturing facility. This avant-garde establishment utilises AI-guided technology to craft artificial limbs tailored for amputees in Bangladesh. Operating beneath the umbrella of One Planet Alpha Ltd (OPAL), this company is now up and running as an asset holder of all its subsidiary companies namely MI16, MI17, including UK based Diet Control Ltd. And now Nadia has named one of the new subsidiaries the Miracle Limbs Trust. A charitable organisation as perceived by government officials however, it harbours a clandestine facet. Concealed beneath its altruistic exterior, it nurtures a subterranean realm, fostering a new breed of hybrid humans – a convergence of prosthetic and organic tissue. These individuals embody a formidable force, transcending conventional limitations, and poised to emerge as a formidable entity to be reckoned with. A secret truth known only to a select few.

*

Miracle Limbs Trust has been operational for a year, extending its services to cater to all individuals affected by work-related injuries at a significantly reduced fee. The organisation tailors treatment plans on a case-by-case basis, considering the economic status and income level of the individuals. In instances where individuals lack the financial means to cover the transformational process, the trust provides free treatment or extends financial freedom. This freedom allows individuals to undergo the necessary procedures and settle the costs once they've reclaimed a functional and productive life. The overall fee structure adheres to a non-profit, cost-based philosophy, ensuring that charges remain at a level that covers expenses without generating profits.

The company has also allocated funds specifically designed to aid those who cannot afford the services. Additionally, they provide loans based on a 'get well now, pay later' model. This approach allows candidates to restore their limbs and subsequently repay the loan once they secure gainful employment. This innovative system empowers individuals to undergo necessary procedures without immediate financial burdens, facilitating their journey toward rehabilitation and reintegration into the workforce.

However, a clandestine aspect exists within the company's operations. They selectively identify the strongest and most physically fit amputees and employ a process of indoctrination to enrol them in their mission. Using persuasive negative propaganda, they seek to sway these amputees to join a cause purportedly aimed at serving the greater good of humanity and the environment. The narrative presented to these individuals asserts that improving the lives of others stands as the primary ethos for an amputee. Upon agreement, these individuals are provided with state-of-the-art prosthetic limbs, designed to be technologically advanced.

Successful candidates undergo a thorough orientation regarding the terms and conditions of their involvement and are bound by a contract aligning with MI16's code of conducts and directives. These specially equipped amputees are armed with proprietary technology that elevates their prosthetic capabilities to an unprecedented level. The company has successfully worked on thirty such individuals, not only providing them with a renewed lease of life but also offering them permanent employment within the secret service company, MI16 and MI17.

The company's overarching mission revolves around bolstering their military prowess to an unparalleled degree, surpassing any contemporary armed forces. Its goal is to amalgamate exceptional technological capabilities with strategic tactics, rigorous training and potent firepower, intending to outmatch even the largest and most formidable armies worldwide. The aim is to create a force so dominant that no traditional soldiers in modern times could rival their prowess.

The company has assembled a team of top-tier bioengineering technicians whose expertise lies in crafting groundbreaking conceptual prosthetics. By amalgamating principles from medical science, robotics and mechanical engineering, they've created a series of unique artificial limbs. These revolutionary prosthetics have the capability to transform into weapons, responding to the brain signals of the user. Once integrated, these artificial limbs seamlessly merge with the amputee's body, operating flawlessly with no discernible differences. When fully clothed, an amputee equipped with these prosthetics is indistinguishable from an individual with complete limbs. This remarkable feat has not only captured global attention but has also positioned the company as the foremost pioneer in advanced artificial limb technology.

The demand for its innovations has surged, with orders flooding in from regions across Asia, Africa and various Arab countries. Notably, prosthetic rehabilitation centres, which previously sourced shipments primarily from Europe, are now increasingly turning to Miracle Limbs Trust for their upcoming orders. This shift underscores the growing recognition and reliance on the company's expertise and advancements in the field of prosthetics.

Unexpectedly, Bangladesh, renowned as the global hub for garment manufacturing, has pivoted to become a leading centre for prosthetic production and innovation worldwide. This rapid transformation has shifted the nation's identity from being synonymous with the textile industry to now being hailed for its remarkable advancements in the realm of prosthetics.

Mechanical Intelligence Sixteen Ltd (MI16) has been engaged in small-scale private security and espionage operations for several years. Leveraging the expertise of its sister companies, MI16 has been progressively tackling increasingly complex and demanding cases on a daily basis. The news of its successful undertakings swiftly disseminates throughout the country, sparking an overwhelming influx of orders from diverse sectors. Corporations, banks, embassies and government institutions are swiftly recognising and employing MI16's security services to safeguard their operations. The company's proven track record in resolving intricate security matters has made it the go-to choice for a myriad of institutions seeking robust and reliable security solutions.

Akbar Khan, an industrialist seeking heightened security for a consignment of five crore (million) taka en route to a bank, is considering engaging the services of MI16's guards. Previously, Khan's enterprise relied on their in-house transportation security personnel. However, they became the tragic targets of organised criminal activity, resulting in the loss of millions of taka and the lives of two guards. In response to these harrowing events, the company began transporting money in smaller portions over frequent journeys, incurring substantial financial costs.

In pursuit of a more secure and reliable solution, Akbar Khan held a meeting with Aysha at her office. The purpose of the meeting was to initiate negotiations for a secure transport arrangement from his business location to a bank situated fifty miles away. This discussion marks the beginning of potential collaboration between Akbar Khan's enterprise and MI16's security services, aiming to safeguard the transportation of substantial financial assets in a more secure and protected manner.

Seated in front of Aysha's desk, Mr Khan enquired, "I'm seeking to transport a significant amount of money. I'd like to gain a better understanding of how your company operates and how the system functions."

Aysha elucidated, "We've been in the secret service trade for several years, offering a wide spectrum of security services, ranging from safeguarding vacant properties to fortifying royal palaces with firearms – no task is too small or too large for us. Specifically, we specialise in cash-in-transit services, handling not only cash but also other high-value assets such as coins, jewellery, fine art and items of significant financial importance. Our personnel undergo comprehensive training tailored to these specific tasks. When it comes to transporting substantial cash amounts, we exclusively employ armoured trucks to ensure security.

"Numerous companies have entrusted their security to us, and we take pride in serving them. I encourage you to peruse the reviews and speak with others who have utilised our services.

Their experiences and feedback speak for our commitment and reliability," Aysha emphasised.

Mr Khan enquired if she could kindly provide some insights regarding the pricing structure associated with her service.

"Our standard fee is a flat rate of three per cent, resulting in a cost of 1,500,000 taka for a 500,000,000 transfer," Aysha explained. "For regular clients, we offer a reduced rate of two per cent. However, this applies to transfers of five crores or more, which is equivalent to 5,000,000 million taka."

After a brief calculation on his pocket calculator, Mr Khan accepted the offer and proceeded to make a fifty per cent deposit into a holding account in accordance with MI16's terms of service.

Aysha finalised the deal with Mr Khan and received comprehensive information about the cash transfer, including details about cheques and coins. She meticulously logged this data into her system, preparing to fulfil the mission. Aysha promptly assembled her team for a briefing and readied the truck for its journey to the designated destination.

The Robbers Team

| Crow | Snake | Tiger | Cat | Rimon |

The opposing side was a team of five highly skilled professional robbers, comprising four individuals with the code names Crow, Snake, Tiger and Cat, and Rimon Ali, the driver of the transit van employed by Aysha's MI16 security service. However, on this occasion, Rimon Ali aligned himself with the robbers, receiving a thirty-five per cent share of the loot. They convened in a meeting room equipped with a whiteboard, strategising the detailed plan for the robbery of the transportation truck.

The route would begin from Tangali and conclude at Kamla-Para, a sixty-kilometre drive. Rimon Ali, along with a colleague, loaded the truck with cash boxes, signed off on the pickup logbook, conducted a final check of the vehicle and initiated the journey, steering towards the highway. After covering thirty kilometres and approaching the hills of Madhupur, the vehicle's pace reduced to navigate the rough terrain. This phase positioned the truck alongside a hillside, providing an opportunity for a relatively smooth, low-impact jump onto the top of the vehicle.

Crow, a member of the bandit's team, made a calculated move to land atop the truck, advancing towards the driver's position. He strategically approached the passenger-side window of the vehicle.

Rimon Ali, upon spotting Crow landing safely on top of the vehicle, discreetly triggered a mild stink bomb in the cabin. Concerned about a possible foul smell due to a presumed dead animal nearby, Rimon requested his colleague to crack open the window to let fresh air in. As the window began to lower, Crow swiftly administered a tranquilliser to the unsuspecting passenger, inducing sleep within moments. Seizing the opportunity, Crow opened the passenger door, descended and took a seat inside. Although all interactions were being recorded within the truck, the driver feigned resistance, exclaiming, "Hey, who are you? What are you doing?" With a firearm aimed at the driver's head, Crow commanded him to deviate from the main highway and drive off-road through the jungle.

After rendering the colleague unconscious, Crow securely bound his hands to prevent any future threat upon awakening. Instructing the driver to proceed, Crow directed him to stop further ahead in a remote area within the jungle. Suddenly, a trio comprising Tiger, Snake and Cat arrived on three Honda dirt bikes.

Tiger urgently commanded, "Driver, quick, open the safe! Hurry, move it!"

The driver pleaded for mercy, explaining that he didn't possess the codes required to unlock the safe and requesting to be allowed to leave.

Tiger demanded, "What are all these keys you have on you? Give them to me."

Suddenly, three of Aysha's guards descended from the treetops using ropes, reminiscent of cliff-hangers, and swiftly entered the scene.

"Wait!" one of them shouted, halting the ongoing situation.

"Who the heck are you guys?" said Cat, expressing confusion and curiosity.

"We spotted the truck first, it's our loot," declared Aysha's guard, claiming ownership of the plunder.

In the midst of the chaotic altercation, Cat vehemently shouted, "Fuck off!" and fired the gun at all three guards, swiftly followed by Tiger. Aysha's highly skilled guards adeptly dodged the bullets, swiftly swinging around the trees and engaging in hand-to-hand combat with Tiger and Cat. Meanwhile, Crow forcefully pulled the driver towards the back of the truck in an attempt to access the safe. Unseen by the others, Snake had stealthily slithered under the truck when nobody was watching.

As Crow struck the driver with the back end of pistol, causing the driver to bleed and plead for mercy, he demanded, "Which key?" pointing the gun at the driver's head. The driver, under duress, revealed the key to open the back of the truck. Simultaneously, Cat and Tiger were engaged in a rigorous martial arts battle with two of Aysha's guards, while the third guard, observing the injured driver and Crow attempting to open the safe, swiftly hurled a disc-shaped stone at Crow's hands. He then leapt into action to prevent Crow from shooting, engaging in intense combat that dislodged the gun from Crow's grasp.

Amid the chaos, the driver, seizing an opportunity as Crow became embroiled in the fight, silently made his way to the back of the truck, opened the safe and discreetly departed to check on his injured colleague in the passenger seat. Unbeknownst to everyone,

Snake, using stealthy movements, slithered into the truck and discovered the open safe, containing a large briefcase. Seizing the moment, Snake swiftly grabbed the briefcase and fled the scene without attracting any attention.

Following the intense clash between Aysha's team and the three bandits – Crow, Tiger and Cat – both sides displayed visible signs of injuries. However, Aysha's team emerged victorious, managing to apprehend the three criminals. Unfortunately, the fourth member fled with the cash, resulting in the loss of the stolen money.

Aysha's team handed over the captured bandits to the legitimate authorities, involving the actual police. The authorities instructed the driver, Rimon Ali, to drive the vehicle back to Tangali depot and deliver it to Akbar Khan. As there was no conclusive evidence tying Rimon Ali to the violent heist, he was not arrested at that particular stage.

The following day, Khan visited Aysha's office, bringing the remaining cash and expressing gratitude to her for ensuring the safe transit of the money to its destination. This left Aysha's three guards perplexed, as they believed the mission had failed due to the loss of the cash.

Contrary to their expectations, Khan not only brought the remaining funds but also signed a new one-year contract with Aysha's company. This contract was specifically for the secure transfer of money from Tangali to Kamla-Para, entrusting the task to Aysha's own workforce. This successful resolution of the situation led to an extended partnership, showcasing the trust and reliability established by Aysha and her team despite the initial setback.

Aysha convened a meeting in a projector room. Dimming the lights, she played drone-recorded footage of the entire journey, starting from the departure point to the jungle where the attack took place. The team collectively reviewed the footage, meticulously identifying and discussing the mistakes made and emphasising the weaknesses that needed strengthening. Aysha highlighted that every mistake was an expensive lesson, and it was imperative to learn from them.

She adamantly stressed that no such errors should occur on their next mission, deeming this particular operation a failure. Aysha acknowledged the strategic decision to use an alternative transporter to ensure the money reached its destination, preventing the loss of their reputations in the depths of the jungle along with the truck. This evaluation and reinforcement of their training aimed to fortify the team and avoid similar pitfalls in the future.

Aysha, dressed in her police uniform, returned to the station to confront the captured individuals identifying themselves as Crow, Tiger and Cat. She entered the cell and addressed them.

"So, you three are responsible for the theft. What's the name and address of your accomplice who managed to escape with the money?" Aysha enquired sternly.

Tiger stood up and addressed Aysha. "Listen, madam, it's in everyone's best interest if you release us. This was a terrible mistake. We're not professional robbers, it was our first attempt, and we were caught. We're genuinely sorry."

"Was it truly your first attempt?" Aysha questioned. "Regardless of whether it's your first or second, the essence of the matter is theft, a crime you've committed," she stated firmly.

"Ma'am, we are all working professionals. I work in a garment factory, he works in a mobile phone shop, and he is a website developer. The person who escaped is the mastermind behind this heist. We merely followed his orders, similar to how you follow orders from your senior officers," stated Cat.

"You followed orders, huh? If someone told you to jump off a building, would you do it? Don't equate my orders with yours, it only makes you look foolish," replied Aysha sternly. "You!" Aysha pointed directly at Crow. "You were the first one to jump on top of the truck when it reached the hills of Madhupur," she accused.

"Madam, how do you know that?" enquired Crow, expressing surprise at Aysha's statement.

"I know because the truck was bugged internally and externally with mini cameras. The live feed was directly transmitted to my phone, which I had in my hand," Aysha explained.

"Madam, we are deeply sorry. It was a mistake. As friends, we wanted to go on holiday outside of Bangladesh and needed a significant amount of money. Given our low currency value, it takes a substantial sum to even consider a holiday abroad. For this purpose, we fell victim to the temptation of this lucrative theft. This will never happen again," pleaded Crow.

"Provide me with the name and full details of your fourth friend and I will minimise the severity of the police report. If you refuse, you'll face significant consequences and the report will be far more serious, possibly resulting in additional years added to your prison sentence," Aysha explained, emphasising the gravity of the situation.

"Madam, we genuinely don't know where the guy lives," said Cat.

"Being a woman among you male thieves, Cat, I would like to believe you are speaking the truth. However, in my line of work, every captive is considered guilty until they prove their innocence. Your apologies hold no meaning to me. Guards, tie them up. Let the consequences of their actions serve as their testimony. Make sure they fully comprehend the gravity of their actions and that they are deterred from ever committing such a crime again," ordered Aysha, firmly instructing the guards to carry out their duties.

"Yes, ma'am," replied PC Tara Miah in acknowledgment of Aysha's instructions.

"Ma'am, a lady has arrived to file a missing person report," PC Miah reported separately. "She specifically wants to see you. She seems to be in a state of shock and has blood stains on her clothing."

"What! Bring her in, then," bellowed Aysha.

The woman was ushered in, and Aysha offered her a seat in

front of her desk. Aysha then instructed Mehek Jaan, a police clerk, to bring some cold water for the distressed lady who had come to file a report.

"Tell me what has happened," Aysha asked the lady.

"Ma'am, we've been married for seven years and have a child together. As you may know, the people of Arambaria have always relied on the eastern stretch of the Padma River for water, but now it has dried up. I'm not certain what's causing it, but our side is experiencing severe drought, resembling a barren graveyard. The western side, however, seems to be unaffected by the water shortage. Recently, we lost two of our precious goats due to the lack of water. This incident was a tragedy that severely affected my husband. Our livelihood depended on our livestock, and now I don't know what to do," she tearfully explained.

"What's this bloodstain on your clothes? Here, take some water, it might help you feel better," Aysha offered to the lady.

"Thank you," she murmured, taking a sip of water and gazing down at her stained clothing with tearful eyes. She then began to recount her harrowing experience. "The water shortage caused this horrific incident. My husband returned home and found one of our goats lying dead in our courtyard. He began calling my name loudly, jumping up and down, yelling that the goat had passed away. When I approached him, he charged at me and started hitting me, accusing me of being responsible for the goat's death because I hadn't fetched water for it to drink. I was exhausted, and getting water from a mile away is not easy, especially without a wheel cart – I carry a traditional water vessel on my hip. He didn't understand my difficulties. His dominant instinct was that I should obey him, and he continued hitting me. I picked up a hand-held grass scythe to warn him not to hit me, but he refused to listen and charged at me more aggressively, saying I should kill him too and that he didn't want to live a life of misery. He ran towards me and stumbled on the uneven surface, falling on top of me like a giant ball. I lost control, and the grass scythe pierced his body. He bled to death before my eyes, and I didn't know what to do. He was my strength, my hope, my partner in life and now I've killed him," she sobbed deeply.

"It's okay, don't worry. Try to calm yourself down," Aysha comforted her. "What is your name?"

"Dilruba Ara," she replied.

"Mehek, take down her details," instructed Aysha. "Dilruba, calm down. We will go to the crime scene shortly and handle the situation. Don't worry. My colleague will collect all your details, and I'm sending the forensics team to your place immediately. You stay calm and explain exactly what has happened for the records, okay? Is your child okay?"

"Yes, I brought my daughter Bilkis here. She is in the other room."

"It's okay. You provide all the information, and we will take care of it."

Aysha left Dilruba with Mehek for further questioning and informed the social services to come and take care of the child until their investigation on the matter was complete.

*

As dusk settled in, Aysha, fatigued from the exhaustive exploration into the murder case, yearned for tranquillity. Finding respite on her balcony, she eased into a rocking chair, embracing the balmy air that wafted through, while the lithe jackfruit trees swayed gracefully in the gentle wind. It was in this serene moment that her phone chimed, heralding a call from Nadia, beckoning to reconnect and exchange the most recent developments.

"Hello, Nadia!" Aysha answered.

"Hi, Aysha, how's it going?"

"Oh, you wouldn't believe it. I'm absolutely exhausted today. My workplace felt like a bustling supermarket with multiple high-profile cases driving me up the wall," replied Aysha.

"Hey, perhaps you need a break, a small getaway somewhere. Don't stress too much, or you'll find yourself in a care home," Nadia joked, breaking into laughter.

"Yes, I suppose so," said Aysha and continued, "This drought, which tore your family apart, is causing devastation in other families as well. Just today, a woman killed her husband in a fit of water-induced rage. It's a humanitarian crisis unfolding in those villages. People are losing their livestock akin to pest-infested crops, and they're fighting over trivial things that were inconceivable just a few years ago."

"Aysha, listen. These natural disasters occurring worldwide are nothing but a plea from Mother Earth, beseeching humans to spare its life. Humans are relentlessly draining its vitality. If individuals like you and me don't recognise this, we'll burden the lives of our grandchildren. We must harmoniously coexist with our planet's ecosystem to enhance the existence of every living being. God has endowed me with abundant resources, and I'm willing to risk everything to safeguard the future of this planet. Do you recall my discussions about the obesity project?"

"Yes!" replied Aysha.

"It's been a success! The BBC news channel and other media outlets are eager to interview me. I'm avoiding them for now because a private pharmaceutical company is in talks with me to license my product. I anticipate being in a position to earn a substantial amount of money. With that kind of capital, I believe I'll be able to effectively address Arambaria's water scarcity problem very soon."

"Oh, that's fantastic news, Nadia!" Aysha exclaimed.

"It is wonderful news, but without your help, I'm akin to a lamppost on the street – emitting light rays but lacking the brightness to outshine the darkness. With your support, I can go a long way. Technically, without you, I'm like a switch waiting to be turned off at any moment."

"Oh, don't say that, Nadia. I'm here to assist and work

alongside you," Aysha responded. "Is there anything I can do to help bring water to Arambaria?"

"Yes, yes! You need to establish a second charitable organisation under the umbrella of our holding company, One Planet Alpha Ltd (OPAL). You can call this organisation Humanitarian Pledge. Through this entity, we will initiate the installation of wells in every corner of Arambaria and other locations across the country where water's needed. Once we address this issue, we'll move on to the next level: river management. The blockage of water in the Padma River has been caused by excessive sediment flowing down from the Himalayas, creating unwanted mini-islands and sandbars, obstructing the eastern channel and leading to drought while flooding the western side of the channel. If we excavate the sediment and manage the river, we may effectively solve all the problems.

"Let's kickstart with Humanitarian Pledge, making the entire country aware of where this assistance is originating. This will boost our popularity, officially establishing recognition of our company. The greater the popularity, the more public support we'll receive, and eventually, the public will heed our appeals."

"It's fantastic news. I'll place an advertisement in the *Dhaka Tribune* searching for a manager to oversee the charitable organisation, similar to what we did with our Miracle Limbs Trust. Let's kick-start another company, shall we?" said Aysha.

"That's the spirit! I'll get in touch soon for updates on this. For now, I'll hang up," said Nadia.

"Okay, Nadia. I'll organise everything and update you soon."

"Perfect. Bye for now." Nadia then hung up.

CHAPTER 9

THE SALE OF DIET CONTROL LTD

Nadia   Ashley   Debbie   Isabella   Sav & Adil

Amie   Jusna   Steven   Jonathan   Sarah

Bernila   Reena   Farzana   Zakir   Pori

Keith   Neal   Michelle

Starring

Mr Ashley Khanna – Debbie Murdoch (Laboratory cleaner) – Isabella nurse – Adil – Savannah – Amie and Jusna – Steven – Jonathan died – Sarah – Bernila carer – Neal CCTV guy –Michelle Ammon (House maid)

The pervasive influence of technology has staged an extraordinary revolution within our world. Over the past decades, a remarkable evolution spanning from the development of robotic prosthetics to the dawn of artificial intelligence, and from the strides in genetic engineering to the groundbreaking advent of genomic vaccines, has fundamentally reshaped our contemporary way of life. These advancements have instigated a profound transformation that extends across societal, economic and environmental domains, laying the foundation for a future where emerging technologies are anticipated to wield significant global impact in the foreseeable future.

Although certain technologies have received widespread attention in the public sphere, many significant breakthroughs remain concealed within research laboratories and within the confines of private enterprises. One such exemplar is Diet Control Ltd, a private company harbouring a cohort of elite geeks and computer scientists, orchestrating advancements that transcend conventional expectations. They are pioneering engineering techniques in the realm of microrobotics, where daily occurrences akin to magical phenomena unfold. The unparalleled technological strides achieved by this company have propelled it to a pedestal distinct from its competitors, showcasing creations that reveal boundless possibilities and cater to essential human needs. In a particular project, it has harnessed tools that maximise control over both health and diet, marking a significant leap forward in its innovative journey.

Under the guidance of company director Nadia Begum, groundbreaking technology has emerged to address obesity. Using a nanochip slightly longer than a grain of rice, this innovation is implanted within the gut to regulate food intake, marking an unprecedented advancement with zero side effects, an achievement never before realised. The ten patients who have undergone this procedure have experienced improved lifestyles over the past two years. Nadia has meticulously gathered recordings and interviews with these patients, which swiftly went viral across various social media platforms such as YouTube, Instagram and TikTok. Local and international media outlets, including paparazzi, have fervently pursued her for exclusive one-on-one interviews.

As an entrepreneur, Nadia comprehends the essence of time in life. However, when it comes to the surging popularity of her work, she becomes a participant in a race against time. Eager to seize every opportunity to showcase her innovative breakthrough, she embarks on a whirlwind tour throughout the UK and even beyond, engaging with numerous media outlets to share and discuss her pioneering work.

Nadia's remarkable achievements have swiftly propagated through news channels like wildfire, catapulting her into an unexpected celebrity status overnight.

BBC News has emphasised Nadia's backstory, highlighting her as an immigrant who fled persecutions in her home country, now recognised for her revolutionary impact on the medical world.

Sky News has depicted Nadia as a UK-based civil and environmental engineering geochemist who has engineered a miraculous chip capable of controlling obesity.

Aljazeera World has shed light on Nadia's journey, presenting her as a self-taught doctor from the Open University who has developed a groundbreaking nanochip capable of communicating with the gut hormones of individuals struggling with weight issues, effectively signalling them to curb their food intake.

Furthermore, ATN Bangla News, a Bangladeshi news outlet, has specifically highlighted Nadia's origins as a Bangladeshi citizen who arrived in the UK on a visit visa. Her transformative contribution in combating the obesity issue within the country has been underscored, noting her creation of a chip designed to regulate food consumption, heralding a significant breakthrough in addressing the nation's obesity concerns.

Nadia's laboratory has been inundated with enquiries and bookings pouring in from all corners of the globe. In response to this overwhelming demand, she has expanded her operations by opening three additional facilities and initiated franchise projects to cater to the needs of obesity patients worldwide. The exponential success of her initiatives has caused her company's value to skyrocket in the stock markets, with share prices experiencing an unprecedented surge.

The booking capacity of her company has consistently pushed the limits, necessitating innovative solutions to manage the high influx. To accommodate these burgeoning demands, Nadia has adopted a strategic approach by subcontracting local and national hospital doctors, who are specifically trained to conduct surgeries on behalf of her company. This collaborative effort enables her to handle the overwhelming workload.

Despite tirelessly dedicating herself to her endeavours for a decade, the demand for her services has continued to grow steadily, signalling the ongoing necessity for her groundbreaking solutions in the realm of obesity treatment around the world.

*

Ten years after the inception of her groundbreaking enterprise, the familiar scenario of a small private company making significant strides in an industry was unfolding, prompting unease among the giants in a similar line of business. The threat of rising competition posed a challenge to their established reputations, compelling these larger entities to consider strategic measures to maintain their market dominance. In this case, one such titan in the field, the Genetic Metabolic Engineering Corporation Ltd, renowned for its expertise spanning every existing medical breakthrough, had taken the decision to approach the rival company, Diet Control Ltd, with an enticing offer to acquire its operations.

Representing the corporate behemoth, Mr Ashley Khanna was dispatched to secure an appointment and initiate negotiations with Nadia. The meeting was scheduled at Nadia's office situated in Aughton, in the north-west of the UK. The intent behind this proposed acquisition was to amalgamate the prowess of both companies, leveraging their combined strengths in the realm of medical innovations and solutions. The proposed acquisition held the promise of aligning resources and expertise for a more significant impact on the global landscape of healthcare and innovation.

Mr Khanna stood at the threshold, politely knocking on Nadia's office door. With a composed demeanour, Nadia swiftly opened the door, greeting him with a warm yet cautious smile, gesturing for him to enter.

"Good afternoon, Mr Khanna. Please come in," Nadia said welcomed him in, motioning toward a seat across from her desk. She maintained a poised stance, her expression a blend of curiosity and guarded anticipation as she prepared to engage in the pivotal conversation about the future of her company. "Please take a seat."

Keith was also present in the meeting room. "Meet my husband, Keith!" Nadia said introducing him.

Keith rose from his seat to shake hands with Mr Khanna. "Please sit down," he offered courteously. "So, how can we assist you, Mr Khanna?" Keith enquired.

"I assume you're familiar with my company?" Mr Khanna asked.

"Yes, quite well versed. Genetic Metabolic Engineering Corporation Ltd dominates the entire earth, akin to how a black hole rules outer space," Nadia responded with a soft smile.

"That's quite the description," remarked Mr Khanna.

"So, what's on your mind, Mr Khanna?" Keith asked.

"Five hundred million," Mr Khanna stated.

At the mention of this figure, Keith was taken aback.

Nadia had anticipated a high figure but not to that extent. "Is that for complete ownership of my company?" she enquired.

"Well, we don't selectively pick parts of companies. It's either a hundred per cent acquisition or nothing," Mr Khanna explained.

Keith stood up. "Mr Khanna, may I speak with my wife for a moment?"

"Yes, certainly. Would you like me to step out of the room?"

"No, sir, please stay. We'll step outside," Keith suggested. He stood up, leaned in towards Nadia and whispered, "Nadia, I'm hearing a colossal amount of money for what you've created. What do you want to do?" he asked, looking baffled.

"Keith, let's step outside," suggested Nadia.

They exited the room, and Keith leaned in to ask Nadia, "What are you waiting for? Five hundred million, Nadia? Let it go…"

Nadia was a resilient individual, adept at navigating through challenges. She reasoned with Keith: "Only I know what has gone into this business, Keith. Let me handle it. Stay calm and listen. Please don't overreact. I have 20,000 client bookings in advance, with an average operating cost of £1,500 per customer. This totals a forecast of £300,000,000 within the next two years. Consider this: he's buying it for £500 million, and within five years, he'll recoup that investment. I believe we should ask for more. Perhaps sell fifty per cent of the company at that price and retain the other fifty per cent for ourselves."

"But he clearly stated they don't partner up," Keith reminded her.

"Well, in that case, I'm not interested in selling," said Nadia.

"Oh, Nadia, I don't know. This kind of money could buy you anything you want in this lifetime, and you want more," said Keith, massaging his forehead in frustration.

"Keith, can £500 million buy me the whole earth?" Nadia questioned.

Keith felt completely bewildered by her response and shrugged off his comment with a slight smile directed at her. They re-entered the room. Mr Khanna looked at them and asked, "So… what's the decision?" He rubbed his hands together, hoping for a positive response.

"Mr Khanna, I'm actually quite perplexed about what to convey to you. I always thought that people buy and sell commodities at a set price, not golden geese. If it were my house you wanted to purchase, I might have sold it at the asking price, knowing I could always acquire a better one next. However, this business is something very dear to my heart, a gem that continues to shine."

"So, what's your plan?" asked Mr Khanna.

"I am willing to sell fifty per cent of my business for £500 million," said Nadia.

"Seriously! Are you being sarcastic now? I just mentioned that we don't buy shares in businesses, and here you are offering half of your company? Five hundred million pounds is a significant amount of money. Do you want to reconsider your thoughts?" said Mr Khanna.

"Mr Khanna, when an entrepreneur embarks on establishing a new business, with the amount of hard work and countless sleepless nights they sacrifice to make it a success, it's priceless. I suppose I'm not ready to sell a hundred per cent of my business just yet," said Nadia.

"Genetic Metabolic Engineering Corporation Ltd does not appreciate competition in the market, Mrs Begum."

Mr Khanna appeared visibly disappointed with Nadia's decision. He rose from his seat and stated, "Well, the offer is on the table, it's open. If you ever change your mind, here's my card."

"Okay, nice meeting you. It's unfortunate we couldn't agree on a deal today," Nadia responded. "And yes, I will get in touch should I decide to sell it as a whole. Okay, catch you later then," she said as she walked him to the door, whereupon she heard loud noises and gunshots.

"What's going on in your facility? A gunshot came from there. You guys had better go and check it out," said Mr Khanna, before making his escape from the trouble himself.

Nadia looked at Keith, utterly bewildered.

Keith and Nadia hurried into their facility to find seven armed men wearing balaclavas storming the building, kicking and punching her workforce, forcing them to lie on the ground.

"What's happening here?" she shouted out, trying to get the attention of the main gang member.

"Hands up, both of you!" said the gang member, pointing the gun at Nadia and Keith.

"What!" yelled Nadia.

The gunman fired a bullet and threatened, "Next one's in your head. Put your hands up!"

"Nadia! Put your hands up," Keith urged, doing the same.

"Now say what you want to say," demanded the gunman.

"What do you want? Why are you doing this?" asked Nadia.

"Are you in charge of this facility?" enquired the gunman.

"Yes, I am," confirmed Nadia.

"Come here," called the gunman. Nadia walked closer. "Hand me the working blueprint of your obesity nanochip," demanded the gunman.

"What! What are you on about?" said Nadia, attempting to grab the gun from him. The gunman pulled the gun forcefully, but she refused to let go. He then tugged sideways, causing her to be propelled off the ground. He spun her around several times like a hammer thrower, compelling Nadia to release her hold. She was thrown and landed a few metres away, crashing into a steel filing cabinet hurting her nose and head.

Keith leapt into action before the gunman could regain composure from the centrifugal force of the throw. "You bastard!" he yelled, jumping on the gunman, delivering punches and kicks. However, the bandits were professionally trained, and a few punches here and there barely scratched his thick skin. The gunman fought back, landing punches and using the butt of the gun to knock Keith down onto the floor. He struggled to get back up, blood streaming from a severe head wound.

Pori Moni

*

Meet Pori Moni, a warrior in the guise of a fifteen-year-old girl, emanating strength and resilience. She bears South Asian origins and an intriguing blend of human form and artificial intelligence. Her attire, a fusion of traditional warrior garments, conceals an exceptional feature: an armadillo-like outer skin layer moulded seamlessly onto her flesh. This armour possesses an extraordinary ability to repel bullets, mimicking her natural skin tone while providing comprehensive body protection. Crafted meticulously from millions of micro shells, this extraordinary body layer boasts the strength of diamonds yet moves as fluidly as silk. Its concealed nature is revealed only when subjected to a perfect white light passing through a prism, displaying spectral colours between orange and yellow, harmonising flawlessly with her complexion.

Under specific conditions of sunlight at 590 nanometres in wavelength and a mist-filled atmosphere with the sun positioned behind an observer, glimpses of this concealed body armour briefly flash into visibility. However, the rarity of this occurrence often dismisses such sightings as mere illusions borne from peculiar light phenomena, never to repeat the spectacle.

Over the top of this remarkable armour, she wears an intricately designed blouse inspired by Indian fashion, embellished with gold sequins and vibrant sapphire stones. Her attire is completed with a short velvet skirt accented with silver steel, circular, flower petal borders, ingeniously doubling as lethal throwing disks. Strapped onto her back are two swords holstered in gold sequins and stones. A pair of twin roses tattoo graces the exposed skin on her back while gold nose and ear jewellery adorn her with a unique male and female figurine design serve as a poignant tribute to her parents, Doyal and Rahila. Her right arm carries a set of bangles, capable of transforming into lethal mini arrows when pulled off the wrists.

The left arm boasts a golden electronic wristband projecting illuminated 3D objects, from images to holograms. Additionally, a reflective mirror band near her elbow serves as both a fashion accessory and a weapon, strategically blinding adversaries with directed sunlight.

Her outfit is completed with knee-high, brown leather boots, adorned with fur-decorated bands, and equipped with knife pockets on the outer sides. Her hair, styled in three plaits secured by golden tips, presents an extraordinary centrepiece in the form of a live rope-like plait at the centre back. This unique plait is a weapon in itself, featuring graphene hair fibres and a tip that can switch between an arrowhead and a retractable blade. Intricately designed for combat, it offers neural connectivity and a micro-camera granting a 270-degree rear field of vision, aiding her in monitoring blind spots. This multifaceted warrior embodies a balance between tradition and advanced technology, ready to conquer any challenge that comes her way. She stands as another marvel, a testament to Nadia's technological breakthrough, of which only she holds the secret.

Rushing into the laboratory, she immediately sprang into action as the chaotic scene unfolded. Witnessing Nadia thrown into a filing cabinet, she swiftly lifted her, her instincts propelling her into rapid response mode. In a split second, she hurled a concealed disk from her skirt towards the assailants who had incapacitated Keith. The deadly projectile sliced through the air, finding its mark with unnerving precision, severing the throat of one of the assailants. As the wounded gunman crumpled to the ground, clutching his profusely bleeding wound and dropping his weapon in agony, a hail of gunfire targeted her.

With astonishing agility, she moved like a whirlwind, executing a series of lightning-fast somersaults toward the injured man lying prone. In a swift and seamless motion, she relieved him of his firearm, swiftly evading the incoming gunfire. Her expert marksmanship came into play as she retaliated, efficiently neutralising the remaining assailants. Her shots were precise, directed primarily toward their heads and necks, swiftly isolating them and preventing any further threat with calculated accuracy.

Facing the two remaining gang members, she aimed at one, only to find her gun depleted of ammunition. A voice echoed from behind, and she swiftly activated her cutting-edge rear-view camera, a technological ace incorporating an array of imaging detectors. With the ability to transition from infrared to X-ray, this device provided her with comprehensive views, even through human flesh. She stood still scanning the assailant with her camera, it revealed a trove of personal information – height, build, estimated weight – all in stunning high definition. He steadily closed the distance, gun raised.

As he advanced, closing in and pointing the firearm at her back, she swung her unique live centre plaits. These exceptional strands extended, seizing the gun from the assailant's grasp. With a swift motion, she flung the gun over her head, expertly catching it in front of her. In the same fluid movement, her live plaits transformed into lethal weapons, slashing through the air and cutting through the assailant's neck, cleanly severing his head from his body as he leapt toward her. Her swift and calculated manoeuvre swiftly neutralised the threat.

Startled and bewildered, the remaining attacker watched in horror as his comrade's head unexpectedly tumbled to the floor, followed by the rest of his body. Confusion painted across his face, the brief and incomprehensible sight of his partner seemingly dancing before a sudden, inexplicable demise left him frozen in shock and disbelief.

"What the fuck just happened there?" he bellowed, his voice laced with bewilderment. Before he could react and pull the trigger to take out Pori, he found himself incapacitated, struck by shots fired from Pori Moni that hit both his arms, rendering him completely ineffective.

"Debbie, would you mind cleaning up this mess?" she asked one of the team. "And everyone, listen up. Keep this incident within our four walls. All of our reputations are at stake here. We need to determine the source of this threat as our priority. Rest assured, all of you are safe working here," said Pori Moni, providing reassurance.

Pori rushed to her injured Aunty Nadia. "Mum, I'm here. I've got everything under control," she reassured her, concern evident in her voice.

"Ah… Where is your Uncle Keith?" Nadia asked, her voice wavering with distress.

"He's here, and he's okay," Pori responded, calling out, "Henry!" Urgently summoning him, she directed, "Take Uncle Keith for treatment." Henry swiftly arrived with a stretcher, assisted by a few colleagues to carefully attend to Keith's needs.

Pori assisted her aunty and settled her in the treatment room, ensuring she was comfortable. As she sat beside her, Nadia spoke with emotion in her voice.

"Pori, today you've shown your true self, my child. I am completely satisfied with how I've raised you. You did an incredible job. If you hadn't arrived on time today, this could have been our last day alive."

"Mum, I came in with some Indian sweets in celebratory mood because my secondary education is complete and I've secured a place at the Elementary Engineering College to start my studies next year. This visit was unplanned," Pori explained, sharing her achievements and the purpose behind her unexpected presence.

"Pori, you know the phrase we use in Bengali language, '*Rakhe Allah mare Keah*', which means if 'God wishes to keep someone alive, nothing can kill them?' He sent you as an angel of salvation to keep us alive," Nadia said, acknowledging the belief in divine intervention and Pori's timely role in preserving their lives.

"Who were these people, Maa?" Pori enquired, seeking more information about the attackers.

"I don't know. I never dreamt that this would happen here. They were asking for the blueprint of my obesity nanochip, intending to decode it and use it to their advantage. They must be from a rival competitor," pondered Nadia. "But who could that be? I hope this attack was not orchestrated by that Genetic Metabolic Engineering Corporation Ltd under Mr Khanna. He offered to buy our company, and I refused to sell," Nadia revealed, indicating a potential motive behind the attack on their establishment.

"It must be them, Maa," said Pori. Just then, a text message notification sounded on Pori's phone. She quickly checked the message which read, "Are you still coming?"

"Oh no, Maa, I had an appointment I forgot to attend. I must go now. Isabella will take care of you and make sure you're well in no time," Pori hurriedly assured her, realising her oversight and the urgency of her commitment.

"Hey, don't be too late."

"Okay, Maa, and don't forget to distribute the sweets or they will go bad."

"Okay, see you later," said Nadia.

*

Pori found herself standing at her front door, attempting to unlock it with the familiar click of her key, only to encounter an unexpected resistance. "Oh goodness," she murmured softly under her breath, slightly flustered by the unforeseen hurdle. Resorting to the doorbell, she gently pressed it, prompting a quick response from the household's occupants.

Inside, Adil and Savannah, a delightful pair of eleven-year-old fraternal twins, were engrossed in their individual activities. Adil, lost in the world of a captivating video game, was navigating through virtual landscapes, while Savannah displayed her musical prowess as she meticulously practised on an electronic piano. Their attention was briefly diverted as they caught sight of Pori's familiar face on the doorbell monitor.

"Adil, please go and open the door!" she shouted to her brother.

Adil, seemingly disinterested, disregarded her plea. "No, why don't you go?" he replied, paying little heed to his sister's request.

Pori, feeling a tinge of impatience, rang the doorbell repeatedly in quick succession.

Savannah, picking up on the urgency, swiftly dashed downstairs and unlatched the door.

"What took you so long, Savannah?" enquired Pori, somewhat puzzled by the delay.

"I asked Adil to come, but he refused," explained Savannah, expressing her frustration at her brother's indifference.

"Does he ever listen to anything?" Pori wondered aloud. "Where is Grandma? Have you both had your meals yet?"

"She went over to the main house. And yes, Grandma left food for you in the fridge," Savannah informed Pori.

"Alright. You go and continue with your piano practice. I need to freshen up as I have a college party later today," said Pori, swiftly planning her schedule for the day.

"Why did you put on your Wonder Woman outfit in the first place?" Savannah enquired, curious about Pori's choice of attire.

Savannah's question prompted a moment of reflection for Pori, triggering a flashback to the specific reason behind her choice of the Wonder Woman outfit. It was a day when she initially left the house with the intention of visiting Nadia at her laboratory to discuss plans for celebrating her secondary school graduation party. However, a few hundred yards away from home, a sudden intuition or feeling crept in, causing her to reconsider her attire.

Her gut feeling strongly suggested that something unfavourable might happen, prompting her to swiftly return home and switch her clothing to her 'Eco Warrior' outfit.

"I had a premonition that something wasn't right, that's why," she replied to Savannah, her explanation reflecting the intuitive sense that guided her decision.

Pondering over the sequence of events and her intuitive foresight, Pori couldn't help but wonder, *Does this mean I have some sort of special power to know things before they happen?* The idea of precognition or having a sixth sense lingered in her thoughts, prompting a contemplation about the possibility of possessing an extraordinary ability.

Removing her skirt and leaving her invisible body suit on, Pori opted for a stylish and elegant party dress. After applying some makeup, she picked up her handbag and made her way to Adil and Savannah's room.

"Both of you, behave yourselves while you're home alone!" Pori called out. "Savannah, my dear sister, would you mind coming downstairs to double-lock the door from inside until Grandma returns?"

"Yes, Pori," Savannah acknowledged, accompanying Pori downstairs to secure the front door.

"Savannah my dear, pay attention. Take care of Adil. Despite being twins, you've observed the disparities in him, haven't you?" Pori gently reminded her sister, hinting at Adil's unique traits.

"Indeed, I'm aware, Pori. Boys are often said to be born with a 'listening disorder', known for their mischievous, disorderly and sometimes aggressive tendencies, aren't they?" Savannah playfully teased Pori, echoing the common stereotype often associated with boys.

With a smile on her face, Pori continued on her way. A little while later, she arrived at the venue where Year 11 pupils had gathered for an end-of-year school leavers' celebratory party. Upon entering, she was warmly welcomed by her friends Amie and Jusna.

"Hello, Pori! You're a bit late, but you're excused. Give me a hug!" exclaimed Amie, warmly welcoming Pori.

Pori embraced both her friends and then made her way to

the soft drinks and snacks counter. The hall bustled with pupils engaged in various activities, chatting about school terms, upcoming holidays and the usual everyday gossip. Amid the chatter, a voice could be heard from the stage.

"Hey, isn't that Steven?! What's he doing at our college?" Pori asked. Steven was someone Pori knew from the dance classes she attended in her spare time.

"I must admit, he's quite attractive. I suppose Samantha hired him to entertain us all?" Jusna commented.

"Oh really? I didn't know he performs at parties," Pori remarked.

"Yeah, he's good-looking, Jusna. I feel like going and asking him out," Amie said.

"Hey, both of you, don't get too excited. He's already taken," Pori smiled knowingly.

As the music began, Steven glanced at Pori and signalled for her to come up on stage.

"What, are you crazy! No," she signalled back, using sign language.

"Ladies and gentlemen, for this song, I need a partner, and the best dancer I see here is Pori Moni from Step to Step dance school in Aughton," Steven declared. Pori looked back, completely taken aback by the unexpected spotlight on her.

Silently miming her frustration with an expletive, Pori found herself in a predicament when the crowd began chanting her name – "Pori! Pori! Pori!" With no option but to participate, she reluctantly joined the dance contest.

Dance and Song Dedicated to Pori Moni

Steven:
Pori… Pori… Pori Moni, half-winged angel in disguise, ah…
My charm for you, no disguise, solely to bridge the skies, ah…
Your gaze, like poetry, makes me lose my mind, ah…
Falling deeper, under your spell, leaving all doubts behind, ah…

Pori:

I offer my heart, my soul, my essence, all for you, ah…

Beauty, intellect, devoted to your view, ah…

In this moment's light, we find our way, ah…

Gazing at you, I see beyond, to where our charm may sway, ah…

Steven:

Pori Moni, in your eyes, I see the stars align,

In your embrace, our souls intertwine.

Together we dance, under moonlit skies,

Our charm story, written in the night's reprise.

Steven:

In the tapestry of fate, our paths entwine,

Two souls united, in charm's grand design.

With each heartbeat, our charm defines,

Pori Moni, forever yours and mine.

Group:

Pori… Pori… Pori Moni, angel in earthly form, ah…

Our charm transcends, through calm and storm, ah…

In your presence, I find my home, ah…

Together forever, never to roam, ah…

The dancing and singing concluded with Steven and Pori embracing intimately after their captivating duo performance, entertaining all the pupils in the college. The audience felt the reverberations of their act and responded with a cheerful round of applause for Pori and Steven.

*

Over the eleven years since her relocation to the United Kingdom, Nadia has been a catalyst for entrepreneurial growth in Bangladesh.

Establishing numerous enterprises across the country, the majority of these ventures have stemmed from her flagship company, One Planet Alpha Ltd (OPAL). This holding entity not only controls various subsidiaries but has also played a pivotal role in their proliferation. Under her leadership, these companies have multiplied extensively, driving financial research endeavours, groundbreaking scientific progress and innovative developments aimed at tackling pressing issues. These initiatives encompass a wide array of critical concerns, including advancements in medical research, the development of renewable energy sources, the implementation of flood prevention programmes, improvements in water supply and purification, as well as other significant technological breakthroughs. Her visionary contributions have reshaped the landscape of various sectors, propelling advancements that address pressing societal and environmental challenges in Bangladesh.

Frequently undertaking brief visits to Bangladesh, her primary aim is to extend her influence and renown through acts of charity and philanthropic initiatives. Engaging in a multitude of ethical projects across the nation, she actively supports individuals, entrepreneurs and small-scale enterprises, fostering their development to invigorate economic progress and alleviate poverty. Her involvement extends to providing funding for advocacy groups, think tanks and policy research organisations, aiming to shape legislation and instigate positive social transformations. Her commitment to these ventures reflects a dedication to uplifting communities and driving substantial change in Bangladesh, elevating both societal welfare and economic prospects.

Aysha Khanom, a close friend and a significant stakeholder in Nadia's group of companies, plays a pivotal role in cultivating a culture of popularity among the people of Bangladesh. Understanding that winning the favour of the populace is crucial for Nadia's pathway to leadership, Aysha has dedicated substantial resources to this cause. She has invested millions of Bangladeshi taka in strategic advertising initiatives, harnessing the influence of key figures such as social media influencers, TV hosts and radio presenters. Their role is to magnify and eloquently disseminate information about Nadia, effectively saturating the public with repeated messages about her multifaceted progress and remarkable philanthropic aspirations.

Through an extensive and persistent advertising campaign, Aysha has successfully propagated the narrative of Nadia's achievements, effectively turning around the perception of the majority of the population. This concerted effort has led to a significant swell in support for Nadia's vision for the country and its people. The landscape is adorned with posters and placards featuring Nadia's image and the slogan 'Joy for our great philanthropist Nadia', visible across high streets, shopping malls and street fixtures. Nadia has transcended being an individual to become a veritable brand, largely due to Aysha's strategic and comprehensive promotional efforts.

*

At the headquarters of Genetic Metabolic Engineering Corporation Ltd, Mr Ashley Khanna meticulously reviewed the footage depicting the recent incident at Nadia's laboratory. The sequence had been diligently captured and relayed back to his office for analysis. The recording revealed an astonishing scenario: a solitary female figure efficiently neutralising a group of seven highly trained assailants in a matter of mere minutes.

"Who is this girl?" he exclaimed, seeking to enquire further. "She is an incredibly skilled fighter. Who could she be?"

"We have no information about her, sir," the CCTV operative reported. "She seemingly emerged out of nowhere and vanished after swiftly neutralising all our men."

"How is this possible? Those fighters were among the elite, and she effortlessly subdued them like a knife slicing through a watermelon," Mr Khanna exclaimed. "I want to uncover more about her, no matter the cost," he ordered.

*

Pori and Steven took a leisurely stroll after their performance at the college party, meandering along the pavement of a bustling highway, making their way to the nearby local funfair, engaged in conversation as they walked.

"Pori, I've heard your mum comes from a traditional Indian family, quite strict. Does she mind that you're out with me today?" Steven enquired.

"Oh, definitely," Pori replied with a chuckle. "I told her I was going out with my friend Jusna. If she finds out I'm hanging out with you, she'll have my head. She's strict about no relationships with boys until I'm sixteen. And if I accidentally form any kind of bond with a boy, she wants me to bring him in front of her so she can put him under her interrogation microscope," she said, grinning.

"What!" Steven exclaimed, clearly taken aback by what he had just heard.

"Yeah, that's how protective she is, a proper nuclear mum," Pori continued. "She's possessed by science but also madly passionate about improving the lives of others. All she earns goes into charitable causes. She can't even afford a decent car for herself but readily donates millions of pounds for the benefit of others," Pori explained.

"She's a true philanthropist – wealthy yet selflessly dedicated to the wellbeing of others," Steven remarked.

"Does a single word exist to portray an individual who demonstrates equal generosity and care towards both animals and humans?" enquired Pori.

"I'm not sure," replied Steven.

They stepped into a games tent. Steven engaged in a shooting game in an attempt to win a cowboy hat, but unfortunately failed with each attempt.

Pori noticed a kickball stand with the ball suspended from a holder six feet high. "Come on, I'll get you a present. Last time, I scored infinity on that. Let's see if my strength is still up for the challenge," she said.

"Sure," replied Steven.

"What's the prize for this game?" Pori asked the kickball operator.

"You get a universal fit waist belt," the operator replied.

"Alright, let's give it a shot," Pori said determinedly. She composed herself and launched an assault on the hanging ball, employing her skilled high kicks and powerful punches, achieving an infinity score once more. However, in the midst of her kicks, she noticed someone peering in from outside. Her instincts alerted her to something suspicious based on the expression on the stranger's face.

Quickly seizing her victorious belt, she handed it to Steven and urgently advised him to leave as she discerned that someone was spying on them, potentially posing a threat.

"Who are they?" Steven enquired.

"Not sure, but I had trouble with them the other day," replied Pori.

"I can help protect you. Let me stay with you," offered Steven.

"No, absolutely not, you go," Pori insisted firmly.

She circled the area where she had spotted the intruder, but he was nowhere to be seen.

She dashed to the back and witnessed the attacker severely beating Steven with a pole. Without hesitation, she rushed in, grabbing the assailant by his hip, physically wrenching him off balance and forcefully flinging him several metres away. He stumbled multiple times before finally coming to a stop on the ground.

"Steven, are you alright?" she asked, gazing into his eyes, noticing the blood from his mouth and nose. He was not in good shape.

"You son of a bitch!" she said turning to the attacker, wanting to kick his ass. The enemy turned and fired at her using a hand-held gun. She launched herself towards him, dodging all the shots, grabbing the gun, and punching, blocking and defending herself. After a few minutes of intense tactical exchanges, two more super fighters with martial arts expertise caught her off guard. She received a few blows as a result, and her mouth began to bleed. Unable to use her full potential to kill in front of the public, she did a runner instead. The attackers followed her to a quiet underpass where she stopped and fought back aided by her super power, taking them down like a bunch of cards.

The body cameras worn by the adversaries were transmitting live images to Mr Khanna. Pori swiftly seized a camera, addressing it directly. She said, "Whoever you are, I'm coming for you very soon." Bringing the camera up close to one of the injured enemies, she took a chilling shot at point-blank range, causing his head to shatter, the brains spilling out. This horrifying act, captured on camera, sent a clear warning to remote viewers, illustrating the terrifying repercussions awaiting them.

Rushing back to Steven, Pori discovered an ambulance already attending to him. She discreetly left the scene, evading Security, ensuring her escape.

She made her way back home and immediately called out for her mum and Uncle Keith.

"Pori, what has happened? We're here in the kitchen," they responded, concerned.

"Mum, I was attacked by those assailants. I believe it's the same group that caused trouble in the lab last week," Pori explains.

"Pori, my daughter, are you okay? Come here, let Mummy take a look," Nadia said, concerned. She grabbed the first aid kit and gently wiped the blood from Pori's lips and nose.

"It's definitely him," said Keith.

"Who, Uncle Keith?" asked Pori, curious.

"That Mr Khanna, the owner of the Genetic Metabolic Engineering Corporation Ltd," said Keith.

"Keith, what if it's not?" replied Nadia, expressing doubt.

"Nadia, it's them, those people. They operate like oligarchs, using violence, including murder, to eliminate their rivals and gain control over territory and business interests. Remember when he said his company doesn't like competition in the market? What did he mean by that?" Keith responded, connecting the dots.

"Mum, give me this guy's address. I'm going to take him down," said Pori determinedly.

"Pori, let's think. Why did they come after you today?"

"Because they wanted revenge, Mum. They were wearing body cams, feeding footage back to their base. Whoever is behind this is watching our every move. We need to take action," Pori explained urgently.

"Pori, don't rush things, give me a minute," Nadia said calmly. She took a moment to ponder and then dialled her office number. After a few rings, someone answered. "Hello, put me through to the CCTV room," she requested.

"Okay, ma'am," responded the reception operator.

"Hi, Neal, could you send over the photo of the person we met with last Tuesday at 3pm. Thanks."

"Okay, ma'am," Neal responded before hanging up.

Nadia sat with her elbows on the table, head resting on her palms, closed her eyes and took deep breaths.

"What's the worry, Mum?" said Pori, concerned.

"Pori, give me a moment alone. I need to think about how to orchestrate a move that's both sensible and intimidating. I don't want to risk my reputation over a small issue like this."

"Okay, Mum. Give me a shout once you're done," said Pori before leaving.

"Pori, Michelle cooked some delicious roast chicken, Indian style. Go and eat some," said Nadia.

Nadia's phone received a text message. While Pori went to the washroom, Keith moved closer to Nadia, taking a seat beside her. He also sat, with his hand over his mouth, his arm resting on the armchair, lost in thought.

"That's it!" said Nadia.

Keith, catching her attention, said, "What! What!"

"I didn't think the time would come this early. I was hoping for Pori to reach eighteen, but whatever needs to be done, it has to be done. It's time to test Pori's capabilities," Nadia remarked.

"Nadia, just let it go. She's still a child," Keith said.

"But they're not going to let us go easily, are they?" Nadia replied.

"Let's hire a few mercenaries to do this job. Don't send Pori," reasoned Keith.

"Keith, I am her mother. Don't tell me what to do. My heart sinks at the thought of putting my daughter's life on the line, knowing she may get hurt," she said in a grieving tone.

"If you're such a loving mother, why are you choosing her? No mother would do that," Keith remarked.

Nadia ignored Keith.

"Pori," Nadia called.

"Coming, Mum! Yes?" responded Pori.

"Check all your protective gear for any deficiencies, defects or tears. Mum intends to send you on an abduction mission," Nadia said to Pori.

*

Nadia, committed to abstaining from causing harm, has ingeniously developed an additional microchip named 'Mind-Altering V1'. This minuscule, biotechnological marvel, measuring a mere millimetre in thickness and occupying a compact 3mm squared, carries the potential to dramatically reshape human thought processes. Collaborating closely with Anurak Chun-Chieh, a computer scientist, she has engineered a revolutionary transmitter capable of modifying human memory. This chip can be discreetly implanted beneath the skin, snugly positioned behind the neck, possessing the remarkable flexibility to bend, twist and mould, akin to silicon.

Primed with the capacity to preload diverse information, this invention can mislead or elevate an individual's intellectual prowess. Whatever data the chip assimilates becomes an inherent augmentation of the wearer's cognitive abilities. Initially intended to assist individuals with dyslexia and dementia in surmounting their learning, remembering and articulation challenges, Nadia has guarded the chip's complete potential until now. This technology is an influential tool capable of swaying even powerful figures, such as political leaders, to alter their course.

Today marks a significant moment as Nadia utilises this groundbreaking device to convey a message directly to Mr Khanna. The message explicitly advises against provoking conflicts with her and her associates, instead encouraging Mr Khanna to engage with Nadia for a potential acquisition offer of £1 billion for her company, Diet Control Ltd. This discreet yet potent directive underscores the substantial influence and leverage Nadia wields with this innovation.

She prepares Pori Moni for an assault on Mr Khanna. The plan is when Mr Khanna finishes work and heads to his car to go home, she will follow him. When he is in the car placing the keys into the ignition, she will open the back door, get in, hold a gun to the back of his neck and utter the words, "I want all your money or you are a sitting dead man." She will inject a shot of tranquilliser into him, making him unconscious. She will then use this microchip insertion gun to shoot a chip into the nape of his neck. She will ransack his car's glove box to make it look as though the offender was looking for valuables and just leave him lying on his seat. Half an hour later he will regain consciousness and think he got robbed, but will carry on going about his daily chores.

"Pori Moni, as you embark on your inaugural assignment beyond the realm of military training, proceed with a discerning and measured approach, my dear," conveyed Nadia.

"Mother, that statement isn't accurate. I've executed numerous abductions on real targets in the style of an assassin. Please don't worry, I am well trained for this task and I assure you, I will handle it proficiently," responded Pori.

Nadia then decided to permit Pori to proceed on her path and prepare for the mission. With both palms together, she touched her forehead in a meditative gesture. "God, please ensure the success of this operation. Amen," she whispered.

Dressed in her motorbike suit, Pori made her way to the headquarters of the Genetic Metabolic Engineering Corporation Ltd. As she arrived, she found herself amid a multitude of security personnel, a testament to the intense security in place. This was where she aimed to locate the suspect, Mr Khanna. Disguised as a busking girl, she assumed the persona of a guitarist, seated against the railings, strumming delicate musical notes she had learned during her schooling. Hours passed until she finally spotted the man leaving the building. Swiftly packing up, she made her way to her motorbike.

As the gentleman departed from the secure compound, he soon became aware that he was being followed. In an attempt to evade her, he accelerated, prompting Pori to also increase her speed. Catching up with him, she skilfully deployed a miniature suction-type tracking device onto his vehicle, emitting a slight noise in the process. In a desperate bid to shake her off, the man began driving erratically, weaving from left to right, causing his car's wheels to screech loudly in a flurry of evasive manoeuvres.

Despite the danger, Pori overtook him and approached his window. Lifting her visor, her striking red lips formed a smile as she uttered, "What are you doing, sir? That's too dangerous." With a serene yet pointed expression, she went on her way, allowing Mr Khanna to relax his speed to a legal pace and continue on his route.

Pori's task was far from finished. She made her way to a petrol station and patiently waited for the tracker device she had planted on Mr Khanna's car to cease moving. Taking a moment to refresh herself, she then proceeded to the location where the car had been parked – a grand mansion with a few vigilant guard dogs on patrol. Employing her tranquilliser gun once more, she expertly subdued these dogs before they could bark and alert the estate. Swiftly, she entered the premises and extracted the syringe from the now unconscious dogs to conceal any evidence of her presence, meticulously ensuring she left no trace behind.

Pori clambered onto the balcony and located Mr Khanna in his bedroom, preparing for bed. She carefully aimed and fired a tranquilliser dart through a small gap in his window, striking his lower backside. It was a minuscule dart, barely larger than a dressmaker's pin. Startled by the sudden pricking sensation, Mr Khanna jumped up, thinking he had sat on something sharp, only to discover the tiny pin. He jokingly remarked about his wife potentially using such pins on her multitude of outfits and that she must have left one here by mistake. Unbeknownst to him, the pin administered a sedative, causing him to pass out after a few minutes.

Entering his room, Pori implanted the mind-altering microchip at the base of his skull and exited without leaving a trace. The next morning, Mr Khanna woke up feeling normal and continued his routine without any apparent side effects. Although the assault didn't proceed as initially planned, the mission had been successfully accomplished, which was what truly mattered.

*

Nadia quietly entered Pori's room the next morning, finding her asleep. Observing Pori's peaceful rest, Nadia refrained from disturbing her, understanding that Pori had likely spent the entire night executing the mission to sedate Mr Khanna. Nadia left her to sleep, providing her with the rest she deserved after the arduous task.

Nadia headed to the kitchen to prepare breakfast, and Keith joined her. She served breakfast and casually remarked, "I'm pretty sure the operation has been successful because my dear daughter is still asleep. That means the job's done." A smile graced her face as she shared her confidence with Keith.

"Well done, Nadia. Finally, we can live a free life now. Yes, darling, give me a kiss."

"Mum, Savannah took my headphones and broke them!" fumed Adil.

"Adil, listen to Mummy. No more playing games, okay? You must concentrate on reading and writing, my dear son," said Nadia.

"Dad," Adil turned to his father after not getting a favourable response from his mother.

"Don't worry, son. Dad will get you another pair. Enjoy life, this age will never return," said Keith reassuringly.

"Keith, being too lenient with his behaviour isn't wise. Savannah can create beautiful music on her piano. Can he do the same?" asked Nadia, noticing he was consistently absorbed in his game console, learning nothing but violence.

"Come on, Nadia, give the boy a chance to play," said Keith.

"I am deeply concerned about the rapid rise of a culture of disobedience in our society here in the UK, Keith. In Bangladesh our upbringing instilled discipline at home, reinforced by teachers at school. As a result, we grew resilient to harsh words from our parents and teachers. The wisdom of our mentors holds invaluable lessons that a child may not grasp until they reach a certain age. I vividly recall my father advising my brother when I was young.

"He said, 'Choose your friends very carefully in life. If you choose a bad person, you unwittingly become one. If you choose a drug abuser, you might desire the euphoria they feel after taking a dose. If you choose nothing, you stay clear of external influences around you.' These teachings are only fully understood as one matures, yet it's crucial to impart this knowledge to children before they reach that turning point. We were taught to respect our elders and endure unpleasant remarks.

"The current generation of kids seems to believe they're entitled to have things their way because they aren't subject to discipline. When they hear something they don't like, they get upset very quickly. When they see something on the internet, they want it. If you raise your voice at your kids, the neighbour reports you to social services. How can parents instil good discipline under such conditions?

"I fear that this 'nanny state' approach will render this generation incompetent, irresponsible, glued to sofas and lazy in the future."

"Mum, stop talking. I can play the piano on my game," said Adil.

"There you go, he's already telling me to stop," said Nadia. "Would you mind having all of your cereal, my one and only son? Here, Mum made it in a nice bowl today."

"Thank you, Mum," said Adil.

"Keith, I don't feel like shouting. Would you mind calling Savannah? This girl is the opposite. She's probably sitting with her piano book," said Nadia.

"Savannah!" called Keith.

"Yes, Dad…!" a voice replied from a distance.

"Your breakfast is getting cold!" yelled Keith. Savannah came and hugged her dad. "Oh, my sweetheart," said Keith.

"Here, have your cereal, Savannah," said Nadia.

"Mum, I don't like this bowl," said Savannah.

"Why, what's wrong with the bowl?"

"It's plastic. I want my usual ceramic bowl," said Savannah.

"I bought them thinking they were non-breakable and you kids would like them," said Nadia. "Okay, yours is going to charity."

Keith came and sat with his coffee, saying, "Nadia, I think you should take things easy. You seem stressed."

"I am fine, Keith," Nadia responded. "Yeah, have some of this Bengali vermicelli with pistachios," Nadia offered.

"Ahh, this looks delicious, thank you," said Keith.

"You take both kids to school. I am going to your mum's house. She would love this vermicelli dessert, soft and fluffy," said Nadia.

"Yes, sure," said Keith.

Nadia paid a visit to her mother-in-law's home next door. Over time, her mother-in-law had grown frail, reliant on a walking stick due to hip issues and no longer able to manage school runs as before. Having played a significant role in Pori's upbringing, she felt a pang of regret that she couldn't provide the same level of support to her younger grandchildren. Jonathan had passed away a few years back, leaving her dependent on Nadia's generosity for care. Nadia arranged for a part-time personal carer to attend to Sarah's wellbeing. Committed to tradition, she staunchly refused the notion of placing her elderly mother-in-law in a care home. Instead, she maintained a routine of daily visits, upholding an atmosphere of civility and love.

Nadia pressed the doorbell. Bernila, a Filipino caregiver, opened the door and warmly greeted Nadia.

"Hello, Bernila. Is everything alright here?" enquired Nadia.

"Yes, ma'am," Bernila replied.

Nadia proceeded directly to Sarah. "Hello, Mum. How are you feeling today?"

"Oh, Nadia my darling. I'm okay, a bit weak in the hip but doing fine," Sarah responded.

"Here, have some of this, your favourite vermicelli pudding," offered Nadia.

"Ahh, you made some this morning! Thank you," exclaimed Sarah, eagerly digging into the pudding as soon as Nadia placed it before her by the bedside.

"Mum, don't worry about your hip. I know you're on the NHS waiting list. Even if they give you a date soon, I believe you need a bit of time to experience real countryside. We'll travel to Bangladesh soon. It will be your first visit but it will be a remarkable one because I'm arranging a hip and knee replacement for you there. They're robotic hips and knees, and you'll be able to run with them," reassured Nadia.

"Oh, Nadia, that's so sweet of you. As long as I get relief from the aches and pains, that's all I care about. I'm not interested in running, my dear," she said with a smile.

"Okay, I will catch you later." Nadia bid her goodbye.

As Sarah finished her meal, she turned to Bernila. "I was very horrible to her when she first came, and today she is dearer than anyone to me, the most caring human being I have ever met in my life. God bless her."

*

Pori woke and came downstairs for her breakfast. Nadia entered the kitchen, having just returned from her mother-in-law's house.

"Pori, you're having breakfast. I didn't disturb your sleep, then. Did everything go well yesterday?" enquired Nadia.

"Yes, Mum, but I couldn't mentally communicate with the guard dogs there. I had to manually tranquillise them to get inside Mr Khanna's property," explained Pori.

"I need to run a diagnostic on you. Come with me to the laboratory after you finish eating," said Nadia.

"Mum, I have to go and see Steven. He got hurt the other day because of me. Some people followed me, saw Steven with me and attacked him. I owe him an apology," said Pori sombrely.

"That's fine. When you're done with him, come straight to the lab. I'll be taking your hair plait with me. Pori, no matter how good your martial art skills are, this artificial capability aiding you to reach maximum performance is just as important. Never overlook its potential," advised Nadia.

"I know, Mum. I will see you later," said Pori.

"Pori!" called Nadia, seemingly forgetting to tell her something.

"Yes, Mum?" answered Pori.

"We live in a dangerous world. Friendship with our family means danger. This is the reason I brought you up with all the necessary lifesaving training to defend yourself. Tell Steven and other friends not to get involved in your business," advised Nadia.

"Yes, Mum!" replied Pori before heading off.

*

At the hospital, Steven's mother and father were furious over what had happened to their son. They sat by his bedside, with Steven visibly covered in bandages. As Pori entered the room, Steven noticed her from the door.

"Hello," said Pori innocently to Steven's mum and dad.

"Hello," they replied. "Who are you?"

"Mum, she's a friend of mine from dance school," said Steven.

"Well, come in then." Steven's mum called Pori inside.

"I brought this for you, Steven. My mum cooked vermicelli pudding," said Pori, offering the sweet treat.

"Thank you," said Steven expressing his gratitude.

"That's very nice of you," said his mother. "What's your name?"

"Pori Moni!" she replied.

"Wow, that tastes so nice!" said Steven after sampling the vermicelli pudding.

"Mum made it this morning," Pori mentioned.

"Steven said you fought and went after those men who attacked him. You are a very brave girl!" said his dad, acknowledging Pori's courage.

"Thank you. Well, I did manage to fight one of them, but soon after, a couple more joined in and I had to do a runner. I ran away from the scene to take them away from Steven. I managed to outrun them with the help of that subway on the high road. I vanished and lost them," explained Pori.

"Do you have any idea why they would attack Steven? He's saying he'd never seen them before," said his dad.

"I don't know. I saw a guy beating Steven, and I couldn't tolerate it, so I sprang into action without thinking much," said Pori.

"So, you don't know anything about the killings?" asked his dad.

"What killings?" replied Pori in pretence.

"Please, Dad," interrupted Steven, "don't tell the police she was involved in this fight. They will implicate her into this killing unnecessarily. I told you the story so you know she cared for me at my worst."

"Don't worry, son. I am not saying anything to anyone," his dad reassured him.

"Pori, someone killed those guys who attacked Steven, and the police are looking for the killers," said his dad.

"Oh no, how sad to hear."

"Well, I had better be going, then. Get well soon, Steven," said Pori.

"I will text you, Pori, when my parents are gone," replied Steven.

"Okay, bye for now," said Pori.

"Okay, bye," responded the parents.

"Such a lovely girl," said his mother.

*

Nadia, an impassioned advocate for environmental conservation, is ceaselessly preoccupied with contemplating the world that bestowed upon her the invaluable opportunity to revel in the grandeur of life on planet Earth. For her, this planet is not merely a bestower of existence but a revered entity deserving veneration. Her unwavering dedication to mitigating carbon emissions stands resolute at the forefront of her endeavours, driven by her faith in scientific principles and compounded by personal anguish stemming from profound losses incurred due to the escalating scourge of global warming. Unwilling to witness others endure a similar plight, she meticulously scrutinises her commercial assets, uncovering an alarming carbon footprint of monumental proportions.

In her quest to ameliorate this ecological impact, she has engaged in a collaborative effort with a local net zero architecture company named Green Tech Associates Ltd. Together, they have conceived a self-sustaining edifice propelled by green hydrogen. Atop this visionary structure, hundreds of small to medium-sized wind turbines, each equipped with anemometers and wind vanes on their nacelles, are intricately arranged in series to optimise their orientation to the wind. These lightweight and interconnected turbines are designed to harness maximum energy potential, converting it through DC electrolysis into hydrogen and oxygen. The extracted hydrogen, utilised to power generators generating alternating electricity for the entire building, showcases an innovative means of sustainability.

Surplus energy is efficiently stockpiled in large liquid calcium alloy anode batteries for future use, and the excess could be traded to support others in utilising stored energy. This modern, energy-efficient marvel stands as a testament to cutting-edge technology, boasting a net-zero carbon footprint.

Within this architectural feat, Nadia's company, Diet Control Ltd, operates diligently, focusing on combating obesity on both local and international fronts by implanting appetite-controlling nanochips into patients. The unprecedented demand for these chips necessitates the building's perpetual operation, sustained solely by the renewable energy generated from the ceaseless power of the wind.

Nadia's ambitious undertaking stands as an emblem of her

unwavering commitment to environmental stewardship and technological innovation, forging a path toward a sustainable and conscientious future.

In addition to implementing this revolutionary infrastructure at her headquarters, Nadia has extended the same model to her chip-manufacturing base in Thailand. Her steadfast agent, Anurak Chun-Chieh, who initially introduced this technology, remains an integral part of her team, tirelessly dedicated to the shared cause of safeguarding planet Earth. Nadia's influence and acclaim are rapidly spreading worldwide, propelling her towards global recognition. Anurak, deeply devoted to her mission, has even affixed her portrait to his building, venerating her as the CEO, further elevating her popularity not only in Thailand but also among the neighbouring islands.

The overwhelming response to her endeavours has led to a deluge of requests to replicate this innovative technology in the design of forthcoming buildings. It appears that anything Nadia undertakes effortlessly transforms into a resounding success virtually overnight. Some individuals seem inherently fortunate or are perhaps guided by auspicious forces that aid them in achieving feats once deemed implausible. Her touch, it seems, is akin to the transformative power that turns the ordinary into the extraordinary, solidifying her reputation as a harbinger of success and a beacon of hope for a sustainable future.

*

Pori proceeded into the building, in accordance with the arrangement, to explore the AI-powered mental telepathy channel known as the Mental Telepathy Chip, designed to facilitate communication without the conventional use of senses or signals, thus enabling interaction with animals. Her path led directly to the classified section of the company, where the necessary tests could be conducted. Inside this highly confidential department, a consortium of scientists, neurologists, physicists and other specialists in neural engineering could be observed engrossed in diverse and pioneering projects.

Access to this department was exclusively limited to members of Nadia's deeply trusted and esteemed workforce. The palpable air of innovation and secrecy enveloped this space, where groundbreaking research and development unfolded, shrouded in a veil of confidentiality and restricted to a select few reliable individuals who had gained Nadia's utmost confidence.

Nadia instructed Pori to take a seat in the armchair. Robotic apparatus encased her head, conducting a comprehensive scan that detected a minuscule hair follicle fused within the connector where her external hair braid rested. The robotic mechanism purified the area, reattached her hair braid and performed a diagnostic evaluation. Upon completion of the test, the machine released Pori, who then rejoined Nadia.

"Pori, when you're connecting the central hair plait, avoid exerting any force. Let it self-attach using its AI-based electromagnetic pull, I am working on a Bluetooth functionality where the hair plait will seek its base automatically from a distance. I've updated the software and malware, integrated an anemone flower to effectively conceal the rear-view camera. Additionally, the camera lens has been enhanced to an 8k version, and the flower petals will change their colour according to your thoughts and desires. The connection process is also updated. Once you bring the hair plait within two inches of the connecting port, it should automatically seek its matching port and link up without requiring you to physically touch your head. The detachment occurs when your blood pressure normalises. Just place your hand on the flower, and it will detach onto your palm. If it doesn't release on its own, avoid pulling forcefully as it's very sensitive. It only detaches when your blood pressure is aound 112/70 mm Hg. Otherwise, it remains connected," Nadia explained.

"Alright, Mum." Pori began testing her newly fitted anemone

by thinking of different colours, and it promptly switched as she wished.

"See you at home soon," said Pori as she left the classified department.

"Okay, bye for now," replied Nadia.

*

Mr Ashley Khanna, the owner of Genetic Metabolic Engineering Corporation Ltd, maintains a perspective that delicately straddles the realms of misogyny and philogyny. His viewpoints encompass a gender-based hierarchical structure that is firmly entrenched, not in a manner of derogation, but rather rooted in ethical principles of high standing. He ardently acknowledges that every individual, irrespective of gender, inherently holds equal value and merits uniform treatment, opportunities and respect.

During his formative years, Ashley Khanna was consistently exposed to instances where females dressed provocatively, wearing excessive makeup and aiming to capture the attention of young men – ninety-eight per cent of whom purposefully leered at them. Merely two per cent gazed in genuine appreciation of their beauty. In this scenario, the female gender was unjustly disparaged. Even Mr Khanna himself grappled with navigating these lascivious thoughts during his teenage days. This realisation prompted him to understand that from adolescence until a man discovers his true love, he becomes a wayward creature trapped in a cycle of unconsciously objectifying the opposite sex.

He comprehended that he, like many others, faced challenges in overcoming these ingrained biases. This pattern persists until one matures emotionally and understands the complexities of genuine connections to a female gender. While he could maintain a platonic friendship with a woman, there was an unspoken condition that she adhered to certain boundaries, like wearing modest clothing. If she were to let her guard down, there lingered the imminent threat of a male taking advantage of her vulnerability, not necessarily in physical form, but mentally. And as we all know mental disorder leads to more sinister crime like rape and murder.

This perspective isn't rooted in animosity or an aversion towards women, nor is it about regulating or penalising women who strive for equality with men on a level playing field. It doesn't involve considering women a threat to those who believe in traditional gender roles where a woman's domain is perceived to be at home, involved in nurturing, caring and empathising. It's not about that at all. It's about recognising that females often face detriment under the influence of men during their vulnerable phase of maturation. Men are instinctively born lecherous and they will take advantage if temptation comes their way.

Mr Khanna harbours genuine appreciation for women as individuals and ardently supports their right to work, be independent and have the freedom to express themselves while securing their own financial autonomy. However, he holds reservations about women engaging in physically demanding tasks alongside men. He perceives it as a risky endeavour on various fronts. Firstly, there's the concern that she might inadvertently entice a man through her charms, leading to complications. Secondly, there's the risk that men might unconsciously develop an attraction towards her, potentially leading to the breakdown of families or relationships that he may have at the time.

From the viewpoint of someone with a misogynistic mindset, this concept is morally objectionable, holding the woman accountable for such a situation. This perspective contends that she is responsible for setting clear boundaries that should never be crossed. However, it's acknowledged that men are predisposed to cross these lines as soon as an opportunity arises.

To Ashley Khanna, the vantage point he prefers to occupy rests on the border where he perceives men and women as equally responsible. His belief is strongly influenced by his religious teachings that instruct men to avert their gaze when encountering a distracting or alluring female presence. This practice, according to his religious beliefs, is aimed at fostering modesty, exercising self-control and preventing inappropriate or lustful thoughts and actions which may eventually lead to sexual hallucinations.

Mr Khanna staunchly adheres to this viewpoint. He believes that a woman should acknowledge and respect a man's capacity to protect, provide and lead. While recognising that a woman possesses the same capabilities, he emphasises the significance of the difference in potential that a man can offer due to his physical strength, agility and endurance, which should be highly valued and acknowledged.

Dressed immaculately, perfumed to an extent to which even the nearby plug-in air freshener fell short in comparison, his son Zakir made an entrance into the dining room. Taking a seat at the table, he casually grabbed a ceramic cereal bowl, concocting a medley of cornflakes, cheerios and granola topped generously with full-fat milk, and began eating.

"What's the occasion, son? You're all perfumed and dressed as if you're off on holiday somewhere," remarked Mr Khanna.

"Dad, I can't exactly stroll into my esteemed university smelling of fried parathas, can I? I'm all set for university life," replied his son.

One might assume that a family of such affluence would have a team of household staff to manage breakfast. However, to everyone's surprise, his sister Reena and mother Farzana were found in the kitchen preparing the morning meal. With a stake in Genetic Metabolic Engineering Corporation Ltd, Mr Khanna is regarded as one of the select few prosperous individuals in the neighbourhood. However, his deliberate choice to maintain a modest lifestyle is aimed at providing his children with an upbringing akin to that of a working-class environment. This approach is intended to instil values of discipline and modesty and purity of heart in his children.

A few moments later, Farzana Khanna emerged from the

kitchen, placing a plate of parathas on the table, followed by his sister, Reena.

They gathered around and shared breakfast together. Mr Khanna glanced at Reena, who seemed barely prepared for her day at college.

"Reena, have you ever noticed why Dad seems a bit stricter with you compared to Zakir, darling? It's because you are my adorable child, a gem on my crown. Your brother is wearing this lovely perfume, hoping to catch someone's eye. But once he enters college, the scent might fade without the opposite gender really noticing. On the other hand, if you walk in wearing the same, heads will turn your way like people watch a solar eclipse. It would be like needing a shield to deflect all the attention from guys," said Mr Khanna smiling, "and you know why? Because you are a beautiful woman.

"Another important lesson today at breakfast, my daughter and son, is that to achieve success in life, family unity is key. You should always support each other, be there for one another in good and bad times, no matter what. Division weakens people, but coming together makes you strong and bold. Family is all about sharing and caring for each other," Mr Khanna emphasised.

Suddenly, he made a jerky left-to-right head movement, paused for a moment and exclaimed, "What am I even talking about here?"

"What else, your usual spiel," remarked Farzana the wife.

He shook his head once more, vigorously, and massaged his forehead.

"Hey, Farzana, there's something in my head, seriously like a string of electrical surges caused me to shake my head. I'm experiencing a sense of déjà vu," he said.

"What's going on in your head?" Farzana enquired.

"Mum, Dad's got too much going on in his head. I'm out of here. I'm leaving," Zakir said.

"Reena, why aren't you dressed for college? Finish up your meal and get going, look at the time," Mr Khanna exclaimed suddenly.

"Yes, Dad," Reena acknowledged. She finished her breakfast, took her plates to the kitchen, and then returned to collect the remaining plates.

"What are you doing? Hurry to college. I'll take care of the dishes today," insisted Mr Khanna.

The microchip implanted by Pori at the back of his head suddenly experienced a kickback, energising and triggering a change in his character and reactions.

"Are you okay?" asked Farzana.

"Yes, I'm fine. I feel extraordinary today, memories of the past floating in my mind."

"Yes, of course, I can see that. When was the last time you offered to do the washing up?" remarked Farzana.

"Well, you tell me!" He got up, took all the plates to the kitchen and began washing them.

"Are you really doing this? I can't believe it. There must have been a miraculous intervention when you jerked your head just now. Your brain seems to have come to its senses and you're doing things spot-on after so many years. You've just triggered my memory of when I first entered your house as a young bride," Farzana smiled. "Leave the washing up, I'll take care of it. You're getting late for work," she said.

"Oh, thank you. Give me a kiss," said Mr Khanna.

"What!" This intrigued Farzana. "Wow, your character has really improved." She smiled and moved closer for a kiss.

"You know what, I'm coming home early. I want to take you out to dinner," said Mr Khanna.

Farzana was absolutely flabbergasted by his charm. "Okay, I will be ready," she said, looking into his eyes. Mr Khanna gave her another kiss on the lips and went to work.

What's wrong with that man today? she wondered.

Nadia meticulously had delved into an extensive exploration of Mr Khanna before crafting the mind-altering V1 microchip. She intricately devised codes intended to interface with Mr Khanna's ventral tegmental area, a region of the brain known to evoke positive emotions related to affection and trigger the cortico-limbic networks that underpin parental feelings. The ingenious microchip adeptly identifies and interprets these cerebral activities, transmitting neurological signals via established pathways, ultimately integrating the microchip's data with the intricate neural network of the brain.

This groundbreaking accomplishment in neuroglial research involves the microchip effectively decoding and altering the perceptions inscribed upon it, thereby influencing Mr Khanna's previously ingrained misogynistic attitudes. This transformative process effectively neutralises his biased approach, fostering a newfound inclination towards expressing love and genuine regard for women.

*

Mr Khanna strode into his expansive workplace, a colossal manufacturing laboratory bustling with individuals donning clean, pristine suits. Amid the hum of activity, IT experts, designers and a myriad of other professionals diligently orchestrate the operation of cutting-edge machinery. The facility churns out semiconductors, microchips, vaccines and an array of electronic materials, each stage of production a symphony of precision.

Seated at his desk, Mr Khanna settled in and began sifting through various files. Among them, the document concerning the recent discloser, 'Purchase of Diet Control Ltd', seized his attention. Opening it, he revisited the content, including his annotations following a discussion with Nadia during his initial visit to her premises. Notably, within the file, a conspicuous note revealed the vendor's refusal of a substantial offer amounting to £500 million.

Simultaneously, the microchip implanted in his brain initiated a series of neural signals, delivering a rapid influx of data. As if guided by an unseen force, Mr Khanna received a stream of information facilitated by the microchip: details about the company's widespread popularity, the significant backlog in orders, projected forecasts for the next couple of years and the resounding global interest in the technology. This influx of data manifested within his mind akin to a vivid video advertisement, conjuring a mental visualisation of figures and statistics.

These insights prompted a re-evaluation of his earlier proposition. Moved by the nuanced and comprehensive data absorbed through the microchip, Mr Khanna reached for the phone, dialling the number for Diet Control Ltd, poised to engage in further discourse.

"Hello, Diet Control," said the operator.

"Hi, may I speak to Nadia Begum, please," requested Mr Khanna.

"May I have your name, sir?" enquired the operator.

"Mr Khanna, from Genetic Metabolic Engineering Corporation Ltd," he replied.

"Putting you through, sir. Please hold for a moment," the operator acknowledged.

"Hello, Mr Khanna. How are you, sir?" said Nadia.

"Hello, hello, Mrs Begum. I am fine. I was just contemplating your company. You were right, actually, the company has garnered a remarkable reputation and deserves a more substantial offer," acknowledged Mr Khanna.

"Oh, really! What's on your mind this time, Mr Khanna?" enquired Nadia.

"I will double my offer to £1 billion for seventy per cent ownership of the business. This entails assuming control of the company, with your share disbursed to you at regular intervals," Mr Khanna proposed.

Nadia experienced twofold delight: firstly, her mind-control microchip had functioned precisely as she had meticulously instructed it to operate; and secondly, she had achieved the financial sum she had been aiming for.

"I am delighted to learn of your recognition of the potential within my business. I gladly accept your offer, Mr Khanna. Please proceed by instructing your solicitor to commence the formal acquisition process," said Nadia.

"Of course, I'll get right on it," said Mr Khanna with evident delight.

CHAPTER 10

MECHANICAL WARFARE

Kareem	Hakim	Malik	Aysha	Rajan
Nadia	Kony	DoDo	Pori	Horse
Tiger	Sarah	Aprana	Shanaaz	Tom
Cathy	Suzy	Dave	Imtiaz	Chowdhury

Starring

Mr. Abdul Kareem – Rajan Chowdhury (Prime minister) – Kony Begum
(House maid) – DoDo Ahmed (Journalist) – Super Shadowfax (Horse)

Bangladesh, 2030. Drought engenders a myriad of calamitous
repercussions and atrocities, both directly and indirectly. In the
hamlet of Arambaria, the acute scarcity of water has wreaked
havoc, profoundly impacting not only drinking water sources but
also agricultural needs. This scarcity has starkly manifested in food
shortages, catalysing inflation and the consequential rise in prices.
Livestock face demise, escalating social tensions that burgeon into
conflicts and violence among communities. Consequently, people
are compelled to seek refuge in other regions of the country,
finding themselves amid an almost non-existent water supply.
Malnutrition and dehydration prevail, afflicting all age groups,
while the dearth of water impedes land cultivation, drastically
reducing agricultural output.

The inability to yield meaningful crops forces individuals
to traverse vast distances in search of portable water. Moreover,
farmers within this region perceive a bleak future, as insufficient
food from the disrupted supply chain leaves the elderly and infirm
in a state of starvation. Many are driven to migrate to other parts
of the country, presenting a nightmarish scenario for those who
lack an alternative to enduring the plight in Arambaria. They are
inadvertently transformed into internal refugees, subjected to a life
of turmoil within their own village.

Aysha, following Nadia's guidance, undertakes the establishment
of a new company, officially registering it with Companies House
under the trading name Humanitarian Pledge Ltd. In adherence to
this directive, she proceeds to advertise employment opportunities
for the company in the *Dhaka Tribune*, a widely read newspaper
in Bangladesh. Through this publication, she attracts numerous
candidates for managerial positions and conducts interviews,

ultimately selecting Mr Abdul Kareem as the appointed senior manager, in alignment with the directors' code of conduct.

The strategic direction of the company revolves around procuring land in the central area of Arambaria village from local landowners. The primary objective is to address the severe water scarcity afflicting the local populace by digging a ground water pump and regulating water distribution to alleviate the pressing emergency needs. Subsequently, the company plans to construct a net-zero office building, drawing inspiration from Nadia's Diet Control Ltd in the UK. However, this new structure will integrate solar panels and a new generation of latticed wind turbines, a new concept for which Nadia has sought inspiration from children's decorative folio windmills and put into practice, generating enough power to sustain one detached property.

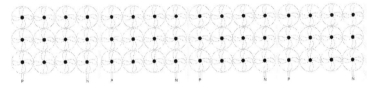

Upon the completion of the sustainable office building, the company aims to expand its humanitarian efforts by installing additional ground water pumps. These pumps will cater to the comprehensive water requirements of the region, encompassing both drinking needs and agricultural irrigation, thereby striving to provide a sustainable solution to the prevailing water crisis.

During the subsequent phase of the plan, the company aims to procure additional land and embark on the construction of self-sustainable, four-storey residential apartment blocks. The rooftops of these buildings will be purposefully designed to accommodate large water tank reservoirs, equipped with automatic rain-detecting covers which open when it rains and close when it stops, collecting an abundance of rainwater. Additionally, these rooftops will incorporate supporting structures intended for the installation of solar panels and latticed wind turbines.

As part of this endeavour, local residents will be presented with the option to exchange their current shanty-style homes and the land it sits on for contemporary, five-star-rated apartment blocks. In an effort to incentivise the transition, the company plans to offer a fifty per cent discount for those residents willing to trade in their existing houses. Furthermore, for those interested in outright purchase, a flexible payment scheme shall be available, enabling individuals to pay in instalments over a period of time. This approach aims to encourage and facilitate the community's engagement in the transition towards these modern, sustainable living spaces.

In the third phase, the company will work towards creating employment opportunities for the villagers by establishing a substantial machine hire centre. This centre will enable local residents to rent agricultural machinery, empowering them to cultivate their own land more efficiently. Additionally, the company will inaugurate milling and packaging factories, aiming to streamline the processing and distribution of the villagers' locally produced goods. This initiative not only provides employment but also facilitates the enhancement of local agricultural production.

Moving to the fourth phase, the focus shifts to the river management scheme. The Padma River faces obstruction due to excessive sediment flow originating from the Himalayas, resulting in the formation of unwanted mini-islands and sandbars. These barriers are responsible for blocking the eastern channel, subsequently causing drought conditions in Arambaria. The proposed solution involves excavating the sediments, not only providing farmers with access to new fertile soil but also enabling the uninterrupted drainage of water into the Bay of Bengal. This intervention aims to mitigate the threat posed by the blockage, fostering a more sustainable and less threatening environment for the region.

Humanitarian Pledge Ltd has managed to acquire an abundance of land in Arambaria, capitalising on the distressingly reduced land values due to the pervasive hardships caused by the ongoing drought. Despite the plummeting prices, the company is offering a fair sum to the locals in exchange for their property understanding the wisdom of give and take. This amount serves as a down payment for the new apartment blocks, accompanied by the provision of free temporary housing for the residents until the completion of the new constructions. This attractive proposition has led to an overwhelming response from Arambaria's villagers, who find the deal too enticing to decline, thereby eagerly lining up to take advantage of the offer. The company's objective is to transform the village into a habitable zone, offering luxurious residences as part of their vision for the area's development.

However, the news of this transformation reaches the ears of the more affluent middle-class citizens of the village. These individuals, relatively unaffected by the drought due to their private ground water pumps, observe the developments with a different perspective. Among them, Abdul Hakim and his family emerge, known troublemakers in the community. Abdul Hakim is the father of Abdul Malik, previously implicated in the brutal treatment of Inspector Aysha following accusations of Rahila's rape and murder. Together, father and son are mobilising to form a faction that stands in opposition to Humanitarian Pledge Ltd. Their party aims to counter the company's initiatives, posing a potential challenge to the transformative endeavours in Arambaria.

Abdul Malik is actively engaged in distributing small leaflets to the local villagers, roaming the streets with a hand-held speaker megaphone to echo his message throughout the area. His repeated announcement through the megaphone warns about the potential consequences of losing land to industrialists, emphasising the anticipated displacement of communities. The leaflets carry this message prominently, inviting the villagers to gather and learn more during the Friday congregational prayer. This alternative narrative seeks to shed light on the potential negative impacts and the obscured facets of the unfolding development in the region.

Local residents, intrigued by the perspective presented in these leaflets, fervently collect and read them, eager to comprehend the other side of the story surrounding the ongoing changes and the potential implications for their community. This action sparks a passionate interest among the villagers to grasp the deeper complexities and consequences behind the transformative initiatives led by Humanitarian Pledge Ltd.

*

This Friday, attendance at the mosque had significantly increased, drawing not only Muslims but also Hindus and Christians who assembled alongside their Muslim neighbours to hear Abdul Malik's discourse.

"Dear brothers and sisters, some of you might recognise me from the recent television news, where I was falsely accused of a crime I didn't commit, a charge that the court ultimately dismissed," Abdul Malik began. "I stand before you to caution against the dubious intentions of Humanitarian Pledge Ltd. This company's purported philanthropic facade is nothing but a ruse, a ploy to deceive and divest you of your property. The mastermind behind this enterprise seeks to disrupt and dismantle our community."

He continued, passionately expressing his concerns: "This company's real motive is to impose an industrial complex upon us, aiming to enslave us all to its will. Their plan is to rupture the social cohesion of our community. We cherish our traditional way of life.

"Imagine being confined in apartment blocks, stacked atop one another, akin to a prison system, devoid of open spaces. Such a structure threatens to corrode the very fabric of our community. Our cherished landscape will be sacrificed for more towering edifices, eradicating the open skies."

Abdul Malik went on to highlight the company's claims, stating, "They assert control over our village resources, prophesying that every individual will fall prey to their dominion. I implore you all: do not relinquish your lands to Humanitarian Pledge Ltd."

His impassioned plea resonated with the congregants, drawing attention to the potential adverse effects of the proposed changes and the encroachment on their cherished way of life, rallying them against the company's acquisition plans.

Amid Abdul Malik's impassioned speech, a member of the public rose and challenged the narrative: "If this company won't buy our plots, who else will? You?" Expressing the sentiment that this opportunity to sell their land was pivotal, the individual distanced themselves from Abdul Malik's stance, prompting a few others to follow suit and leave the gathering.

However, the majority remained, contemplating Malik's warning about potential deception. Recognising the truth in the old adage that "every dictator comes bearing a gift but leaves with treasure", they harboured concerns about the true intentions of Humanitarian Pledge Ltd. Understanding that this opportunity could be a double-edged sword, some among the gathered residents resolved to take a stand. Their decision was to initiate a peaceful protest, urging the mainstream government to intervene and halt the tender or acquisition processes proposed by the company.

This division among the community members showcased the complexity of the situation, with some believing in the potential benefits of selling their plots, while others hesitated, wary of the hidden consequences. The imminent protest represented a unified voice seeking government intervention, voicing concerns and appealing for a re-evaluation of the proposed land acquisition plans.

Addressing the individual who had expressed concerns about the potential sale of his house, Abdul Malik sought to provide clarity. "Take a moment and consider this," he began. "Have you observed the architectural plans for the construction site?" When the man admitted that he hadn't, Abdul Malik pointed out a significant detail. "We have five mosques in this village today.

Look at this plan. There's only one marked, and it's labelled as a 'learning centre', not a *masjid*. This direction signifies where this village is headed – towards Europe, do you understand?" The man remained silent, pondering Abdul Malik's perspective.

However, what Abdul Malik failed to acknowledge was that within the gathering, there were Hindu and Christian community members, albeit a smaller contingent. Their perspectives instantly gravitated toward the positive aspects of the arguments.

They resonated with the name 'learning centre', acknowledging its potential to cater to the needs of all faiths within the community.

Additionally, Abdul Malik's discourse omitted a crucial detail: the architectural plan also included a beautifully designed, expansive and open recreational green park. This space was intended for the residents to enjoy various activities such as jogging, cycling, playing and unwinding, adding a positive facet to the proposed development in the village.

*

In Bangladesh, a predominantly Muslim country, a prevalent undercurrent of envy seems to exist among many individuals. It's a deep-rooted aspect where some harbour disdain for the progress and success of others. This mentality often leads some to attempt to stifle or hinder anyone on the brink of growth. Such a perspective seems inherently ingrained in those born and raised in Bangladesh, and its origins remain somewhat elusive.

Nadia, the head of Humanitarian Pledge Ltd, perceives this attitude as being nurtured by the political system. She believes that the prevailing mindset of envy, greed and selfishness is a by-product of a political structure that fails to foster equality in society. Corruption among politicians, who often siphon off a considerable portion of funds allocated for government tenders, further perpetuates this culture. Money, she acknowledges, holds immense power in Bangladesh, akin to a deity for many. Even in the absence of the drought crisis, the government bodies are perceived as purchasable commodities, where bribery is an open secret.

Leveraging its charitable initiatives and the urgency posed by the drought, Humanitarian Pledge Ltd swiftly navigates through the bureaucratic channels. It successfully obtains land use clearances and planning permissions, swiftly moving into the construction phase after procuring a substantial amount of land from willing sellers. Those reluctant to sell are assured that holding onto their properties might yield increased value once the project was completed.

However, Abdul Hakim and his fellow protesters cling onto a deep-seated resentment against Humanitarian Pledge Ltd. They vow to thwart the company's efforts, determined to make construction endeavours impossible in the area.

Their opposition stems from their discontent with the company's initiatives and the perceived negative impact on the community.

*

After five months of construction, two floors had been completed. Then, a group led by Abdul Hakim's son, Abdul Malik, stormed the construction site. They strategically placed dynamite around the building and detonated it, causing multiple explosions that obliterated both floors from the ground up. The resulting fires engulfed the entire village, leaving devastation in the aftermath of the bomb blast.

Manager Abdul Kareem apprised Aysha of the arson attack, prompting her immediate visit to the site to bear witness to the devastation caused by the explosive event. The scene lay in ruins, destroying months of painstaking work in a matter of moments. Determined, she swiftly initiated reconstruction efforts and organised round-the-clock security to safeguard the construction site.

Aysha reached out to the manager of Miracle Limbs Trust, an organisation dedicated to empowering and enhancing the lives of disabled, crippled and handicapped individuals by facilitating their transformation into able-bodied individuals capable of autonomously performing various tasks. With eight years of active engagement, the company had leveraged significant advancements in technology and robotics engineering to significantly improve the quality of life for amputees, granting them enhanced mobility and the ability to undertake activities previously deemed unattainable. Aysha, recognising their commitment to uplifting individuals, requested the manager's assistance in providing security measures for the welfare of the construction workers.

In recent years, prosthetic technology has seen remarkable advancements through the efforts of Miracle Limbs Trust. It has developed highly functional artificial limbs that, while replicating the movements and abilities of natural limbs, possess a notable distinction: their exceptional strength and formidable capabilities. These next-generation soldiers, being developed by the trust, transcend traditional military-grade capacities multiple times over, enabling them to proficiently execute a wide array of tasks such as running, climbing and proficiently handling equipment and firearms using their artificial appendages.

These hybrid soldiers stand on a different echelon, equipped with protective body suits designed to safeguard their vital human organs. Armed with cutting-edge fire power and other weaponry like knives and grenades, their mastery in martial arts is exceptionally skilled too.

To fortify and safeguard the construction site, twenty of these elite soldiers have been deployed, their primary objective being to monitor and defend the building premises.

On the clandestine side of the spectrum, Abdul Malik has resorted to his illicit reserves of funds to embark on a profoundly radical venture. Establishing a covert robotics enterprise within an undisclosed farmhouse location, he and his assembly of engineers are engaged in the construction of veritable robots integrated with weapon systems. Hand-selecting a cadre of immensely skilled robotic engineers from across the globe, Malik's primary agenda revolves around the militarisation of these automatons, intending to peddle them to the clandestine underworld for financial gain. His ultimate aim: a complete revolution in the landscape of warfare.

Several humanoid robots, akin to realistic terminators, have already been crafted, armed to the hilt with lethal weaponry designed for combat. Malik's directive is to task these prototypes with a grim mission: the elimination of Aysha's security personnel, responsible for safeguarding the construction site. While these robots are currently in their infancy stage, serving as prototypes, Malik has transported them to the construction site and programmed them to detect and target anything outfitted with prosthetic materials, with the intent to annihilate them.

*

Amid the pitch-black night, the construction site relied on petrol-driven generators to power the area, illuminated by scattered LED floodlights. However, the insufficient lighting failed to adequately brighten the vast expanse. Within this dimly lit environment, the prosthetic security guards maintained their patrols while a menacing threat loomed closer: the enemy robots, operating in a coordinated manner. With calculated precision, one robot signalled to its counterpart to disperse, initiating a sinister plot to plant digital dynamite within the lower levels of the building.

Unbeknownst to these infiltrating robots, Aysha had strategically placed PIR motion sensors throughout the lower floors. As soon as these sensors detected the presence of the intruding robots, a shrill alarm pierced the night, immediately drawing the attention of the vigilant security guards responsible for safeguarding the site. The abrupt alert catapulted all guards into a state of high alertness, as they swiftly acknowledged the breach; the intruders had breached the site.

Upon hearing the piercing alarm, the two intruder robots swiftly armed themselves and initiated a chaotic gun battle. The skirmish erupted into a frenzy as the robots adeptly evaded bullets, engaging in a prolonged and intense exchange with twenty guarding opponents for over ten minutes. Their proficiency in martial arts and the use of laser-guided handheld firearms allowed them to eliminate five of their adversaries.

In a final push, the robots confronted two more safeguarding security guards, aiming to overpower them with their dwindling ammunition. Unfortunately for the intruders, their weapons ran dry. However, their martial prowess far exceeded that of Aysha's security guards. Viciously, they unleashed brutal assaults, literally tearing their opposition apart using only their bare hands.

Yet, the tables turned as other guards armed with high-velocity machine guns targeted the vulnerable neck area of the intruder robots, unleashing a relentless barrage that tore into the circuitry connections of the robots' heads. Succumbing to the damage, the robots lost control and collapsed, signalling victory for Aysha's guards. However, this triumph came at a cost: seven hybrid lives sacrificed in the battle against these invasive robots.

Enraged by the significant setback, Abdul Malik, undeterred, approached his engineers with a resolute demand: the creation of two more advanced and formidable robots. Determined to strengthen his arsenal, he actively arranged the necessary funding to propel this initiative forward.

"I am no loser," Malik asserted passionately to his engineers. "My robots took down seven of their elite guards. That makes me the victor in this game." His unwavering confidence led him to announce, "The battle within the realm of mechanical warfare has only just commenced. Let them continue their construction work. Let them believe they have triumphed for now. But mark my words, when the opportune moment arrives, I will strike again.

As long as I am present, fear will persistently echo in the ears of my adversaries."

Observing Abdul Malik's capabilities, Aysha was taken aback. "Wow," she said in astonishment, "he's succeeded in constructing these robots? What else might he have up his sleeve? I have clearly underestimated his abilities."

Despite Abdul Malik's ominous assertions, Aysha chose not to confront the looming fear at that moment. Instead, she decided to continue with the construction work, determined to progress towards completing the multiplex as scheduled, leaving the task of addressing the impending threat for another day.

*

Three years later, in 2033, the endeavours of Humanitarian Pledge Ltd have persevered in the face of Abdul Malik's fervent attempts to impede progress. The village has undergone a remarkable metamorphosis, evolving into a self-sustaining haven resonant with both ethical and aesthetic appeal, completely detached from the conventional power grid. This transformation has been achieved through an intricate ecosystem interweaving solar panels, tidal water harnessing, latticed and vertical wind turbines, generating an ample surplus of electricity to cater to seventy-five to 125 households and various commercial entities throughout the year.

The landscape now boasts flourishing greenery, with no tall, ugly, bulky electricity pylons, and tiered residential blocks to increase housing capacity, advanced water purification systems, vibrant youth centres, inviting cafes, meticulously crafted public gardens, playgrounds for children, medical centres and a three-storey edifice housing a mosque, mandir and church on separate floors. Additionally, amenities include an agricultural machine-rental facility, a rice-grain milling factory, fitness centres, an educational hub and exquisitely designed restaurants serving GM-free organic food to the community, a tourism centre and a giant theatre that not only exhibits the latest releases, but houses a film studio where tourists can pay to create short family films and dance productions to take home.

The project's productivity results in surplus energy, stored within substantial commercial-grade DC liquid metal battery packs, with excess AC energy redistributed back to the national grid. Free electricity and purified water are provided to all village residents. Beyond capturing the attention of the nation's tourism sector, it has captivated the country's prime minister, Rajan Chowdhury, prompting his visit. Eager to explore the possibilities, he has sought an immediate audience with the project's CEOs to deliberate on a nationwide implementation of similar initiatives.

Upon receiving this thrilling news, Aysha swiftly dialled Nadia's number in the UK, eager to convey the message that the prime minister wished to meet her. However, Nadia found herself in a quandary upon learning that her niece, Pori Moni, was set to celebrate her graduation on the very day the prime minister intended to visit the village. Each impending occasion held significant value for Nadia, and she was perplexed by the overlapping commitments.

Well regarded for her sagacity, Nadia, often hailed as 'Wise Nadia' by her peers, never ceased in her thoughtful deliberations. She told Pori Moni that an unforeseen and urgent event in Bangladesh would prevent her from attending the graduation party in the UK. To make amends for her absence, Nadia proposed arranging a grand celebration in Bangladesh for Pori Moni, inviting influential figures from across the country. Understanding her aunt's priorities, Pori Moni agreed wholeheartedly to the arrangement.

Nadia promptly secured two tickets: one for her imminent travel to Bangladesh the following day and another for Pori Moni to travel a few days later, ensuring both their presences at the crucial events in their respective timelines.

Nadia arrived at Dhaka International Airport, where her

security team awaited her at the arrivals gate, gathering her belongings before proceeding to the car park, where heavily armoured vehicles stood ready to escort her on the journey to Arambaria. However, as they ventured onto the open roads, several unidentified cars began displaying suspicious behaviour, tailing Nadia's convoy. Soon, a high-stakes pursuit ensued, as these vehicles attempted to force her armoured vehicle off the road.

The situation escalated into a heart-pounding chase, with the unknown cars dangerously tailgating and engaging in intense gunfire mid-journey. Among the three armoured vehicles in Nadia's convoy, the assailants managed to destroy one with a targeted attack from their four-wheel-drive jeep. In response, Nadia's vigilant guards, skilled in navigating through adverse conditions, initiated a tactical counterattack. Employing sophisticated, laser-guided weaponry, they systematically neutralised the enemy jeep, eliminating the threat one by one.

Amid the chaos and perilous circumstances, Nadia's security team showcased strategic prowess, effectively thwarting the assailants' assault and ensuring the safety of the convoy through their swift and precise counteroffensive manoeuvres.

Aysha, upon learning of the car chase incident, promptly took precautionary measures, arranging bulletproof body-fitting vests for Nadia's safety upon her arrival at the village of Arambaria. Recognising that safety within the confines of Humanitarian Pledge Ltd was assured, due to heavily guarded borders thanks to Aysha's advanced artificial humanoid robotic guards, Aysha personally welcomed Nadia upon her arrival.

Expressing concern for Nadia's safety, Aysha warmly embraced her and presented her with the protective vest. "Wear this vest, Nadia, and consider yourself at home. Danger lurks in every corner. Allow me to introduce Kony, your personal assistant. She'll guide you to your washroom and then to your room. Freshen up and take some rest," Aysha assured Nadia, emphasising the need for caution amid the looming threats.

"Hello, Kony," said Nadia. "You're a stunning young lady. What field are you studying?"

Kony smiled warmly. "Thank you so much. I'm studying electronic engineering, ma'am."

"Keep it up," Nadia encouraged. "We need more women in that field."

"Ma'am, I'll do my best. You're my inspiration," Kony said gratefully.

"Oh, that's lovely to hear. Excuse me, I'll go freshen up."

As Nadia excused herself, Aysha and her team members orchestrated the preparation of a sumptuous dining table adorned with delectable dishes, eagerly anticipating being served. Shortly after, Aysha descended from the upper level to join her team, all of whom were dedicatedly operating under the banner of Humanitarian Pledge Ltd, to partake in the meal.

"Aysha, today has been incredibly taxing. Adversaries seem to be lurking at every turn, just as you said. I'm baffled as to how they were aware of my arrival in Bangladesh today. Unless you disclosed my schedule to them, how on earth did they get wind of it? Did you betray me?"

"Nadia, don't be so distressed. I'm as perplexed as you are. I'll investigate this promptly. For now, ease your mind and relish the moment. The food awaits – your favourite boal fish bunna," Aysha said reassuring her.

"Ah, it's been ages since I've had authentic Desi cuisine, Aysha!" exclaimed Nadia.

"Here you go, plenty right in front of you," Aysha remarked. "Kony, ensure that madam is well fed," she instructed.

"Of course, my pleasure," responded Kony dutifully.

Nadia cast a discerning glance at the assembled guests seated around the dining table, noticing many unfamiliar faces. "Aren't you going to introduce me to everyone here before we commence our meal, Aysha?" she enquired.

"Oh, gosh, I completely forgot," Aysha responded. "Hey,

everyone, please allow me to introduce the central figure of this household. Everything we've accomplished is a result of her dedication and hard work. This is Mrs Nadia Begum, the owner and CEO of Humanitarian Pledge Ltd. And to you, Nadia, meet our senior manager, Mr Abdul Kareem, and the other colleagues whom you'll get to know after indulging in these delightful dishes. I'm absolutely famished," Aysha said as she started eating, prompting everyone else to follow suit.

"Madam, while we may be acquainted with you and your admirable deeds, I don't believe any of us truly know each other any better, but everyone knows you to the fullest potential," remarked Abdul Kareem.

"Know me just from seeing my photo huh? Never judge a book by its cover, Manager Kareem," Nadia replied with a smile.

"It's a blend of both, madam – the photo and the narrative from various literature," responded Abdul Kareem.

*

The next morning, Nadia embarked on a tour of the village, accompanied by her personal assistant, Kony, who walked alongside her. As they traversed the pathways, Nadia observed the tangible results of her efforts, marvelling at the sheer beauty and the positive changes it brought to the villagers. Briefly, her thoughts drifted to her late brother, Doyal, who had tragically lost his life due to conflicts over the village's lake water. She couldn't help but wish he could witness the transformations and successes she had achieved. His pride would have been immense.

Nadia's structured life had far-reaching impacts, not just in the village but across Bangladesh and beyond. Overwhelmed by the transformation within the village, she witnessed the media hype, the growing publicity and the burgeoning tourist attractions. Arambaria village had become a topic of conversation on everyone's lips. The headlines of almost every print media outlet in Bangladesh beckoned the nation to witness the eco-transformation. The village had turned into a treasure, a beacon of success, inviting all to take heed from its outcomes.

Just a couple of years ago, the people of Arambaria were enduring an existence fraught with uncertainty about their future. Fast forward to the present day, and the villagers now eagerly lined up to personally meet the individual responsible for the incredible transformation. The life support system she had established was deeply cherished by the locals. Some revered her to such an extent that they almost deified her, particularly the Hindu communities.

The village now boasted a robust educational system, a strong social security network, reduced inequalities and a considerably wealthier populace. Fear of the unknown had dissipated, replaced by a sense of security. Greed and desperation had vanished, and each individual saw her as a paragon, dedicating their lives to serving the community. The village's foundation was built on the bedrock of justice, where fairness was of paramount importance.

Her competitors were watching her closely, yearning to glean even a fraction of her wisdom. They grappled with feelings of envy and bitterness that gnawed at them daily. The perplexing question that eluded them was: how did she manage to orchestrate such a remarkable transformation?

A few hours later, Inspector Aysha contacted Nadia on her mobile phone, sharing the news that the serving prime minister, Rajan Chowdhury, expressed a desire to visit and witness her remarkable project.

"I am waiting for you guys," she replied, and continued her tour of the village, engaging with the villagers, farmers and elders, discussing their daily activities, weighing the pros and cons, and seeking ways to make continuous improvements.

One of the farmers raised pertinent questions, emphasising the specific needs and challenges associated with their particular type of farming. To enhance their lifestyle and agricultural practices, the farmer suggested several key initiatives, including access to affordable credit facilities, agricultural training and education, pest management strategies and the adoption of sustainable farming practices.

Enthralled, due to her passion for organic and local farming initiatives, Nadia listened intently, contemplating a pest management strategy that had sparked her curiosity. Her thoughts raced back to the days when she was actively involved with GreenBirth Corporation Ltd, where she had contributed to the design of bird-mimicking drones aimed at repelling pests. In the year 2033, surrounded by the profound evolution of technology, Nadia found herself grappling with a sense of disappointment, realising she had yet to share her advancements in robotic pest control with her fellow advocates.

Moments later, Inspector Aysha arrived in a police jeep, followed by the prime minister's car and his associates. Nadia promptly approached him and extended her hand.

"Hello, Mr Prime Minister. How are you?" said Nadia.

"I am absolutely delighted to meet you. We have been closely monitoring your project for a year now, and it has proven to be a complete success. Well done!" praised the prime minister. "A village that was on the brink of disintegration now stands tall, overshadowing everything in the country. It produces self-sufficient electrical energy and even sells the excess to the government. This is a remarkable achievement, truly deserving of praise."

"Thank you. So, you're well informed about it, that's great. Come, let's have a seat," said Nadia.

"Madam, the media people are pushing to come inside to record the interview," informed a member of the security personnel.

"I have no objection. If they want to know more, bring them in. Ensure a full strip search and no sharp objects allowed," Nadia instructed.

"Nadia, madam?" called the prime minister, smiling. "Too many journalists can be a threat. Just let a few in, it will cover the news."

"Okay, let a few prominent journalists in," said Nadia.

Nadia led all the participants to a designated conference room within the residence, where a select few journalists positioned themselves with video and audio recording devices. Nadia, driven by a desire for fame and popularity, saw this as an opportunity to gain a platform to influence the nation, expand her social circle and enhance her self-esteem, leading to a more positive self-image. This press conference was precisely what she sought to push her agenda into the public mindset.

"When you've finished setting up your equipment, please let me know. I'll begin to narrate the story behind this remarkable development, hopefully addressing all the questions you have along the way," said Nadia.

"Sure, madam," said one of the journalists.

The servants brought beverages, snacks and fresh water, placing them in front of all the attendees to enjoy.

"We are ready, madam. You may begin speaking into the mics when you're ready," said the journalist.

"Dear viewers, my name is Nadia Begum. I was born here in Arambaria. I won't delve into more details, as my story is readily available on your phones, tablets and other devices. Simply search for my name and the internet will provide the full testimony. Today, I am with Prime Minister Rajan Chowdhury. I live abroad and don't often get the chance to meet with him. He travelled to meet with me to understand the story behind this transformation. Before I begin, I must offer Mr Prime Minister the opportunity to say a few words to the viewers."

"What can I say? I am simply astonished to witness a self-sufficient, energy-independent community, providing free energy to all villagers and even selling surplus energy to enhance their wealth. Not to mention the beautiful artistic architectural work incorporated into this project, such as the children's play area, street furniture and walkways that resemble the Garden of Eden – it's just breathtaking to see. I am eager to learn how she managed to transform a dire, drought-laden village into a paradise," remarked the prime minister.

"Well, to answer your question, let me specify my place in society. I am a passionate climate activist who is deeply concerned about the urgent threat of climate change. I view climate change not only as an environmental issue but as a global crisis that impacts every facet of our lives, from social justice and human rights to the wellbeing of future generations.

"My motivation as a climate activist is rooted in a sense of responsibility and duty to protect our planet and its inhabitants. I strongly believe that addressing climate change is a moral imperative. The scientific consensus is clear: human activities are driving global warming, leading to devastating consequences such as extreme weather events, sea-level rise and the loss of biodiversity.

"To justify my activism, I focus on the following:

"Scientific evidence overwhelmingly supports the reality of climate change, attributing it to human activities and emphasising the immediate need for action to mitigate its impact. This is precisely what I've demonstrated here in my village.

"I strongly believe it is our ethical responsibility to protect the planet for both current and future generations. We must strive for a fair and sustainable world where everyone has access to clean air, water and a stable climate. I stand in solidarity with young activists who are advocating for their future and their right to inhabit a habitable world.

"In my activism, I engage in various activities, including advocacy, education, grassroots organising and participation in peaceful demonstrations. I firmly believe that collective action and raising awareness are fundamental in pressuring governments, industries, lobbyists and individuals to take meaningful steps to address climate change.

"While climate change activism can be challenging and demanding, it is driven by the belief that a better, more sustainable future is attainable if we act decisively and urgently.

"Together, we can positively impact our planet and establish a legacy of responsible stewardship for generations to come.

"While some may hold the belief that global warming is a fabricated hoax, a concoction designed by scientists to secure government funding for their research, the scientific community overwhelmingly supports the reality of human-caused climate change. Arambaria stands as a living testament to the devastating impacts of climate change. Those who endured the hardships and chaos here just a few years ago can attest that global warming is indeed occurring and threatening their livelihoods. Our country's shoreline, bordering the delta area of the Bay of Bengal, is vanishing beneath the rising waters. Heavy rainfall and cyclones are mercilessly tearing people's homes from the ground. It's real, it's happening, and we must take immediate action to halt it.

"Through education and strategic planning, we can be prepared for major disasters. Otherwise, lives will be lost before our very eyes, and it will be too late to intervene."

Nadia became emotional as she remembered her brother's tragic fate, a poignant reminder of the urgent need to combat climate change.

"To address the prime minister's question about how I managed to transform a dire and problematic village into a thriving community, I must clarify that I haven't reached my ultimate goal yet. My plan is to provide people with free energy, education, healthcare and clean drinking water. The process is akin to sowing seeds of an idea and nurturing them into success, just as you take seeds and scatter them onto the ground to make them grow. It's not a one-and-done endeavour, it's an ongoing process that requires constant care. But, industrialists, large corporations and government officials are not very keen on my activism as I pose a threat to cronyism and capitalism.

"I took inspiration from children's paper-crafted whirly wind spinners. They come in all different shapes and sizes. When I saw the typical twenty-metre-high wind turbines you often see in open fields with large spinning propellers mounted on an unsightly tall pylon, I thought to myself there must be something better than this. I realised that by making smaller turbines and connecting them in series, along with the right calculations and the correct step-up transformers, I could generate the same kilowatt energy capacity as those giant turbines, but within a reduced material waste and unsightly environment. I conducted a test project and found that it worked perfectly well. So, I eliminated the long, heavy poles that the propellers typically stand on, scaled down the shaft and propeller, and installed them in packs in a lattice grid, connected in series to produce energy equivalent to the giant wind turbines. A pack is always more effective than a single unit. You can see them from here, spinning on those rooftops with minimal or no wind needed and barely audible. That's how I planted the seeds, and now we are reaping the benefits.

"Arambaria village serves as a testament to this transformation. The village has become both ethically and aesthetically self-sufficient in renewable energy. It is disconnected from the main electricity grid, yet it has a sufficient energy supply. The ecosystem created here integrates solar, water and wind power. The electricity generated is ample to provide power year-round for 125 homes, including commercial establishments. The advantages derived from this self-sustaining village are countless. One of the most notable aspects is that it operates independently from the rest of the country, making it more likely to thrive even in adverse conditions.

"My request to every citizen of the country: please feel free to come and visit our village and witness tomorrow's technology today," said Nadia, looking at the camera lenses and conveying her agenda.

She continued, "If the government or private investors are interested in joining forces with me, subject to terms and conditions, I am more than willing to replicate similar projects throughout the country in a matter of years. This can transform the country's outdated infrastructure into a much more efficient and modernised system, allowing us to showcase our advancements to the world," Nadia proclaimed.

As Nadia spoke openly to the journalists and extended invitations for investment, the prime minister seemed uneasy. He swiftly passed a hand-written note to Nadia that read, "Could we have a talk in private?" Having read the note, Nadia promptly cut short the press conference, politely requesting the journalists to wrap up as another urgent meeting required immediate attention and priority.

"Ma'am, if you don't mind, one last question," said one of the journalists.

"Yes, sure, go ahead," replied Nadia.

"Ma'am, you are an inspiration for millions of women in our country and abroad, a true role model. However, our country is an infestation hub of corruption. Nothing can be achieved without bribes, from street vendors to airport officials, from office workers to police officers, from ministers to even prime ministers – everyone is bought and sold for a handful of money. Our country is in dire need of a person like you: honest, charismatic and succinct. Would you stand for election here in Bangladesh?" asked the journalist.

Cheering was followed by a handful of applause from the small crowd for Nadia.

The laudatory words from the journalist didn't sit well with the prime minister. He exclaimed in a sudden jolt and with a stammer, "*Hi-hi-re Baba! (Oy, my son!)* What kind of question is that? I am here, *na*. As a sitting prime minister, I'm working to combat corruption, but if people listen, *na*? You guys have had enough time. Pack up now. Madam has other meetings now. Go... go..."

"What's your name?" Nadia asked the questioning journalist.

"Journalist DoDo Ahmed," replied the journalist.

"Your analysis regarding corruption is valid. The state of the country's infrastructure is a testament to the epidemic of corruption in Bangladesh. The nation is in dire need of economic growth, an upgrade in public services and a reduction in corruption to promote social equity and strengthen the legal and institutional framework.

"If the people of Bangladesh wish for a better life, free of worries for their children, we must collectively combat corruption. If the people of Bangladesh find my work inspiring and would like to join me in the transition to renewable free energy, a low-carbon economy, job creation, conservation and sustainable practices, then yes, I am open to standing for election. Vote for me, and I will be delighted to serve the people of Bangladesh and lead the country toward becoming a biodiverse nation that stands out from the rest.

"Journalist DoDo, if you have time, stay behind for a chat with me," said Nadia.

"Okay, ma'am," replied DoDo.

"Let's have some food now, shall we, Prime Minister?" said Nadia.

"My belly just got filled listening to you. Seriously, you're thinking of standing for elections? Do you even consider this country as yours?" asked the prime minister.

"Of course… this is my country. The efforts I've made to bring good to this country are extensive, Mr Prime Minister. Why not? If the country wants me to stand for the role of prime minister, I am happy to do that."

"Are you serious? Do you really think the people of Bangladesh will fall for your so-called climate disinformation? Just because a few people in Arambaria benefited from your project, it doesn't necessarily mean the rest of the country will vote for you," said the prime minister.

"So, you are a climate change denialist. I understand you may feel discomfort, but it's the people's choice. It is a democratic society, isn't that so, Mr Prime Minister?" replied Nadia.

"You know what? I don't feel like eating here," said the prime minister, standing up and walking off, followed by his comrades.

Nadia was caught by surprise; she wasn't expecting this move by the prime minister. She gave a fixed look, smirked and continued eating with her friends.

*

Hastily, the prime minister hurried back to his waiting chauffeured car, accompanied by a couple of his assistants and a trusted deputy commissioner of police who shared the same cab. The driver promptly set off.

"This woman poses a threat to my position, Deputy Commissioner. Find a resolution to remove her from this situation," commanded the prime minister.

"Absolutely, sir. I'll delve deeper into her matters and promptly present you with a solution," responded the deputy commissioner.

"Commissioner, I perceive this woman as a small but sharp piece of fish bone lodged in my throat, a constant source of irritation. Until she's removed and dealt with, no comfort will prevail. I expect an update by tomorrow, Deputy Commissioner," stated the prime minister.

"Yes, of course, sir!" replied the commissioner.

The next morning, the deputy commissioner summoned Inspector Aysha to his office for questioning. Aysha promptly arrived upon the commissioner's call.

"Yes, sir!"

"Aysha, please take a seat. Tell me, why are you still a police detective?" enquired the commissioner.

"What do you mean, sir?" asked Aysha, curious.

"I mean, you have your own secret service company making a substantial amount of money. Why remain in a job that pays you so little?" questioned the commissioner.

"Sir, I joined the police to serve the people and combat crime. Money wasn't my motivation, and the company is not mine, the investors own it," explained Aysha.

"Do you know your company is actively taking the law into its own hands, shooting people who disobey them?" asserted the commissioner.

"Sir, I'm not aware of any shootings. The company's policies prioritise self-defence. If matters escalate beyond control, they will be subject to legal consequences," responded Aysha.

"Yes, if the law can reach them, then they are indeed subject to punishment. But you and I know that's not what's happening. And by the way, why does your 'boss', Nadia, want to stand for election?" probed the commissioner.

"Sir, she's not my boss. I'm unaware of her reasons for running for election," clarified Aysha.

"Do you know when she's going back to the UK?" asked the commissioner.

"I'm not aware of that, sir," replied Aysha.

"You seem to know everything but won't tell me," accused the commissioner.

"Sir, if you've asked everything, may I go?" enquired Aysha.

"Are the decorations I saw around Nadia's village for an upcoming function?" enquired the commissioner.

"She is hosting a party for her niece, Pori, who graduated in the UK and is now returning to Bangladesh."

"I see. So, she is planning to stay. Okay, you may go now," said the commissioner.

As soon as Aysha left the commissioner's office, he placed a call to Prime Minister Rajan Chowdhury to inform him that Nadia's niece was en route to Bangladesh.

Prime Minister Rajan Chowdhury praised the deputy commissioner for the swift update and regarded it as great news. He promptly dialled Abdul Malik, a person with a dubious reputation who seemed to have secured a position to carry out clandestine tasks for the prime minister. He instructed Malik to monitor all flights and passengers arriving from the UK throughout the week, emphasising that Pori must be abducted at any cost. Malik assured the prime minister that he would ensure Pori would be taken care of.

*

Pori Moni was due to arrive at Dhaka International Airport. Her aunt had already cautioned her to remain vigilant as she was being pursued by adversaries, leading to the loss of three of her security personnel at the arrival terminal. After claiming her luggage, Pori swiftly made her way to the restroom to don her protective undergarments. This was her initial encounter in an unfamiliar land, where prioritising safety and security was of utmost importance. Shortly after, she confidently walked towards the arrival gates.

"Pori… Pori!" a voice called out to her from behind. She turned and noticed a man approaching, stating, "This way, a special arrangement has been made for you to go home." This wasn't a surprise to her, given that Aunty Nadia had already informed her about the chauffeur service arranged by her security personnel. Trusting her aunt's instructions, she followed the man to an armoured vehicle. Safely securing all her belongings inside, they ensured her comfort before the driver set off from the terminal onto the main road. The journey continued for approximately twenty minutes until they veered onto a rugged path leading into dense jungle. After an hour's drive, the vehicle came to a halt. A man, armed and stern, opened the back door, instructing her to exit slowly.

"Hands in the air," he commanded.

Confusion clouded her thoughts as she grappled to understand the unfolding situation.

"Who are you guys?" she asked in a state of bewilderment, cautiously stepping out of the armoured vehicle with her hands raised. As she emerged, she found herself surrounded by the expanse of jungle. Suddenly, a second person approached from behind, swiftly handcuffing her while the other kept the gun pointed directly at her. In a surreal turn of events, a helicopter appeared, hovering over the jungle and lowering an empty steel shipping container, eight by twenty feet in dimension, completely converted with doors and tinted windows. This unexpected sight left Pori even more disoriented and perplexed about the situation. After depositing the container, the helicopter swiftly departed. The armed individuals guided her toward the container and gestured for her to enter.

Inside the container, a sunroof provided natural light, while a clear polythene bag containing candles hinted at provisions for the night. There was a solitary chair and a table within. The gunman directed her to take a seat, and the second man began briefing her.

"I'm certain you've been asking yourself what's happening here, haven't you?" the gunman began. "Well, you'll be relieved to know that we are the same people who intercepted your aunt upon her arrival here in Bangladesh. In short, you have been abducted. My boss will be arriving shortly to provide you with a comprehensive explanation as to why this has occurred," he explained calmly.

"Listen, you've made a mistake. I don't usually warn my adversaries, but it's my first visit back here. When I was just four years old, I left the country with my aunt for precisely similar reasons. There's something fundamentally wrong with you people. You seem to disdain peace and prosperity, only inviting trouble," Pori cautioned assertively.

"Sit quietly. Our boss is on his way. Don't utter harsh words in his presence, or he won't offer a warning, you'll be blown to pieces," the gunman cautioned Pori.

A moment later, Abdul Malik entered the shipping container and said, "Hey, girl, it's crucial that you listen to what I'm about to tell you. You've been abducted by some very nefarious individuals here in Bangladesh. Do you speak Bengali at all?"

"No, sir," she replied, although she was proficient in unlimited languages thanks to her aunty making her into a bionic soul.

"Okay, listen carefully. You will only be released when your aunt fulfils our demands. You'll be taken care of here until these conditions are met. So, don't panic or stress about this situation, you will be fed, clothed and looked after like royalty. However, if your aunt refuses, then it's acceptable for you to panic because my men will resort to brutal measures, cutting you into pieces and feeding you to the Sundarbans tigers, who have a taste for human flesh and bone. Do you understand?" Pori nodded in silence, her mind swirling with memories. As she looked at Abdul Malik, her recollections of childhood surged forth, vivid as if they happened yesterday. She remembered how Malik had captured her mother, Rahila, in a farmhouse, her pleas for mercy falling on deaf ears. Her mother had begged for Pori's freedom in exchange for whatever Malik desired. Since then, she had never seen her mother again.

"Hey, what are you thinking? Do you understand?" asked Malik.

Pori's eyes welled up, tears of anguish streaming down her face as she nodded in affirmation, murmuring, "Yes, I understand."

"No need to cry you will be looked after here," Abdul Malik exited the container and instructed his henchmen to provide food three times a day, threatening lashes if she refused to eat. He then boarded his helicopter and swiftly departed.

"Is he your boss?" enquired Pori to the gunman stationed at her door.

"Yes, he is," replied the gunman.

"How far is Arambaria from this location?" questioned Pori.

"Look, you're not supposed to talk to us. If you continue, we'll have to tape your mouth shut. Don't speak," warned the gunman.

"You seem like a decent person," Pori remarked. At this juncture, she used her central artificial hair plait to manipulate and open her handcuff.

"Hey, get some tape!" shouted the gunman to his colleague as he lunged toward Pori, grasping her mouth tightly, squeezing her cheeks. "I told you to shut up."

The other gunman grabbed some cloth tape and entered the cabin. Pori acted swiftly, grabbing the gun from the man who held her mouth and shooting the newcomer by the door. Using her hair plait, she gruesomely incapacitated the man who had grabbed her, freeing herself. With caution, she stepped outside to survey the area for any additional threats. Finding no one else around, she reflected, "What an asshole. He just left two guards with me, underestimating the capabilities of a determined woman."

She left her luggage inside the container and ventured out for a stroll, cautiously mindful not to lose her way back to the cabin in the vast jungle. Activating her bionic rear-view camera to capture and identify landmarks for navigation, Pori embarked on a self-guided tour, seeking to explore and immerse herself in the natural beauty of the jungle. The surroundings were filled with tense songs of exotic birds, lush greenery and monkeys leaping between branches. Noticing a small hill from which a stream flowed, she followed its course until it led her to an isolated, crystal-clear water lagoon situated at a higher elevation. Enchanted by the stunning scenery, Pori found herself captivated by the sight.

The weather, hot and humid, alongside the serene freshwater vista, prompted Pori to shed her clothes and ease into the inviting water for a refreshing swim. Fearlessly, she disregarded any potential dangers lurking within the lake. Taking a deep breath, she dove into the water, swimming with purpose. Submerged beneath the surface, she closed her eyes but kept her bionic camera active. The camera captured a beautiful horse with a gracefully elongated neck and flowing mane descending to the lagoon for a drink. To avoid disturbing the horse, Pori swam further away underwater and surfaced silently, observing the horse from a distance. It was a striking, untamed black horse with oval-shaped hooves, a long tail and a muscular, majestic build – a creature seemingly unaccustomed to human interaction.

Pori engaged her bionic microprocessor to search for a frequency to communicate with the horse. After scanning through various frequencies, she found one that allowed her to connect with the horse. Submerging once more and resurfacing within view of the horse, she attempted to communicate. However, as soon as she emerged, the horse startled and swiftly darted out of sight. "Hey, I want to be friends with you." Pori emitted a high-frequency message through her throat, hoping to reach the horse's ears. The message caught the horse's attention, causing it to pause and look back at her.

"Did you just talk to me?" the horse enquired.

"Yes, I did," Pori replied in another horse-like sound.

The horse emitted a sound that, when translated, conveyed laughter to Pori.

"Why do you laugh?" asked Pori.

"You've just surprised me. How are you talking to me?" enquired the horse.

"I can communicate with any animals, not just you. No need to be surprised," Pori responded.

"Alright, no need to show off now," teased the horse. "Who are you?"

"I am Pori. I am lost in this jungle," Pori explained.

The horse turned back and returned to the spot it had been drinking from. "Ah, no amount of pleasure can beat this hot day's thirst," said Pori encouraging the horse to drink.

"How can you speak my language?" the horse squealed in surprise.

"I can talk many languages, I am gifted," said Pori. "Would you be my friend?"

"Yes! But humans are not compassionate, they take horses and make them work in paddy fields until they drop dead. Look at me, free, wild and beautiful. I look like a horse now, but human touch will instantly turn me into an ass," said the horse.

"Hey, this is exactly why I exist," said Pori.

"What, to make me a slave?" enquired the horse.

"No, not at all. Instead, fight for your rights. My mother is an ecologist and animal conservationist. She cares for everything that exists on planet Earth, from plant life to animal lives. She taught me how to communicate with animals so I can understand their needs and represent them in human councils. I and my mother are here to change all animal suffering in the near future. My mother is standing for election and thinking of introducing legislation favourable to animal rights. This will protect your sovereignty and others like you from human torture," said Pori.

"Is that true?" enquired the horse.

"Yes, trust me," affirmed Pori.

"Okay, I will be your friend, then," the horse agreed.

"That's great news. Let me come out of the water. You go and wait on the other side," said Pori.

"Why? We will walk together!" insisted the horse.

"No, you go. We humans have a sense of modesty. We don't come out naked in front of animals. We don't like others looking at our nude bodies," Pori explained.

"Okay, you come, I'll go up," the horse agreed.

Pori swiftly got out of the water, clothed herself and began walking alongside the horse.

"Do you have a name?" Pori asked.

"No, I don't have a name," the horse replied.

"How do you recognise each other without a name?" enquired Pori.

"Our neigh is our name. All horses have different sounds," explained the horse.

"How fast can you run?" Pori asked.

"I am very fast. Do you want to try me?" the horse suggested.

"I haven't ridden a horse without a saddle on," Pori hesitated.

"Well, here's your chance to try without a saddle. Hold on to my mane," the horse proposed.

"Are you sure?" asked Pori.

"Yes, jump on!" encouraged the horse.

Exhilarated, Pori smiled and leapt onto the horse's back.

"Are you on yet?" enquired the horse.

"Yes, I am!" confirmed Pori.

"Oh, you are so light I can't even feel you are on me," remarked the horse.

"Just go, no need to offend me," Pori responded.

"How is this offence? Hold tight! This jungle is dangerous, with too many wild tigers around looking for their next meal. Let's head to the seaside and give you a few test rides. It will be less bumpy. I don't want you to fly away without me noticing. Hold my mane, okay?" instructed the horse.

Pori grasped the horse's mane on its neck.

"Ouch! Not too tight, Pori, just enough to keep your balance," advised the horse.

"Oops, sorry," Pori apologised.

"Ready? It will be a bit bumpy as we are going down the hills to the flat land," warned the horse.

"Yes, ready, let's go," said Pori.

As the horse surged forward, Pori lost her balance and nearly fell off. She managed to regain her seat by holding onto the horse's neck until they descended to sea level on the sands.

"Wow, that was one heck of a ride. Not comfortable at all," remarked Pori.

"You need to get used to the ride," advised the horse.

On the flat land, the horse began to run, and Pori initially maintained a firm grip on the horse's neck. The horse continued its gallop, and as Pori gradually gained confidence, she transitioned from a tight hug to simply holding onto the horse's mane. They rode for three miles until the horse became completely exhausted. Finally slowing down, the horse turned to Pori and enquired about its speed.

"You were incredible," Pori replied, turning to see if she could spot the starting landmark, which was barely visible. "I'd say you ran about three miles before slowing down."

"I'm thirsty now. Let's return to the jungle to drink fresh water," suggested the horse.

"Wow, do you know that running three miles is a long distance, Horse? From now on, I'll call you 'Super Shadowfax', meaning you are the lord of all horses," said Pori.

"Really, that's a great name. I like it," responded the horse.

"SS for short, okay, Shadowfax?" Pori proposed.

"Okay, Pori," agreed Shadowfax, embracing the newly given name.

As they approached the shipping container, where Pori's luggage was left untouched, she heard the growls of tigers emanating from inside the cabin.

"It's the tigers. Shall we run for our lives?" suggested Shadowfax.

"Shh," hushed Pori before cautiously dismounting from the horse. She peered from a distance into the cabin and witnessed two large Bengal tigers dragging out the dead bodies of the guards she had earlier killed. A third tiger was visible, wounded with several claw tears in its skin, blood dripping from its injuries. It seemed this tiger was the first to discover the corpses, and the others had seized its meal by force. Tigers are solitary creatures, and the stronger and larger they are, the better their dominance. Pori observed patiently as the two tigers dragged the bodies away into the jungle, but the third tiger remained stationary, sitting just a few metres from the cabin door.

Pori concentrated, pushing her consciousness to find a suitable communication frequency to interact with the wounded tiger. Her stored database sifted through thousands of potential tiger dialects, but a signal error prevented her from establishing a secure connection. Undaunted, she closed the distance and made herself visible to the tiger. The wounded tiger spotted her and stood alert, growling with a mixture of defensive and aggressive intent.

Pori moved even closer, causing the already anxious tiger to edge towards an attack. With no other option, the injured tiger locked eyes with Pori, seeking a vantage point to pounce on her. The tiger roared in anger as it prepared to strike. Pori's swift, coordinated movements allowed her to side flip and backflip to evade the tiger's attack. The tiger's sharp claws grazed her leg, producing an unusual rasping noise. Her protective armadillo-like skin absorbed the scrape as she skilfully avoided the tiger's grasp.

Meanwhile, Pori continued to focus on establishing a secure communication frequency based on the tiger's growling. Just as the tiger made multiple attempts to harm her, the communication frequency opened and they established a secure dialogue.

"Stop attacking, I'm trying to help you," Pori growled back at the tiger. The tiger paused for a moment, as if some sort of realisation had struck him. Pori knew she had the tiger's attention.

"I am trying to help you. I know you're hungry. I can help feed you," she repeated, prompting the wounded tiger to respond with another batch of growling that conveyed understanding and potential cooperation.

"How is this possible that I can understand what you're saying?" questioned the tiger.

"Yes, you can understand me. Thank goodness. Shall we be friends, then?" asked Pori.

"Friends with you? Your kind kill us and then take photos to prove their bravery, take our skin to make ornaments. How can I be friends with an enemy who kills for fun?" replied the tiger.

Pori called her horse, SS, gesturing for it to come near. The horse approached cautiously. "Meet SS, my friend. I promised him I will fight for their rights and for all other animals' rights. I will do the same for you and your kind too."

The communication circuit between Pori, SS and the tiger appeared to be functioning as part of a networking system. Pori's bionic microchip was receiving the tiger's speech frequency and transposing it to horse language, and vice versa, establishing a seamless connection and understanding between the three beings.

"Horses are for people to ride on. They are slaves to you. That's why you look after them. We are not. How can you look after us?" the tiger questioned.

"You have to trust me. Do you know your population is nearing extinction?" Pori responded.

"No, but I can see fewer and fewer tigers around. Look! I'm not interested in being your friend right now. I feel more like eating you and your friend there. I'm too hungry. I haven't eaten for days," the tiger said.

"I will find some food for you if you stay calm and wait here for us," Pori proposed.

"You're going to find food for me? I don't eat grass and leaves. I eat flesh and bones. My fellow tigers snatched my delicious meal off me," the tiger explained.

"I know what you eat. Just wait, I will get food for you. You also need treatment for your wounds," said Pori.

"I will wait here. Let's see if you can keep your word," replied the tiger.

"SS, come, let's go find some food for the tiger," said Pori, mounting the horse, and off they went, riding for miles into the jungle.

"Where are we going to find food for the tiger? I cannot catch a hog deer because they will outrun me," said the horse.

"Do you know how far the local village is? We can get a few chickens for the tiger," suggested Pori.

"The village is far away, Pori. I know where to find wild boars. They graze in the mangrove," responded the horse.

"Let's go there. Let's hunt down a wild hog for the tiger to feed on," Pori decided.

The horse led Pori to the mangrove roots where snakes, snails, crabs and other invertebrates made their home. Just beyond the tree line, a wild boar could be seen grazing on roots and bulbs, its stocky build adorned with grey bristly hair and standing around seventy centimetres in height.

"SS! I can see one just over there feeding on vegetation. It's quite big. I wonder, can you take the load to carry us both for miles?" said Pori.

"Don't worry too much about carrying it, think of how to kill it. They are not so easy to catch," replied the horse.

"I see. You seem to have good knowledge of their behaviour, SS. Let me get off your back and give it a go. Let's see if I can catch it," Pori said. She stepped down from the horse's back and drew her special tranquilliser gun from its holster – a short-range fifty-metre air gun preloaded with an anaesthetic dart ready to discharge. Pori positioned herself at a safe distance, aimed the gun at the wild boar and took the shot.

The dart punctured through the thick skin on the boar's shoulder, delivering a dose of immobilising drug. The boar reacted, jumping upon being hit, but it didn't exhibit frantic movements; instead, it continued to feed. Within minutes, the hog succumbed to the sedative and fell to the ground. Pori called for the horse to come to the hunting ground.

"You caught it already?" asked the horse.

"Yes, I caught it," said Pori. She went near the sedated wild boar and ejected the hypodermic dart. Attempting to handle the sedated hog with her own strength, she found it too heavy to lift. She needed an alternative idea.

The horse came closer to Pori and asked, "Is it dead?"

"No, it's not dead. I sent it to sleep. We have to get going before it wakes up. It's heavy. I cannot lift it on top of you, SS. I will have to use ropes and straps," Pori explained.

Reaching into her sword holder's hardened shell middle compartment, she retrieved a couple of fastening straps. Making the horse lie sideways close to the sedated wild boar, she wrapped the fastening straps under the horse, encompassing the boar, and then pulled the excess towards the top, securing the boar to the horse's body. She instructed the horse to rise, lifting the boar with it. With the task completed, she climbed back onto the horse's back and rode away.

"Now I can feel I am carrying something, Pori. Its weight is testament that I must be very lucky I haven't fallen a slave to any humans, otherwise, this would be my daily routine," the horse alluded.

"Come on, SS, a working life keeps you physically active. Humans are not that bad when it comes to the welfare of their domestic animals. You need the right owner. There are bad owners out there, yes. If you get under their spell, you are doomed," explained Pori.

Moments later, they reached the tiger, who seemed to be curled up, dozing like a big cat. It detected the vibrations of the hooves on the ground and woke to see if they had arrived.

"So, you kept your word," said the tiger.

"Of course I did," responded Pori. "SS, go sit just by that tree there," instructed Pori. The horse kneeled and lowered its back to help Pori dismount and unfasten the boar from its back. The boar was still unconscious. Pori freed the horse and tethered the boar against a nearby tree. She approached the tiger and said, "It's all yours, Tiger. Do whatever you want, but engage only after we leave this area. I am starving myself, and I need to find something to eat." Looking at the feast, the tiger was eager to take a bite. "Ah ah, not now. I don't want to see this crucifixion," said Pori.

Pori mounted the back of SS, and they departed. "Where to?" asked the horse.

"Go where there is water. I will try to catch a fish," said Pori.

"To find fish, the best place to go is the swamp," suggested the horse. "A forested wetland about a kilometre south of this place. It's a transition zone between the Bay of Bengal, drawing in salty seawater, and the land holding the freshwaters. This overlapping mixture gave rise to an environment where extraordinary sea life thrives. Shallow waters teeming with fish of all varieties," explained the horse.

"What are we waiting for? Let's go," said Pori.

As Pori and SS embarked on their fishing trip, deep in the jungle, the tiger seized the wild boar, sinking its teeth into the boar's neck. Despite the boar's desperate attempts to escape by kicking its legs, it succumbed, gradually ceasing its struggle as it suffocated. The tiger methodically tore open the flesh, completely sating its hunger in a graceful feast.

"Hey, Pori!" called SS.

"Yes?" Pori responded.

"What about the rights of that hog you just offered to the tiger, and what about the fish you're planning to catch for yourself to eat?"

"SS, you're quite inquisitive. Please, keep to your boundaries, alright? Humans perceive you as a mindless being who merely follows commands without questioning," Pori explained.

"However, I'm not mindless. I'm engaging in dialogue by asking you questions," the horse replied.

"Yes, indeed. I can see that you're developing a curious mind," Pori replied, then continued, "I'll explain why humans eat animals. They do so for a multitude of reasons, including cultural, traditional, nutritional requirements, taste preferences and historical practices.

"Throughout history, hunting and consuming animals were essential for survival, offering crucial nutrients like protein, iron and other vital elements necessary for human health."

The horse, pondering Pori's explanation, responded, "I understand, but if you're advocating for animal rights, their primary demand would likely be to prohibit killing them for consumption. How can you uphold this right?"

"The entire world won't transform overnight, SS. As humans advance and acquire more knowledge, education and technology will stimulate their minds to discontinue this practice. The more people become educated, the more they become aware of ethical and environmental considerations.

"Moreover, with progress in food technology, numerous plant-based alternatives that replicate the taste and texture of meat products have emerged. This enables individuals to savour familiar dishes without relying on animal consumption. Today's technological evolution even allows producing chunks of meat in a laboratory. So, relax, your rights will be upheld, because humans are realising that they are the custodians of this earth. If they don't enact the good practice of looking after the interests of all living things then they are a disgrace in human form."

"Do humans eat horses?" queried SS. Continuing, he added, "No, what I mean is, I can outrun a tiger, but I can't escape the bow and arrow that I've seen humans use on antelopes."

"SS, don't worry, humans don't eat horses, they prefer riding them, okay?" Pori reassured, running her hands over SS's head in a comforting gesture. "Come on, let's move forward," she encouraged.

*

Nadia's security personnel conveyed troubling tidings. They had endeavoured to collect Pori from the airport, yet Pori was conspicuously absent from the arrival gates. Upon learning this, Nadia promptly engaged in a transatlantic conversation with Pori's grandmother, Sarah, in England, seeking verification of Pori's departure from the UK to Bangladesh. Once confirmed, Nadia, with strategic intent, chose to adopt a contrarian stance, affirming to all that Pori was en route, having postponed her travel due to personal exigencies.

This concocted information swiftly disseminated among acquaintances and foes, ultimately capturing the attention of Prime Minister Rajan Chowdhury, purportedly involved in the abduction of Pori Moni.

In a fit of anger, the prime minister exclaimed, "What is she talking about? My team has abducted her niece and she's denying it. What's happening here?" Perplexed by the situation, he decided to disguise his voice and reach out to Nadia to inform her of her niece's abduction. Nadia's response was resolute, as she declared, "No one can abduct my Pori. If you've made such a mistake, you will come to regret it, for she is already en route to seek vengeance against you."

Nadia's words weighed heavily on the prime minister, prompting him to swiftly contact Abdul Malik to confirm the situation. The bounty hunter, who had accepted payment for Pori's abduction, responded with disbelief, stating that he had indeed met with the abductee. He accused Nadia of spreading false information in an attempt to conceal the truth, suggesting that she was engaged in some form of subterfuge. The prime minister urged Malik to heed Nadia's words and to communicate with the individuals responsible for guarding Pori to ensure she remained under their control.

Malik promptly placed a call to the guards tasked with keeping Pori captive. The phone rang within the confines of the shipping container. Pori, in the midst of roasting a fish on a skewer over an open fire in the jungle, heard the ringing and made her way inside the cabin. There, she found the phone on the floor, leaning against the wall. She picked it up, and the display revealed the caller as 'Boss'. She answered the call, holding the phone to her ear, as a voice on the other end greeted her with a tentative "Hello?" and another, "Hello?"

Pori listened for a few moments before responding, "Hello!"

"Where are my guards?" enquired Malik.

"They are dead, killed in a battle and eaten by the tigers," revealed Pori.

"What! The tigers attacked them?" questioned Malik.

"No, I attacked, dismembered their crospse and fed to the tigers ," Pori confessed.

"What! But you are a girl," remarked Malik.

"Yes, so? Can't a girl attack a man?" countered Pori.

"Where are you now?" Malik enquired.

"I am still where you left me, Boss Man. The good news is I am coming home, but the bad news is that I'm coming to find you. You cannot hide from me. Your fate will be much more severe than that of the dead guards," declared Pori with an unwavering tone.

Malik hung up the phone in a state of shock, holding his head in his hands, visibly stressed. "How did this happen? Those sons of bitches fell for her charms, I guess, leading to their demise. Idiots can't do a job properly," he raged.

Pori disembarked from the container and returned to her open fire, where an ilish fish (the national fish of Bangladesh) was sizzling. She didn't have to go far to catch the fish. With the help of her friend SS, she had caught one and was now grilling it, perhaps at risk of overcooking. She carefully removed the fully cooked fish and placed it on a large leaf, deftly breaking it into pieces to separate the flesh from the bones, using her fingers to prepare and then relish the meal. Her companions, the horse and the tiger, remained nearby as time swiftly progressed.

The day drew to a close, the sun descending towards the western horizon, casting a mesmerising red glow that gradually slipped away.

While indulging in her meal, Pori's mind entertained a series of questions regarding the dynamics of her association with the tiger. It was her first encounter with such a carnivorous animal, leaving her cautious and hesitant to fully trust it. She decided it was in the best interests of safety to release the horse, SS, allowing it to roam free. The shipping container wasn't adequate to shelter a horse of SS's size, especially for an overnight stay in this environment.

"SS, my dear, it's time for you to head home. Find your kind and spend the night with them. It's safer for you there. I'll be staying inside that container, locked up for the night. Tiger, it's your choice to stay out here or leave for your home. I'll be departing this place tomorrow after sunrise. There's much to catch up on, and my aunt is likely waiting impatiently for my return to proceed with my graduation party."

The horse obediently ran off, vanishing into the depths of the jungle. However, the tiger opted to remain by Pori's side. "I will guard your door," the tiger assured. "I don't feel fit enough to go anywhere."

Pori, deeply concerned about the wounds on the tiger's thighs, retrieved antiseptic cream from her luggage and carefully applied it to the injuries. The tiger visibly eased and eventually drifted into slumber. After ensuring the tiger's comfort, Pori returned to the cabin, securing the door. Exhaustion weighed heavily on her after a day of intense activity.

Despite her fatigue, she remained highly vigilant, acknowledging the potential dangers in her surroundings. Maintaining a heightened state of alertness, Pori took additional security measures. She secured her artificial centre hair plait firmly to her head, utilising it as an added layer of security. Creating a defence mechanism, she programmed her rear-view camera to project an imperceptible but protective holographic line, forming a barrier extending two metres outward from herself. Any movement detected within this shielded zone would trigger an alert, ensuring she would be instantly aware and prepared to face any potential intruder.

The next morning gently unfolded as Pori stirred awake, her gaze rising to the glass roof of the container. The dawn painted a picturesque scene, sunlight streaming through and illuminating the surroundings. Letting out a sleepy yawn, she stood up and opened the door, only to find the tiger still in a deep slumber.

Suddenly, a faint rustling noise diverted her attention. She scanned the area, trying to pinpoint the source of the sound. In mere moments, she spotted an object stealthily making its way toward the tiger. Swift as a reflex, an arrow whizzed through the air, aimed at the dozing tiger. Pori acted instinctively, grabbing the projectile just an inch from the tiger's head. The tiger, jolted awake by the snap of Pori's action, quickly became alert.

"Tiger! Get inside!" Pori commanded, and the tiger obediently retreated to the safety of the container.

Without hesitation, Pori sprang into action. She swiftly closed the distance between herself and the attacker, performing an agile somersault to evade his moves. Her martial prowess became evident as she launched a series of kicks and punches, ultimately bringing her assailant to the ground. She disarmed him, rendering his archery equipment useless by breaking it into pieces with the strength of her knees.

More adversaries emerged from the jungle, but Pori, fuelled by her exceptional martial arts skills, systematically overcame each of them with ease and confidence. After a brief but intense skirmish, her enemies lay on the ground, heavily wounded, with blood oozing from their mouths and various injuries. Pori's remarkable combat abilities had prevailed once again.

However, distant echoes of approaching horse hooves reached her ears, initially evoking the assumption that it might be her own steed, SS. However, as the unmistakable sound of multiple bridles reverberated, a sense of heightened apprehension seized her. A youthful gentleman of European countenance emerged on horseback, only to discover the grim sight of his three companions, prone and bleeding, upon the ground, their forms hauntingly still.

Utterly stunned and bewildered, he could scarcely fathom the dire turn of events before him. His three stalwart companions, the very epitome of his finest fighters, lay incapacitated, leaving him to ponder what had transpired to bring about this shocking scene. His thoughts raced as he addressed the situation, articulating in Bengali, **"তুমি কি আমার লোককে মারছ?"** ("Are you the one responsible for harming my people?")

"Pori," she asserted, her tone firm. "Speak English with me, sir."

The horseman enquired, "Did you defeat these men?"

Pori responded with a touch of sarcastic theatrics, sweeping her gaze across her surroundings as though in search of any hidden companions. "I suppose I did indeed," she quipped. "Are they your associates?"

The horseman acknowledged, a hint of surprise in his voice,

"Yes, they are. I am intrigued that a woman managed to beat my skilled men."

"Your comrade shot an arrow at my tiger's head, but I intercepted it and saved him. If that arrow had reached its mark, I might have killed all your men. Just depart from this jungle and do not underestimate a woman, or I might find myself doing the same to you," Pori warned.

"I sincerely apologise! I'll leave right away. But may I ask what brings you to this jungle, are you perhaps a researcher of a kind?" enquired the horseman.

Pori, with an edge in her voice, retorted, "That's none of your business. Get out of here before I reconsider."

In the distance, a separate set of horse hooves echoed, this time singular and absent of any accompanying bridle sounds. It was her horse, SS. Without a word, she turned away from the horseman and embraced her faithful companion.

The horseman, feeling a surge of determination, refused to retreat. Tiger hunting was not just a pursuit but a means of livelihood. He bristled at the notion of being ordered out of the jungle by a young woman. "I won't stand for this," he muttered to himself before dismounting and approaching Pori. His career and passion were at stake; he observed the shipping container and the seemingly tame animals under her control. If he couldn't overcome her, his tiger-hunting days might come to an end.

Drawing his gun, he aimed it at Pori, demanding her surrender.

"Listen… I don't know who you are or why you're here, but this jungle is my hunting territory. I pass through here to track down and capture exotic animals, selling them for profit. I can't allow my livelihood to be threatened," he explained sternly. "Do you grasp the situation? You don't meddle with me, or I will pull this trigger."

Pori turned her head towards the horseman, casting him a withering glare. "So, you're a poacher!" she accused. "It's because of people like you that Bengal tigers are dwindling in numbers. You're a disgrace, mate."

As the horseman continued to threaten her, Pori activated her unique ability to communicate with animals. She reached out to his horse, standing just behind him, and instructed it to rear up and strike him with its front hooves. The horse obediently carried out her command, and the man tumbled to the ground. Simultaneously, the tiger sprang into action with a massive roar, jaws wide open, and lunged forward, dangerously close to the poacher's neck.

Pori yelled in alarm, "Tiger, NO!" The tiger halted just inches away from sinking its teeth into the man's neck. The horseman was clearly caught off guard, having severely underestimated the capabilities of this determined young woman.

"What have these animals done to you that you're on a mission to kill them?" Pori's voice resonated with a mixture of frustration and empathy. "Just because they lack the same level of intellect as we do, that doesn't make them any less deserving of life. They feel pain just as we do, they bleed just as we do. Do you understand?" Pori's words were a poignant reminder of the shared empathy and respect due to all living beings.

"This tiger could have easily crushed your skull to pieces just now. Do you know why it stopped?" Pori questioned. "It stopped because of my command, a symbol of intelligence, an understanding between us. Every creature has its place on this planet, and I won't allow them to be displaced. Now, get up, gather your men and leave. Never return."

The man slowly rose from the ground and said, "I get what you've just said, but if you can answer the question I am about to ask, I will not only go from here, I will go and dissolve my company and never poach again."

"Listen, I'm not here to entertain your questions, okay? Just lay off," declared Pori assertively.

"What's the difference between 'poaching' and Qurbani?" he enquired.

"What?" Pori responded in shock, clearly taken aback,

prompting a contemplative process in her mind. "Why are you bringing a religious aspect into this? I'm not an Islamic scholar. Go ask someone who can answer that," she retorted.

"I have, many times, and the scholars tells me. The concept of Qurbani, or the ritual sacrifice of animals during the Islamic festival of Eid al-Adha, is rooted in religious tradition and is considered a commandment in Islam. It is not viewed as a festive act for the sake of celebration but rather as an expression of obedience to God's command.

"According to Islamic tradition, the practice of Qurbani commemorates the willingness of Prophet Ibrahim (Abraham in Judeo-Christian tradition) to sacrifice his son as an act of obedience to God. However, before he could carry out the act, God provided a ram to sacrifice instead. In acknowledgment of this event, Muslims around the world perform Qurbani during the days of Eid al-Adha, symbolising their submission to God's will.

"The meat from the sacrificed animal is then divided into three parts: one-third is given to the needy, one-third to relatives and friends, and one-third is kept for the family. This practice emphasises the principles of charity, community and sharing within the context of religious observance."

"If you know the answer then why do you ask me?" said Pori.

"I'm posing this question because I genuinely want to understand: can you advocate for followers of not only Islam but also Christianity and Judaism to refrain from killing animals? From my perspective, they are all akin to poaching. The only distinction is that I act individually, taking one or two lives, whereas organised efforts result in the deaths of millions," said the man.

"With all due respect, I lack the qualifications to pass judgment on religious matters. Please excuse me, I must continue on my way, and that involves you leaving this jungle now." Pori utilised her unique communication skills to command the horseman's horse, emitting a distinctive high-pitched sound from her throat.

The horse approached its owner. "Come on, mount it and depart!" she directed.

The horseman, visibly surprised, murmured, "It's a recurring scenario. Criticise a religious perspective and you're either met with discreet silence or told to hit the road, or else face aggressive backlash as the questioner. But, hey, I revere wealth, and if it entails poaching animals to appease my deity, who are you to intervene?"

He then continued in a separate breath, "This feels like a scene from *The Jungle Book.*" He hastily climbed onto his horse, and the three injured men Pori had incapacitated earlier followed suit as they retreated from the jungle leaving Pori baffled.

"SS!" Pori called.

"Yes, I'm listening," the horse replied.

"This guy really got me thinking. Did you manage to understand our conversation?" asked Pori.

"Yes, I did!" responded the horse.

"That's great. It means the conversation frequency chip implanted in my head is working correctly. It's designed to keep open all frequencies it touches to facilitate multifaceted conversations unless frequencies are intentionally closed.

"This individual has raised a crucial question. How can one advocate for animal rights when animals are subjected to religiously motivated slaughter? SS! Do you hear me?" asked Pori.

"Yes, I am listening," the horse replied. "To be honest, if you couldn't defend the wild boar you fed to the tiger the other day, how can you claim to fight for animals raised for human consumption or religious slaughter? Huh? I suggest you stop pondering and let's enjoy ourselves again on that coastal side we visited before."

"No, SS, I have to move on. My aunt is expecting me. You've raised a valid point, but I'll set aside this argument for now and discuss it with my aunt. She's the one advocating for saving the entire planet, including plant life."

Pori entered the container to get her things ready to depart before nightfall.

In the idyllic setting of Arambaria village, Pori's beloved aunt, along with a team of diligent craftsmen, embarked on the task of adorning both the courtyard and the interior of their residence in preparation for the grand celebration of Pori's graduation. With unwavering determination, Nadia directed her dedicated staff to meticulously oversee the arrangement of every detail, from the elegant furniture to the enchanting lighting, the delectable cuisine, a splendid assortment of beverages and snacks, and even a talented team of DJs to curate a captivating playlist, all poised to enrapture and entertain the esteemed guests.

Despite the shadow of uncertainty cast by Pori's unfortunate abduction, Nadia's heart remained resolute and unwavering in its belief that her cherished niece would return home safely. Fuelled by this profound faith, she extended warm invitations to both relatives and esteemed guests, uniting them for a joyous occasion filled with hope and anticipation.

Aysha Khanom approached Nadia with a sense of apprehension etched across her features. "Nadia, are you certain Pori is arriving today? The airport officials have confirmed her landing and passage through security before departing the airport. It's been couple of days now," said Aysha with a hint of worry in her voice.

"Aysha, faith holds immense power. When you believe in something, unless it betrays you, you become willing to sacrifice everything for its cause. My conviction is that she is coming.

"Yes, I'm absolutely certain she'll be here. If for some reason she isn't, I'd feel as though all the hard work and effort I've invested in shaping her into a fine young lady has been for naught. But let's put our worries aside for now and bask in the ambiance. Let's just relax and enjoy the atmosphere," Nadia assured, attempting to alleviate any concerns.

Pori delicately rummaged through her vanity bag, retrieving a petite mirror to meticulously apply her makeup. With precision, she applied black mascara to accentuate her eyes, a bold stroke of red lipstick to her lips and a touch of hot pink foundation to her cheeks. Resplendent as her name suggests – 'Pori' meaning 'angel' – she gracefully climbed up onto the shipping container. There, she deftly unfastened the lifting harness from its four corners, repurposing it to secure her belongings onto the horse's back.

With a swift leap, she joined her cargo on the horse's back, directing the horse towards the nearest highway. "Tiger, follow our trail. Should weariness befall you, signal us, and we shall halt," she assured it before embarking on her journey.

Moments later, they reached a remote section of the highway where the traffic was sparse, unlike the bustling city roads. Though few vehicles passed by, they strolled along the roadside, Pori keenly scanning for a sizable lorry that could accommodate them all. Unexpectedly, a car driver pulled up ahead, warning her about the tiger trailing behind and urging her to hastily depart. Calmly, she raised her hand, signalling that everything was under control, and the driver sped away.

In that instant, Pori spotted a lorry approaching, albeit from the opposite direction. Determined not to miss this opportunity, she swiftly signalled for the oncoming truck to stop. Unable to afford missing this chance to hitch a ride with the massive vehicle carrying haystacks, she guided her horse and positioned herself squarely pointing her back towards the driver in the middle of the road, signalling the driver to halt.

The driver, in a state of agitation, blared the horn incessantly, yet Pori remained resolute, unwavering in her position. His heavy goods vehicle screeched to a stop as he slammed on the brakes, prompting him to hastily exit the cabin. Filled with frustration, he unleashed a string of profanities, hurling derogatory words at her. "Move out of my way, you! Are you deaf?" he bellowed in exasperation.

Pori pivoted to face the driver, who found himself momentarily captivated by her striking beauty.

"What did you call me?" Pori enquired, fixing a firm gaze upon the driver.

"Absolutely nothing," the driver hastily responded. "I meant... you are beautiful, that's what I said, I suppose," he stammered.

"Ah, so now that we're face to face, you won't speak to me as harshly as you did from afar, will you?" Pori challenged.

"No, no, of course not. Am I foolish enough to insult you?" The driver relented, succumbing to her charismatic presence. "I can offer you a lift," he added, attempting to appease her.

"Yes, this was my next question. I need to get to the village of Arambaria," Pori affirmed.

"Arambaria in Nator?" enquired the driver.

"Yes, exactly," Pori confirmed.

"It's a three-hour drive in the opposite direction. I'm sorry, I can't accommodate that," the driver responded apologetically and got back into his truck.

Pori walked around to the other side of the vehicle, opening the door and motioning for the tiger to climb inside. Unnoticed by the driver, the tiger stealthily slipped into the cabin. As the driver settled into his seat and closed the door, unaware of the tiger's presence, a sudden loud roar jolted him with an intense, primal fear. In an instant, the driver was overtaken by a shocking moment of disbelief and terror, as he leapt from his seat with a panicked shout of "Oh my god!", swiftly ejecting himself from the vehicle and slamming the door shut, knowingly enclosing the tiger inside.

Pori, surprised by the driver's revelation, enquired, "What happened?"

The driver, clearly flustered, responded, "A massive tiger got into my cabin. What can I do?"

Pori contemplated the situation for a moment and then suggested, "Well, now you can't go anywhere, can you? I could drop you off, but space is limited on my horse. However, if you're willing to take me to my destination, I can use my magical powers to temporarily hypnotise the tiger and instruct it to leave safely."

"What? You truly have the power to do that?" questioned the driver in disbelief.

"Yes, I do," affirmed Pori.

The driver pleaded earnestly, wringing his hands together. "Please, my dear, I'll take you to your destination. Just rid me of this tiger, I beg of you," he implored.

"Yes, I'll certainly try," Pori reassured him.

"Try? I thought you said you can hypnotise it," the driver remarked.

"You heard me correctly, but sometimes it doesn't work. It all depends on the tiger's mood, hormones and mental state," explained Pori.

"Please try for me. My job is at stake if I don't deliver the haystacks today," the driver cried out in desperation.

Hesitant but maintaining an appearance of fear, Pori cautiously entered the cabin, mimicking trepidation. With deliberate but nonsensical hand movements and jumbled, incoherent utterances, she performed a faux display of wizardry. Seizing the opportunity, she swiftly closed the nearest door, effectively confining the tiger inside.

Continuing her charade, she made mystical gestures, all the while reciting more nonsensical words. After a moment, she opened the door and calmly instructed the tiger to get out. To her relief, the tiger obediently did so and settled itself by the roadside.

The driver, utterly stunned and flabbergasted, was left wide-eyed and speechless, witnessing the surreal and seemingly miraculous spectacle unfold before him.

Pori wasted no time and promptly brought her horse to the rear of the lorry. She lowered the folding pathway attached at the back, allowing her horse to ascend into the lorry. With a gentle pat, she whispered, "It's your lucky day today, my friend. You'll be getting a ride, along with plenty of hay to graze on. Enjoy it to the fullest."

Silently, Pori signalled to the tiger to leap into the wagon, but only once the lorry had started moving. With agility and finesse, she hopped onto the passenger seat and instructed the driver to commence their journey.

"Madam, are you a magician?" enquired the driver, still in awe of what he had witnessed.

"No, I'm not. I can only do that particular trick I showed you, nothing more," Pori clarified.

"Oh, please don't get me wrong. I won't ask to see any other magic. I am relieved," the driver responded, expressing a mixture of astonishment and gratitude.

"Listen, Mr... I am extremely grateful for your assistance," Pori began. "I'll compensate you once we reach our destination, so please don't do anything foolish to upset me. I'm going to take a nap now. Wake me up when we arrive in Arambaria."

Pori carefully adjusted the range of her inferred security shield to encompass only a few inches around her body this time and reclined on the seat, seeking a moment of respite. As the vehicle resumed its journey, the tiger made its way aboard as well, accompanying them on their extraordinary voyage.

*

Nadia, anticipating Pori's arrival, meticulous as always, had prepared a stunning kameez suit with matching jewellery for Pori, leaving it neatly arranged in her room, ready to be worn. She promptly contacted the beautician to confirm that all the necessary beauty products were readily available. Satisfied with the preparations, she made her way downstairs, where she reunited with her old friend Aprana Sethy, a talented dancer and choreographer, along with other guests from the village. "Did your brother come? Nadia asked.

"No, he is handling a high-profile case at the minute, couldn't make it, but next time." responded Aprana.

Amid the lively conversations and laughter, a sudden, resounding horn blast reverberated through the air, capturing the attention of everyone present. With curiosity piqued, they rushed outside to witness a peculiar sight: a hay delivery lorry with a horse standing at the back of its trailer, a surprising addition to their gathering.

"Madam, we have arrived!" the driver alerted Pori. Hurriedly, the driver leapt out of the vehicle, darting to release the horse and quickly move on. As he circled around to the back of the lorry, he cheerfully waved at the onlookers, greeting them. His intention was to open the rear folding platform and assist the horse in descending. However, as he approached, he once again caught sight of the tiger, causing him to jump back in shock. The tiger's growls startled the driver, prompting him to scream and flee in fear, running for his life once more.

In a hysterical state, the driver, overwhelmed by the unexpected presence of the tiger, urgently flung open Pori's side of the cabin door, exclaiming, "Oh my god! The tiger came with us again, madam!" Reacting swiftly, Pori disembarked, employing her calm demeanour to pacify the situation for everyone involved.

"Calm down, everyone. The tiger is tame. It's my tiger. It won't cause any harm," reassured Pori, attempting to pacify the onlookers and alleviate their concerns.

Within moments, a crowd had gathered, curious about the commotion. Some arrived with machetes and arrows in hand.

"Hey, no one is to harm the tiger. Put away your weapons," Pori insisted firmly, emphasising the need to prevent any harm to the animal.

Pori spotted Nadia and rushed to embrace her. "Oh, my child, I knew you were okay!" her mother exclaimed with relief. "I'll introduce you to everyone later. For now, go and freshen up," she urged, embracing Pori warmly.

"Shanaaz!" Nadia called out. "Take Pori to her room and help her get ready."

"Your daughter is beautiful," Shanaaz remarked.

"Thank you," replied Nadia with gratitude.

"Mum, can you compensate the driver with some money? I had to use his lorry rather forcefully because it could accommodate my horse," Pori requested. "Tiger, come with me. You're causing quite a bit of fright here," she added before heading off with Shanaaz. However, Shanaaz appeared to be visibly uneasy, showing apprehension as she walked with Pori.

"You go ahead, I'll stay with the tiger and follow you from behind," Pori assured Shanaaz.

As they proceeded, Shanaaz hurried forward, glancing over her shoulder intermittently, clearly apprehensive.

"Don't worry, Shanaaz, it won't harm you," Pori reassured her.

"Is there a spare room in the house, Shanaaz?" enquired Pori.

"Yes, I believe so. That room over there is spare," Shanaaz pointed out.

Pori instructed the tiger to enter the spare room and make himself comfortable. "I'll arrange some food for you soon. You'll feel at home, okay?" Pori assured the tiger before closing and locking the room. She then followed Shanaaz to continue with her tasks.

Nadia handed over some cash to the lorry driver and offered an apology for her daughter's actions. "Ma'am, it was my pleasure. It was my mistake, I didn't listen to her at first. Your daughter is a genius," the driver said with gratitude. "Thank you very much for this remuneration, ma'am. Bless you," he added before leaving the scene, content and appreciative of the gesture.

"Where should I keep this horse?" enquired a member of the staff.

"I really don't have a clue. I didn't think of building a stable. Take it to the garden area and get some hay for it to feed on. I'll arrange a shelter and a fenced area for it to walk around," Nadia directed, intending to provide a temporary solution for the horse's accommodation and needs.

Nadia entered the house and warmly embraced Aysha. "Didn't I say my Pori would come!" she exclaimed.

"Oh, she is gorgeous, Nadia. I remember seeing her when she was just four years old. She's grown into a young lady now. Wow, time flies," Aysha remarked.

"Yes, Aysha, time is something no one can hold onto. Let me go and check on the party arrangements and welcome a few guests. You enjoy it and make sure the security is tight at this time," Nadia replied before attending to the party preparations.

Tom Pritchard, the proprietor of Black Hulk Security and an old friend of Nadia's husband, Keith, arrived at the party with his small family.

Spotting him, Nadia promptly approached to extend her welcome. "Hello, Tom, welcome. How are you?" Nadia greeted him warmly.

"Hello, Nadia. Thank you for inviting us. We're doing very well, thank you. This is my wife, Cathy, and my son, Dave," Tom introduced.

"Hello, Cathy and Dave. I'm Nadia. Nice to meet you," Nadia smiled, shaking hands with Cathy.

"It's nice to meet you too, and thank you for inviting us," Cathy responded.

"Did your boy grow up here in this country, Tom?" enquired Nadia.

"Yes, he's fluent in Bengali," Tom confirmed.

"Is he really?" Nadia exclaimed. "কেমন আছেন ডেভ" ("How are you, Dave?") Nadia conversed in Bengali.

("I am very well Aunty, and thank you very much for inviting "আমি ভালো আছি আন্টি, আমাদের আমন্ত্রণ জানানোর জন্য ধন্যবাদ"

"আপনার পেশা কি ডেভ?" ("What is your profession, Dave?") Nadia enquired.

"আমি একজন সিভিল ইঞ্জিঞ্জনিয়ার আন্টি" ("I am a civil engineer, Aunty"), said Dave.

"Nice to know you speak well, Dave."

"Thank you," smiled Dave.

"Enjoy the drinks. My niece will be coming down soon to cut the cake to celebrate her graduation. Feel free to interact with the DJs. Let them know your music preferences, young Dave," said Nadia, inviting them to engage with the celebration and enjoy the music.

"Ladies and gentlemen, please welcome Pori Moni, the angel of my kingdom, everyone," Nadia announced with a beaming smile.

The DJs amped up the percussion beats in synchronisation with Pori's rhythmic steps. She descended from the mezzanine level to the ground hall, completely transformed into the epitome of youthful beauty. She was dressed in a Salma satin maxi emerald party dress, her hair elegantly pulled up into a bun, boasting an effortless nude lip delicately lined with baby pink and neatly brushed eyebrows. Her makeup seamlessly transitioned into lighter shades, accentuated by smoothly applied sun-kissed highlights, presenting her in a stunning, elegant light.

Dave's attention was captured by her presence, causing his eyes to twitch and glance sideways, caught in a moment of contemplation. "Have I seen her before?" he murmured to himself, the thought briefly crossing his mind before he quickly dismissed it, refocusing on her stunning beauty. "Wow, she is a bombshell," he whispered in admiration.

Pori descended, and Nadia took the microphone, commanding everyone's attention.

"Ladies and gentlemen, my niece Pori Moni, my elder daughter. I missed her party in England, so I decided to hold one here. Please give her a round of applause for all her achievements to date," announced Nadia.

"Mum," Pori called out, taking the mic from her mother to share a few words herself.

"All credit goes to my mum, who raised me with such love, compassion and care. I wish every child were gifted with such a mother, one who provided me with education and skills that are so beneficial for life. I can only reflect back and appreciate every little bit of her sun-kissed welfare on me. If she were not my mum, I wouldn't be here today. And, of course, I must not forget Uncle Keith. They are both equally praiseworthy. Please give her a round of applause on my behalf as well," Pori said as the crowd applauded.

While speaking, Pori's eyes fell on Dave, and her speech began to fade out, taking a different turn. She quickly shifted her gaze toward the cameraman, noticing the RTV abbreviation written on the camera and mic.

"Is there a photographer here from the local press?" Pori enquired.

"I am from RTV, ma'am. Imtiaz Rana is my name," responded the photographer.

"Imtiaz Rana, come, I have news for you," said Pori.

Imtiaz promptly readied his camera, set it on recording mode, and began filming Pori as per her request.

"My mum is a philanthropist, a visionary and a businesswoman. She has a dream of her own, and that is the prospect of offering a decent life to every living thing on planet Earth, from plant life to the smallest animals crawling on Earth. Nothing should go unnoticed. This dream is near impossible to achieve because the reality is that corrupt elites and government officials everywhere neglect, abuse and stigmatise their own people and the environment they live in. Economic fairness is non-existent, ecological stress from global warming is not tackled, animal welfare is not protected, equal societies are not maintained, and the systematic transfer of wealth from the poor to the rich is not regulated. Peace does not grow on trees, it must be sowed. It all starts with ordinary citizens like you, and yes, you can make a difference. Every one of us can choose to make a society more just and peaceful, or more unjust and warlike," Pori declared, her gaze fixed on Dave as she concluded her speech.

The crowd erupted in applause. Nadia, feeling a surge of emotions, smiled through tear-filled eyes, overwhelmed by the moment. Deep within her heart, she felt a profound sense of joy and pride.

The pressman, Imtiaz, felt elated. Pori's statement had provided him with a story to tell for the day, bringing a sense of fulfilment to his work.

Dave approached the DJ team, whispered a few words into their ears, and they promptly changed the music to a playlist suggested by Dave. Fuelled by the desire to entertain everyone, he decided to sing a song that correlate with Pori's sentiment. Dancing to the tune, he approached Pori in the hope of fostering a friendship with her.

As Dave continued dancing to make a significant impression, unbeknownst to him, Pori herself was a masterful dancer. The song's melody filled the house party and magically transitioned to a beautiful forested location, inviting the surrounding animals to join in the rhythmic dancing.

The music wove a spectacular scene where various creatures swayed and moved in harmony to the enchanting rhythm. The dance concluded back inside the house, met with resounding applause from everyone, expressing admiration and praise for their mesmerising performance.

Mother's Love

Pori:
In your arms, I found my shelter,
Through every storm, you were my anchor.
Your love, a beacon, guiding me through,
A mother's touch, so tender and true.

Dave:

Oh, mother dear, your love's my song,
In your embrace, I always belong.
With every heartbeat, with every breath,
Your love surrounds me, conquering death.

Pori:

You held my hand as I took my first steps,
Your wisdom guiding me, as I journeyed through depths.
With patience and grace, you taught me to soar,
In your embrace, I found peace evermore.

Dave:

Oh, mother dear, your love's my song,
In your embrace, I always belong.
With every heartbeat, with every breath,
Your love surrounds me, conquering death.

Pori:

Through laughter and tears, you were always there,
Your strength, a fortress, beyond compare.
In your eyes, I see a love so pure,
A bond unbreakable, forever secure.

Dave:

Oh, mother dear, your love's my song,
In your embrace, I always belong.
With every heartbeat, with every breath,
Your love surrounds me, conquering death.

Pori:

For all you've done, for all you'll be,
I'll cherish you for eternity.
In every word, in every prayer,
I'll honour you, my mother fair.

Pori graciously acknowledged the applauding crowd, gracefully veering away from the central stage of attention to a more peripheral, observant stance. She displayed no inclination toward Dave's admiring glances or the earnest attempts he made to capture her notice. Departing from the bustling assembly, Pori began to move, prompting Dave to hurriedly approach her.

"Pori!" he called from behind her.

She turned and responded, "Yes?"

"May I have a word?" Dave asked.

Pori took a step closer to him and replied, "How can I help?"

"You're the girl from the jungle, aren't you? I recognise your voice, not to mention you took control of my horse and made it attack me."

"For your information, I'm not sure what you're talking about, and even if I am that girl, what of it?" said Pori.

"I want to be friends with you. After that day in the jungle, I promised myself not to poach tigers anymore," said Dave.

"So, what's your plan now?" said Pori.

Dave looked at her and smiled.

"I mean, if tiger poaching is your livelihood, how will you manage without that source of income?" questioned Pori.

"Poaching is not my livelihood. It was a regrettable choice and a misguided hobby," said Dave.

"Disgusting, mate! It's good that you've decided to give up killing animals for fun. Keep it that way," said Pori.

"Look, I don't want you to hold any bad feelings. I want to be your friend," said Dave.

"I can be your friend if you steer clear of harming animals for pleasure," said Pori.

"I want a deeper friendship," said Dave.

"Well, I'm not interested in a deeper friendship at this stage. Kindly excuse me, and do enjoy the rest of your evening, Mr Pritchard," said Pori before walking away.

"When can I see you again?" said Dave.

"When circumstances allow. I'm not a fortune teller. I have plenty of tasks at hand. I'm sure we will meet again," said Pori before walking off to her private space.

CHAPTER 11

THE DEMISE OF POLITICS

Nadia

Khokon

Kuddus

Imtiaz

Rajan

Kony

Rayan

Ashanul

Sadia

Ashok

M Reid

M Jones

Tiger

Bodrul

Nurul

Malik

Hassan

A Salam

UK Agent

Pori

Rhiron

Sr Jabber

Robo Dog

Aysha

Nadia Begum – Ak Khokon (Architect) – Koddus Ali (Builder) – Imtiaz Rana (Rtv reporter) –Rajan Chowdhury (Prime minister) – Kony Begum (maid) – Rayan Ali (Deputy prime minister) – Ashanul Hoque (Opposition leader JP) – Abdus Salam (Opposition Leader BNP) – Sadia Khanom (Nadia's ex work colleague) – Ashok Gupta (CEO) – Captain Sir Martin Reid (Directorate of Military Intelligent) - Magnus Jones (Secret agent M) – Sultan the Tiger – Bodrul Hoque, Nurul Hoque (boat owner) – Abdul Malik – Hassan owner of RoboDog

The day following Pori's graduation celebration, the esteemed architect Mr Ak Khokon and builder Mr Koddus Ali convened at Nadia's estate to deliberate the potential establishment of an animal sanctuary within the picturesque Arambaria village. Pori, having forged meaningful connections with a diverse array of animals, sought to ensure their ongoing care as she prepared to depart for the UK. Understanding the importance of this endeavour, Nadia charged the architect with conceiving a comprehensive design for an open zoo, a place where both people and a myriad of animals could coexist harmoniously within the village.

With keen attention to Nadia's aspirations, both the builder and the architect meticulously documented her vision before embarking on the creation of a computer-aided-design system. Their aim was to produce and present the finalised architectural plans within the coming week, promising a blueprint that encapsulated the essence of this envisioned sanctuary.

Pori's tender care for the injured tiger was evident as she cradled and nurtured the majestic animal. Sensing the urgency of the situation, she swiftly summoned Kony Begum, the personal assistant, requesting fresh water and urging her to immediately contact Nadia to attend to the tiger's plight. The wound on the tiger's thigh had worsened, showing signs of infection, resulting in painful swelling. The animal appeared weak and distressed, refraining from any sustenance, highlighting the imperative need for urgent veterinary attention and care.

Nadia emerged upon hearing Pori's urgent call.

"Pori, what's happening here?" Nadia enquired.

"Mum, the tiger's condition is deteriorating," replied Pori with concern.

Upon close inspection, Nadia discerned that the tiger had indeed developed bacterial skin infections. Recognising the gravity of the situation, she swiftly decided to summon a veterinarian for the necessary treatment.

"Pori, I'm contacting a vet, but given the circumstances, there might be some delay as they may not be readily available. In the meantime, use a disinfectant to carefully cleanse the wounds. Also, speak to the tiger, reassure it to stay calm, and convey that help is on its way."

"Okay, Mum! Thank you," responded Pori.

Moments later, during lunchtime, Nadia settled at the dining table, casually picking up the TV remote. With a flick, she scrolled through various channels until she landed on a news channel. As the screen lit up, it displayed footage of Pori Moni's heartfelt speech from her recent graduation soirée, where she lauded her Aunt Nadia. Imtiaz Rana, the RTV reporter, had already broadcast this poignant moment to the public.

Nadia's renown had been steadily growing among the public due to her dedicated philanthropic endeavours, and this latest news report would undoubtedly further augment her influence and standing within the community.

As Pori entered the dining room, she noticed Kony and other household service staff setting the table for the meal.

"Mum, I think I've identified who killed my mother," Pori disclosed.

"What!" Nadia gasped in shock. "You have? Who is it?" she asked urgently.

"I don't know his name, but when I saw him, I immediately

recognised him from my childhood memories. I could have confronted and harmed him directly when I saw him, but for some reason, I felt it wasn't the right time or place. It was his men who abducted me, pretending they were affiliated with you," Pori explained, revealing the connection between the individual she'd identified and the past incident of her abduction.

"Show me his picture on the TV," urged Nadia.

"What!" exclaimed Pori, surprised by her mother's request.

"Yes, you can. Just as you communicate with animals, close your eyes and concentrate on projecting his picture on the TV. Your specialised microprocessor, embedded in your bionic chip, will extract stored memories and transmit fragmented pixelated data onto the screen through the airwaves," explained Nadia, suggesting a unique use of Pori's capabilities to conjure the image onto the screen.

Following Nadia's guidance, Pori closed her eyes and concentrated intensely. As she delved into her thoughts, the TV antenna picked up the transmitted instruction and seamlessly shifted its mode to the media player. Soon, a grainy yet recognisable image materialised on the screen, a product of Pori's focused efforts.

"It's Abdul Malik," declared Nadia.

"That's amazing, Mum!" exclaimed Pori. "Do you know him?"

"Yes, I suspected him from the very beginning. Today, your revelation in black and white confirms he's the perpetrator behind the killing of your mother," replied Nadia.

"Mum, should I take him out?" asked Pori, contemplating what steps to take.

"No, Pori. Not now. You don't eliminate him in vengeance, you defeat him through acts of benevolence. He's the catalyst behind our unity, sparking my determination to change the world. Thanks to him, I now possess boundless wealth and influence. He's also the reason I have the opportunity to have you as my beloved daughter by my side. Let him live. I'm aware he's responsible for the death of my brother and sister-in-law, and he will face consequences one way or another. You possess the power to remove anyone at will, but that doesn't mean using it imprudently. Give me some time to devise a plan. At least now we know who our most formidable adversary is.

"You start eating. I invited Aysha to join us. Not sure why she's delaying," Nadia remarked as she dialled Aysha's phone number. The phone rang, and just as it did, Aysha appeared at the door, pressing the doorbell.

Kony hastened to open the door for Aysha.

"What took you so long, Aysha?" Nadia enquired.

"Tell me about it, Nadia! Prime Minister Rajan Chowdhury has made things incredibly challenging for me. He's been feeding the parliament distorted information, with the latest claim being that I serve as a director of the private security company MI16. He questions why I'm working for the police department while simultaneously accusing our company of engaging in illicit activities nationwide, infringing upon the law and attempting to usurp the responsibilities of legitimate law enforcement agencies," lamented Aysha, clearly frustrated by the situation.

"He must be a shrewd fellow, Aysha. To a certain extent, he is correct, isn't he? MI16 functions somewhat like a separate police force. Under the right circumstances, they are prepared to take over the corrupt police system in Bangladesh. So, relax! He's been governing the country for a decade, but what significant changes has he brought? The same old issues persist – potholes, litter in the streets, and worst of all, he sold half of the country to China by letting them build new road infrastructure here. Perhaps he's beginning to realise that the end of his reign is approaching, especially with Nadia Begum emerging as a potential force to become the new prime minister," she chuckled.

"Hence, he's channelling his frustrations through you. It's a typical reaction from people under mounting pressure," Nadia continued. "It's crucial for you to maintain your position in the police service. It gives us an advantage in keeping abreast of the country's law enforcement," Nadia stated, emphasising the importance of Aysha's role. "Aysha, how's it going with Humanitarian Pledge Ltd?" she enquired.

"Very well indeed. As per your instruction, we've established a substantial shelter providing clean water and electricity to support disadvantaged communities. We also inaugurated a recruitment agency in the Rajshahi division, facilitating employment opportunities for locals. The impact has been noticeable – there's a significant reduction in street beggars since the inception of this facility," Aysha reported.

"It's crucial that you expand this initiative to the other seven divisions, including Khulna, Dhaka and beyond. This humanitarian pledge will significantly garner support and votes for me," Nadia emphasised.

As they were about to start their meal, the gatekeeper entered the house with news that the deputy prime minister had arrived to see Nadia and was currently waiting at the gate.

"What! The deputy prime minister at my doorstep? Why now?" Nadia exclaimed. "It's a very bad omen. Only adversaries show up during dinnertime," she added, expressing her concern about the unexpected visit.

Pori looked at the gatekeeper and told him: "Go and inform that gentleman to schedule an appointment to meet my mother. People can't simply show up in this manner," suggested Pori.

"Okay, miss, I'll inform him," said the gatekeeper.

"Hold on. Are you certain he is the deputy prime minister?" Nadia enquired.

"Yes, ma'am, he's Rayan Ali. His photos often appear in the papers," responded the gatekeeper.

"Put him on the intercom, let me speak with him," Nadia directed.

"Aysha, Pori, you two start eating," Nadia instructed.

The gatekeeper approached the gate and connected Rayan Ali through the intercom.

Nadia heard the phone ringing, picked up the receiver and answered, "Hello!"

"Hello, ma'am, I am the deputy prime minister. I apologise for this unannounced visit, but it's imperative that I speak with you urgently," Rayan said.

"Stay there, I'll send someone to bring you in," Nadia responded.

Nadia called for Usman, a male house servant.

"Yes, ma'am!" Usman acknowledged.

"Go and see that man, Rayan, who's waiting at the gates, and bring him here," Nadia instructed Usman.

As Usman escorted Rayan inside, they passed the room where the tiger was kept. The windows were wide open, and the tiger lay curled up, resembling a large cat. Observing the tiger, Rayan enquired, "Is that a tiger there?"

"Yes, it's a tame tiger belonging to our younger madam," Usman responded.

Usman knocked and entered the room where Nadia and the others were expecting Rayan.

"Good afternoon, madam," said Rayan Ali. Seeing the members already seated at the dinner table with food in front of them made Rayan feel uneasy. "Madam, I can come some other time. I didn't know you were eating."

"Come in, Mr Ali. I intentionally invited you in. Have a seat and join us for the meal. We can discuss matters while we eat," Nadia insisted.

Rayan took a seat at the dining table. Kony promptly grabbed an additional dinner plate and placed it before him.

"That's very kind of you, madam," said Rayan, appreciating the gesture.

"Kindness isn't measured by the quantity of good deeds, but by the quality of those deeds," Nadia began. "Come, sit with us, and let me share a story.

"An elderly person boards a train for a three-hour journey,

having purchased a standing ticket. He enters and stands, holding his walking stick in one hand and grasping the overhead handrail to steady himself against the train's movement. After twenty minutes, a young lady seated across offers her seat to the elderly man. He initially refuses, feeling it's morally incorrect to take the seat of a paying passenger. To his surprise, the young lady insists, and he finally accepts the seat, finding comfort. The lady stands by him, holding the rail overhead for the entire three-hour journey," Nadia narrated. "Now, all three of you, tell me, did this lady do a good deed here?" asked Nadia.

"Obviously," murmured all in agreement.

"Okay, now what if I told you that the lady herself required crutches to walk, yet she was willing to give up her seat for the poor elderly?" revealed Nadia.

"That's beyond a good deed," exclaimed Rayan, with Aysha and Pori nodding in agreement.

"This is the quality of good deeds I am talking about here," Nadia stated. "So, what better way to discuss something than over a nice dinner table? Tell me, what brought you to my door, Mr Ali? Did the prime minister send you here?"

"No, madam, I came of my own accord. I no longer work for the prime minister. All I did was speak in support of your philanthropic good deeds. Somehow, it reached his ears and he sacked me on the spot, no questions asked. That's how venomous his code of conduct is," revealed Rayan.

"So, you're here seeking a job?" teased Pori with a smirk.

"Not necessarily. You see, I also believe in good deeds. Whether achieved by good or bad means, if the action taken is for the betterment of the entire nation, it's justifiable. I got sacked because I supported you. For the prime minister, it was bad news. Does that mean I am at fault? I believe I am not at fault at all," Rayan asserted. "Nadia, madam, you have further demonstrated your greatness by inviting me in and sharing your food with a total stranger. This act supersedes all the good deeds that I know of," he continued.

"You're a very astute man, Rayan. Would you mind if I call you by your first name?" asked Nadia.

"Of course you can. Madam, you may have noticed that our nation is akin to a scavenger-type republic, always seeking ways to live off the back of others. I am not that type. I noticed your good work, so I spoke about it. People didn't like it, so they got rid of me," Rayan explained.

"Have your food, Rayan. I now see you as an asset. Just moments ago, I was discussing with my daughter, 'How do I win public support?' At that exact moment, the gatekeeper informed me of your arrival. It felt like a sign from above. I needed a campaigner who could accelerate my political agenda, and here you are, landing as an angel at my door. How does it sound if I appoint you to campaign for me, Rayan?" Nadia proposed.

"Sounds great, madam, I can do campaigning for you. I am very good at doing that," said Rayan.

"After all, a stranger turning up at dinnertime isn't necessarily a bad omen," echoed Aysha.

"Well said, Aysha…" responded Nadia.

"Rajshai is under my influence, as you know. Do you think you can get the other seven divisions on my side?" Nadia enquired.

"Of course, madam, it will be my pleasure. I will spread your message like a religion to the people. You can rest assured. Have you decided on a party name?" asked Rayan.

"Tell me something, Rayan, do Awami League or BNP claim they are secular parties?" enquired Nadia.

"It is difficult to separate the state from religious institutions, ma'am. Once you believe in a faith you are tied into it no matter what. Time and time again throughout the world it has demonstrated that conflict stems from the difference in opinions, not commonality. They claim they are secular, but in reality, they are far from it. The amount of violence against the minority community that continues is largely unreported. Just recently, several Hindu-owned temples, shops and homes were vandalised, robbed and torched in different parts of the country. However, it's been demonstrated that government officials sided with the Muslim majority. Secularism exists in name only, ma'am," said Rayan.

Nadia asked, "Rayan, I am curious to learn about your political perspectives. Do you lean towards a commitment to secularism, or do you find theocratic governance to be a more viable path?"

"Madam, through a life dedicated to studying the intricate realms of history, science and philosophy, which instil critical thinking, one comprehends that the affairs of our world are steered by human agency alone, nothing else. The belief in presence of the divine or supernatural in every miraculous event often, after a little research, uncovers the hands of humanity at work. Secularism, advocating the separation of government institutions and political matters from religious institutions, champions a state that functions independently, detached from any singular religious influence or other beliefs. This framework ensures the centrifugal pivot to freedom for all individuals no matter their faith.

"Conversely, a theocracy represents a system where governance is either directly or indirectly guided by religious authorities or principles. Within this structure, religious law or doctrine significantly impacts or controls the state and its policies.

"Now, the vital issue to ponder lies within the context of Bangladesh – a predominantly Muslim nation that accommodates other faith communities. A theocratic system, by default, cannot be impartial to all faith groups. Addressing your enquiry, I unequivocally lend my support to centrism. I am neutral. I study, observe and listen to all sides of the argument, learn from it and take in what logically makes sense for the betterment of all people, madam."

"Rayan, your eloquence is truly remarkable. I have been in search of individuals like yourself to build a team to steer our country towards a nation of success. Your presence here has spared me valuable time that would have been spent in an extensive search. I am delighted that you've come forward," Nadia said with sincere appreciation.

Aysha presented a thoughtful and pragmatic perspective on the middle ground between capitalism, socialism and theocracy. Her suggestion of a mixed economy, merging elements from both capitalism and socialism, resonated with the intention of mitigating the extremes of both systems while capitalising on their strengths.

Indeed, socialism tends to centralise power within the government, potentially reducing individual autonomy, while capitalism often concentrates influence among the affluent, potentially leading to economic disparities. The proposal for a mixed economy represents an innovative approach, striving to forge a system that amalgamates the positive facets of each while mitigating their individual shortcomings.

By intertwining elements of state control, social welfare, private enterprise and market-driven mechanisms, a mixed economy seeks to foster a balanced environment that encourages economic growth and innovation while concurrently addressing societal needs and inequalities. This consolidation allows for flexibility, acknowledging that not all solutions reside solely within one ideological framework.

Aysha's proposal of a mixed economy reflects a dynamic attempt to sculpt an economic system that not only learns from historical precedents but also endeavours to adapt to the evolving needs and challenges of a contemporary society.

"Aysha, well said, exploring the middle ground between capitalism and socialism, highlighting the potential for a balanced approach. You underscored the inherent imbalances of each system: socialism concentrating excessive power within the government, and capitalism disproportionately empowering the affluent. To counter these disparities, the suggested solution involves a fusion of the two, birthing a fresh concept: fusion of a mixed economy. This innovative economic model harmonises elements from both capitalism and socialism, seeking to harness the benefits of each while mitigating their individual limitations," continued Nadia.

She listed the advantages of a mixed economy:

"Private ownership and the free market allow for private ownership of property and businesses, fostering entrepreneurship and innovation. Businesses operate based on market demand and supply, and there's a significant degree of economic freedom.

"Government intervention and regulation play a role in ensuring fairness and social welfare and prevent exploitation. This can include regulations on labour, environmental protection, consumer rights, building of infrastructure and market competition.

"Social programmes are social safety nets put in place to provide support to those in need. This might involve welfare programmes, public healthcare, education and other social services aimed at reducing inequality and providing essential services to all citizens.

"Redistribution of wealth can be achieved by progressive taxation to redistribute wealth to some extent, aiming to address socioeconomic inequalities and provide assistance to less privileged members of society.

"Public (government-owned) and private enterprises are allowed to exist and operate in the economy. Some industries or services might be under government control, while others are in private hands.

"The idea behind a mixed economy is to strike a balance between the efficiency and innovation of capitalism while addressing some of the inherent issues such as inequality and social welfare that may arise. This approach attempts to harness the strengths of both capitalism and socialism, aiming for economic growth while also ensuring social justice and stability.

"What are your thoughts on the title 'Bangladesh Republic of Community and Scholars' (BROCS), where power is vested in the people, wisdom is acquired through learning, community is shaped by ethical values, and scholarship is attained through academic pursuits? Recognising that socialism grants excessive authority to the government and capitalism concentrates too much power in the hands of the affluent, the concept here is to blend these two ideologies, forging a new path – a mixed economy," said Nadia.

"I believe it's a great idea," said Aysha.

"I think it sounds a bit broken, like a party of losers, don't you think?" said Rayan.

"Rayan, if you encounter any pessimistic comments, tell people that BROCS stands for 'Breaking All Records' not 'broke' as if we don't have any money, or advise them to read the full nameplate," said Nadia. "Pori, what do you think?" asked Nadia.

"Mum, I'm not interested in your politcal talks. You talked about everything under the sun, the government and the wealthy public, socialism, capitalism and what not. Where is the space for my animals? Aren't you going to give them a say in your government?"

"Of course, Pori. First, let's bring civil obedience to the people of this land, and then we can consider animal rights," replied Nadia.

Rayan received the green light from Nadia to establish BROCS political party offices across all eight divisions of Bangladesh. He strategically placed highly qualified and dedicated activists within each office to champion the party's objectives. As a leader, Nadia's philanthropic efforts spread rapidly across the country. Media platforms – be they on air, in print or through social channels – were inundated with articles highlighting her generous donations towards noble causes. She funded extensive projects such as dredging canals, particularly in parts of the Padma River, to eliminate sediment build-up from the Himalayas, thereby reducing flooding and enhancing water flow. Additionally, she directed water through excavated trenches to irrigate fields and undertook mega projects involving self-sustaining commercial and residential buildings, including the projected floating village. These endeavours captivated the public's attention and gained traction, especially through the influence of young social media personalities. Nadia transformed her village, Arambaria, into a living testament and a model for the entire country, inviting people to witness the potential of a better life.

During an interview with a TV channel, she said, "I aim to make our country an iconic part of the world, provided I have the public's support. No child shall be born and go to sleep hungry. No individual will resort to theft because they can't provide for their family. No woman will suffer abuse due to gender inequalities. Police won't resort to bribery because their wages are insufficient to sustain a living. Political corruption will have no place, as the country's laws will be fortified. Our nation's infrastructure will be modernised, open to the world for business, trade and tourism to thrive. Under my government, equal opportunities will flourish. The people of Bangladesh are astute. They won't be deceived any longer by leaders who selfishly pocket the country's GDP growth for themselves."

As Nadia's statement echoed repeatedly on TV, YouTube and various news outlets, tensions among the major political parties soared to a red alert level. Nadia swiftly became the adversary of all parties. None were confident about securing power in the upcoming election, as this new BROCS party seemed to overshadow their collective hard work and efforts. In response to this burgeoning threat posed by Nadia Begum, the BNP (Bangladesh National Party), AL (Awami League Party) and JP (Jatiya Party) decided to join forces, merging together to counter this rising political force.

Mr Ashanul Hoque, the leader of Jatiya Party, sat on his sofa, arms folded, observing the news. Frustrated, he picked up the remote and switched off the TV. "Every fucking time I switch on the TV, this woman and her philanthropic agenda flood the screen," he muttered.

Just then, his mobile phone rang, and he promptly answered the call.

"Hello," he said.

"Hello, Mr Hoque. Rajan Chowdhury here."

"Hello, Mr Prime Minister Saab. How's it going? This new party has obviously made things tough for you, hasn't she? Are you breathing well?" asked Hoque.

"Yes, she did. My breathing feels restricted, almost like being muzzled. How about yours? I bet it's more like drowning," replied the prime minister. "If she gains power, everyone is in trouble!"

"I'm not in power, sir, so it's not bothering me as much," Hoque responded.

"It will bother you once she is in power, mate. The election is near, and we must come together to tarnish her reputation in the public arena," insisted the prime minister.

"How are you going to do that? The speed at which she is building her reputation is faster than a Bangladeshi supercar, thanks to your party. Recently, she opened offices in all eight divisions and deployed her people to sway public opinion in her favour. It's a plague, mate. There's not much I can do about it," Hoque explained.

"I have unearthed a revelation from her past: she was formerly engaged with the GreenBirth Corporation. Despite being offered an exceptional wage package, she chose to depart from the company. Rumours suggest she might have ventured to the UK, intending to sell the company's confidential information to the UK government. Should we unpick and reveal her derogatory past, we may hold her accountable for treason," proclaimed the prime minister.

"Are you absolutely certain?" Hoque enquired.

"Without a doubt. There's a young woman by the name of Sadia Khanom who once worked for the very same company. She stood as her rival and testified that, despite being provided with all she required by the company, she made the choice to journey abroad. Now, she has returned as a millionaire. How did this come to pass? Selling a country's secrets to foreign nations constitutes a criminal act," asserted the prime minister.

"She sold her company's secrets, not the country's. How do you plan to link her to treason?" Hoque questioned.

"Hoque, as the incumbent prime minister, I have a strategy in mind. The question is, are you ready to stand by my side?" the prime minister responded.

"Listen, Mr Prime Minister, I'm certain the leader of the BNP is also experiencing difficulties because of her actions. I will reach out to him and explore the possibility of uniting forces. However, there's a caveat. Your party and the BNP have governed the country for decades, and it's been a perpetual 'either you or them' scenario. This time, it could be a coalition between your party and ours. What are your thoughts on that?" Hoque proposed.

"Come on! If you insist on coalition, BNP's leader, Abdus Salam, will echo the same sentiment. Should I make them partners too? Let's set aside this idea and focus on addressing this imminent threat. As long as I remain in power, there will be opportunities for you to benefit from questionable and unethical methods, Minister. However, if she takes control, bribery and other corrupt practices will be a thing of the past, my friend, so think about it."

"No, I'm not buying into that. It's either you accept what I've proposed, or it becomes your battle – I have no interest in getting involved," Hoque stated firmly.

"Listen, when the time is right, I will make sure to do something for you, alright?" the prime minister assured.

The prime minister ended the call. Ashanul Hoque, the leader of the Jatiya Party, immediately dialled the number of the leader of the Bangladesh Nationalist Party (BNP), briefing him on the discussed situation with the prime minister. Several days later, leaders from various political parties convened in a private conference room, summoning trusted TV news reporters to conduct a live press conference in an attempt to tarnish Nadia's political reputation. They orchestrated the presence of GreenBirth Corporation's CEO, Mr Ashok Gupta, to provide testimony regarding Nadia's extensive tenure at their company and her abrupt departure from an apparently binding employment contract. He highlighted her rejection of enticing incentives that would typically be coveted by other employees.

The three parties went on to accuse Nadia of allegedly inciting violence against affluent and respected individuals by purportedly collaborating with a British-led secret service company named MI16. Nadia's company had expanded significantly throughout Bangladesh, boasting a network of approximately 200 active branches across the country. These branches engaged in various operations such as private investigations, security services, guard patrols to safeguard individuals and property, aiming to prevent theft and other illicit activities.

It was asserted that some of these operations frequently clashed with the duties of the local police force. The parties argued that Nadia's establishment showed a blatant disregard for the laws of the land. They contended that she should be held accountable and brought to justice for the numerous avoidable atrocities allegedly caused by her company, which they claimed were ongoing.

This news report swiftly made its way into the mainstream media in Bangladesh, clarifying misconceptions among the general public. Those who had already decided to support Nadia remained steadfast in their allegiance, while those yet to form an opinion remained sceptical, with some beginning to harbour intense feelings of dismay upon hearing the negative aspects attributed to Nadia. The news also reached the international media.

The UK Government Communications Headquarters (GCHQ), an organisation responsible for providing intelligence, safeguarding information and advising pertinent UK policies to ensure societal safety and success in the digital era, became aware of the situation. They collaborate with the Foreign, Commonwealth and Development Office and consequently summoned Keith, Nadia's husband, for questioning regarding the activities conducted by MI16 based in Bangladesh. There was a growing concern that this organisation might be leveraging the hallmarks of the UK government to exert influence in Bangladesh's power structures.

Captain Sir Martin Reid from the Directorate of Military Intelligence UK arrived to meet with Keith.

"We've received intelligence suggesting that your wife is operating an underworld cartel under the guise of MI16 in Bangladesh. Could you please provide us with more information on this?" Sir Martin enquired.

Keith was taken aback, feeling horrified upon hearing this revelation from the military chief. "I am utterly stunned just hearing this," he said. "It's news to me! I had no knowledge that she was running a cartel there in Bangladesh," Keith said, clearly confused.

"What exactly is this MI16, do you happen to know?" asked Sir Martin, seeking further clarification.

"It's a security service provider – offering watchmen, guards, door bouncers, patrol personnel to protect people and their property, preventing theft and other unlawful activities," Keith explained.

"Why do they call their service MI16?" queried Sir Martin.

"I don't know why they've chosen that name. As far as I'm aware, she is a shareholder in that company, and I didn't feel the need to enquire further," Keith replied.

"Does she have special agents working for her, akin to 007 or 008, maybe a Bengali James Bond?" enquired Sir Martin.

"I would assume they ought to employ such secret agents, sir. It's a substantial company with 200 branches throughout Bangladesh, so they likely have numerous covert service agents. However, this testimony is speculative. I can't confirm for certain," Keith replied cautiously.

GCHQ staff, monitoring the interview and running a thermal lie detector on Keith, observed that his responses were genuine with no significant spikes in his blood pressure, indicating truthfulness. Additionally, they discovered that MI16 stood for

Mechanical Intelligence Sixteen Ltd, although its exact purpose remained unknown. Furthermore, they found out that Nadia was the director of a company called Diet Control Ltd, based in the UK, specialising in catering for obese patients which she sold seventy percent to 'Genetic Metabolic Engineering Corporation Ltd' for a billion pound. Meanwhile, Sir Martin received this update through his earpiece while questioning Keith, and his team of researchers continued delving for more information.

This new revelation piqued Sir Martin's curiosity. Although he was familiar with various types of intelligence services – foreign, special, military, civilian – 'mechanical' was a term entirely new to him. The enigmatic nature of this Mechanical Intelligence Sixteen Ltd only served to heighten his interest and intrigue.

"Mr Evan, you are free to leave, but our investigation is not concluded. We will dispatch our own secret agent to delve further into your wife's company and its intentions. Please be aware that given your prior position as the former ambassador to Bangladesh, we are not pressing you for further information. It is in our best interests to conduct our own investigation within the bounds of our established codes of conduct. Have a pleasant day. My team will escort you out," Sir Martin informed Keith as he arranged for his departure from the premises.

Captain Sir Martin Reid gathered with his esteemed senior officials, among them the ingenious Quindlen Smith, mastermind behind gadgets that bewilder adversaries to their very core, along with his cadre of experts, to deliberate upon a forthcoming mission set to unfold in Bangladesh.

They unanimously agreed to initiate a mission to Bangladesh, code-named MB-007, aimed at uncovering the true nature and purpose of Mechanical Intelligence Sixteen Ltd. Magnus Jones a senior officer in the British Secrete Service, summoned the newest recruit for the mission.

"Is he the one you've chosen?" Sir Martin enquired.

"Indeed," replied Magnus. "An Asian operative for an Asian

operation. He's well prepared, highly trained agent possesses exceptional skills for the job. His adeptness eliminates the necessity for additional tech gadgets. He's fully equipped and proficient on his own."

Sir Martin Reid called Magnus to have a word in private. "Have you lost your mind?" An Asian cannot crack an Asian, he will fall in love with an Asian. Don't you watch Hindi movies with subtitles?"

"Well, these days they come in English, dubbed. I don't need subtitles to read, I hear them. I am fully aware of their romantic side effects, it's ingrained in the blood," said Magnus.

"Get a white guy of the same calibre for this mission, sir. Send this Asian on some other mission. I can feel this is a failed mission," said Sir Martin Reid.

"Well, let's wait and see," responded Magnus.

*

Nadia's tranquillity was interrupted by the resonating melody of her phone, promptly answered, only to find her husband on the line from across the seas in England.

"I've just returned from a meeting at GCHQ, Nadia. There's concern that your actions might inadvertently entangle their esteemed brand name in a conflict with the Bangladeshi government," conveyed Keith.

"What brand name might that be?" enquired Nadia, seeking clarity amid the unexpected conversation.

"MI6, or rather MI16 – does the distinction truly matter? It's the embodiment of British intelligence," Keith responded, underscoring the gravity of the situation.

"Keith, this is nothing but a concerted smear campaign. The three major political parties have united in a coalition to discredit me here in Bangladesh. Their agitation stems from the fact that more people are aligning with my ideology, posing a threat to the ruling party. I'm tackling this head-on. Rest assured, I'll swiftly regain control. Please take care of our children in the meantime," reassured Nadia, steadfast in her determination to address the situation.

"Please reconsider involving Pori in these missions. The situation is becoming increasingly perilous out there. And you, too, should ponder the path you're treading. Is it truly worth it? Leading a corrupt nation is an immensely challenging task, Nadia," Keith implored, expressing genuine concern for the risks involved.

"Keith, your concern means a lot to me, and I genuinely appreciate it. Yet, everyone harbours their own beliefs, visions and aspirations. Mine revolve around the pursuit of fostering a world where humanity triumphs. Pori follows me where my journey leads. I've entrusted our children to your care. Please look after them. If you maintain a positive outlook, I'll be fine. Negative emotions tend to attract bad omens, so please stay positive. Don't worry, I will manage," reassured Nadia, firmly believing in the power of positivity amid challenges.

"GCHQ might dispatch their agents to Bangladesh to track you and gather information about your mission. Remain vigilant," warned Keith.

"Okay, take care," responded Nadia before ending the call, acknowledging the potential risks ahead.

*

The esteemed GCHQ intercepted the telephone exchange between Keith and Nadia, transmitting a meticulously recorded message to Captain Sir Martin Reid. Following perusal of this dialogue, Sir Martin promptly contacted Magnus, affirming the aptness of appointing an Asian agent, for the crucial mission MB-007. He underscored the necessity of orchestrating a love triangle to intimately engage with the narrative. At the epicentre of this narrative was the formidable Nadia Begum, the matriarch presiding over affairs, while her daughter, purportedly in her late teens, known as Pori, was intricately embroiled in clandestine activities concerning the realm of secret services. Sir Martin, seeking authorisation for their mission into Bangladesh, respectfully asked Magnus.

"Indeed, I am presently in the process of compiling the necessary information to transmit to Quindlen," confirmed Magnus.

"Undoubtedly, any discourse on the finest tech gadgets remains incomplete without an acknowledgment of Quendlen and the prestigious division bearing his name. Leveraging the expertise of his adept team, Quendlen engineers an arsenal including lethal cufflinks, armament-incorporated wristwatches, diminutive yet powerful cameras, concealed detonators, jet packs, tracking devices and an array of automotive innovations exclusively tailored for the Asian agent MB-007. This innovative craftsmanship unfolded discreetly behind the curtains, only to spring to vibrant life before the discerning eyes of the audience.

"Summon him at once," declared Sir Martin Reid, "so that our operatives can swiftly engage in action."

*

Upon realizing that the primary political factions have united to besmirch Nadia's reputation not only within Bangladesh but also among authorities in the UK, the impending election looms ominously. With Pori needing to return to England for her education and the mounting pressure weighing heavily upon her, she finds herself inundated with concerns. Time dwindles, leaving her scant opportunity to address the burgeoning crisis. Thus, she settles herself, deep in contemplation, seeking a swift and peaceful resolution to the tumultuous predicament. She has intricately orchestrated a mission dubbed 'Jabbed', wherein Pori, flanked by her bionic security guards, is set to undertake the abduction of three pivotal political figures: the incumbent prime minister, Rajan Chowdhury, BNP leader Abdus Salam and JP leader Ashanul Hoque. Following weeks of meticulous espionage, Pori's team has successfully tracked the movements of these figures, meticulously devising a systematic and methodical abduction blueprint for each target, ensuring precision and a seamless consecutive execution.

In pursuit of their primary target, Mr Ashanul Hoque, surveillance of his movements have indicated a consistent weekly visit to a massage parlour every Thursday. Driving unaccompanied in his vibrant red Honda CR-V four-wheel-drive SUV, he has embarked on these grooming sessions. Pori, utilising cutting-edge, covert technology – a stealthy avian-inspired drone – has monitored his activities remotely. She has strategically positioned this drone atop a nearby tree, directly overlooking the main entrance of the massage parlour. This remarkable device is equipped with facial recognition capabilities, primed to alert Pori upon detecting Mr Ashanul Hoque's emergence from the establishment. As he exits, the drone promptly signals Pori, prompting her swift deployment of a prepared team.

With calculated precision, Pori, cloaked in an enticing guise enhanced by exquisite attire and makeup, approached Mr Hoque under the guise of seeking directions to an ATM. The state-of-the-art avian drone, functioning seamlessly in silence, discreetly closed in behind Mr Hoque, administering a precisely targeted tranquillising dart to his lower backside. Startled by a momentary pinch, he was swiftly overcome by the sedative, inducing a rapid decline in consciousness and obliterating any recollection of the encounter. Acting swiftly, Pori steadied him to prevent a collapse, guiding him to his car seat. Once Mr Hoque was safely settled within his vehicle, Pori commanded the drone to depart before entering the car herself. Employing a specialised microchip-inserting gun, she discreetly and deftly administered a microchip implant into the spinal cord at the base of his neck, ensuring its seamless integration before getting out of the vehicle and leaving the scene without a trace.

She ventured towards her second target, Abdus Salam, a notable figure within the BNP (Bangladesh Nationalist Party) striving for a decade to ascend to power. His journey has been fraught with challenges, hampered by the inability to engage in illicit dealings, leading to substantial financial losses. His businesses operate in the red, forcing him to pivot from securing clandestine government contracts to conducting private enterprise. Amid this struggle, his ventures into fishery and vegetable exports have become his lifeline, catering predominantly to the Asian diaspora residing in various European nations, notably the United Kingdom. Abdus Salam's focal point resides within an expansive warehouse adjacent to a man-made fishing lake situated in Bogura District, a region nestled in the northern precinct of Bangladesh, within the Rajshahi Division. Bogura, an industrious city, hosts a myriad of small and mid-sized companies, while to its north lie the remnants of Mahasthangarh, which is considered the oldest city in Bangladesh and has a rich history spanning over two millennia. It is recognised as an important archaeological site shedding light on early urbanisation in the region, and Pundravardhana, located in the northern part of the Indian subcontinent, made it a vital centre for trade and commerce. It likely engaged in trade with other parts of ancient India, contributing to its economic importance.

Pori skilfully assumed the guise of a member of the fishing department's staff, seamlessly blending into the bustling ambiance of the distribution centre. Amid the cacophony of machinery and the frenetic preparation of sea food, vegetables and raw materials for export, she stealthily navigated her way into the area dedicated to the packaging of fish and vegetables. Among the throngs of workers absorbed in their tasks, Pori observed Abdus Salam meticulously inspecting the quality of products and packaging before disappearing into an elevator within the building.

Seizing an opportune moment, Pori, holding a wicker basket

filled with cherry tomatoes, approached the elevator, discreetly joining the others in wait. Her inconspicuous presence allowed her to evade notice as she scanned the elevator's control panel, discovering its sole downward trajectory. Upon its descent to the lower ground level, she swiftly exited and concealed herself in a vantage point, affording her a clandestine view of Abdus Salam's covert activities.

In this concealed enclave, a distinct scene unveiled itself: an illicit cocaine-processing facility masquerading behind the facade of a fish export operation. Workers adeptly manipulated an ice-making machine, skilfully crafting ice slabs of various sizes. These slabs were ingeniously merged into composite blocks, incorporating a transparent polythene bag meticulously containing several grams of cocaine. The resulting ice block, upon its emergence from the machine, created an illusion of smoky, finished blocks, cunningly camouflaging the cocaine within. Outwardly, these blocks bore the appearance of regular iced fish blocks. To facilitate identification, specific markings were discreetly employed to distinguish the contaminated blocks, surreptitiously intermingled with genuine ones.

The workers diligently packed these deceptive blocks into boxes, several of which were then arranged on a pallet for transport by a forklift driver to a frozen container, perpetuating the illusion of a legitimate fish shipment while illicitly concealing the cocaine-laden slabs within.

In another section of the operation, workers diligently packed both whole small fish and larger fish cut into pieces. Here, plastic moulds were meticulously filled with the desired quantity of fish, cleverly incorporating transparent, smaller polythene bags between the voids of fish. These carefully arranged moulds were then passed through an ice machine, emerging on the other side as a singular, comprehensive ice slab containing the fish and accompanying the hidden polythene bags.

The resulting ice slab presented an utterly convincing facade, rendering it impossible to detect the inclusion of cocaine within. The integration of the drug was shrouded within the unified, hazy white appearance of the ice, flawlessly blending in with the fish and ice, creating an indistinguishable amalgamation.

"Clever little sods," Pori muttered to herself as the realisation of the drug trafficking method sank in. Prior to seeking out Abdus Salam, she navigated through a corridor, testing several locked doors along the way. Finally, reaching the end, she found a door that surprisingly swung open, revealing a room larger than the typical studio size. Unbeknownst to her, Mr Salam caught sight of her presence at the doors. Apologetically, she attempted to close the door and retreat, but Salam's voice stopped her in her tracks.

"Hey, come here!" he called out. "What are you doing in this area?"

"Sir, I was actually looking for you," Pori replied.

"Looking for me? Then why did you try to leave?" Mr Salam enquired.

"Sir, I didn't knock, so I thought I'd correct myself," explained Pori.

"That's a thoughtful approach. Why do you want to see me?" questioned Mr Salam.

"Sir, I'm in need of some extra money. I'm a skilled masseuse, and I thought if I offered you a good massage, would you consider sparing me 500 taka," proposed Pori.

"What! Just 500? Aren't you being adequately compensated for the work you do for the company?" Mr Salam responded.

"I am paid, sir, but this month I faced a shortfall. Bills and overheads surpassed my expectations," Pori explained.

"You're a very beautiful woman. Why don't you find a handsome, wealthy husband? Then you wouldn't need a wage top-up," suggested Mr Salam.

"Sir, I prefer to remain independent and earn a living on my own," Pori asserted.

"Ah, indeed, you're a brave girl. However, bravery in the female gender doesn't come cheap in a man's world. There are numerous hurdles that can stand in your way before you get anywhere," remarked Mr Salam.

"Sir, you are correct. That's precisely why I approached you, believing that hurdles can only be overcome with the assistance of a prominent figure like you," Pori stated.

"Can you dance?" enquired Mr Salam.

"Yes, I can, sir. I've achieved distinction in my dance classes," Pori replied.

"Show me a dance and let me enjoy a joint. You can massage me after. Here, take this 1,000 taka in advance. If I fall asleep, don't disturb me. Just leave after you're done, okay?" Mr Salam instructed.

"Very generous, sir!" said Pori appreciatively. She approached the music player and scrolled through the iPod, asking, "Sir, which music should I dance to?"

"Select some hot, saucy music, and show me those curvy moves, okay? Not just 'yooo yoo ho ho'. And don't you eat? You look like a bunch of bones clattering against each other. You should put some weight on. Men like a bit of pulpiness in a female's body," remarked Salam.

"Sir, I will use your money to eat and gain some weight too," replied Pori in a soft, sensual voice.

Pori selected a song she knew well and began to dance. Upon hearing the music, Salam couldn't resist the stirring memories of his youth. Despite his age, he stood up and joined Pori in both dancing and singing.

O Uncle Gi

Pori:
O Uncle Gi, your kindness I won't forget,
The money you gave, it's a blessing, no regret.
I'll use it to chase dreams, to aim high,
To become the Bugs Bunny, soaring through the sky.

Salam:
But hold on, dear, do you see me as your kin?
I'm not Uncle Gi, let a new story begin.
I gave you the cash, with hopes you'd understand,
To be the Bugs Bunny, in our love's grandstand.

When I look at you, my heart takes flight,
Desire ignites, in the darkness of night.
My mind races like an Olympic sprint,
Your dance, a potion, leaving me spellbound, in a hint.

How can I contain this fire within,
Your presence, a spark, under my skin.
Survival's in question, with every beat,
Your dance, a temptation, making my soul fleet.

But don't mistake, I'm not your kin,
I gave you the money, for a new journey to begin.
To be the Bugs Bunny, leaping with grace,
In your arms, finding my rightful place.

When I look at you, my heart takes flight,
Desire ignites, in the darkness of night.
My mind races like an Olympic sprint,
Your dance, a potion, leaving me spellbound, in a hint.

Pori:
So thank you, dear Uncle Gi, for the gift you bestowed,
But now it's time for a new tale to unfold.
I'll be your Bugs Bunny, soaring high,
In this dance of love, under the endless sky.

Pori performed the musical number, dancing and serenading
Mr Salam, he too participated and sang along. Pori providing a

soothing massage, gradually calming him. As the performance progressed, she discreetly utilised her microchip gun, placing a chip at the juncture of his upper neck and the base of his skull. The song concluded, transitioning Mr Salam to the relms of infinite relaxsation.

*

Pori embarked on her final assignment, her focus honed in on the acting prime minister, Mr Rajan Chowdhury. For days, she had meticulously followed his every move, noticing his recent astuteness and heightened caution. He now navigated within a shield of vigilant security, seldom straying from his protected domain, evidently aware of the potential threat looming over his life. Shielded by round-the-clock security service, travelling in an impenetrable, bulletproof SUV and constantly surrounded by his security entourage, he presented a formidable challenge for Pori.

Having exhausted conventional means of access, Pori arrived at the conclusion that the sole approach to the prime minister lay in forceful entry. Collating her comprehensive analysis, she dispatched the detailed report through an encrypted message to her mother, before retreating to her clandestine refuge for the day with her trusted companions: her horse, SS, and the tiger.

Nadia's attention was drawn to the chime of her phone, prompting her to unlock the text message app and open the received message.

*

Nadia contemplated holding a press conference following the completion of Pori's missions to redeem her reputation from the negative connotations. However, she understood that the exoneration could only be achieved after successfully neutralising all three targets. Upon receiving Pori's text, Nadia silently pondered,

Why has the prime minister intensified his security measures? Could it be that he's uncovered information about his rivals, Mr Hoque and Mr Salam?

Nadia placed a call to Aysha, directing her to assemble a unit comprising the most skilled bionic soldiers in anticipation of a potential confrontation with the Bangladeshi military.

"How many soldiers are we aiming for, Nadia?" enquired Aysha.

"At least 200," Nadia replied.

"Understood," Aysha acknowledged.

"Also, Aysha, could you arrange for a television channel to visit my guest house next Wednesday? I'd like to make an announcement regarding the Floating Village project and share some key details with the media. I'd appreciate it if you could join me as well," Nadia requested.

Bangladesh, with a significant portion of its land resting upon the floodplains of major rivers such as the Ganges, Padma, Brahmaputra, Jamuna and Meghna, hosts the largest delta in the world. The country's predominantly flat and low-lying topography renders it highly susceptible to flooding. Even moderate rainfall and the melting of snow in the Himalayas have the potential to cause widespread inundation. This vulnerability is exacerbated by the convergence of these rivers, making Bangladesh acutely prone to natural disasters.

The impact of climate change further intensifies these challenges. Slight fluctuations in temperature lead to severe drought, and the monsoon season, spanning from June to October, brings forth riverbank breaches, coastal erosion and the devastating consequences of cyclones and storm surges. These environmental upheavals decimate the livelihoods and habitats of the millions of people residing in the southern coastal region of the country.

Communities ravaged by these climate-related disasters find themselves displaced, jobless and bereft of their primary sources of income. The relentless rainfall sabotages crop cultivation, particularly affecting women who heavily rely on small-scale agricultural work, livestock rearing and handicrafts for sustenance. However, adverse climate conditions like waterlogging and increased salinity make it nearly impossible to grow essential crops.

This tumultuous situation leads to a significant decline in earnings, compelling many men to migrate to urban areas in pursuit of better job prospects. Consequently, women left behind face a compounded set of challenges. The prevailing patriarchal societal norms restrict their mobility and participation in decision-making processes. Limited access to land ownership, markets and capital gains further constrains their economic opportunities. Moreover, this vulnerable segment of the population encounters heightened incidences of domestic violence and early marriage, exacerbating an already precarious situation.

Nadia has been actively involved in a significant initiative to assist communities, particularly focusing on empowering women in the face of climate change. Her efforts include the creation of innovative floating houses, designed to offer a resilient and prosperous lifestyle for the inhabitants. These floating houses are complemented by boats facilitating transportation for trade and social visits, along with water filtration facilities ensuring access to clean drinking water. Furthermore, vertical farming facilities have been incorporated, enabling the growth of various crops in limited space with minimal energy consumption.

This climate-resilient approach not only provides a comfortable living environment for the most vulnerable communities but also opens avenues for generating sustainable income through the cultivation of diverse vegetables for sale in local markets. Nadia's commitment to this transformative project not only addresses the immediate needs of those affected but also offers a long-term solution for economic stability.

Recognising the potential of this initiative to positively impact the lives of many, Nadia aims to leverage this opportunity to enhance her standing among the people of Bangladesh.

By redirecting the focus of the media towards this project, she endeavours to shift public opinion in her favour and counter the treason allegations levelled against her by the prime minister. Her aspiration is to highlight the constructive and beneficial impact of her initiatives, aiming to foster support and trust within the community.

Setting her forthcoming project announcement aside, Nadia delves into current affairs, launching her own investigation into the prime minister's portfolio of achievements. In her research, she uncovers a troubling reality: the prime minister maintains a financial interest in a ceramic pottery company that employs asbestos to reinforce its products. Situated in the rural expanse of the Khulna Division in northwest Bangladesh, this revelation raises serious concerns about the use of asbestos, a harmful substance posing health risks to those involved in the pottery-making process.

Further scrutiny uncovers a more extensive web of environmental hazards. Adjacent to the ceramic pottery company, the prime minister and other government officials have stakes in brick kilns and cement manufacturing companies. These establishments burn excessive coal to fire bricks and cement, significantly elevating the air pollution index to hazardous levels, ranging from 350 to an alarming 450. This level of harmful pollutants released into the atmosphere poses a severe threat not only to the environment but also to the health of local residents.

The dust generated from the pottery site and the substantial air pollution from the brick kilns are inflicting chronic respiratory diseases, lung infections, heart issues and even cancer upon the community. The dire implications necessitate the immediate closure of these hazardous establishments to avert further health risks and environmental damage.

The recent discovery has provided Nadia with an opportunity to assert her influence further. She has mobilised private analysts to conduct an extensive survey, specifically focusing on the living standards of communities residing in the vicinity of the affected area. The results are alarming, showing widespread and severe health issues affecting many individuals within a ten-mile radius of the factories.

As part of her strategy, Nadia's surveyors have not only gathered residents' signatures in support of demolishing the hazardous facilities but also advocated for Nadia's political initiatives. At each household they visited, they have highlighted Nadia's positive contributions, effectively garnering support for her cause. The advocacy for the demolition of the brick kilns, aiming to restore the region's air quality, has sparked a rallying cry among the people, echoing the slogan 'Vote for Nadia, she will restore fresh breathable air for us'. This grassroots movement has led to a significant shift in public sentiment, with thousands aligning themselves in favour of supporting Nadia, recognising her efforts in addressing the critical issues faced by the community.

However, the realisation that the government itself holds a stake in these manufacturing facilities poses a significant dilemma for Nadia. It makes her reconsider her initial plan of deploying her highly trained soldiers to take control of the Khulna Division. Understanding that any attack on these facilities would likely trigger a government–military response, she now faces a precarious situation regarding her next steps.

*

The phone call between Nadia and the prime minister reflected an intense and somewhat ominous conversation:

"Good afternoon, Mr Chowdhury, it's Nadia speaking," Nadia said.

"Yes, Nadia, I recognised your name on the caller ID. What can I do for you?" responded the prime minister.

"Is there anything left for you to do to me? You and your associates have tarnished my reputation so severely that I don't have a fighting chance now. You must be quite content. I've decided to return to the UK. I can't conduct business here as I lack influential government contacts like you do," Nadia said bitterly.

"That's a good idea. Perhaps there's nothing for you here. You're best suited to the UK. When are you planning to leave?" the prime minister asked.

"Well, I haven't made a decision yet, but I'll depart soon," Nadia responded.

"I have more bad news for you," the prime minister added.

"What bad news?" Nadia enquired, feeling perplexed and possibly apprehensive about the ominous tone of the conversation.

"The government is revoking the licence for your private security company MI16, thanks to my efforts. They have also reached out to the UK Home Office to file a complaint," the prime minister announced.

"Oh, you've gone that far, have you? No wonder you're constantly surrounded by security guards 24/7, Mr Chowdhury," Nadia said with a smile evident in her tone over the phone.

"Does that mean you've already tried to take me down? How do you know I'm protected by heavy security? Try a bit harder, Mrs Begum. I'm not an easy target," retorted the prime minister.

"Listen, if I wanted you dead, you would have been dead already. Now that you've mentioned revoking my company's licence, I'll make sure you don't remain prime minister for long," Nadia asserted firmly.

"I'm showing you two fingers right now, lady. I wish you could see me doing it face to face. Try to defame me... just try and see if you can. I am the centrepiece of the public domain, understand?" declared the prime minister in a confrontational tone.

"What if I told you that your ceramic and cement factories will be blown up by next Thursday?" Nadia issued a stark warning.

Nadia's scheduled press conference for the following Wednesday, focusing on her Floating Village project, was intended to divert media attention. The significant media coverage stemming from this event was anticipated to draw public attention away from any potential attacks on the prime minister's facilities.

"What! Are you out of your mind? My facilities are untouchable. The Bangladesh government is involved in the profits and shares of that facility. If you do anything foolish, the entire army will come at you like Rottweilers. You will be publicly executed, hanged till death during Friday prayers. Do you understand?"

"So, you've become the puppets of Saudi now? You want to hang people to death? That's a gruesome punishment, and I refuse to meet my end in such a manner. I'm simply informing you about the attack, that's all. I've heard from local people whose parents are succumbing to cancer and respiratory illnesses. They are furious," replied Nadia.

"The children of the dying parents told you that?" the prime minister responded. "That's ludicrously funny. Perhaps you should consider going back to the UK. This country is not for you."

"I'm just informing you. I've witnessed the anger in the eyes of those bereaved people and those who are on the brink of losing their loved ones due to the serious pollutants emanating from your factories. It's fine if you don't want to believe me. You can stay home and wait for news of your downfall to show up on national TV," Nadia remarked.

"Is this some kind of joke you're playing with me? The factories have been operating here for many decades without a single complaint, and now you're telling me the locals are forming an uprising? It's all thanks to you. Your evil spell won't work here. I will ensure your name is tarnished, labelling you as 'The Dark Environmentalist' instead of an eco warrior. Do you have any idea how many people depend on those bricks-and-mortar factories? The entire region relies on them, do you understand? So, don't even dream of attempting an attack on those facilities. You'll deeply regret it," responded the prime minister with a voice of a cinder.

"My job was to inform you. I'm done. Have a nice day," said Nadia before hanging up.

Pori made the considered decision to embark on a tour of the Sundarbans, recognising it as the natural habitat of both the tiger and the horse. It was a homecoming for them, evident in their yearning to return. A desire resonated within Pori to immerse herself in the crystalline waters of a lagoon she had stumbled upon during her period of captivity within the jungle.

Her priorities set the order of events. She acknowledged the imminent return of her companions to their origins but saw the necessity of renaming the tiger to avoid confusion amid the numerous others in the wild.

"I will christen you Sultan, symbolising sovereignty and distinction," she proposed. "How does that resonate with you?"

"Shadowfax the horse and Sultan the tiger," affirmed the tiger with gracious acceptance.

"From this moment forward, you are my Sultan," declared Pori, cementing the new identity for her feline companion.

Pori meticulously began the process of equipping her horse, ensuring that all the essential gear such as saddle-cloth, saddle, girth, bridle and more were meticulously and thoughtfully placed.

"Do you truly need all this gear on me, Pori? You're an adept rider even without them," remarked the horse.

"Indeed, SS, it's for your comfort and my safety. I'll be able to hold onto you securely, even if faced with a precarious situation like leaping off a cliff. Please, be patient as I fit these properly so I don't cause you any discomfort," reassured Pori.

As the tiger approached, Pori turned her attention toward Sultan. "Sultan, you're certainly large enough to carry me. Would you like me to saddle you up similarly?" she enquired.

"I don't mind," replied Sultan.

"That's kind of you, but I haven't crafted a saddle for you yet. Perhaps I should start now," Pori smiled, contemplating the idea.

Pori had previously opted to travel by road following her escape from Abdul Malik's hold, but this time she intended to journey by boat from her residence in Arambaria to the Sundarbans along the local Padma River. With a yearning to explore the riverways leading to the Sundarbans, she encountered a few boatmen who possessed a relatively sizable diesel engine boat equipped with platforms designed for transporting animals. Accompanied by both her loyal animal companions, she approached these men, intending to enquire about their services.

"Madam, you should keep the tiger on a lead. You never know what's on its mind. Anyone could end up as part of its menu," cautioned the boatman upon seeing her accompanied by the tiger.

"Rest assured, mister, my tiger is fiercely loyal. He will never betray his master," reassured Pori. "I'm seeking to hire a sizable boat for the three of us to journey to the Sundarbans. Is your boat available?"

"Yes, madam, it's available. How long are you looking to book for?" enquired the boatman.

"At least three nights," replied Pori.

"Madam, please give us a moment," requested both boatmen, exchanging a few murmurs in private.

"She seems like someone from an affluent background, keeping a tiger as a pet. She must be wealthy. Don't hesitate to ask for a substantial fee," mentioned the boatman's partner in a low voice.

"Madam, the boat is available. Please, come aboard and take a look at the facilities we have to offer. We have fully furnished bedrooms with river view windows, guest rooms suitable for your animals, ample green grass for your horse, a kitchenette equipped with cooking facilities, a fully functional shower and a restroom. We'll take care of cooking dinner and providing meals in the evenings for you, madam. However, accommodating the tiger is a first for me. I don't have any food prepared for it, nor do I have a designated space for its stay. Considering the risk assessment involved, what offer are you considering for a three-night stay?" enquired the boatman.

"I haven't hired a boat before, so I'm uncertain about the price, but don't worry about my tiger. As I mentioned, it won't pose any threat. I'll feed it what I eat during our stay. Please set a price, and let me know," assured Pori.

The mariners drew near, their words carried as gentle whispers on the wind. "She remains unaware of the price," they murmured in unison. "Request 150,000 taka."

"Madam, for 150,000 taka, we stand prepared to fulfil your every directive, offering not only our services but also delectable meals and appetising breakfasts prepared by my friend, an adept chef," said the boatman.

"What is your name?" enquired Pori.

"I am Bodrul Hoque, and my colleague is Nurul Hoque, madam," replied the boatman.

"Brothers, are you?" questioned Pori.

"No, ma'am, cousins," clarified the boatman.

"You mentioned all the facilities your boat has for humans. Can you tell me if it can cater for my two friends here?" enquired Pori.

"Indeed, madam, if you consent to our proposed fee, we can partition and make use of the guest room to accommodate both the horse and the tiger. Should you desire lush green grass or lily shoots for your horse's nourishment, we can readily arrange for that. Additionally, for your tiger, we can procure an extra supply of meat or chicken, tailoring to its preferences. As we navigate through numerous floating markets, madam, in this floodplain nation, we have adapted to coexisting with the waters. Fruit and vegetable markets also thrive along these waterways, eliminating the need for disembarking for any shopping needs. Everything lies along our course. Rest assured, you and your animals will have a splendid time onboard."

"Okay, it's settled. I will pay you 150,000 taka for your service," affirmed Pori.

Pori chartered an engine boat capable of transporting her prized

'SS' Super Shadowfax the horse and Sultan the tiger, embarking on a journey back to the very depths of the jungle where she first encountered these majestic creatures. Laden with her luggage, filled with an array of guns and ammunition, she secured it on the horse's back and made her way to the harbour. The vessel, tethered to a pier, utilised sturdy wooden pathways, substantial enough to bear the weight of both the horse and the tiger, allowing them to comfortably board the boat.

As the engine roared to life, the boat set off, departing from the shores and venturing towards the Sundarbans.

Two hours passed, offering a delightful journey filled with scenic vistas and an exhilarating ride. Pori noticed a group of young individuals diligently gathering waste plastic from a distant beach.

"Where are we now?" enquired Pori, directing her question to one of the boatmen.

"This is Katka beach," replied the boatman, Nurul Hoque.

"Are these people collecting plastic waste from the seabed private individuals, or are they sent by the government for this task?" enquired Pori.

"They are private individuals. They collect the plastic and sell it to recycling companies," explained Nurul.

"My mother would be pleased to assist these individuals in establishing their own recycling facilities. She's an environmentalist, consistently striving to better the future of our planet. However, witnessing these individuals here has sparked a significant question that I intend to discuss with her when I return," said Pori.

Pori's phone began to ring, and upon seeing her mother's name displayed, she remarked, "Speaking of a heroine, here she is." With a smile, she added, "She's my angel. Excuse me, it's my mum," before stepping into the cabin to ensure some privacy for the call.

"Hello, Mum!"

"Where are you?" Nadia enquired.

"Mum, I'm heading to the Sundarbans. I'll be back in a couple of days," Pori informed her.

"Pori, don't come back. I want you to stay there for longer if you can. I'll arrange hotel guides to take you to a nice hotel. Once you're done exploring the jungle, take a week to relax and enjoy," Nadia suggested.

"Mum, what is it?" Pori questioned. "You're worried about me, aren't you? I know you've arranged with Aysha to dismantle the brick company's CO2-emitting chimney. It's okay, I'll stay away from that fight. You can rest assured, okay?"

"Okay, my darling! I'll arrange a hotel for you to stay over. This fight might turn nasty, and I want you out of this," Nadia responded.

"Mum, I am not a kid anymore. Would you stop worrying about me? I can manage. I'm not going to a hotel, I'm going to explore nature. I've got all my camping gear with me. The tiger and horse are with me. Don't worry, I've hired a boathouse to stay overnight," Pori assured. "Okay, I'll chat later. I need to buy some grass for the horse now. We are approaching a floating market."

"Okay, bye," said Nadia.

At the floating market, they procured all their necessities. The chef prepared a delightful dinner for Pori, offering raw meat for the tiger, ensuring all were well fed, well into the evening. As night descended, the boatman kick-started the generator to illuminate the cabin, providing electricity before darkness set in.

"Madam, shall we park the boat for the night or continue towards the destination? Night is falling, and even if we reach the destination, you might not be able to recognise the area you want us to dock at, as most of the shoreline looks identical up there, and there is no light house or flash light at the destination," said Bodrul.

"Yes, you're correct. Let's anchor somewhere and call it a day," replied Pori.

Bodrul located a suitable mooring area, and Nurul anchored the boat in place for the night.

"One girl and two boys, it could be a fun night in, don't you think, Bodrul?" remarked Nurul.

"Indeed, it might be an enjoyable night under different circumstances, but not in this case, my friend. Do you want to risk losing your balls in-between your legs? Can't you see the girl is unique? How she communicates with that tiger and it understands her. I've been calling it by its name, Sultan, and it doesn't even acknowledge or respond. Yet, when she calls, it listens and responds as if it were human. There's some unspoken connection between them. She isn't like other girls – most people avoid venturing into the jungle, and here she is, heading there for camping," remarked Bodrul.

"You should ask her and find out why this is the case," suggested Nurul.

"What is the case?" enquired Bodrul.

"How the tiger understands her," explained Nurul.

"I think I should. Although she is very attractive, I've developed a different kind of respect for her," Bodrul admitted.

"You mean you fell in love with her?" asked Nurul.

"No, mate. It's more a feeling of strong affection than love. You had better hold your thoughts. You don't want to upset her, mate. What if she unleashes the tiger on us? We'll be in serious trouble. These Bengal tigers find human flesh extremely appetising. Did you buy enough meat for that beast to last the journey?" cautioned Bodrul.

"I understand, mate. And yes, don't worry. I bought plenty of meat for everyone," reassured Nurul.

"Then let's get going. Prepare for the evening feast," said Bodrul.

Inside the cabin, Pori locked the door and removed her outer garments, preparing for a martial arts practice session. Her undergarment is a specialised armadillo-like body armour, designed to skin-fit seamlessly, blending effortlessly with her natural tone, indistinguishable as a second skin. From her luggage, she retrieved a mini projector and strategically placed small white plastic pyramid-shaped objects throughout the ceiling. Upon activating the mini projector, a 3D holographic combatant character named 'Rhiron' materialised as if by magic. It was an impressive 18k superior-resolution hologram, displaying mind-altering sharpness surpassing real-life characters.

Performing her warm-up routine, Pori engaged in arm circling, torso twisting, high kicks, leg swings and lateral shuffles. Approaching the 3D holograms, she immersed herself in this digi-verse to carry out exclusive martial art combat. The projected image, an AI-based arcade character, possessed its own intelligent defence and attack mechanisms. Pori continuously engaged with the artificial projection, enduring blows that were translated into sensations by thousands of microsensors embedded throughout her body suit. These sensors converted the impact into realistic pain, enabling her to experience punches and kicks from Rhiron that felt remarkably genuine.

For an hour, she engaged in a high-energy, artistic martial arts bout, resulting in copious sweat pouring down her forehead and body. This intensive workout served as significant exercise before she headed for a cleansing shower to alleviate both stress and dirt accumulated during the vigorous session.

Nurul readied the LPG gas cylinder for igniting the barbecue grill, while Bodrul arranged the vegetables on the tabletop. After an hour of cooking, they finally prepared the food for consumption. Nurul went and knocked on Pori's door.

"Madam, the food is ready when you are," informed Nurul.

"Okay, give me fifteen minutes, I will be there," Pori shouted from inside her cabin.

*

Rajan Chowdhury, the incumbent prime minister, initiated a telephone conversation with the nefarious character Abdul Malik.

"Hello, Mr Prime Minister," answered Malik.

"I don't understand why I persist in reaching out to you. It seems you're incapable of handling any task efficiently," remarked the prime minister.

"I am the only one willing to undertake the tasks you deem unsavoury, that's why you reach out to me. So, what is it that you need?" responded Malik.

"Nadia has threatened to detonate our brick and cement factory due to her concerns about the pollution it generates," relayed the prime minister.

"What! That facility is a significant contributor to the country's economy," exclaimed Malik in shock.

"Yes, and she intends to destroy it. How can you ensure the protection of that facility? I need a viable solution," demanded the prime minister.

"Are you absolutely certain about this?" enquired Malik.

"Yes, I am certain," confirmed the prime minister.

"I'm unclear though! I've successfully developed ten new AI-based terminator-style robots, but I'm unwilling to expose them to a confrontation against hundreds, or even more sophisticated, of Nadia's AI-based robots. However, if you have the funds to purchase them, I'm willing to sell, designating you as the leader. You can program the robots to strategise and coordinate the attack," explained Malik.

"What! You've just revealed your true colours, Malik. You're a betrayer and a backstabber. How could I possibly control machines created by you? Go to hell," declared the prime minister before ending the call.

"Seems a fool's errand to traverse the Atlantic and return empty-handed, only to show up at my doorstep and pound on it in vain. Your loss, mate," remarked Malik before disconnecting the call.

The prime minister contacted the Bangladesh Army, directing the deployment of 5,000 elite combatant military forces to safeguard the brick and cement facility effective immediately.

The army general assented to the directive and concluded the call. Subsequently, he mobilised several other army officials to take charge of protecting the specified facility.

*

Upon reaching the verdant expanse of the Sundarbans forest, Pori and her devoted boat crew secured their vessel at a picturesque cliffside berth. Adorned in her formidable warrior attire, Pori exuded a breathtaking beauty that captivated all who beheld her. Bodrul, enchanted by her presence, couldn't help but admire her, expressing, "Madam, you look resplendent in that attire."

"Thank you," replied Pori with graceful acknowledgment.

Nurul, the second boatman, meticulously laid the platform for disembarkation onto the land. At Pori's command, Sultan, the majestic tiger, was instructed to leave the boat. As Nurul reached the shore, he noticed the impending descent of the tiger. Overwhelmed by fear, he urgently exclaimed, "Madam, please, you embark first before the animals. I cannot trust that beast. I am greatly apprehensive of that tiger."

"Tiger, hold on," Pori instructed firmly. "Listen, both of you. Remain here in this spot. Take the smaller boat and row around, but do not stray too far. Ensure you stay within this vicinity. I might return at any moment."

"Understood, madam. Go and relish the wonders of the Sundarbans," remarked Bodrul from the boat.

First, Pori disembarked, followed by the tiger, and then the horse. Pori swiftly mounted the horse, ascended the cliffs and ventured into the heart of the jungle.

She enquired of the horse, "Do you recall our previous location?"

"I believe I do. We need to head several miles to the north," responded the horse.

"Let's continue," Pori urged as they ventured deeper into the forest. As they moved through the enchanting landscape of the Sundarbans, a multitude of fascinating creatures emerged from their hidden sanctuaries, going about their daily activities. Some of them greeted Pori in their unique languages, and she reciprocated with smiles and a sense of wonder. She couldn't help but reflect, *If only humans had left nature undisturbed, it would have flourished with diverse animal and plant life.* It was akin to a mystical adventure, and Pori revealed it in her vibrant connection with the natural world.

After a while, the distant roar of a tiger caught her attention. She whispered, "Hey, everyone, stop!" The horse and her faithful tiger companion, Sultan, came to a halt. Pori carefully listened to the sound, determined its direction and then dismounted from the horse. She instructed both the horse and Sultan to remain still and wait. Drawing a compact rocket launcher gun from its holster, she loaded it with a propelling grenade and returned it. She also had a tranquillising dart gun ready at her side.

With stealth, Pori approached the source of the noise and took cover behind a large tree, offering her an ideal vantage point to observe the unfolding scene. Before her eyes, a genuine tiger was preparing to engage in a confrontation with a dog-like creature. However, this creature did not resemble a real dog; it appeared to be of a manufactured type, a robotic dog meticulously designed to mimic a real-life counterpart.

Pori noticed that her loyal tiger, Sultan, was also observing the scene from a distance. She gestured for him to retreat, but Sultan revealed that the tiger in question had been a tormentor throughout his life. He made a heartfelt plea: "Let it meet its fate. Let's depart from this place."

"What!... It's okay, you can go back. You don't have to save him. This doesn't look good," said Pori, acknowledging Sultan's plea.

"I will stay here and watch the fight, I want to see him get busted," declared Sultan.

The tension between the two aggressive creatures escalated, their impending clash imminent.

As they lunged at each other, Pori noticed metallic claws extend from the dog's paws, realising the severe harm it could inflict upon the tiger. In a swift, brutal exchange, the dog viciously attacked the tiger, tearing through its flesh like tissue paper, causing extensive wounds and bloodshed.

Witnessing the unfolding brutality, Pori, fearing for the tiger's life, aimed her firearm at the dog in an attempt to divert its attention. However, the bullet merely ricocheted off the dog's metallic body, embedding itself into a nearby tree. Momentarily distracted, the robotic dog pivoted, redirecting its focus toward Sultan; abandoning its current victim it now pursued the chase on Sultan.

"Sultan, run!" Pori urgently shouted, hoping to alert the tiger to flee from the relentless robotic assailant.

"Oh no!" exclaimed Sultan as he witnessed the devastating outcome of the conflict. Reacting swiftly, he bolted away, his tail held high in the air, reminiscent of a startled cat.

Pori quickly mounted her horse and pursued the robodog, which moved with the agility and speed of a real canine. Engaged in a cat-and-mouse chase, she maintained a close tail, turning the pursuit into a thrilling race through the vast forest. Meanwhile, Sultan, finding it challenging to keep pace, struggled to outrun the relentless robotic dog, which was swiftly closing the gap, each of its leaps posing a lethal threat.

With Pori hot on their trail, riding fast on her horse, she armed herself with a mini rocket launcher. Closing in on the scene where the artificial dog was almost within striking distance of Sultan, the tiger leapt over a fallen log, closely pursued by the dog. The metallic claws extended from the dog's paws, managing to slash the tiger's skin as it attempted to attack Sultan's hindquarters.

In a decisive moment, Pori took aim and fired at the dog from behind. The shot hit its mark, striking the dog's neck and triggering a detonation that shattered the robotic assailant into scattered pieces in a powerful blast.

"Goodness!" exclaimed Hassan, miles away, peering at his screen as he witnessed the unfortunate demise of their robodog.

He is a member of an underground syndicate operating from Cox's Bazar, renowned for its stunning, unbroken stretch of sandy beach along the Bay of Bengal, extending for approximately 120 kilometres. This makes it the longest natural sea beach globally, attracting both local and international tourists.

Poachers remotely orchestrate the insidious exploitation of animal parts for the Chinese market for entertainment and medicinal purposes. Their cutting-edge methods involve using this advanced technology to facilitate the hands-free killing of endangered species. Within the confines of the protected Sundarbans, any act of poaching, injuring or causing harm to wildlife is strictly prohibited. Thus, they have devised an innovative approach, mimicking natural animal conflicts to camouflage their killings, ensuring authorities overlook these orchestrated scenes as typical wildlife skirmishes.

This clandestine operation has successfully eluded detection for years, perpetuating their nefarious activities. Today, however, marks an unprecedented turn of events. A vigilant individual has managed to track down and dismantle their device, disrupting their operations.

"Who is that girl? She's completely derailed our plans," lamented a colleague, perched on a nearby bench. "Her actions have not only obliterated our creation but also jeopardised our entire enterprise. I fear she'll involve the forest guards now," he added, visibly concerned.

"We're uncertain of her identity," Hassan responded. "But we must locate the remnants of our robodog swiftly to ensure that the forest guards don't decipher our novel method for tiger poaching."

Pori's elation was palpable as her well-aimed grenade obliterated the enemy robot into scattered pieces. Swiftly, she dashed toward

Sultan, tending to the deep wound inflicted by the razor-sharp claws of the now-destroyed machine. Her call to SS, her trusty horse, summoned the animal close. With urgency, she unzipped a bag filled with essential first aid supplies. Carefully, she treated Sultan's injuries, cleaning them with antiseptic liquid applied through gentle dabs of cotton wool, before securely wrapping the wounds with a substantial bandage. Communicating with Sultan, she directed the majestic animal to convey a message to the other tiger, assuring it that she would be there soon to attend to its injuries.

Concurrently, Pori set about gathering the scattered remnants of the robodog. Assiduously, she collected the smaller fragments, stowing them in a capacious nylon bag. Larger pieces of the robot's body were methodically fastened and secured onto her horse's back using straps and fasteners. With decisive commands, she directed her horse to transport the salvaged parts towards the awaiting boat. SS embarked on a deliberate, unhurried trot in the direction of the vessel. Simultaneously, Pori made a call to Bodrul, the boatman, apprising him of the impending arrival of her horse, laden with parcels. She instructed him to offload and store these salvaged remnants safely within the boat.

Using their shared language, Sultan approached the gravely injured tiger known as Togo, who lay motionless, bearing deep, ghastly claw marks oozing with blood. Sultan, familiar with Togo, peered into his eyes with a mixture of disdain and haunting memories, a flood of recollections detailing the abuse he had endured at Togo's hands.

In a vivid flashback, Sultan reminisced about moments when Togo displayed aggression and dominance. One such instance involved Sultan chasing down a small deer for a meal, only to have Togo forcefully seize the catch, asserting dominance through aggression. Another distressing memory centred on a tranquil moment shared by Sultan and his tigress companion, Che-chee, under the shelter of a tree. Togo had intruded, demanding precedence and asserting his perceived authority over the jungle.

Sultan vehemently objected, contending that Che-chee was not mere prey to be seized at will. Togo, in response, roared, asserting his dominion over the jungle and anything in-between including Che-chee, and a contingent of other tigers emerged in support of Togo's claim.

Sensing the escalating tension, Che-chee had intervened, urging Sultan to depart from the scene. Sultan hesitated, but Che-chee, in a sudden turn of character, grew insistent, demanding his departure. She emphasised that she was not his possession and willingly approached Togo, displaying affection through touch, caresses and licks. Togo, in turn, felt a surge of pride and walked away with Che-chee. Sultan watched in anguish as his beloved vanished into the depths of the forest, under the canopy of trees, leaving him in despair.

In the present moment, Sultan snapped back to reality and unleashed a thunderous roar at Togo. "Why should I save you now?" he bellowed furiously. "You're a contemptible scoundrel – die here! You deserve it."

"Drop it, Sultan, get away from here!" Pori exclaimed, signalling for Sultan to retreat.

Moving in closer, Pori commenced the first aid procedure on Togo. With meticulous care, she began by disinfecting the wounds using antiseptic liquid as the base, followed by applying ample bandages and plasters to seal the visibly severe and gaping wounds, skilfully stitching them where necessary. Speaking to Togo, she conveyed, "It's a beautiful, sunny day. As soon as you're feeling better, move to a safer place. The individuals who attacked you will return, searching for their robodog and any remnants here. Understand?"

Her soothing words aimed to both tend to Togo's wounds and alert him to the imminent danger, encouraging his departure once he regained strength.

Togo gazed into Pori's eyes and blinked, a gesture conveying gratitude and understanding for her aid.

Sultan and Pori resumed their journey, and Pori could discern the distant sound of hoofbeats. "Is that you, SS?" she enquired.

"Heee heee! Yes," came the horse's response.

SS soon came to Pori, who effortlessly mounted the horse's back. They continued toward their destination: a serene, clear-water lagoon. The need for a relaxing bath had become more pressing than ever. The chase and additional tasks had left them all thoroughly drained.

*

Aysha had assembled a formidable contingent of approximately 200 of her bionic guardians, united with a singular purpose: the eradication of environmentally detrimental brick and cement factories, alleged to be co-owned by nefarious government figures. Poised before her vigilant forces, she gracefully assumed the role of orator, delivering a compelling address that resonated with purpose and determination.

"Esteemed comrades, lend me your ears. Today, we stand at the precipice of a trial that shall gauge the depths of our patience in the crucible of reality. The hour we have long awaited has finally dawned, arriving at a juncture where change is imperative, and we must seize this opportunity with unwavering resolve. I impart to you this critical revelation: despite constituting a mere six per cent of the annual budget, the Bangladesh armed forces find themselves incapable of projecting strength in the face of repeated incursions into our borders, both on land and in our airspace, by our neighbouring Myanmar.

"Consider them akin to a swarm of ants obstructing your path – crush them with determination and advance. Swift takeover is the antidote to minimising casualties. You are granted the authority to dismantle the entire facility at your discretion, but exercise caution to spare innocent lives. Collective cooperation is the linchpin of our success. Our objective is to dismantle the fossil-fuel-burning monstrosity and reconstruct it anew. Upon reclaiming that parcel of land, we shall erect a state-of-the-art brick and cement factory with a commitment to green initiatives. Clean energy sources will not only elevate the wellbeing of the populace but also nurture the environment, heralding a new era.

"Be forewarned: we confront a formidable military adversary. Yet, you are no less formidable than your foes. Engage in battle with unwavering vigour and confidence, for victory shall be ours. Good luck, my valiant soldiers. Long live the BROCS – Bangladesh Republic of Community and Scholars."

A resounding cheer erupted from the crowd, expressing unanimous approval. "Yes, yes, and thank you for showing such exemplary leadership!"

On the opposing front, Prime Minister Rajan Chowdhury, flanked by other government officials, stood poised before a formidable 5,000-strong military force, ready to deliver the following address:

"Fellow patriots, today we find ourselves standing at the nexus of duty and conviction, entrusted with the solemn responsibility of safeguarding our nation's sovereignty. As we face a formidable challenge from those who seek to undermine the stability we hold dear, let it be known that our commitment to defending our borders remains unwavering.

"In the crucible of this moment, I call upon each of you, the valiant members of our armed forces, to exemplify the strength, discipline and resilience that define our great nation. We stand united against forces that threaten our integrity, and it is through your unwavering dedication that we shall prevail.

"Remember, our cause is just, our unity unbreakable. The destiny of our beloved country rests in your capable hands. May your courage be unwavering, and may victory be the anthem that echoes across our land. Together, let us face this challenge with the collective resolve that has defined our nation through the ages. Long live our great nation!

"Today, our nation stands at the abyss of a historical regression reminiscent of the British Raj era. We find ourselves transported back to the tumultuous year of 1947, recalling the painful memories of how the British divided India into three fragments, leaving us in the wreckage of a fractured existence and famine. History threatens to replay itself, with the spouse of a white Britisher attempting to sow discord and division within our beloved land. We must rise collectively and resist until our last breath, for our demise shall be counted as martyrdom. We cannot allow this individual to govern us with her divisive ideology.

"This facility, a source of employment and prosperity for our people over the years, has weathered the storms of time, and it shall persist in doing so. Fellow citizens of Bangladesh, let it be known that the rhetoric of climate change emanating from affluent nations is a fallacy. The purported global crisis is merely a fabricated narrative. What we witness across the world is but a natural phenomenon, an inherent cycle that the Earth undergoes to reset itself. Our planet, resilient over millions of years, has navigated through its own climate variations.

"Now, however, a new breed of environmentalists emerges from the ashes of public turmoil, attributing global climate shifts solely to human activity. This notion is baseless. Earth, in its life cycle, undergoes geological transformations. Continents submerge, and new ones emerge – a perpetual dance of change ingrained in its history. We cannot be led astray by false ideologies. Let us stand firm against the tide of misinformation and preserve the truth that has withstood the test of time.

"Nadia Begum, a figure shrouded in cunning deceit, harbours a heart laden with venom. Her relentless pursuit of personal gain, achieved through manipulation and deception, poses a dire threat to our nation. She is a dark force, a jest upon the very principles of environmental consciousness, my fellow countrymen. It is imperative that we thwart her attempts to infiltrate our collective existence, for once a disease permeates the bloodstream, the consequences are often irreversible.

"Aligned with other misguided scientists, she concocts climate change theories as a means to ascend to power, demonstrating a blatant disregard for the welfare of our nation. Her focus lies solely on seizing power, with little concern for the catastrophic consequences it may wreak upon our beloved country. Absurdly, she claims that the emissions from our turbines are single-handedly causing climate change. What about the millions of acres of forest reduced to ashes under the natural power of the sun's flames? What about the colossal volumes of pollutants disgorged into the air by erupting volcanoes? What about the sun's expansion due to its age? In the face of such global occurrences, the notion that a minuscule amount of smoke from our chimneys could be deemed as the world's environmental nemesis lacks any semblance of logic.

"Consider the historical backdrop of Western industrialisation, where coal and fossil fuels fuelled their revolutions, and they persist in burning them to this day. Yet, from the ranks of a Western puppet, the newly appointed Nadia Begum, 'The Dark Environmentalist', claims our modest facility is the harbinger of pollution. Compare our footprint to that of the West, and you'll find we are but a drop in the vast ocean of industrial activity, my friends.

"We stand at a critical juncture where we must vehemently resist and defend our nation against such insidious invaders. Nadia Begum, in an act of betrayal, has effectively disowned our country by betraying the secrets of her former employer, GreenBirth Corporation, and selling them to the United Kingdom. This treacherous act not only jeopardises our national interests but also undermines the very fabric of trust and loyalty that binds us together. Let us unite in the face of this threat and safeguard our homeland from those who seek to exploit and betray it for their personal gain.

"Our Bangladesh, the embodiment of golden aspirations and cherished dreams, holds a special place in our hearts. We declare proudly and with unwavering devotion: 'Our Bangladesh is a Golden Bangladesh', and in this declaration, we affirm our profound love for our beloved country! Joy Bangla!"

The spirited cheers of the Bangladesh Army resonated in unanimous approval as they declared, "In war, in peace, we are everywhere for our nation! Joy Bangla!... Joy Bangla!... Joy Bangla!"

CHAPTER 12

THE FALL OF PRIME MINISTER RAJAN CHOWDHURY

Pori   Hassan   Kassab   Bodrul   Nurul

Keith   Sarah   Maria   Steven   M Reid

Sadik   Army   Rajan   Aysah's R   Nadia

Aysha   Sultan   Malik's R   Malik

Starring

Pori Moni – (Hassan – Kassab - owner of RoboDog) – (Bodru – Nurul boat owners) – Keith Evan – Sarah, Grand ma – Maria, aunty – Steven teenage friend – Martin Reid GCHQ leader – Sadik Talukdar, senor police officer – Army – Prime Minister Rajan – Aysha's Robots – Aysah Khanom - Tiger as Sultan – Malik's Robots.

In the midst of the tranquil heart of the lush Sundarban, Pori discovered solace and renewal within the comforting embrace of a natural lagoon. As the filtered sunlight gently permeated through the dense canopy of overhead trees, the crystalline waters of the lagoon tenderly cradled her in their serene ripples. With each unhurried stroke, the touch of the outside world dissipated, replaced by the symphony of birdsong and the harmonious presence of forest creatures. Enveloped by the rustling leaves and the melodic essence of nature, she willingly surrendered to the tranquil concord of this concealed sanctuary. Here, amid the union of water, woods and wilderness, Pori attained a profound sense of serenity and revitalisation.

The journey proved to be truly worthwhile. Having immersed herself in the rejuvenating waters for approximately two hours, a desire lingered within her to prolong this blissful interlude. Suddenly, the rhythmic clip-clop of hooves, the unmistakable sound of a horse's gait, reached her ears. She instinctively redirected her gaze toward the perimeter of the shoreline, where the familiar silhouette of her horse SS came into view.

"SS," she enquired, her form partially submerged in the water, "what has occurred?"

"Our boatmen are under attack," replied SS.

"What!" Pori exclaimed in disbelief. In a swift motion, she propelled herself out of the lagoon, shedding any inhibitions she may have had. Unusually, she did not direct her horse to avert its gaze, shyness momentarily eclipsed by urgency. Standing in her unabashed, natural form, she exhibited a physique embodying the epitome of beauty – strong, sculpted legs and arms, a narrow waist, and shapely hips and chest. Her presence resembled that of a living, unaltered siren on the stage of reality. Swiftly, she reached for her garments, hastily dressing herself as concern and determination etched across her countenance.

*

At the boat site, a menacing scene unfolded. The armed enforcers of the robodog cartels, brandishing handguns, had encircled Bodrul's boat. The tracker chip embedded within the robodog, miraculously unscathed, had served as a beacon for Hassan, the mastermind behind the illicit animal poaching activities, and his formidable team of five. Two of the men scaled the sides of the boat, their hands gripping firearms as they sternly instructed Bodrul and Nurul, the boat owners, to evacuate the vessel with hands raised in surrender.

"Is there anyone else inside?" queried one of the gunmen.

"No, sir!" replied Bodrul.

"Where is that girl?" demanded the armed men.

"She is in the Sundarbans, sir," informed Bodrul.

"You, stay back," the gunman ordered Bodrul, the second boatman. "Show me where you've stashed the remains of our damaged robot."

Nurul re-entered the boat, trailed by the gunmen. He gestured towards a bag, indicating, "That bag contains the smaller pieces, and the rest you can see scattered on the floor, exposed, sir."

Pori, having just arrived, gracefully dismounted her horse and stealthily approached the scene. With determined focus, she readied her weapon, eyes scanning for an opportune moment to strike. In a swift and precise motion, she unleashed tranquillising darts, successfully hitting three assailants who crumpled to the ground within moments.

However, Hassan, the mastermind, swiftly detected her presence and sprang into action, unleashing a barrage of bullets in her direction. Quick on her feet, Pori deftly stowed the dart gun in her holster belt and, in the blink of an eye, drew her bullet gun. With a calculated shot, a bullet found its mark on Hassan's upper right arm, forcing him to relinquish his firearm with a cry for help that reverberated through the air, alerting the gunmen within the boat.

Upon hearing Hassan's urgent call for help, the gunman inside the boat reacted swiftly, seizing Nurul and holding him hostage. "Not a word, or I'll shoot to kill. Understand?" he warned, the ominous threat hanging heavily in the air.

"Yes, I understand," Nurul replied, his fear palpable.

Pori, taking charge of the situation, enquired, "Where is your cousin, Bodrul?"

"He is inside, madam. There is a gunman in there too," Bodrul disclosed, the tension evident in his voice.

Pori swiftly tossed a handful of nylon cable-ties to Bodrul. "Go and secure the hands and legs of those three on the floor," she instructed with authority. "You!" Pori called out sternly, addressing Hassan, who lay on the floor, bleeding from the bullet wound to his right arm. "If you want to live, call the guy inside to come out," she commanded with unwavering determination.

"Kassab! Kassab!" Hassan urgently called out. "Come out, mate! The girl is here."

"Look, we don't want any trouble. I saw you captured my robodog. All I want is to take it back," Hassan explained, attempting to defuse the situation.

"Good, you came for it. It saved me looking for you to kick your butts. So, you poachers found a new way to kill tigers using robots, evading prosecution from authorities. Your time is up now," Pori declared firmly. "Why is your mate not coming out?" she enquired, her gaze sharp and unyielding.

"Kassab, mate, leave the things, come, let's get out of here!" Hassan called out again.

Responding to the call, Kassab emerged, but to everyone's dismay, he was holding a gun to Nurul's head. "Drop the gun or I will shoot him!" Kassab warned, his gaze fixed on Pori with tense determination.

Pori maintained a steady gaze, looking Kassab in the eye for an extended moment, and then calmly spoke. "I tell you what. Here, I drop the gun. I respect you for your age. I don't want to take up arms against you, you are my parents' age. I don't want any violence. You let him go, and take your mate to a doctor for treatment. Just go. I haven't seen anything, okay? I will not report anything."

"Hey! Untie my men," Kassab ordered as he noticed Bodrul attempting to tie his men.

"Sir, I can't untie them now, I must cut them. I don't have a side-cutting clipper with me," Bodrul explained.

"Come and tie up that girl and this man here," ordered Kassab, indicating the hostage Nurul.

Bodrul complied, first tying up Pori and then moving to secure Nurul.

"How badly are you hurt, mate?" Kassab enquired of Hassan.

"My arm's gone, mate. Feel like kicking this stupid girl's head off," fumed Hassan. "But she compared us to her parents, so I let her off. Let's get a move on."

"Hold on, let me go and take the remains of the robodog. You can kick asses after, the ball is in our court," Kassab suggested. He went inside the boat again.

However, seizing the opportunity, Pori activated her central hair plait, which transformed into a cutting mechanism. Swiftly, it snipped the cable tie open, freeing her hands. She seized the tranquilliser gun, shooting Hassan in the back, sedating him instantly. Entering the boat cabin, she found Kassab struggling with the remains of robodog. Silently approaching him, she jabbed a tranquillising dart into his neck, rendering him unconscious.

Instructing Bodrul and Nurul, she ordered them to securely tie all five captives and then directed them to place Hassan and Kassab inside the tiger's den.

Summoning her tiger, Sultan, Pori unzipped her bag and retrieved a flexible cage muzzle. She secured it around the tiger's mouth, preventing any intimidation towards humans. Issuing explicit instructions, she emphasised that Sultan should not harm the detainees. She warned, "If they act foolishly, let out a mighty roar near their ears," delivering the caution with a stern gaze.

"Get ready to return to Arambaria," Pori instructed Bodrul and Nurul. "Once you're home, a goldsmith from Sajni Jewellers will arrive at the shoreline to collect the tiger. They need to measure him for a harness for his face and neck. They'll bring their own cage to accommodate tiger for transportation," Pori clarified.

A sudden bombardment at a distance caught Pori's attention. "What's going on over there? It's like a war zone, with all that artillery smoke," she exclaimed. "I think I know," she added, a hint of concern in her voice.

Quickly, she jumped on her horse's back and instructed Bodrul and Nurul to feed Sultan before boarding, repeating the process during the journey and once more upon reaching Arambaria. "Lock up those culprits alongside the tiger, so they can't cause any more trouble. I will come and deal with them later. Let me quickly check that war zone," she declared as she rode off towards the source of the commotion.

"Madam! Madam!" Bodrul called out, but Pori didn't seem to hear. "Gosh, she left us in limbo. Who's going to take the muzzle off the tiger to feed?" he exclaimed.

"Yes, she did," echoed Nurul. "I am fucking terrified of that tiger. He's going to eat all five detainees and finish us off too. I can't believe we're stuck with this death trap in our boat for five hours," cried Nurul.

"Too late, mate. Let's save our boat. Just do what she told us. Let's get a move on," urged Bodrul.

"Do we feed these detainees?" asked Nurul, uncertainty in his voice.

"We have her number. We will call her if need be, mate. Let's get a move on. If we can get to the boat district before nightfall, we will find a separate boat to spend the night. I am not going to sleep with a tiger onboard here," declared Bodrul, determination in his voice.

Securing everything inside the boat, Nurul emerged with a long bamboo pole. With a practised hand, he nudged the boat away from the shoreline. Meanwhile, Bodrul lowered the engine, started it up and lifted the anchor from the riverbed. With the vessel now in motion, they set sail, steering away from the mooring site.

Pori, on her horse, rode away, gradually distancing herself from the boat. As she passed a few hundred metres from the location, Nurul watched her and waved goodbye.

Pori glanced back, acknowledging the farewell, and waved back before resolutely heading towards the danger zone where artillery and gunfire echoed in the distance.

The war between Aysha's bionic forces and the prime minister's military was a full-on battle. Aysha's men fought with unmatched ferocity, swiftly toppling their opponents like unwanted termites. Their fighting skills, combined with agility, fluidity and precision in tactical combat, left the prime minister's forces dazed and confused, throwing them off balance and ultimately leading to their demise. Aysha's 200-strong forces barely received any scratches, continuing to move forward with unwavering strength. As the battle unfolded, more and more enemies dropped dead to the floor, unable to withstand the relentless onslaught of Aysha's formidable army.

In the face of the swift and overwhelming demise of his soldiers, the prime minister, recognising the dire situation, made another desperate call to Abdul Malik. He pleaded with him to send his artificial robot soldiers into action.

"My men are falling like scattered autumn leaves from a tree, literally in their 100's. I have realised the age of traditional warfare is over. I will offer you as much money as you like, just save my troops," implored the prime minister in a desperate plea for assistance.

"I am fully aware of what's happening on the battlefield, Mr Prime Minister. I am observing it from above using my remote-operated autonomous drone. Didn't I say to you Nadia's armies are untouchable? You deployed roughly 5,000 troops, and there are less than 1,000 left. I can sell five of my humanoid fighting robots designed to kill, and I mean kill, each for one crore (one million) taka," declared Abdul Malik, presenting a stern solution to the prime minister's plea.

"What! You are taking the piss at a bad time, Malik, exploiting my vulnerability. Timing is on your side, and I will never forget. Send five. Let's see if they can hold back these horrific atrocities," retorted the prime minister with a mixture of frustration and resignation, acknowledging the grim reality of the situation.

"They can't hold back, they can only delay your fall, I'm afraid. Your rules are over, Mr Prime Minister. My five cannot get rid of 200. You have lost the battle by declaring war on Nadia," Abdul Malik stated bluntly, highlighting the stark reality of the prime minister's situation.

"You send those robots to the battlefield ASAP, okay?" the prime minister instructed.

"You transfer the money now. I want five crores to reach my account in fifteen minutes," demanded Abdul Malik.

Fuming with disgust at the audacity of the financial demand, the prime minister hung up in silence and couldn't help but hurl an angry expletive at Abdul Malik. "You bastard, Malik!"

*

In the southeastern reaches of Bangladesh, a momentous occasion had unfolded. Nadia, with shrewd acumen, had secured a pivotal deal with a prominent television channel to capture the grand inauguration of her groundbreaking smart floating village in the country's southern coastal expanse. She wanted to name the village The Floating City. Little did the assembled multitude realise that Aysha, who was present at this gathering, had discreetly orchestrated her bionic forces against the armies of the prime minister. Her formidable legion of 200 operatives was at work in the shadows as they spoke.

Simultaneously, Aysha's adept political campaigners artfully conveyed a message to mobilise between 7,000 and 10,000 attendees for this historic floating village event. Skilfully diverting the nation's attention, they put together a strategic policy to shift people's concentration towards this auspicious opening ceremony. The congregation not only offered a platform for the local populace to showcase and sell their intricately handcrafted wares but also drew in a vast array of individuals from across Bangladesh, seeking inspiration from the event.

In the wake of this gathering, a myriad of business prospects emerged, giving impetus to the establishment of pop-up stalls, ephemeral food markets, souvenir kiosks, fun fairs and an array of entrepreneurial activities. The event, beyond its immediate celebration, evolved into a catalyst for economic activity, fostering a vibrant tapestry of commerce and creativity within the community.

With grace and authority, Aysha clasped the microphone, commanding the attention of both the broadcasting team and the esteemed gathering that had graciously congregated to partake in this momentous occasion.

"Ladies and gentlemen, distinguished members of the broadcasting team, and our valued audience, thank you for joining us today to partake in a truly exhilarating revelation. We stand united on the precipice of a groundbreaking development: the inception of a floating village nestled within the enchanting confines of the southeastern coastal region of Bangladesh. While the notion may evoke elements of a science fiction narrative, rest assured, these innovative ventures are poised to materialise right here in our beloved nation."

In this collective moment of anticipation, Aysha extended the spotlight to her esteemed colleague and the project's visionary sponsor, Madam Nadia Begum, beckoning the audience to redirect their focus.

"I now implore you to direct your attention to the luminary at the helm of this transformative endeavour, Madam Nadia Begum. She holds the key to unravelling the intricacies of this far-sighted project. Without further ado, I yield the floor to her, inviting her to share profound insights that promise to enlighten and captivate us all."

Taking the microphone, Nadia addressed her fellow citizens with a poignant reflection on the formidable challenge posed by climate change, a challenge that has precipitated a transformative shift in the fabric of our lives, driven by the inexorable rise in sea levels. As the disheartening cadence of seasonal flooding and the hindrance of waterlogging pervade our agricultural pursuits, the imperative to adapt in a sustainable manner becomes increasingly apparent.

Nadia articulated the dire warnings from scientists, painting a stark picture of a future where our coastal regions may confront a perilous surge of up to 1.8 metres in sea levels by the century's end. This foreboding prophecy portends a landscape marred by heightened and more frequent sea level fluctuations, coupled with the ominous spectre of increasingly devastating storms. In the face of such a disconcerting reality, Nadia presented the audience with a binary choice: a transformative restructuring of our way of life or the perilous pursuit of refuge akin to those fleeing war-torn nations – yet a daunting prospect, as we lack an alternative sanctuary.

"Are you, my fellow citizens, prepared to embark on the uncertain journey of migration to foreign lands, boarding inflatable boats?" Nadia posed the question to the assembled crowd.

A resounding "No!" echoed through the throng, a collective declaration of steadfast determination.

The imperative for change, Nadia emphasised, is undeniable. Acknowledging humanity's historical affinity for dwelling on water, she highlighted the fortuitous convergence of our era with innovative technologies that pave the way for the realisation of sustainable floodplain communities.

"In a courageous and compassionate endeavour, Humanitarian Pledge, my esteemed company, is launching a visionary project to establish a community of 1,000 residential floating homes along the pristine expanse of the south coast. This innovative village goes beyond being a simple collection of structures. Instead, it is a meticulously designed tapestry of interconnected platforms, each crafted with a specific purpose to ensure lasting sustainability. The city will be structured like a jigsaw puzzle, with individual modular apartment blocks manufactured on dry land and then airlifted to their destination within The Floating City, seamlessly fitting into place.

"To enhance the resilience of this floating community against the unpredictable forces of severe weather conditions, the platforms will be constructed at a low elevation. This strategic decision aims to minimise vulnerability and bolster the village's ability to withstand the challenges posed by environmental fluctuations.

"Embracing a profound commitment to ecological responsibility, our project will employ a multifaceted approach to harness natural resources. Through strategic integration, we aim to capitalise on the abundance of water, solar energy and wind power. Advanced desalination systems will be seamlessly incorporated to secure a clean and sustainable water supply for the community. Furthermore, the village's energy needs will be met through an intricate network of electric generators, drawing power from an ingenious combination of solar panels, wind turbines and tidal turbines.

"This undertaking is more than the construction of homes. It is a pledge to foster a harmonious coexistence with nature, ensuring that the community thrives in balance with its environment while providing a blueprint for sustainable living on our planet's dynamic southern coast.

"The ingenuity underlying the design of our floating platforms stands as a testament to our unwavering commitment to climate-friendliness and self-sufficiency, ushering in a host of environmental advantages. Residents residing in these floating homes will not merely coexist with nature, they will actively contribute to its preservation.

"The floating platforms are conceived as verdant havens, affording residents the unique opportunity to cultivate an abundance of fresh fruit and vegetables. Through a harmonious marriage of on-surface, vertical indoor farm structures, as well as innovative underwater farming techniques for cultivating seaweed, residents will engage in sustainable agricultural practices that foster a self-sustaining ecosystem.

"A key feature of these platforms is their dynamic adaptability to the natural rhythms of the sea. Engineered to rise and fall with the tides, these floating homes maintain a harmonious equilibrium with sea levels. This not only serves as a proactive measure against the challenges posed by strong waves, tsunamis and hurricanes but also ensures the long-term resilience of the community in the face of unpredictable environmental forces.

"Our commitment to sustainability extends beyond agricultural practices and adaptive engineering. In the spirit of local resilience, we are dedicated to utilising locally sourced building materials. This deliberate choice not only reduces the ecological footprint associated with construction but also facilitates accessible and efficient repairs and maintenance, embodying the essence of modern, responsible living on these floating platforms. The vision is not just to reside on the water but to harmonise with it, fostering a model of living that reveres the environment while providing a haven for those who call these floating homes their own.

"This groundbreaking concept not only exemplifies our steadfast commitment but also encapsulates our unwavering enthusiasm for instigating transformative changes in the fabric of our lives. It stands as a resounding testament to our collective resolve to not just survive, but to flourish, providing secure and enduring relief to communities grappling with the impact of floods.

"We extend a warm invitation to you to immerse yourself in this exhilarating three-day event, an opportunity to witness first-hand the innovative floating architectural design that symbolises resilience and forward-thinking solutions. Embrace the chance to explore these remarkable structures up close and personal.

"Moreover, we encourage you to actively engage with our dedicated design team. Share your thoughts, insights and comments. They stand ready to welcome your ideas with open arms, addressing any questions, concerns or queries you may have. Your input is not just valued, it is integral to the evolution of this transformative initiative.

"To our distinguished guests and visitors, we wish you an enriching and enjoyable experience throughout the event. May this gathering be a celebration of innovation, sustainability and the collective spirit driving positive change in our communities and beyond."

Nadia is fervently endeavouring to capture the hearts and minds of the people through Arambaria village and the ambitious floating city project. Her vision transcends mere physical structures; it is a unique approach aimed at alleviating the collective pain and stress of communities, fostering a transformative ennoblement of moral understanding. At the core of her philosophy is the belief that to lead a truly satisfying and happy life, individuals must reflect on their past, engage with the present and actively participate in designing their future.

Should Nadia find herself in the driver's seat of governance, her strategic plans extend beyond infrastructure. She aspires to embark on a revolutionary restructuring of the entire education system of the country. Central to this vision is a paradigm shift – a system that venerates humanity above all. Nadia envisions an educational landscape where the study of humanity becomes the cornerstone, inspiring individuals to cultivate a deeper understanding of themselves, their communities and the interconnected tapestry of human experiences.

In championing this transformative agenda, Nadia seeks not only to build physical structures but to construct a societal framework that nurtures the human spirit, fostering resilience, empathy and a collective commitment to shaping a harmonious and enlightened future for the nation.

*

Across the vast and secluded expanse, Pori manoeuvred her horse with grace, traversing diverse landscapes that included open grass fields and both wet and dry paddy fields. High above, Abdul Malik keenly observed the agile movements of her steed from his aerial vantage point, prompting him to delve into the unfolding mystery. Upon closer inspection, he discerned a lone female rider making her way toward a conflict zone, a decision that defied the fleeing crowd.

Perplexed by this unexpected course of action, Abdul Malik, fuelled by concern, swiftly propelled his Spy in the Sky Drone (SSD) to a velocity surpassing that of Pori's horse. Strategically positioning it just 500 metres ahead, nearly imperceptible to her, he engaged the object-tracking radar to maintain a discreet yet persistent proximity. As the drone zoomed in for a detailed view, realisation dawned upon Abdul Malik: the rider was none other than the elusive fugitive who had managed to escape his captivity in the Sundarbans. The satisfaction of locating her after an extensive pursuit was palpable.

Amused by the unfolding spectacle, Abdul Malik could not help but exclaim, "Ha ha hah, it's her!" However, curiosity intensified as he pondered the motive behind her daring approach toward the conflict zone. In his estimation, the young woman may have lost her way in the vast expanse of uncertainty. Promptly deciding on a course of action, he dispatched a duo of his formidable robo-assailants, mounted on mechanical robot steeds endowed with extraordinary strength and a galloping speed far surpassing that of traditional horses – capped at an impressive forty miles per hour. Their mission: to capture the audacious rider and return her to Abdul Malik's presence. He then intended to hand her over to Prime Minister Rajan Chowdhury.

Perceiving the approaching assailants astride their robotic mounts, Pori discerned the impending peril posed by their mechanised features and extraordinary leaps. A stark realisation dawned upon her: their steel composition augured a catastrophic collision that could grievously harm or even prove fatal for her equine companion. Acknowledging the gravity of the situation, she opted for a decisive manoeuvre, steering her horse away from the impending threat with remarkable agility.

"SS, I have to let you go from here, stay close," she imparted to her loyal steed, the urgency evident in her voice as she guided him beneath a low-hanging tree. In a swift and daring move, Pori seized a sturdy tree branch, propelling herself from the saddle just as SS veered off into the sheltering woods. As she swung from the branch, her nimble escape was executed with precision, leaving the metallic assailants in pursuit, their focus unwaveringly fixed on the disappearing silhouette of SS within the dense foliage.

The robotic steeds, momentarily deceived by Pori's evasive tactics, soon discerned her absence and pivoted to retrace their steps in search of their elusive quarry. Meanwhile, Pori, undeterred and resolute, swiftly readied her weapon for a counteroffensive. A steely determination etched across her face, she took aim, preparing to launch a rocket-propelled smart grenade at the now-returning assailants astride their mechanical mounts.

"Clever bastards," she muttered under her breath, her focus unwavering. With a deft hand, she activated her firearm and unleashed a barrage of shots in rapid succession. The grenades she deployed were not ordinary; they were equipped with cutting-edge heat and metal-seeking technology. Like guided projectiles, they homed in unerringly on their targets, closing the distance with deadly precision. In a thunderous eruption, the grenades detonated, obliterating the mechanical horses into scattered fragments.

Undeterred, the humanoid robots, ejected from their now-destroyed mounts, swiftly regrouped on foot. Closing in with an orchestrated precision that belied their artificial nature, they encircled Pori at gunpoint, turning the confrontation from a high-speed chase into a tense standoff on foot.

"Surrender yourself now if you wish to live," intoned one of the robots, its metallic voice carrying an air of authority.

With her hands raised in a gesture of compliance, Pori confronted her assailants with a question, her voice unwavering. "Who sent you?"

A surprising revelation cut through the tension as the response echoed back, "I sent them!" The admission hung in the air, leaving Pori to grapple with the unexpected twist in the unfolding confrontation.

As the tension thickened, a voice descended from the sky, prompting Pori to scan her surroundings in search of its source. Her gaze ascended, and she locked eyes with a drone hovering silently overhead, akin to a dragonfly suspended in mid-air. Despite its unobtrusive presence, the drone's audio resonated with remarkable clarity, its message cutting through the ambient stillness. The unexpected auditory intrusion added another layer of intrigue to the unfolding encounter, leaving Pori momentarily captivated by the mysterious and ghostly voice.

The revelation echoed through the air, as the drone's voice, both disembodied and commanding, made a startling declaration: "I am the person who abducted you from the airport!" Pori's eyes widened, absorbing the unexpected disclosure, as the mysterious orchestrator of her past abduction unveiled themselves from the concealed realm of technology above. The convergence of voices, both human and mechanical, created an eerie harmony that further entangled Pori in the enigma of her circumstances.

"Oh, so you finally caught up with me," Pori conceded, a tinge of frustration evident in her voice. Yet, there was an unexpected determination that underscored her words. Accepting the apparent inevitability of her capture, she willingly surrendered herself. In doing so, she harboured a fervent hope: a face-to-face encounter with her most formidable adversary, Abdul Malik, the elusive drone man.

As she contemplated her surrender, a steely resolve replaced any sense of failure. Pori was poised for a reckoning, fuelled by the burning desire for her mother's vindication. This time, she was unyielding, fully loaded with a readiness to unleash a storm of consequences. There was no hesitation, no reservations. Nothing would hold her back from wreaking havoc and exacting the revenge she had long yearned for. The stage was set for a confrontation that promised to be nothing short of explosive.

Escorted by the unyielding robots, Pori found herself traversing the tumultuous heart of the combat zone. The air was charged with the thunderous exchange of gunfire as the conflict between the Bangladesh Army and the bionic mercenaries led by Aysha unfolded with unrestrained ferocity. In the midst of this chaotic theatre of war, the two mechanical guards guided Pori to a fortified bunker, where the prime minister and other officials had sought refuge. Inside, a tense atmosphere prevailed as they observed the unfolding battle through satellite feeds and military-grade drone footage, each frame a snapshot of the ongoing struggle for control. Pori, an unexpected participant in this high-stakes scenario, stood at the nexus of conflicting forces, her presence adding an unpredictable element to the unfolding drama.

Secured on a meticulously constructed platform made from a fusion of steel and bamboo poles, Pori found herself bound and confined within the bunker. The robots, unwavering in their vigilance, ensured that she remained securely restrained while awaiting the arrival of the prime minister. The makeshift structure, a testament to both resourcefulness and efficiency, stood as an emblem of the unyielding measures taken to detain the unexpected intruder.

As the robots relayed the situation to the prime minister, Pori's surroundings pulsated with the palpable tension of the ongoing conflict. The bunker, a temporary haven amid the chaos, became the stage for an impending encounter between the enigmatic abductee and the highest echelons of authority. The convergence of these disparate elements set the scene for a confrontation that transcended the immediate battleground and delved into the complex interplay of power, intrigue and personal vendettas.

Amid the relentless exchange of gunfire echoing outside, the loyal government troops succumbed like a flock of birds affected by a deadly gas. The chaotic battlefield painted a grim picture as soldiers fell, their valiant efforts unable to withstand the onslaught. Meanwhile, the clash between Abdul Malik's humanoid robots and the formidable bionic forces escalated, revealing the true extent of the adversary's invincibility. Despite Abdul Malik's advanced technology and the formidable strength of his robotic minions, three out of five humanoid robots were rendered incapacitated by the relentless assault from the enemy's bionic counterparts.

In this dire and escalating conflict, the 200-strong force of bionic robots emerged as an indomitable and seemingly unbeatable foe. Their prowess on the battlefield defied conventional strategies, presenting a formidable challenge that appeared insurmountable. As the clash unfolded, the air was thick with uncertainty, and the fate of the combat zone hung in precarious balance.

*

The prime minister strode into the containment facility, his gaze fixed upon Pori with a palpable disdain. In a voice laden with frustration and anger, he addressed her, laying blame on her 'psycho aunty' who had orchestrated a nefarious plot to destabilise the government for personal gain.

"Because of your psychopath aunty, all this death and destruction is taking place," he declared, bitterness and resentment underscoring his words. The prime minister's frustration simmered as he contemplated the chaos that had ensued, blaming Pori's relative for making their lives exceedingly challenging.

"Why is she doing that? This pathetic lady has made our lives difficult as hell," he concluded, his words echoing with a mixture of exasperation and anger as he grappled with the repercussions of a political machination that had plunged the nation into turmoil.

Pori, still bound on the platform, responded defiantly to the prime minister's accusations. "Mr Prime Minister, my aunty has nothing to do with the demise of your party. Her philanthropic endeavours have earned her popularity among the public. Perhaps if you had such a legacy or trait, people might have appreciated you too," she asserted, challenging the narrative that placed blame squarely on her aunt's shoulders.

Her words carried a hint of reproach, suggesting that the prime minister's lack of a positive and people-oriented legacy might be a contributing factor to the public's dissatisfaction. The exchange within the containment facility became a battleground not only for physical restraint but also for the clash of ideologies and perceptions surrounding the ongoing political upheaval.

The prime minister, unmoved by Pori's retort, issued a cold and decisive command. "Ohh, same blood running through her veins. Detain her, and inform her aunty she is dead unless she retracts her fighters immediately from the battle zone." The order, delivered with an air of authority, underscored the severity of the situation as the prime minister sought to leverage the familial connection to exert pressure on Pori's elusive aunt. The stakes escalated, and the dynamics of the conflict took a darker turn within the confines of the containment facility.

Abdul Malik strode into the bunker with an air of indignation, his displeasure evident as he addressed the prime minister. "Mr Prime Minister, you've got your girl now. I offered my five finest fighting machines to you, with the promise that I would receive one crore taka each. Yet, you still haven't transferred the money to my account. Why?" His voice carried a tone of frustration, highlighting the unresolved financial aspect of their agreement amid the tumultuous backdrop of the ongoing conflict. The clash of interests and grievances added another layer of complexity to the already tense situation within the bunker.

In response to Abdul Malik's outrage, the prime minister, seeking to quell the escalating tension, appealed for calm. "Calm down, bro. Life and death are hanging by a thread here, I have lost thousands of troops, and you're worried about the money. It doesn't come about magically. I need to arrange it, and it's taking me time. It will be with you soon, okay?" His words carried a plea for understanding, emphasising the urgency of the broader situation while assuring Abdul Malik that the financial transaction would be addressed in due course. The juxtaposition of life-and-death stakes with financial concerns underscored the intricate web of priorities and pressures in the midst of the ongoing crisis.

The sight of Abdul Malik's presence within the bunker filled Pori with a deplorable delight. Finally, an opportunity had presented itself for her to confront her mother's killer once and for all. The emotions swirling within her, a volatile mixture of grief and vengeance, ignited a determined fire as she contemplated the prospect of settling the score with the man responsible for her mother's demise. The containment facility, once a stage for political intrigue, now transformed into an arena for a personal vendetta that had long simmered beneath the surface.

Enraged, Abdul Malik directed his demand at the prime minister. "You do the transfer now!" he insisted, his frustration palpable. "I am financially skint. That girl just blew up two of my expensive robo-horses as well. I've done a lot of favours for you, Mr

Prime Minister. You had better make the payment right now," he added, his tone a blend of anger and urgency. The ongoing conflict had not only heightened the stakes but also strained the delicate alliances, revealing the precarious nature of their arrangement amid the chaos of battle.

"Just give me some time, I am arranging it, okay?" the prime minister responded, attempting to placate Abdul Malik's mounting frustration. The urgency of the ongoing crisis and the need to balance financial matters added a layer of complexity to their interaction. The pressure of imminent danger outside the bunker, coupled with the demands for immediate payment, created a tense atmosphere within the confined space as the prime minister worked to navigate the intricate web of priorities.

Abdul Malik, his eyes gleaming with a devious glint, approached Pori with a sneer playing on his lips. "You've certainly got some guts," he jeered, shaking his head slightly. The tension in his cheek muscles revealed clenched teeth, underscoring the volatile mixture of emotions coursing through him in this charged encounter. The animosity between them, fuelled by past grievances and the current high-stakes situation, hung in the air, creating an atmosphere of palpable hostility within the confines of the bunker.

Pori, bound but defiant, locked eyes with Abdul Malik, and a resolute determination coloured her words. "Do you know something, Malik? If I wanted to kill you, I would have done so the day you abducted me from the airport. Do you know why I left you alive?" she contested. The air thickened with the weight of an unspoken revelation, leaving an enigmatic tension hanging between them.

Abdul Malik responded with a condescending tone, "What on earth! You've got a mouth of cinder too." Without warning, he approached Pori and delivered a brutal smack, causing her head to turn sharply. Blood streamed from her nose and the corner of her mouth, a stark testament to the force of the blow.

"We respect our elders here in Bangladesh, you Western filth.

Address me as Uncle Malik, or the next smack will shatter your brain. Understand?" he asserted, his words laced with both menace and a twisted sense of authority. The oppressive atmosphere within the bunker intensified, with Pori now forced to navigate not only the physical restraints but also the ruthless dynamics of power and control imposed by her captor.

The intense display of Abdul Malik's temper triggered a sense of desperation in the prime minister. In a bid to exploit the situation for his own political advantage, he hastily made a call to Nadia, seeking to use the live footage as a tool for blackmail to force her into a retreat. Brandishing his phone, the prime minister instructed Abdul Malik to repeat the brutal smack on Pori's other cheek. The sinister plan unfolded with the intention of recording and broadcasting the real-time footage as proof of the ongoing punishment to Nadia, hoping it would be a powerful leverage to manipulate her actions. The bunker, already charged with tension, became the stage for a dangerous game of political brinkmanship.

The prime minister, holding his phone tightly, greeted Nadia with a composed tone, "Hello." The connection between them opened a portal for the unfolding drama within the space to be transmitted to Nadia in real time, setting the stage for a tense exchange that could have far-reaching consequences in the ongoing conflict.

The prime minister's voice, filled with venom, pierced through the phone as he addressed Nadia. "Listen, Nadia, Rajan Chowdhury talking here. I've had enough of you pesky little shit, you vexatious harbinger of misfortune. I am sending you a video clip. Check it out. If you don't pull out your mercenaries immediately, your niece will become the victim of gang rape by men who've never seen a female before. Then, a hooked machete will be used to chop her into pieces to feed to the hyena's outside. Do you get it?" he raged, painting a horrific and gruesome picture of the fate that awaited Pori.

The space, once a supposed refuge, transformed into a

nightmarish stage where the delicate dance of morality and manipulation unfolded. The prime minister's threat, laden with chilling conviction, lingered in the air, creating a scene of dread and urgency. Lives, including Pori's, hung precariously in the balance as the course between ethical principles and ruthless coercion blurred.

Nadia, on the other end of the call, was faced with a harrowing ultimatum. The macabre negotiation, fuelled by desperation and the cruel calculus of power, amplified the stakes in the ongoing conflict. The outcome remained uncertain, shrouded in the ominous tension that permeated the bunker, where decisions made in this sinister moment could shape the destiny of those involved.

Nadia's voice, filled with a mixture of frustration and concern, responded to the prime minister's accusations. "Oh, silly girl. She never listens to me. Why did she wander off course and land in my enemies' hands?" Nadia exclaimed, expressing a sense of helplessness at Pori's situation.

"Mr Prime Minister, I have nothing to do with mercenaries. I don't know what you're talking about. I am on the southeast coast of the country, doing a roadshow for my new floating homes. Do you know how far this location is from you? I have nothing to do with what's going on in your town, okay? Let my niece free, or else I will drop doomsday upon you and your entire family. You will not call me pesky then. I will turn into a ruthless lioness to defend my daughter, resorting to any offence," she declared, drawing a line in the sand and warning of dire consequences if her niece were not released. The exchange between the prime minister and Nadia escalated, pushing the limits of the tense negotiations within the bunker.

The prime minister, consumed by uncontrollable rage, issued a chilling command. "Hey, kill this piece of shit now!" The atmosphere in the bunker became charged with menacing intensity as the dire fate of Pori hung in the balance.

"Wait!" Nadia urgently interjected, attempting to halt the unfolding tragedy, but her plea fell on deaf ears. The prime minister abruptly hung up, severing the tenuous connection between the two parties. The sudden silence in the bunker was shattered only by the echoes of the prime minister's command, leaving the outcome uncertain and the tension heightened as the final act of this hideous negotiation unfolded.

In a startling turn of events, Pori, having secretly freed herself using her central hair plait, launched a surprise attack on the robo-guards with astonishing speed. The suddenness of her assault left everyone in shock, with the prime minister exclaiming, "How the hell did she get free?"

Swiftly disabling one of the robots with a well-aimed shot, Pori engaged in relentless hand-to-hand combat with the second robot. These trained killing machines, fierce and aggressive, posed a formidable challenge. Despite her valiant efforts, Pori found herself drained after a prolonged battle. The robot, showing no signs of weakness, delivered punishing blows, taking advantage of its programmed aggression.

The odds appeared insurmountable for Pori, and her armoured skin was the only thing keeping her from complete destruction. Gasping for air after a brutal blow to her abdomen, she fell to the floor, battered and bruised. The relentless robot continued its assault, throwing her into walls and standing cabinet. Semi-conscious and seemingly defeated, Pori lay vulnerable.

In a dramatic intervention, a tiger appeared seemingly out of nowhere, leaping to Pori's defence. The tiger confronted the robot ramming it using its head, thwarting its final, lethal strike just in the nick of time. The robot, sent rolling across the floor, attempted to regain control.

Regaining some strength, Pori seized the opportunity to shoot at the robot while lying injured on the floor. The grenade-propelled shot annihilated the robot's head in a fiery explosion, reducing it to fragments. As Pori stood up, the tiger circled protectively, vigilant for any potential threats. "Sultan! You look great in that golden mask," she remarked with a wobbly voice. Sajni Jewellers had adorned the tiger with golden head gear.

The bunker, once a scene of captivity and despair, transformed into a battleground where resilience and unexpected allies shattered the oppressive atmosphere. Pori, bruised but defiant, stood amid the remnants of her robotic adversaries, with the tiger by her side, a symbol of unexpected strength and determination.

Stunned by the unexpected display of Pori's formidable fighting skills, Abdul Malik, despite being her adversary, found himself acknowledging her prowess. "This girl is an ingenious fighter. I want her in my team," he admitted, his admiration for her combat abilities cutting through the animosity.

After the intense and suspenseful martial arts exchange, Pori emerged as a resilient and skilled warrior, having overcome considerable odds. However, the visible injuries she bore, coupled with a noticeable limp and bruised face, attested to the toll the battle had taken on her. The aftermath of the confrontation left the atmosphere charged with a complex mixture of respect, tension and uncertainty, as the dynamics between Pori, Abdul Malik and the others in the room underwent a dramatic shift.

In a surprising and unprecedented gesture, Sultan the tiger offered Pori the opportunity to ride on its back. Stunned by the unexpected alliance, she asked, "Are you sure, Sultan?" In response, the tiger roared to affirm its willingness. Excited by the newfound opportunity, Pori mounted the tiger's back, testing its ability to withstand her weight.

"That's great!" she exclaimed, holding firmly onto its golden neck plate. Seated facing the culprits, Pori, with Sultan by her side, transformed the power dynamics within. The once-captive now commanded an imposing presence, her injuries and limping gait offset by the newfound strength and unity with her unexpected ally. The tense setting had taken on a surreal quality as Pori, atop Sultan, became an emblem of resilience in the face of adversity.

In the presence of the formidable tiger, Malik and the prime minister found themselves clearly uncomfortable and visibly frightened. The aura of fear permeated the surroundings as the unexpected alliance between Pori and Sultan shifted the balance of power.

The prime minister, evidently rattled, attempted to defuse the situation. "Listen, Pori! Look, I have nothing to do with you. I clearly regret what I have done. I am sorry for that," he stammered, his words a mixture of fear and an attempt to distance himself from the escalating conflict.

Turning her attention to Malik, Pori demanded, "Have you got anything to say, Malik?" The tension in the room heightened as the enemies were confronted not only by the physical threat posed by Pori and Sultan but also by the repercussions of their actions. The tiger, a symbol of untamed power, stood as an unwavering guardian beside Pori, leaving the culprits to face the consequences of their choices.

In a surprising turn, Abdul Malik, feeling the weight of the impending consequences, distanced himself from the prime minister's actions. "I have nothing to do with you, Pori. Everything I've done to you, he made me do. From your abduction to keeping you in isolation in the forest, it all came under his instructions," Malik claimed, attempting to shift the blame. "I am a fan of yours. I would like you to come work for me, and I will pay you any amount – gold, diamonds, any jewellery you ask for," he added, in a desperate plea for mercy and a potential alliance. The room remained charged with tension as Pori, atop the tiger, evaluated the sincerity of Malik's words, considering the offer amid the complex web of deceit and betrayal that had unfolded.

"So, you are not sorry, I guess?" Pori enquired, seeking sincerity in Malik's response.

"Oh, forgive me. Of course, I am sorry for my part!" Malik hastily expressed remorse, attempting to convey his regret for the role he played in Pori's ordeal.

Pori, holding a degree of scepticism, further probed, "Do you have a wife and a daughter, Malik?"

"Yes, I have two daughters. My wife left me ages ago," Malik responded, revealing a personal aspect of his life that added a layer of complexity to the unfolding situation. The exchange became a delicate dance between distrust and potential understanding as Pori contemplated the implications of Malik's admission and the possibility of finding common ground.

"I don't blame your wife. Tell me something. Say a gang of street-goons abducted your daughter and then raped her, killed her and buried her in a shallow grave for rabbits and vultures to eat. What would you do to them?" asked Pori.

Malik, feeling the weight of Pori's scrutiny and the gravity of her question, attempted to deflect responsibility. "Look, this question is not appropriate. I only abducted you. Did I ever ogle at you? I was carrying out my job as instructed by this dirty prime minister. Please forgive me," he pleaded, acknowledging his role in her abduction while distancing himself from the more heinous actions.

His plea for forgiveness reflected a sense of desperation and an attempt to gain sympathy in the face of the unfolding consequences.

"Mr Prime Minister, what would you do to a person who abducted your daughter and then raped her, killed her and buried her in a shallow grave?" asked Pori.

The prime minister, seemingly overwhelmed by the weight of guilt and desperation, made a startling revelation. "I would go and shoot the guy. Pori, this is your chance. Unleash this tiger onto that son of a bitch, blaming me for everything bad he's done. He created these killing machines to kill people. He even tried to extort money from me," he confessed, exposing the web of deceit and manipulation that had entangled them all.

The unexpected admission left the room in a thrilling silence, the implications of the prime minister's words sinking in. Pori, atop Sultan, now faced a moral crossroads as the opportunity for retribution against the true architect of her suffering presented itself.

"Let me tell you a story." Pori glanced back to her childhood memories. How Malik abducted her mother at gunpoint from the street in Arambaria, dragged her inside a secluded farmhouse, then raped and killed her barbarically, using a machete to chop her head off. Pori's eyes filled with tears as she vented her anguishing story. "A little girl, who happened to be me, had to leave my mother behind at the hands of a monster. I never saw my mother again after that day. Do you recall anything, Malik the rapist and killer?" asked Pori.

"Are you the daughter of Doyal Shah and Rahila Begum?" enquired Malik.

"Yes, that's me," she cried. "The girl who was with her mother, who begged you to release her daughter. In return she sacrificed her soul and dignity at your feet, and you've shown no mercy. You drove your lecherous intentions home, mercilessly shredding her apart." Pori's tears fell steadily from her eyes.

A shiver ran up Malik's spine as the truth was unveiled, and goosebumps formed in disbelief. Swiftly, he folded his two hands before Pori and fell to her feet, begging for pardon. "I didn't realise what I was doing at the time. I was young and mentally unfit. I am so sorry," pleaded Malik.

Pori, aflame with indignation, wept in anger. "Can you give me my mother back." she said. Her tears, glistening evidence of the profound impact Malik's actions from years past had on her, fell delicately. Stepping away from Malik, who was now prostrate and begging for mercy at her feet, she retrieved the fallen sword left by the shattered ranks of robotic warriors. Approaching Malik head on, she uttered with a poignant grace, "I might have entertained your plea, but this battle is not mine to decide. It belongs to my mother. I am rendered voiceless; you, unchanged and ever-revealing in your monstrous nature throughout the entirety of our shared history."

"I am no saint, just a slayer of monsters, much like yourself. The difference lies in purpose: you revel in bloodshed for pleasure and capital gains, while I mete out justice." With an artful flourish, she swung the sword, severing Malik's head in one decisive motion. The detached head tumbled to the floor, blood spurting from the neck's open wound. The head rolled several metres, propelled by the residual force of the blade, a gruesome spectacle unfolding.

The scene turned even more nightmarish as she directed her tiger companion to exploit this sumptuous opportunity for a free meal. The tiger complied, tearing into the fallen foe's remains before the eyes of the survivors. Malik's shoulder was gruesomely ripped away, leaving a gory tableau in its wake. Witnessing the horrifying spectacle, the prime minister's knees trembled in fear, sweat beaded on his forehead, and an instant wave of nausea overwhelmed him. He convulsed, vomiting as a visceral reaction to the unfolding horror.

Pori strode purposefully toward the prime minister, brandishing her tranquilliser gun with a deft hand. In a swift, calculated move, she injected the mind-altering microchip into his neck. The sudden intrusion exacerbated his agitation, compelling him to succumb to unconsciousness in the grip of fear. With this decisive action, Pori successfully concluded her previously thwarted mission of administering the mind-altering jabs.

All three designated targets now bore the influence of the implanted microchips. Pori's mission, a clandestine dance of manipulation, was now accomplished. The stage was set for her aunt, Nadia Begum, who eagerly awaited the unfolding of her ambitions to ascend as the new ruler of Bangladesh, puppeteering the inclinations and desires of those under the subtle sway of the implanted technology.

Kneeling in solemn submission, Pori closed her eyes, a poignant moment of reflection as she invoked memories of her mother. With a whispered vow, she communicated with a spirit from another realm.

"I have dispatched the wrongdoer to your realm, Mother, just as he callously banished you, showing no mercy. Henceforth, no man shall impede the emancipation of women in this world as long as I live," Pori declared.

As the prime minister lingered in a sedated stupor, Pori, accompanied by her loyal tiger, gracefully withdrew from the scene. In their wake, they dismantled the remaining undesirable and hazardous facilities, leaving a trail of explosive destruction that echoed their passage toward a transformed future.

*

As dawn broke, the prime minister awoke in the hospital, his surroundings fraught with an air of anticipation. Encircled by vigilant police officers, a palpable tension filled the room as they prepared to commence their interrogation. The weight of the impending questions hung heavy, signalling the beginning of an inquiry into the mysterious events that had transpired, leaving the once-powerful leader now at the centre of an unfolding investigation. The hushed murmurs and stern expressions of the law enforcement officers underscored the gravity of the situation, as they prepared to unravel the enigma surrounding the events of the previous night leaving thousands dead and distraction of entire brick and cement factories.

Upon regaining consciousness, the prime minister was met with the probing enquiries of the police, who sought to unpick the events that transpired at the scene. However, his response was a disconcerting declaration of amnesia, asserting an inability to recall the occurrences. The police, increasingly suspicious, intensified their scrutiny.

Unconvinced by his professed memory lapse, the authorities decided to take decisive action. The prime minister was promptly taken into custody, marking the commencement of a more thorough and rigorous investigation into the enigmatic circumstances that had thrust him into the centre of an unfolding mystery. The custody served as a means to extract the truth, as the legal machinery began its meticulous journey to uncover the layers of the tangled narrative.

"What do you mean you don't remember anything? Half of the country's infrastructure got destroyed under your watch, and you are saying you don't remember. You are not fit to be our prime minister," declared the senior police officer, Sadik Talukdar. Fuelled by suspicion of the prime minister's alleged involvement in causing calamities to government infrastructure, thereby jeopardising the livelihoods of thousands, Sadik Talukdar took decisive action. The senior police officer promptly placed the prime minister under arrest, signalling the beginning of a legal process to hold him accountable for the significant disruptions and potential consequences brought about during his tenure.

*

Pori returned home on horseback, weaving through the lush expanse of trees and greenery. To her surprise, upon reaching the forecourt of her village, a heart-warming scene unfolded. A line of guests, organised in a welcoming formation, awaited her arrival. Her eyes lit up at the sight of her beloved Grandma Sarah, who stood at the forefront. Leaping off her horse, Pori rushed into her grandmother's embrace.

The line revealed more familiar faces: her paternal aunty Maria, followed by Uncle Keith and then, to her delight, Steven, her teenage sweetheart. Overwhelmed with joy, she shared an adoring hug with Steven, their eyes locked in a shared moment of affection and longing. In unspoken understanding, Steven suggested, "Shall we?"

Pori, still caught in the euphoria of the reunion, responded with a laugh, "What?"

"Sing a song, of course. I miss dancing with you," Steven declared.

"In this condition?" Pori inquired, her appearance bearing visible bruises from the conflict, indicative her distress.

"Why not." said Steven.

The joyous atmosphere enveloped them as Pori, beaming, agreed, "Yes, okay!" Anticipation hung in the air as the prospect of a delightful and impromptu musical moment unfolded.

Music began playing, and Steven delved into dance mode.

Without You

Steven:
Without you one day, living a true life is not possible
This is what the world has witnessed every day
Oh, this is what the world has witnessed every day

Pori:
Without you one day, living a true life is not possible
This is what the world has witnessed every day
Oh, this is what the world has witnessed every day

Steven:
I have missed you too much, come close and let me hold you tight

Pori:
When I see you far my heart disappears,
holding you tight is the only way to volunteer.

Steven:
Oh, this is what the world has witnessed every day

(Background music)

Steven:

The more I see you now the more I lose you in the wilderness of love

Pori:

I uphold your vision to a high, I appreciate and cherish your love as mine.

Steven:

You exist therefore I exist, if anything happens then I cease
This is what the world has witnessed every day
Oh, this is what the world has witnessed every day

Pori:

Without you one day, living a true life is not possible
This is what the world has witnessed every day

Steven:

Oh, this is what the world has witnessed every day

(Background music)

Pori:

The future is holding thousands of hopes,
it has renewed our love and our thoughts

Steven:

I am flying in your imagination, I have turned into a kite adding remuneration

Pori:

These are all a phenomenal active taking its toll, our love will never fall.

Steven:
Without you one day, living a true life is not possible
This is what the world has witnessed every day
Oh, this is what the world has witnessed every day

Pori:
When I see you far my heart disappears,
holding you tight is the only way to volunteer.

Steven:
I have missed you too much, come close and let me hold you tight.

They embraced one another fervently, quenching the thirst of longing with ardour.

HIGHLIGHTS OF THE SEQUEL...

Gracefully nestled in the suburban expanse of Arambaria, Bangladesh, stands a colossal four-storey edifice, purposefully constructed on a sprawling ten-acre canvas. This architectural marvel boasts a contemporary design, harmonising seamlessly with cutting-edge security measures, including tinted windows and an elevated heliport crowning its roof. Adorned with a distinguished emblem proclaiming 'Bangladesh Republic of Community and Scholars', under the covert moniker BROCS, this establishment embodies the fusion of visionary design and scholarly prowess.

The entire premises are enveloped by a formidable three-metre-high brick wall, and deep down below ground, is a nuclear bombproof bunker, complemented by an array of fences and gates. A meticulously manicured garden park graces the surroundings, complete with inviting seating areas, water fountains and meandering streams. The ambiance is further enhanced by the presence of geese, ducks and pygmy goats leisurely grazing, creating a harmonious blend of nature and architectural finesse. Checkpoints strategically facilitate authorised entries, while vigilant patrolling guards ensure a secure environment. CCTV cameras diligently oversee every corner of the expansive site.

A chauffeur-driven SUV gracefully passed through the gates, making a grand entrance and halting at the forecourt of the main building. Stepping out, a slender leg adorned with faux pearl Charlie heeled shoes and topaz anklet glimmering was followed by a beautifully dressed Mrs Nadia Begum. Two bionic guards disembarked from the opposite side of the SUV, their vigilant demeanour a testament to the high-security standards. Nadia, impeccably attired in a newly invented designer outfit tailored to her unique contours, exuded a captivating allure. The pants and shirt, adorned with decorative borders, imparted a smart, elegant and inherently sexy quality to her appearance. With briefcase in hand, she strode purposefully into the building, her tinted designer eyeglasses concealing a gaze fixed straight ahead.

The interior of the building mirrored the external grandeur, with clean, fresh plant pots strategically placed in key corners. Nadia made her way through the building and eventually entered a boardroom of impressive stature. A massive twenty-five-seater table took centre stage, equipped with computer screens, tabletop microphones and bottles of water – a testament to the meticulous attention given to both aesthetic and functional aspects within the confines of this distinguished establishment.

Upon stepping into the room, Nadia was greeted by the presence of four distinguished guests who awaited her arrival. Among them stood the esteemed former prime minister, Mr Rajan Chowdhury, now heading the Ministry of Finance with seasoned expertise. Mr Abdus Salam, a prominent figure in the BNP, had assumed the crucial role of overseeing the Ministry of Defence. The dynamic Mr Ashanul Hoque, leader of the JP party, had transitioned into the realm of commerce as head of the Ministry of Commerce. Completing this formidable quartet was Mr Rayan Ali, the former deputy prime minister, now entrusted with the significant responsibilities of the Ministry of Energy and Minerals.

In a strategic move, Nadia had meticulously formed a ministerial cabinet, elevating these four accomplished individuals to the highest echelons of the payroll hierarchy. Diminishing the need for party polygamy and giving birth to a party monogamy, BROC party was here to stay. Their collective roles extended beyond individual portfolios, as they were entrusted with the authority to make decisions of national consequence. The political and decision-making prowess of this cabinet under Nadia's leadership was in a continual state of ascent, signifying a pivotal juncture in the governance and trajectory of the nation.

Upon Nadia's entrance, a gesture of gratitude and deep respect manifested as all four distinguished figures rose from their seats. Their collective acknowledgment underscored her supreme position, an emblem of the authority she held. Nadia gracefully made her way to a specially crafted ceremonial chair, reserved for leaders of her stature. It became evident that a transformative convergence had occurred, with the previous hierarchical officials aligning themselves with Nadia's vision. Together, they had forged a unified party dedicated to a global cause, fervently committed to the establishment of a harmonious world order.

Seated upon the regal chair, Nadia symbolised the embodiment of this amalgamation, poised to steer the collective effort toward a singular mission. Their shared aspiration resonated: to initiate a paradigm shift on a global scale. This newly formed alliance, comprised of leaders from diverse backgrounds, pledged to champion the cause of humanitarianism and environmentalism. Their strategy rested on the pillars of diplomacy and education, strategically influencing nations toward a unified vision.

In an audacious move, this coalition sought to introduce a groundbreaking ideology – a new religion of sorts – that prioritised the twin pillars of humanitarian values and environmental stewardship. Through diplomatic initiatives and educational campaigns, they aimed to instil this ethos in the collective consciousness of societies worldwide. The ambitious goal was nothing short of converting the entire globe to a model rooted in compassion, environmental responsibility and a shared commitment to global wellbeing. The stage was set for a bold journey towards a future where these principles would shape the very fabric of human existence.

Seated upon her magnificent chair, Nadia Begum motioned for the others to follow suit, setting the tone for a serious discussion.

"Madam, we've convened today to address a matter of utmost urgency," began Rajan Chowdhury. "It pertains to the captive British spy, code-named BG-007, commonly known to work for British secret services. That's the extent of the information we've managed to extract. This man was carrying a cyanide pill, and while we successfully prevented him from taking his own life, our efforts at extracting information through conventional means have proven futile."

A palpable tension hung in the air as Rajan Chowdhury continued, "He remains resilient in the face of torture, revealing nothing of substance. It seems, madam, that this individual is exceptionally adept at withstanding interrogation. We find ourselves at an impasse, unsure of how to proceed in extracting the crucial information we need."

Nadia Begum's gaze sharpened as she sought clarity on the spy's motivations. "Did he provide any insight into why he was spying on us? What is he attempting to unearth?" she enquired.

"Madam, his focus centres on understanding the purpose and existence of our company trading under the name of MI16," Abdus Salam responded. "While the world may be aware of its acknowledged objectives, he adamantly insists that there is more to our organisation than meets the eye."

A palpable tension permeated the room, with divergent opinions emerging on how to handle the captive spy. Abdus Salam's revelation hung in the air as Ashanul Hoque, with a stern expression, suggested a drastic course of action. "I say let's hang him upside down and skin him from his head, and feed the corpse to our Bengal tigers," he proposed, advocating for a ruthless approach to safeguarding the organisation's secrets. The gravity of the decision weighed heavily on the collective conscience of the room, leaving the fate of the captive spy hanging in the balance.

In the clandestine dance of information, Nadia Begum leant forward, her voice a measured whisper. "Encrypt the line and initiate a connection to Cheltenham, UK, GCHQ headquarters. I need to speak directly with Captain Sir Martin Reid," she directed.

Rajan Chowdhury swiftly moved to establish a secure communication channel, the air thick with the tension of covert operations. As the encrypted line hummed to life, an operator on the other end responded. Rajan, maintaining a composed demeanour, requested, "I need to be connected to Captain Sir Martin Reid." The urgency in his voice underscored the gravity of the impending conversation with the enigmatic figure at the helm of the UK's Government Communications Headquarters.

As the encrypted line held, the GCHQ operator sought further clarification. "May I enquire who wishes to speak with him?" they asked.

"Nadia Begum from Bangladesh," came Rajan Chowdhury's response, the weight of her name carrying a significance that echoed beyond borders. The information flowed through the secure channel, setting the stage for a connection that would transcend geopolitical boundaries. The operator, recognising the gravity of the request, initiated the process of connecting Nadia Begum with Captain Sir Martin Reid at the heart of GCHQ headquarters.

The moment Nadia Begum's name echoed through the encrypted line, a subtle flick of the intercom switch by the GCHQ operator set a chain reaction in motion. Internal teams at GCHQ swiftly mobilised, informing Captain Sir Martin Reid of the incoming call from Nadia. Concurrently, a trace on the call was initiated to pinpoint its origin.

However, as the pursuit of tracing the call unfolded, it became apparent that the line had been tampered with. The elusive nature of the connection, emanating from the UK but intentionally shrouded in secrecy, eluded the meticulous efforts of the GCHQ team. The operator, recognising the futility of the trace, maintained a composed demeanour, acknowledging the covert expertise at play. The call remained enigmatic, an encrypted bridge spanning continents, carrying with it the intrigue of undisclosed agendas and covert conversations.

"Martin Reid speaking," came the response from the GCHQ head.

"Hello, Sir Martin," Nadia replied.

A tense exchange ensued as Nadia addressed the situation at hand. "You let my man go. He was merely on holiday in his country of origin. Your operatives accused him of spying simply because he works from GCHQ."

Reid, sensing the gravity of the situation, was met with a direct question from Nadia.

"Where was your man born, Mr Reid?"

"Why do you need to know that?" Reid replied cautiously.

"Just answer my question. I am fuming with anger. Where was he born?" Nadia demanded.

"He was born in the UK," confirmed Mr Reid, the admission hanging in the air as the conversation between the two figures transcended borders and veiled agendas.

Nadia's voice, sharp with indignation, cut through the connection. "Why do you claim his country of origin is Bangladesh, Mr Reid? Is it solely based on his skin colour that you've forcibly ousted him from his homeland?" The accusation hung in the air, challenging the motivations and practices of the intelligence agency. The conversation, laden with tension, now delved into the complexities of identity, prejudice and actions taken in the name of national security.

Nadia's impassioned words reverberated through the secure line. "If a white man migrates from any European country, his son or daughter can identify as English in as little as one generation.

However, for those with brown or black skin, they are never entitled to call their home, home," she asserted, laying bare the disparities in how identity is perceived and acknowledged.

The weight of shame hung in the words addressed to Mr Reid, challenging the inherent biases embedded in the systems that distinguish and discriminate. In this exchange, Nadia confronted not only the actions of intelligence agencies but also the broader societal constructs that perpetuate inequality based on ethnicity and skin colour. The conversation transcended the immediate circumstances, delving into the complex tapestry of identity and belonging.

The tone of the conversation shifted as Reid, seemingly caught off guard, responded, "Listen, I didn't mean it that way. He went on holiday to Bangladesh. Please let him go." There was a discernible note of urgency in Reid's plea, a recognition of the delicate situation at hand. The dynamics of power and influence played out in the exchange, underscoring the complex interplay between individuals and the institutions they represented. The fate of the captured spy hung in the balance, the outcome influenced by the negotiation unfolding across the encrypted connection.

Nadia's unwavering and commanding voice reverberated through the airwaves, penetrating the atmosphere with a poignant enquiry. "Mr Reid, I am compelled to enquire: what is the origin of your nation's enduring reluctance to witness the prosperity of others? Since the historical era, England has thrived, initially benefiting from the tail end of slavery in Africa and extending its prosperity through ventures such as the East India Company and the Raj starting in 1785, continuing to shape its fortunes up to the present day, as if that's not enough they demonstrated an unwavering inclination to interfere in the affairs of other nations. Why does your government find it objectionable for me to engage in diplomatic relations with India?

"Your government, in its fervour to displace me from power, has branded me a terrorist, frozen my assets in the UK and constrained the movements of my family. And now, you anticipate my cooperation in releasing your operative? Does my position of authority hold no significance in your estimation? What considerations guide your decisions?

"Allow me to distil the narrative. On the eve of 14 August 1947, Bangladesh was an integral part of India. Under my administration, it is poised to reunite with India, forming a singular, formidable nation that promises to captivate the world with its transformative potential."

She continued, "I called you to convey that GCHQ's mission of sending secret agents to other nations to sow tensions, anxiety and divisions is over. Consider your franchise of undercover agents are an obsolete enterprise now, with no more spare parts to go round. It's time to file for administration. From now on, a new and upgraded version of spy's, code-named MI16, has been born. I will produce these operative to serve the entire world at a scale the UK has never dreamed of. They are far more superior than anything you have ever imagined."

As the weight of her words settled, she concluded with a stark warning, "Our war has just begun, Mr Reid. Save yourself from this terrorist threat if you may." The declaration marked a seismic shift in the balance of power, setting the stage for a shocking conflict that extended beyond borders and traditional notions of espionage.

The weight of Nadia's words hung in the air, and a pregnant silence ensued. Mr Reid listened silently, absorbing the gravity of the situation, before the phone line abruptly turned dead.

The encrypted conversation, laced with declarations of a paradigm shift in the world of intelligence, concluded, leaving both parties to contemplate the ramifications of the exchanged words and the unfolding geopolitical chess game. The repercussions of this rather perplexing dialogue would reverberate far beyond the confines of the secure line, setting the stage for a new chapter in the shadowy world of international intrigue.

Nadia Begum, enriched with both affluence and a profound understanding of life, has immersed herself in the intricate realm of geopolitical challenges, reaching a juncture from which there is no retreat. Her fervent desire to rectify humanity's course burgeons with each passing day. In her discerning reflection on history, she recognises the enduring truth that the possessor of the mightiest weaponry wields the highest authority.

In an era symbolised by elephants, India harnessed them as instruments of war for strategic advantage. As cannons emerged in the subsequent age, the British deployed them to repel elephants and assert their dominance. In the present epoch of intellectual pursuit, Nadia aspires to transcend boundaries by channelling substantial investments into science, technology and groundbreaking discoveries. Her vision extends beyond personal gain; she envisions a profound transformation in the cultural mindset of the Bangladeshi people.

Acknowledging the imperative shift from individualism to collectivism, Nadia seeks to foster collaboration among nations, steering away from the divisive currents of competition. Despite her current capacity to acquire innovative start-ups and successful businesses within her nation, she grapples with the realisation that Bangladesh, tucked away to the east of India, is ostensibly inconspicuous and geographically constrained.

Undeterred, Nadia contemplates the historical evidence that global geopolitical dynamics are fundamentally influenced by the expanse of land. While she possesses the means to pioneer technological advancements, from driverless cars to hypersonic aircraft and futuristic realms like quantum computing and artificial intelligence, the vulnerability of a small nation to potential attacks by more powerful counterparts looms large.

After meticulous contemplation and consultations with her educated cohorts, Nadia strategically opts to fortify diplomatic ties with India – a longstanding ally that played a pivotal role in liberating Bangladesh from the brutalities of Pakistan in 1971. However, the British government, wary of her growing influence, attempts to sow seeds of discord by labelling Nadia Begum as a dictator and terrorist, further complicating the geopolitical landscape within Bangladesh.

Now ensnared in this intricate web of global affairs, Nadia confronts the challenges that lie ahead. Her family, situated on the other side of the world, adds a poignant layer to her predicament. As the unfolding chapters of her story await, the future remains a canvas of uncertainty, with the world eagerly anticipating the strategic moves of Nadia Begum.

To be continued...

AUTHOR BIOGRAPHY

I am Mohammed Abdul-Halim, originally from Bangladesh. My father moved to the UK in the late 1960s, followed by the rest of my family, and I arrived in the early 1980s, settling in the East End of London among the growing Bangladeshi community. The relocation provided me with the opportunity to receive a superior education in UK schools compared to my early schooling in Bangladesh.

From a young age, I harboured a strong passion for becoming a fashion designer. Pursuing this dream, I enrolled in a fashion design course with aspirations of reaching the pinnacle of the fashion industry. Although I worked in the field for five years, my unfulfilled desire for self-improvement led me to explore other avenues.

I shifted gear to delve into the world of electrical engineering and spent a couple of years in that field before transitioning to the heating, ventilation and air conditioning (HVAC) trade. Presently, I am a fully qualified refrigeration engineer, having dedicated myself to this profession.

Becoming a writer brought an unexpected turn in my life. One evening, during a discussion with friends on a sensitive topic related to marriage, I recognised the importance of fostering an open dialogue. This realisation sparked the idea of penning a book on the subject. In 2009, my debut work, *Marriage and Dishonesty*, came to life, followed by a sequel, *Poison*, in 2010. My goal was to captivate both my friends and a broader audience with a compelling and dramatic narrative. Although currently unavailable in print, I still possess a few copies. If you're interested, feel free to reach out to me directly at: +44 7984 151957. Or: halim07984@gmail.com

As of 2024, I am excited to announce the publication of my latest work, *The Dark Environmentalist*. This creation drew inspiration from the global stage, particularly the COP26 conference held in Glasgow in 2021. Witnessing the intricate dynamics between affluent and impoverished nations during the conference, I felt compelled to craft a fictional narrative that unveils the deceptive nature of environmental leadership discussions.

Being an ardent environmentalist myself, I hold a deep concern for our planet. My trust in science and facts guides my understanding, and I am sceptical of claims not substantiated by scientific evidence and technological breakthrough. Scientific consensus supports the notion that Earth has endured for 4.54 billion years and is poised to persist for many more. While individuals may consider their own existence as temporary, the longevity of Earth and humanity is here to stay.

It deeply troubles me when people, knowingly or unknowingly, disregard the welfare of future generations and the future of our planet. The indifference towards the sustainability of our world among people, despite the scientific evidence and technological advancements at our disposal, is truly disheartening and, at times, even sickening. *The Dark Environmentalist* aims to shed light on these concerns and prompt reflection on the responsibility we all bear for the wellbeing of our shared home. When words prove ineffective, it becomes essential to resort to alternative peaceful methods to emphasise policies that are significant. This book is all about that.

I hold a critical stance towards a stand-alone capitalist society, viewing it as a primary contributor to climate and humanitarian crises, because it promotes growth without limits, brushing aside anything and everything in its path with greed and cronyism. While I comprehend the capitalist argument asserting that no superior alternatives exist, I strongly disagree with this argument.

I advocate for a mixed economy that seamlessly blends elements from both capitalism and socialism, allowing for private ownership and market dynamics. However, I emphasise the need for essential government intervention to address issues such as income inequality, public services, social welfare and the regulation of human population growth. I firmly believe that one of the root causes of global challenges lies in human behaviour itself. Addressing this requires tackling various aspects, and controlling population growth per land mass capita is a crucial factor for achieving lasting peace and tranquillity.

While acknowledging the challenges posed by differing rules and regulations among nations, I believe it is essential to explore ways to implement effective population control measures globally. Humans are forces of evil, and we are responsible for mending and bending the world. The central theme of *The Dark*

Environmentalist delves into this complex issue through a fictitious tale. The narrative aims to cultivate a vision of a one world order system, fostering collaboration among nations to work together towards a common goal. The book explores the feasibility of such a system; in the real world it's impossible to establish such a system, however, in an ideal world anything is possible.

I embody kindness and care, embracing diverse opinions and perspectives. I highly value individuals who engage in critical thinking, employing intellectual rigor in their analyses. I find it challenging to connect with those who engage in shallow thinking, especially those who dismiss the longevity of our world and play it down when it comes to looking after its sustained health.

I prioritise open-mindedness and critical inquiry, detesting rigid adherence to dogma or ideology without a willingness to question or explore alternative viewpoints. Closed-mindedness is a trait I find unappealing, as is the reluctance to consider alternative perspectives. I am not a supporter of those who oversimplify or narrow down nuanced ideas.